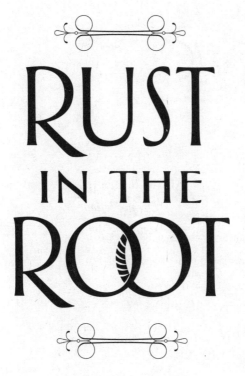

RUST
IN THE
ROOT

Also by Justina Ireland

Dread Nation

Deathless Divide

RUST

IN THE

ROOT

JUSTINA IRELAND

BALZER + BRAY
An Imprint of HarperCollins*Publishers*

Balzer + Bray is an imprint of HarperCollins Publishers.

Rust in the Root
Copyright © 2022 by Justina Ireland
All rights reserved. Printed in the United States of America.
No part of this book may be used or reproduced in any manner
whatsoever without written permission except in the case of brief quotations
embodied in critical articles and reviews. For information address
HarperCollins Children's Books, a division of HarperCollins Publishers,
195 Broadway, New York, NY 10007.
www.epicreads.com

Library of Congress Control Number: 2022935799
ISBN 978-0-06-303822-6

Book design by Jessie Gang
22 23 24 25 26   PC/LSCH   10 9 8 7 6 5 4 3 2 1
❖   First Edition

For the Dreamers

CONFIDENTIAL DOCUMENTATION

Bureau of the Arcane, Main Office
Department of Mystical Divergence
Attn: The Eagle's Aerie
2323 Pennsylvania Ave. NW
Washington, D.C. 20007

To Whom It May Concern:

The narrative contained herein constitutes
the entirety of my report of the events that
occurred between June 5 and June 19, 1937. I
have included examples where necessary, as
directed, including documentation concerning
one Laura Ann Langston, formerly my
apprentice, and now deceased.

I have also appended photographs (many
found among the personal effects of Miss
Langston herself), charts, newspaper articles,
and primary source documents to provide
context for these events—particularly for

members of the Bureau of the Arcane council and the oversight committee who are not practitioners of the mystical disciplines. I hope that this report satisfies the council and fully puts to rest all concerns over the possibility that the mages of the Bureau of the Arcane's Conservation Corps, Colored Auxiliary acted in anything but a professional manner, completing our assigned task as instructed and averting what could have become a national crisis. The actions of a single untrained, wayward girl should not detract from the work of mages who have maintained a sterling record of managing Blights and keeping the US economy humming along.

Any questions may be directed to my office in the Bureau of the Arcane's New York branch.

Yours truly,

The Skylark
July 23, 1937

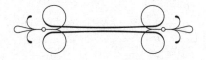

Part 1

GREAT
EXPECTATIONS

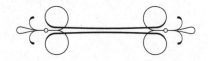

BUREAU OF THE ARCANE AND DEPARTMENT OF THE INTERIOR ANNOUNCE PARTNERSHIP AIMED AT BLIGHT REDUCTION

January 12, 1936, Washington, D.C.—At the urging of President Franklin Delano Roosevelt and with the approval of Congress, the Department of the Interior's Mechomancy Division and the Bureau of the Arcane today announced a collaboration to remediate the scourge of environmental Blights throughout the United States. The Blights, which have continued to manifest in the years since the Great Rust, have remained a threat to the livelihoods of Mechomancers and licensed mages across the country.

Beginning in February, the Department of the Interior will work to place Resonators in all Blight-afflicted regions. These constructs counteract the imbalances and power fluctuations created by damage to the Dynamism that led to the Great Rust. The Resonators will provide much more powerful and efficient corrections to the Blights than that which had previously been provided by the mages of the Bureau of the Arcane, allowing Mechomantic devices to operate within the Blight zones while mitigating their myriad secondary effects.

As many Americans are aware, those living within Blight zones have reported a host of troubling phenomena over time: strange weather patterns; increased rates of sickness, nausea, and malaise; and, in some cases, the mysterious formation of creatures colloquially referred to as Blight Beasts.

Officials believe that these Resonators will allow more Americans to remain living and working within Blight zones. The years since the Great Rust have seen record numbers of Americans abandoning their homes wherever Blights have taken root; despite the efforts of mages to address the Blights through manipulation of the Dynamism, experts say that nearly two million Americans have been displaced since the Blights began appearing in the aftermath of the Great Rust in 1927. These Resonators—which will be produced in significant quantities by the collaboration of eight of the country's largest Mechomancer firms and maintained by the efforts of mages within the Bureau of the Arcane—will finally allow this issue to be addressed on a large scale.

The head of the Bureau of the Arcane, Douglas Adler, praised this new initiative. "Mechomancy is the future of America, and licensed practitioners of the mystical arts are proud to be uniting with the country's esteemed Mechomancers on the Resonator initiatives. We are hopeful that this enterprise will alleviate the impacts of the Blights, strengthen Mechomantic progress across the nation, and put real, honest Americans back to work."

A spokesman for President Roosevelt declared the program one more triumph in his plan to rebuild America in the wake of the Great Rust, and has promised more reforms going forward.

The city never sleeps, but I really need a nap.

Chapter

ONE

I'm not looking for any trouble. I never am. But, somehow, I keep finding it anyway. Or maybe it finds me.

I'd thought New York, full of opportunity and chaos and possibility as it is, might be a place where a colored girl with, if I may be so bold, more than a little talent in the mystical arts could finally catch a break. But even here, talents like mine don't seem to be worth a cup of joe these days—in fact, more often than not, they'll put a target on your back.

As evidenced by the spectacle I'm currently witnessing.

I'm sitting in the corner booth of a no-name diner in Manhattan, trying to ignore the skin-crawl feeling of the white waitress staring at me while I watch the scene unfurl outside. Cops pour out of a nearby building, hauling out mages, using their silver billy clubs liberally whenever someone looks like they might want to put up a fight. The sidewalk is spattered red with the mages' blood, but no one seems to care, pedestrians avoiding the flailing men and women, most of them colored like me.

"Finally rounding up those filthy 'mancers," the waitress says, coming over and leaning to peer out the window as well. There's a slight smile twisting her thin lips. "That speakeasy's been there for over a year now. I'd been starting to think the coppers would never break it up, you know?"

"I . . . yes. Can I get a refill?" I say, pointing to my empty cup. The carafe is in her hand, but she still sighs as she pours half a mug's worth of the oily brew they're calling coffee. It's not good, but at least it's real, not some raveling done by an Illusionist. She waits for a moment at the table's edge, probably expecting me to order food, but when I just give her a tight smile, she moves away, grumbling under her breath about moolies taking up space. The parade of jobless men and opportunity-seeking hucksters that were here when I arrived filed out as soon as the job agencies opened their doors, leaving me alone in the diner, a colored girl at a dirty table nursing a mug of lukewarm coffee.

I lift my one worthwhile possession, a Brownie camera that Pigeon gave me a couple of years ago for my birthday, and snap a picture of the cops manhandling the mages just beyond the window. This is a thing I've done since I got to New York, taking these slice-of-life pictures, as though by documenting my days I can somehow make them worth more. Can't tell you why, exactly. Maybe I imagined that at some point I would develop the photos and flip through them, a picture show of how far I'd come. But I'm right in the same place as when I arrived, more or less. The picture taking is more a silly habit than anything else.

I watch through the window until the last mage is pushed into the back of the police wagon, the portal inside zapping the mages to the local precinct. That could've been me, if I hadn't overslept, if I hadn't had to argue with my landlady about unpaid rent and the rat nesting in the wall of my room, the gnawing keeping me up all night. I could've been right there with the rest of them, spinning charms and raveling hexes, hoping the backlash wouldn't hurt too much, when the police burst through the door. It was only a small disturbance in the Possibilities—a feeling of being watched, you might say—that slowed my footsteps and turned me away from the door of the speakeasy and its illegal charms, sending me into the diner across the street.

Lucky me.

I may have avoided the eager batons of the coppers, but I'm still in a pickle when it comes to my financial situation. I pull out my change purse and count my coins one more time. Two dollars and thirty-six cents. That is all the money I have left, and a dime of it has to cover the coffee.

I came, I saw, I failed spectacularly.

New York was a pipe dream, and now that I'm knee-deep in the muck, I can't help but regret ever leaving Pennsylvania. My sister, Pigeon, always ready to be the voice of reason for her flighty younger sister, warned me that the city was no place for nice girls, but I only smiled and said that was perfect before promising that I'd write every week and send money when I could.

I've sent few letters, and even less cash.

Boy, she's going to get a chuckle out of the mess I made of this one, I think, trying to cheer myself up with memories of Pigeon's characteristic scowl. *Once she's through being vexed with me, that is.*

Country living was easy. Nothing for Floramancers like us to do other than ravel charms for dairy cows and scry the future of a newborn every now and then. Sometimes we'd go out foraging for bits to change into other useful things—acorns and walnuts and the like, which we could ravel into milk buckets or flowerpots or the occasional potpie, nothing fancy. No one wanted Big Ravels in the sticks, and they definitely didn't want the kind of gourmet creations I spent my free time thinking up: magnificent raveled desserts that few chefs, even those trained in the mystical arts, could imagine. It was one thing to turn a walnut into a construct to help around a farm; it was quite another to use that same walnut to create a three-tiered cake that tasted of dreams and happiness. My mother and aunts were good with the Possibilities, and I'd learned a lot from them. But the kind of food I wanted to ravel wasn't the kind you found in Pennsylvania.

And that's why I came to New York. I'd hoped to get an apprenticeship at a bakery, the kind I saw in the food magazines that were sometimes on the rack in the general store. With a bit of training, I knew I could use the finest ingredients and my considerable talents in the mystical arts to create amazing treats, even something otherworldly. Tiny, light tarts raveled from pecans, cakes raveled from a handful of the best almonds, confection spun out of peaches that melted on the tongue and reminded people of their happiest childhood memory.

My plan was to work in such a place just long enough to get a sponsorship and get my license, as everyone knew it was impossible to get a mage's license without a proper sponsor. Prohibition had made anything more complex than household charms illegal, and without a licensed mage to vouch for both my skill and character, I'd never be able to get my certification. Applying for a license from the government without a sponsor was pricey, and they didn't take too kindly to colored folks, so impressing one of New York's mage bakers was my best chance at opening my own treat shop.

That is my best, shiniest dream, the fantasy I spin when I have trouble sleeping. In it, my shop is fancy and cosmopolitan, and so popular that people like J. Paul Getty and Howard Hughes demand my creations for their events. "Get me a Laura Ann Langston confection!" they'd yell into the phone, slamming their hands down on gleaming wooden desks. People from all over would line up each day for a chance to buy a pastry, twisting twice around the block. I'd be in one of those food magazines, and they'd say my treats were "life changing" and "to die for." I'd wear the best fashions from Paris and carry around an ostrich-plume fan just because. Reporters would ask me what Shirley Temple's favorite cake was, and I'd laugh and swat at them with my fan. "I never bake and tell," I'd say with a gleam in my eye, and then lean in and whisper, "but it's raveled from rose petals."

I made the mistake of sharing this with my sister once and immediately regretted it. Pigeon thought it was a silly dream. Why would a colored girl work so hard to open something as useless as a bakeshop? Especially when I could have a comfortable life doing simple charms for the bumpkins in Shrinesville? The kind you didn't need a license for, the kind that wouldn't attract the attention of the Prohibition office's enforcers? She couldn't understand that I wanted Big Ravels, the kind that came with a license and an apprenticeship, the kind that would've been a given if I'd been born white. Pigeon thought I was a fool for leaving the safety of the family farm. She said as much the day of my seventeenth birthday, as I was packing up to head to the nearest Wayfaring station and get beamed to New York.

"Ain't no one going to hire an unlicensed Negro mage, especially not one who happens to be a girl," Pigeon said with a sniff. "All that struggle to make a bunch of fussy sweets? Ridiculous. You'll see. You'll be zapping back here inside of a month. And when you do, I'm going to say I told you so."

Pigeon knew what she was talking about. She usually did. But I couldn't face a long, endless future raveling charms for crops in Shrinesville, Pennsylvania. So I gave my sister a hug and marched out of the house for what I had hoped would be the last time.

It wasn't only big dreams that had made me leave. Pennsylvania was smothering me, keeping me small, and who wanted to live a tiny life?

But now, penniless and out of luck, there's a part of my brain that thinks maybe I'd been wrong to leave. Maybe I should just head home. A few months in the Big Apple had shown me the worst thing they could: that I *was* a silly colored girl with outlandish dreams. If I'd gotten nothing else out of this grand New York experiment, at least I'd gotten knocked upside the head with some common sense. Because here I am, less than four months later, broke as a joke and counting pennies like doing so could make them multiply.

At least I'd lasted longer than Pigeon had expected. That was something.

"Did you want to order food?" The waitress reappears like an apparition and eyes me in that half-defensive, half-angry way white folks always look at Negroes, like I might turn her into a frog and then swipe what's in the till. I consider telling her that the black don't rub off and my ravels aren't the spiteful kind, but that wouldn't assuage her fears. Most likely she's heard the stories, the ones of powerful Negro mages, men and women both, charming white women so they could have their way with them, savage in their appetites. As if the Jim Crow laws in the South would exist if colored folks were that powerful.

The energy that powers Negro ravelings isn't any different than the small bit at the heart of the machines made by the white Mechomancers who ply their trade throughout the city, but somehow folks are okay with the science of Mechomancy and leery of the exploitation of Possibilities. They had been so even before the Great Rust, but when that whole disaster went down, colored folks were an easy scapegoat. How else to explain the Blights that destroyed all Mechomancy but didn't have any effect on the mystical arts? Never mind that there was no evidence that anything we mages did led to the Blights that now dot the country; it was somehow fact that the mystical arts must be to blame. And ever since Congress prohibited the use of anything beyond basic ravels without a license, the cops and G-men have been happy to break the skulls of mages, usually colored, all over the country.

Even here in New York.

Either way, I wouldn't be casting charms on anyone anytime

soon, even if I wanted to. Big Ravels don't happen without a few essentials like joppa seeds and jacaranda vine. And I don't have the coin for either.

Instead of giving the woman a piece of my mind, I just smile. "I'd like another warm-up, if'n you don't mind?" The rumble of my belly is mostly inaudible.

The waitress purses her lips, her pale brow furrowing as she moves off to grab the carafe again. At least her racism is familiar. It was much worse getting turned away by every colored baker I'd asked about a job. For some reason I'd thought Negroes up in the Big Apple would be friendlier, or at least more understanding of my abilities and aspirations than the folks back in Pennsylvania had been. New York's skyline might be dominated by the impossibly tall buildings Mechomancy makes possible, but everyone knows the city is held together with ravels laid over a hundred years ago, ones that prevented the river from flooding and the rats from taking over. Heck, it was just a few years ago that they were having a mystical renaissance in Harlem, folks finding new ways of twisting up old ravels into even better things.

But unlike the Negroes back in Shrinesville, who still relied on the same ravels our families had practiced for hundreds of years, most of the colored folks in New York seemed just as hostile to new mages as white folks. It hadn't been this way before the Great Rust, when the mystical arts and technology still existed in an uneasy harmony . . . but that didn't help me now. People still remembered that day in 1927 when a strange wave of energy washed over the United States, destroying great mechanicals and leaving Mechomancers powerless, their constructs failing in the ebb and flow of the Possibilities, the energy field that powered all ravels. The economy is still recovering a decade later, and with another war brewing in Europe between Mechomancy and the mystical disciplines, well, everyone is a bit on edge. And even colored folks seemed to buy into the nonsense that, somehow, the mystical arts had caused the Great Rust.

Nothing vexed me more than discovering this as I tried to make my way in the city. It didn't make a lick of sense for colored folks to fear the mystical arts, especially in the larger scheme of things. After all, the European Necromancers hadn't been picky about which Afrikans they'd grabbed and thrown on a boat heading west back in the old days, but that didn't change people's silly prejudices. And it wasn't like the Floramancy I did was anything close to the Necromancy that the Ku Klux Klan and their predecessors were known for. But it didn't matter. The whole country was in a quiet war with itself. White folks versus Negroes, the blands who embraced the science of Mechomancy versus practitioners of the mystical arts. It was part of the reason my grand New York experiment had fallen flat. "Mages need not apply" was second only to "Negroes need not apply."

I would've been better off as a leper. At least sick folks get a measure of pity.

I count my coins again, wishing there were some kind of ravel that could duplicate them. But the coins are made of iron and silver—Mechomancy material, impervious to any kind of tinkering within the Possibilities. The only thing I can do is stack them over and over as my mind runs through my limited options.

I have four days until my landlady kicks me out for missing this month's rent. Four days isn't a lot of time, and I'm not even all that sure I'm of a mind to keep paying for the tiny rat-infested bedroom I rent in Miss Viola Swan's Boardinghouse. Not that my preferences make a bit of difference. I need twenty dollars to stay, and I don't have it. Miss Viola had assured me that anything less than twenty-five dollars a month was a steal in Harlem, but that was before I'd seen the place. It is less a boardinghouse and more a kennel, complete with fleas. Walking in and seeing those faded curtains and crooked floors day after day felt like manifesting my failure. The only reason I even have curtains and a threadbare quilt is because of Simone. She used to live in the room next to mine, turned tricks for money—that is to say, she raveled without a license for questionable characters in shady places. I'd been a little sweet on her and thought maybe my feelings were reciprocated a bit. But the police came and snatched Simone up one day, so now it's only me and the rats and a bunch of girls I don't know, most of them hoodlums just crashing at Miss Viola's until the heat dies down and they can get back into whatever skullduggery had landed them in the clink in the first place.

I sigh and stare at my tiny pile of coins. Maybe getting into illegal hexes is the way to go. I am fresh out of other options.

Outside the diner window, the morning foot traffic has died to a trickle, and I briefly consider going back to Miss Viola's, packing my stuff, and heading home. Buck fifty and I could be back in PA by dinnertime, knotting fertility charms out of trumpet vines and casting chicken bones for a look at the future with my rootworker aunts. I'd never be a great mage, never see my desserts in the pages of *Harper's* or the *New Yorker*. At most I'd be a hedge witch. But I could live a nice, quiet life. Comfortable, even. Pigeon would leave off of her "told you so"s after a few weeks. A year at most.

Just the thought makes me want to bawl.

The waitress walks by, and I try to wave her down. "Hey, where's my refill?" I call, pointing to my mostly empty cup.

Her lips tighten, and she shakes her head hard enough that her paper hat wobbles. "We're all out of coffee, and we don't serve troublemakers here. I suggest you finish up and clear on out," she says, before stomping back toward the kitchen, her heels making an angry staccato sound on the cheap linoleum.

I stare after her, trying to figure what it was that turned her so salty, but then I notice the sesame seeds scattered across the table-top. While I was fretting about my options, I must have let my abilities roam, because the seeds—the remnants from someone's sandwich, most likely—have sent exploratory roots skittering across the table, writhing with the energy of the Possibilities. I sweep the seeds into my hand, because I know better than to waste their potential, and stand to leave.

"Yeah, well, maybe you should keep a cleaner establishment," I mutter to no one in particular. I toss a nickel and a dime on the table because I'd never let it be said Laura Ann Langston is a cheapskate, grab the rest of my loot, and make my way out into the morning.

It is nearing lunchtime, and the mechanical district is abuzz.

Mechomancers in derbies and bespoke suits crowd the sidewalks. Their detestable machines glide through the streets, the air thick with the coppery scent of their power. One of Henry Ford's new constructs rumbles past, and I have to keep myself from spitting for luck. Some might think Mechomancy is the other side of the coin to the mystical arts, but there is nothing natural about it. Especially since, for most of American history, it was powered on the backs of colored folks.

Now good old FDR is working to make Mechomancy the cat's meow once more, urging the Bureau of the Arcane to team up with Mechomancers to finally get the Blights under control. I read in the newspaper that Henry Ford is opening a factory in Queens and hiring hundreds of mages to craft his next line of automobiles. And then there's Prohibition, slowly strangling what's left of independent mages. If I wanted an apprenticeship to a mage at a Mechomancer firm, I could've gotten one several times over. But even now, flat broke and juggling pennies, I refuse to apply to one of the Mechomantic employment agencies. Some folks might think Mechomancy is the future, but it seems to me that no matter what anyone says about it these days, it's just an unwanted relic from the past. I prefer work that won't smother my conscience.

I loiter in the doorway of the diner, biding my time and reading the display page on a nearby paper. *Negro Mages Head to Ohio to Quell the Country's Largest Blight*, the headline reads. Under that, pictures of colored folks lining up in a Wayfarer's queue. They're headed west into the Big Deep, the first, and still the worst, of the country's Blights. The higher arts, as folks annoyingly call things like Mechomancy, might not work in a Blight, but the lower arts—the powers that draw from the Possibilities—always have, which is why the Bureau of the Arcane has been recruiting colored folks to help set the Blight to rights.

Good luck to them.

I step out onto the sidewalk, debating whether to head down to Central Park to gawk at the wyverns or maybe head back uptown to Harlem and try to catch up on my sleep, when I realize the sesame seeds in my hand won't hold for later. The burst of potential I woke is anxious for release, tickling my palm with the Possibilities. Without a direction, all that latent energy is a recipe for disaster. Or at least an inconvenience.

A block up the avenue, a grizzled old white man holds down the corner, his clothing threadbare and ragged. "Powerless and hungry," his sign reads. "Just another bland down on his luck." He is covered in grime and barefoot, his face painted with a white scrub of beard. Normally I try not to get mixed up in the affairs of white folks, especially those who openly decry the mystical arts. It has a way of shaking out for the worst. But the man is even lower on his luck than I am, and I feel a measure of pity for him.

"Hey," I say, approaching. The man looks up, his eyes rheumy. "Are you hungry?"

"What do you think?" he grumbles. He smells like a brewery, and I get the feeling that food isn't what sustains him.

I shake the sesame seeds in my hand, cupping them loosely, and call on the Possibilities. I can see where the old man touches the ambient energy that connects all living things, and from there

I can see what he desires. I can feel it, sudsy and bitter, running down my throat, easing hurts and filling my belly.

A couple of rolls of my wrist and each seed hits the ground with a hollow sound, like popping corn, raveling into a bottle of beer. A moment later, the man is surrounded by several full brown glass bottles.

He jerks to his feet, kicking over a couple of the beers as the final sesame seed hits the ground. "Hey, hey! Girlie, you a mage?" There is fear and excitement in his voice, and I decide it isn't worth sticking around to see which one wins out. The last thing I need is a copper collaring me for performing unlicensed ravels.

"Have a nice supper, mister!" I yell over my shoulder before beating feet out of there.

NEGRO MAGES HEAD TO OHIO TO QUELL THE COUNTRY'S LARGEST BLIGHT

June 27, 1937, Pittsburgh, PA—After weeks of reports of new activity in the Ohio Deep Blight, the Bureau of the Arcane has confirmed it is doubling its efforts to mitigate the effects of the country's oldest and most enduring Blighted zone. Multiple teams from the Bureau of the Arcane's Conservation Corps, Colored Auxiliary have been sent in to reactivate and recharge the Resonators placed in the area last year. According to a press release by the Bureau of the Arcane, this action has been taken in response to complaints by local residents that the Blight has continued to grow in both size and intensity.

"We had to get out," said a resident of Collinsville, one of the towns most central to the Blighted zone. In response to hundreds of residents fleeing the area, the Department of the Interior has established a resettlement center just outside of Pittsburgh. Eyewitnesses there have shared accounts of strange happenings, including Blight Beasts, shadowy creatures that stalk untreated Blight zones.

"Crops won't grow, and all our animals got the bloat," said another resident who recently fled. "The government said these Resonator contraptions were going to help, but things just keep getting worse. And now they're sending colored folks in? Don't they have any proper mages?"

When asked for comment, the Bureau of the Arcane simply stated that the Colored Auxiliary represents some of the finest licensed mages in the country, and reiterated that they stand behind the work of these men and women and their command of the mystical arts.

"I think those mages are just making things worse," said a worker in the relocation facility. "In the past month the number of people fleeing the Blight has tripled. Why aren't the Resonators working like everyone said they would?"

Last year, the Department of the Interior and the Bureau of the Arcane announced a joint program to combat the recent surge of Blights in the aftermath of the Great Rust. Blights render Mechomancy inert and have, in extreme cases, been tied to illness and lower crop yields. Resonators, Mechomantic constructs that are designed to bolster the use of the mystical arts to repair the damage to the Dynamism, were installed in the area, but have been experiencing more frequent bouts of ineffectiveness over the last six weeks. Residents in the area have petitioned the governor for help ever since.

"Our prayers have finally been answered," said one displaced resident. "But I worry that it's too late."

There are a thousand ways to starve in the Big Apple,
and a sucker born every minute.
This scam involved hair tonic and a very nice wig.

Chapter
TWO

I opt for heading to Central Park over returning to Miss Viola's. I'd prefer just about anything short of a Klan meeting to returning to my miserable abode. A girl can spend only so many hours staring at the water-stained walls before she considers murder to be a swell idea, and I do not want my next letter to Pigeon, should I ever write one, to be from jail. And besides, maybe something good will happen on the way to the park.

Good things could happen for me—I believe that deep in my heart—and I have half a hope that if I give the Possibilities a chance, they'll finally sprinkle some good fortune down on me. That sort of hope is the only reason I've lasted this long in New York.

A few blocks' walk and I'm at the entrance to Central Park nearest to the unicorn enclosure. I've never much cared for unicorns. They're judgmental jerks in the way that all beautiful cryptids tend to be, always telling a body things they already know and mostly don't care to hear again. But today, after seeing those cops bust up that group of mages, I find I'm not so picky about my company.

A bunch of school kids, all of them white and wearing robes I recognize as being from the Edison Mechomancer Academy, harass a couple of mares for rides nearest the entrance, holding out carrots and sugar cubes invitingly—as if unicorns are just fancy horses. They'll be lucky not to be bitten—or worse. I skirt the group and make a beeline for the back of the enclosure. There is no actual fence for the area, just a bunch of Elementalist beacons, the crystals marking the outline of the enclosure in large quartz stones every few feet. After a quick glance to make sure no one's looking my way, I slip through the barrier. The power scrapes against my skin, harsh and cold. Blands would have to walk the long way around—the enclosure is meant to keep visitors from harassing the unicorns—but I have no problem redirecting the energy through the Possibilities and taking a shortcut to the bench I'm eyeing on the back side of the field, where no one can bother me. The summer sunshine radiates onto it, already hot and sticky even though it is still early in the day.

As I sit, I find a single sesame seed still stuck to my palm. It's a late bloomer of sorts, and the potential in the seed is just waking up.

Apple?

The voice in my head is plummy, and I glance up to see that one of the mares has ditched the kiddos and followed me to the back of the enclosure. The creature has a dappled gray coat and a mane of deep violet, her horn bright silver. She is the most beautiful thing I have ever seen.

"Sorry, I don't have any apples."

But you have Possibilities. Ravel me an apple, love?

This, of course, is the exact issue with unicorns. They are as demanding as they are striking.

I roll the remaining sesame seed into the middle of my palm. I've already done a bit of lawbreaking this morning, so what's a touch more? With the unicorn's insistent influence filling my head, a vibrant red apple appears in my hand.

That looks delicious. You are quite a talented Floramancer. Too bad your dreams of opening your own bakery are dead on arrival.

"Rude," I say, giving the unicorn a glare. "How do you even know about that?" I've never met this particular unicorn before. I'm so annoyed and unbalanced that I consider eating the apple myself, but I don't because that is a great way to tempt a bit of backlash, and a splitting headache is the last thing I need.

The unicorn gives me a smug look before delicately taking the apple with her rubbery lips. She crunches through it happily, and I sigh. If only I could ravel for myself. That is one problem with utilizing the Possibilities: it always has to be directed outward. Ravels done for oneself have a way of backfiring, and every novice learns a thousand cautionary tales before ever spinning a single ravel. I can knit an apple for a unicorn or a case of beer for a hobo, but if I were to try to make anything for myself, it would come out twisted and unnatural. Or worse, it would come out perfectly and my body would pay the price of my selfishness. There are ways to get around it—having a familiar to bleed off some of the chaos, joining a coven when those were still a thing—but neither idea ever really appealed to me. Working with others seemed like a hassle, and why should some cat or dog suffer just because I wanted to ravel myself a new dress or something silly like that?

The unicorn finishes her apple and turns to walk away. She's gone only a few steps when she turns back with a swish of her purple tail.

The Bureau of the Arcane's Conservation Corps, Colored Auxiliary is looking for apprentices. Go to the Flatiron. Today.

"Why would I want to do that?" I ask.

A license is a license, love.

I set my lips in a stern line. The unicorn isn't wrong. Working for old Uncle Sam *could* get me a license—assuming I can stand it that long. The Bureau of the Arcane was still Mechomancy work, just with the government's name on the check. Pigeon had gone on and on about joining up back when the Colored Auxiliary was announced last summer—she never could resist a chance to use her power to help people, infuriatingly so—but we soon realized that it was less real work and more cleanup. Why would I become a housemaid of the mystical arts? That feels less like success and more like settling. If I'd wanted to settle, I would have stayed in Shrinesville.

But the unicorn isn't finished speaking. *That's not why I'm telling you this, though. The strongest mage in Manhattan works there. She needs you. And you need her.*

Normally I wouldn't have trusted a damn thing a unicorn said. Cryptids have a way of twisting things up to suit their whims, and some, like unicorns, have a funny view of time. Meaning, she could be talking about something that wouldn't happen for fifty years. But sudden goose bumps raise on my arms at the unicorn's announcement, making it feel less like advice and more like Prophecy, and no one with half a lick of sense ignores a Prophecy from a unicorn.

Besides, they'll give you a place to live.

"I *have* a place to live!"

If you say so, the unicorn says, before flicking her tail, turning around, and making her slow way back to the group of children.

●●●

I'm somehow even more depressed leaving the park than I was heading in. The Bureau of the Arcane! Honestly. If I wanted to get a job with those Mechomantic bootlickers, I could've done that when I first got to New York and saved myself four months of scrabbling for honest work.

The Bureau of the Arcane says it wants to make life better for mages, but it also advocated for the Sponsorship Law, which requires all mages be apprenticed to a licensed mage for at least a year before applying for their own license. That might sound like a great way to make sure only competent mages are licensed, but it really just makes sure that practically every mage ends up spending some time working for a Mechomancer. The way I want to use the mystical arts has nothing to do with Mechomancy, using the Possibilities to power those mechanical constructs. Why should I hitch my wagon to a mechanical star when there are real stars out there burning bright?

I'm still in a bit of a snit after I've stomped all the way back to Miss Viola's boardinghouse, which is a long way to stomp. The streets have fallen into disrepair and hollow-eyed men and women crowd them. Uptown, where dreams go to die, is where I live.

I climb the steps to the tenement and have gone up only the first two when the door flies open. Standing in the doorway, a bottle in her hand, is Miss Viola.

"Linda!" she says, giving me a gap-toothed grin. Her pale skin twists in a terrifying way. My first impression of Miss Viola had been of an elephant, not because of her size but because of how wrinkled her skin is. She's ancient, and fearsome in that way old people can be. "Where's my rent?"

I give Miss Viola what I hope is a friendly grin. "Well, ma'am, first, it's *Laura*, and second, I'm afraid I'm still looking—"

"Just as I thought," she says. She tosses a familiar bundle at me, and I scramble to catch my few belongings, which have been tied up in the silk handkerchief I use to wrap my hair at night.

"Hey!" I say. "You said I could have until the eighth of the month!"

"That was before I'd found a new lodger to pay for your room," Miss Viola says, drinking deeply from the bottle. "Just found someone who paid me two months' rent up front, and who won't nag at me about some made-up rat keeping them up." She sniffs at me before closing the door.

I grit my teeth and fight back tears. I have nowhere else to go, and everything I own is now in my arms, smelling faintly of mold and stale cigarette smoke. I'm not sad to be done with Miss Viola's, but where am I supposed to sleep?

That's when a haughty voice comes back to me.

The Bureau of the Arcane's Conservation Corps, Colored Auxiliary is looking for apprentices.

They'll give you a place to live.

I sigh. Unicorns.

I turn on my heel and head back the way I came.

This is such a grand city.
It's a shame it's also so ruthless.

Chapter

THREE

The Flatiron Building is a hundred blocks from Miss Viola's, and I consider taking one of the newer portal routes rather than walk. It costs only a nickel. But I have so few coins left that I am loathe to spend a single one, and so I take the leather bus instead, walking two hours through the sweltering heat.

My travels take me past a number of new buildings under construction, all of them being raised by Mechomancers. The steel girders are a dead giveaway, as is the way my belly roils when I pass the men plying their trade, riveting and welding and generally making a big, stinky mess. But none of them are as big a monstrosity as the Empire State Building, which earned the distinction of the tallest skyscraper in the world, to the delight of the Mechomancers who had built it. It was thrown up after the Great Rust, "a triumph of the spirit of the mechanical," one paper had called it, and every time I'm near it, I'm unsettled. Mechomancy always feels like unwashed laundry, sticky and vaguely foul. It clings to my skin and makes me itchy, like the time Pigeon was mad at me for stealing her best hair comb and decided she maybe wouldn't rinse all the lye soap out of my underthings. The Empire State Building is a hundred times more powerful than that. The first time I walked past it I nearly puked, so I've avoided the area ever since. People seem to think that as long as a thing *can* be done, it *should*. But reacting to all the Mechomantic buildings crumbling during the Great Rust by running out to build newer, taller ones seems like all kinds of foolishness to me.

If some Floramancer was out here building skyscrapers from raveled acorns and oaks, they'd be arrested before they could even lay the foundation. Why were things so very different for Mechomancers? No one ever asks a Negro girl from Pennsylvania her opinions on such things, and so I just keep walking down Broadway, getting away from the construction sites as quickly as possible.

It's lunchtime, and the midday sun makes itself known in a real way, hellishly hot as it reaches sharp fingers between the buildings and heats the street below. By the time I make it to the Flatiron, I've worked up a fine lather, and I realize the kind of impression I'm going to make, carrying the entirety of my earthly belongings wrapped in a ratty old silk handkerchief. I stop near a storefront to check my appearance, and indeed, the frizzy-haired colored girl who stares back at me is not an impressive sight. My dress is wrinkled, sweat soaks the material under my arms, and I smell, quite honestly, like salami on rye. Perhaps I should've dropped a little money on a portal ride after all.

I consider raveling myself something new to wear, but even under the circumstances, the blowback wouldn't be worth it.

Nothing to do but smooth my hair under my hat and readjust the hairpins so they cover a bit more of my frizzy braids. I use an unlaundered slip to wipe most of the perspiration off my face, and then repack my bundle of clothing so it looks less like I've just been kicked out of my room and more like I've just arrived in the city, looking to join the Colored Auxiliary. I smile at my still-disheveled appearance in the reflection of the window, but it quickly fades into a grimace.

My talent will have to do the talking for me.

The Flatiron Building is a most peculiar thing, and I have spent a number of afternoons just stopping to gawk at it as I pass while pursuing one fruitless lead after another. It's still standing in the aftermath of the Great Rust because it wasn't built by Mechomancers—it was built by Elementalists, the mages pulling stone and iron together into a structure that vaguely resembles a slice of very tall layer cake. The ravels of it feel cool and crisp, like drinking fresh snowmelt, and that calms my sudden nerves a bit. The Flatiron sits on a triangular lot at the intersection of three streets, and looking at it makes me a little wistful for my mama's red velvet cake.

The jab of homesickness that erupts from the thought nearly makes me gasp with pain. Sudden tears prick my eyes, and for a moment I consider turning on my heel and heading to the nearest Wayfaring station. It's Tuesday, so Mama would be at her weekly church meeting trying to convince Pastor Riley that Jesus Christ was reborn not through the power of Judas's Necromancy or the Elemental abilities of the rest of the apostles, but because Mary was a Floramancer of great strength. Mama was convinced anything could be accomplished with nothing more than a handful of herbs and seeds, including cheating death. Pigeon would be fanning herself and rolling her eyes, ignoring any boy who tried to take advantage of choir practice to flirt with her. "Not in the Lord's house," she would exclaim, even though they'd be necking in an alcove as soon as practice was done.

I take deep breaths until the fear and sadness and longing passes. The people back home are what had sent me running to the Big Apple in the first place, and the sooner I remember that, the better off I'll be. I came to New York to be a great mage, and this might be the chance I've been waiting for these past months. It's not as if I've had any other.

Besides, I was sent by a unicorn, one who seemed to know a bit more about me than was usual. When a unicorn gives a body life advice, they'd do well to heed it.

I enter the building with a renewed sense of purpose, a ravel shivering over me as I do. Most of the buildings in New York have gargoyles or other wards guarding them, looking out for troublemakers. But I have real business at the Flatiron, so after a heartbeat the charm releases me with a slight pop, no worse for wear.

The lobby is underwhelming, consisting of nothing but a plain room and a security guard reading a dime novel at the desk. I give the man my best smile. "Hi, I'm—"

"Fourth floor, all the way at the end of the hall," the man says without looking up. "It'll look like a broom closet, but it isn't. Go on inside."

I walk away without thanking him and manage to keep the look of disgust off my face. Mostly. Psychics are the worst. Always looking into the future but never seeing anything useful.

After an elevator ride up to the fourth floor, I exit into a hallway covered in the brightest yellow linoleum I've ever seen. A pattern of interlocking squares runs across it, and I am wholly absorbed in studying it, convinced it contains a raveling of some sort, when someone clears their throat.

"Can I help you?"

I tear my gaze away from the floor. The hallway leads down to a desk where a colored woman sits clacking away at a typewriter. She's smartly dressed in a dove-gray business suit, a matching hat hanging behind her on the coatrack in the corner. Her hair has been straightened and pulled back into a complicated updo. Gosh, even the secretaries in New York are sophisticated and beautiful and everything I hoped I might be after spending a few months in the Big Apple. Yet here I am, in the same blue sack dress I arrived in, with a pair of ugly brown shoes that I got at the Woolworth's when the bottle caps would no longer stay on my old shoes. My hair is curly from the humidity, and even though I just fixed it, frizzy tendrils escape once more.

"I said, 'Can I help you?'"

The woman hasn't looked up from her typewriter, and a tsunami of doubt threatens to knock me over. The woman looks like a film star—if they let colored women star in movies, that is. Still, I'm feeling a bit flummoxed, my yearning to impress this woman and my need to find employment colliding and, truth be told, making it a bit hard to breathe. "Um, a unicorn sent me," I finally stammer out.

That gets the woman's attention. She stops typing and looks at me with a sharp expression. "What's your name?"

"Laura—"

She holds up a hand. "No. Never give out your real name. Names have power. What are they even teaching children these days?" The woman mutters this last bit before taking a deep breath and letting it out with a sigh. "When I ask your name, I'm asking, what is your mystical name?"

"Oh. I, um, don't have one." Ma didn't truck with such nonsense—most mages back in Shrinesville didn't. Pigeon had taken a new name when she turned eighteen because she was contrary, not because it was expected. Although it could be said that being contrary was a family tradition.

The woman raises a single brow, the movement drawing my attention once more. "Well, that is a surprise. Where did you learn your talents?"

"My ma taught me. She's a root woman back home in Pennsylvania."

"I see," she says, sighing again as she finishes her typing and pulls the sheet from the machine. I don't have a chance to say anything more before the woman stands. "Well, Laura, from Pennsylvania, tell me why you want to join the Bureau of the Arcane's Conservation Corps, Colored Auxiliary."

"Wow. Try saying that three times fast," I joke. When she just watches me, I clear my throat. "Well, I am quite skilled for a young mage, if I may be so bold, and looking to get a license. And I figured that there's no better way to pursue that goal than serving my country." The lie nearly sticks in my throat, and I clear it noisily.

"Serving your country," the woman echoes. She is clearly unimpressed, and a fine bit of panic kicks up in my chest, knocking my heart into my ribs. If I botch this, I have no other options.

A poster catches by eye. Two men—one a skinny man in a silly robe, the other taller in a sharp suit—shake hands under the headline *Mages and Mechomancers: Working Together for a Better America!*

I might not be a very good liar, but I can definitely parse which way the wind blows.

"That's right. I'm especially interested in Mechomancy—have been ever since I landed in New York and laid eyes on the Empire State Building."

She raises an eyebrow. "Is that so?"

"Yep!" I chirp, shifting my weight from foot to foot. "It's just like FDR says: without the work of men like Henry Ford and Howard Hughes, this country would hardly be the most powerful in the world. Mechomancy is what has made America great, and if we can use the Possibilities in service of it, well, that's the ticket for me, ma'am."

"The Possibilities?" she says, a smirk curling her lip.

My face falls, but I catch it almost immediately, and smile humbly. "I'm sorry, I was just . . . That's what we call the Dynamism. Back home, I mean."

"How quaint," she says, and straightens a stack of papers brusquely. "Well, I am very sorry, but I'm afraid we do not have any positions open for a young mage of your particular bent at the moment."

"Wait, what?" I say, but the woman is already sitting back down at her typewriter.

"You are not what we're looking for," she says. "You may go now."

This is all wrong, and the panic comes surging back. If this goes belly-up . . . I realize in that moment that I'd work for a Mechomancer in a heartbeat if it meant I wouldn't have to go home to Pigeon's smug face.

"If you don't mind, I'd like to see whoever is in charge of this outfit," I say, looking around the empty office. "You didn't even give me a chance you show you what I can do." My voice wavers, my anger and fear creating a lump in my throat. I don't cry much, not in front of other people anyway, but sometimes when I get a fit of pique, there's nothing to be done for it. I beat back the tears by focusing on my indignation. Someone has to listen to reason, and if it's not this woman, then there has to be someone else. From what I've heard, the Colored Auxiliary can use all the mages they can get, and I'm no slouch.

I just need a chance.

The woman walks to the door without a response, and for a moment I think she's ignoring me, but then she turns around and gives me a polite smile that chills my bones. "You're talking to the one in charge of this *outfit*. I am the Skylark, Class Four Floramancer, senior agent in the United States Bureau of the Arcane, and head of its Northeast branch's Floramancy Division, head-quartered here in the New York office."

"You?" Her words put me back on my heels.

"Of course. I'm the one who told the unicorns I was looking for mages, though if I would've known what they were going to send my way, I would've been a bit more specific in my request."

I don't know how to respond to that. Truthfully, I'm still a bit in awe of the woman. To think, a Negro woman running something here at the Bureau of the Arcane. I'm suddenly thinking my dreams weren't too big after all. In fact, maybe they're too small.

"I . . . I raveled an apple out of a s-sesame seed," I stammer. "Please, just give me a chance."

"I am afraid not." The woman looks me up and down in a way that makes it clear this decision is not about my skill set. "Good day, young lady."

That's when the world tilts, and I have a moment of queasiness before I find myself staring directly into the sun. I stumble backward and shut my eyes tightly.

The woman teleported me to the sidewalk out in front of the Flatiron.

I'm not given to fits of temper. I swear. More often than not, I keep my cool and just do as I please. But this is more than even I can take. My anger is hot as Hades in August, and I'm half wishing I had an okra pod to show that stuck-up lady just what kind of a mage I am.

"Really?" I yell toward the windows on the fourth floor. "That's it? You didn't even give me a chance to—"

I'm interrupted by strong hands pushing me forward, my chest slamming painfully into the side of the building.

"That's her, officer. That's the girl what raveled me these."

I'm still smoldering with ire as I twist my head around, catching a gander of the old hobo from earlier, his stash of beers cradled in his arms. How they even found me this far downtown is a mystery. Maybe they just wait here hoping to collar colored mages when they get rejected by the stupid Bureau of the Arcane.

I try to plead my case, but there isn't half a chance. The cop trying to imprint my face on the side of the Flatiron cuffs me, the iron burning slightly against my skin as the restraints settle into place. He hauls me backward, his pale face twisted with disgust. The taste of blood fills my mouth, and I spit it out onto the sidewalk. "What the hell?"

"You're under arrest for illicit raveling. Unless you got a license to do that?" He points to the old man hugging the bottles of beer.

I spit out more blood from my split lip, thinking about the flatfoots I watched busting up the speakeasy that morning, and I do the only smart thing.

I lie.

"Wasn't me," I say.

"Doesn't matter," the flatfoot says, shoving me forward. "He says it was you."

"You really ratting on someone who did something nice for you?" I ask the hobo, redirecting my anger and frustration to a target within reach.

"Darky magic is unclean," he says. But that doesn't keep him from clutching the bottles closer as he takes a step backward.

"Is that so?" I say. I don't know what's more offensive, the fact

43

that he called me a darky or that he called manipulating the Possibilities *magic*. Normally I'd let such a thing go, but his words, and the rough handling from the police officer, and the looks I got from that woman not a minute ago, and the frustration of the past few months . . . it's all too much.

The cuffs burn as I reach through the Possibilities, like my wrists are getting spattered with hot bacon fat. The iron is meant to deter what I'm doing right now, but I'm angry enough to ignore it in the name of spite. The cop pushes me forward, but not before I close my eyes, reach out with all of my ability, and tug.

These blands wouldn't know it, but we call what we do "raveling" for a reason. As the charm unspools, each of the beers disappears with a popping sound, until the old man is left holding nothing but a handful of burnt sesame seeds.

The cop pushes me roughly toward a nearby police wagon. The bundle with my clothes is left behind on the sidewalk, but my camera is tucked in my skirt pocket, thankfully. The old man sobs in dismay as he realizes that his beers have all gone back to nothing, and it's the last sound I hear before the doors of the police wagon open and I'm pushed through the portal before me.

Background

Blights began to appear in the United States in 1927 during a "reversion wave," a previously unheard-of phenomenon that is suspected to have been caused by widespread and persistent experimentation with the Dynamism by reckless practitioners of the lower arts—something often referred to as "Wytchcraft." This reversion wave led to a reflexive increase in the ambient energy of the Dynamism, overwhelming the affected areas and rendering inert the mean-level forces used in the technological arts, also known as "science" or "Mechomancy." Colloquially referred to as the Great Rust, this reversion wave led to a number of initiatives in the aftermath of the destruction caused by the total collapse of Mechomantic devices within the affected areas, and the subsequent economic catastrophe it precipitated—something from which we have only in recent years begun to recover.

Although the specific cause of the unusually large Ohio Deep Blight (hereafter in the report: ODB) is not known, we know it appeared approximately two years after the Great Rust, and the bureau has made it a priority to mitigate its effects. It is bureau policy that all Blights can and should be repaired, but the ODB's geographic proximity to Mechomantic manufacturing centers in Pittsburgh, Cleveland, and Detroit have made it a chief concern. The bureau is also concerned with the potential resettlement of those residing within the area, an estimated ten thousand people. The ODB's resistance to the mitigating effects of the Resonators installed last year sets it apart from many others across the nation, and is particularly troubling.

Accordingly, the tempo of operations within Ohio had increased in the months leading up to the incident that is the subject of this report. One of the many reasons I found myself in a position to take on an apprentice in such a hasty manner.

First Impressions

I was not about to engage a half-feral child as my apprentice. I would like to make that clear. I have mentioned this on a number of occasions since the initial inquiry into the events of June 1937, but it requires mentioning once more.

The girl, who went by the name Laura at that point in time, arrived in my office in quite a state, and I had no reason at that moment to engage such an obviously unsuitable candidate as my apprentice, despite the memorandum that had circulated weeks prior.

Chapter
FOUR

The Skylark sits motionless as the Hawk paces back and forth.

No more than a minute after the country girl had been sent on her merry way, and just as the Skylark was sitting back down to her monthly budget report, the Hawk appeared in a cloud of blue smoke and sparkle. Not every mage was so . . . ostentatious. But the Hawk is the kind of man who believes that everything should stop when he enters a room, hence his choice of portal effect. The man made a special trip up from the Bureau of the Arcane head office in Washington, D.C., just to talk to the Skylark in person. Probably because she so rarely answered his phone calls.

The Skylark does not like the Hawk.

She is doing her best to keep a neutral expression as the man begins to lay yet another problem at her doorstep. This is, of course, not new. The Skylark has dealt with dozens of men just like the Hawk in her tenure with the Bureau of the Arcane, and yet she's still here, while many of them are not. It's one of the reasons she's been able to rise to the head of the New York branch. The mystical arts were sometimes dangerous, and men like the Hawk were usually devoured by their own hubris.

"These issues with the Resonators are popping up faster than we can quell them," he growls, still pacing. The Hawk is a short, pale man given to sweating, his bald pate gleaming in the light and his collar soaked from just his few minutes of treading the tiles, but he is also a first-rate Illusionist. It is a fact the Skylark came to learn after working a couple of cases with him, and one of his three quality attributes—the other two being that he does not seem to hold strong notions about either gender or race, and that he is easily pushed aside. The Hawk, for all his annoying habits, truly did promote the mages he saw as the most competent. Something that the Skylark knew was not popular with everyone in the bureau.

"You're referring to Ohio," the Skylark says, her tone mild. When she joined the Bureau of the Arcane a decade ago at her beloved aunt Clem's urging, she'd dreamed of raveling great works and returning to Georgia some kind of hero mage. She thought that a centralized government organization focused on lifting the country up through the mystical arts would benefit everyone, everywhere—not just those near the big cities, or the Mechomancer firms—and no one in her holler would ever want for anything again.

But it hadn't gone that way, and now, every time someone mentioned the Blights, the Skylark felt herself tensing up. In theory, the repair of the Blights was a bureau priority to ensure people weren't displaced and that all could coexist and thrive. In practice, anyone with half a brain could see how the bureau was directing its efforts, servicing the country's Mechomancers rather than elevating its mages—the Ohio Deep Blight being a prime example.

The Skylark hadn't joined the bureau to help Mechomancy recover from whatever had happened during the Great Rust, and she stayed in spite of the way the higher-ups continued to allocate the bureau's resources. She no longer hopes that the Hawk will call with directives to address crop yields on farms in afflicted regions, only for him to deliver another round of Resonator repair orders. By this point, the Hawk's concerns are as unsurprising as they are disappointing.

However, the fact that the Hawk is now in her office rather than sending yet another memorandum with operational instructions is . . . not a good sign.

"The Blight is spreading, Lark," he says. "I don't think our current operations there are working as hoped. It's a real humdinger of a situation."

For once, the Skylark isn't of a mind to argue with the Hawk. She has seen the reports herself. For years, people have blamed the Great Rust on the actions of mages, straining the Dynamism through the intermingling of various forms of the mystical arts. And yet, it didn't take a genius to see that issues with the Blights seemed to coincide with the very same sort of practices that everyone was trying to save. She longed to grab the Hawk by the collar, give him a good shake, and yell, "It's the Mechomancy, stupid!"

The Skylark, however, does none of this. She tried to broach the idea once, and the result was not good. No one is interested in hearing that the constructs upon which the economy is built are the same ones destroying it—just like no one ever felt like discussing the ways in which Mechomancy had been the single most direct driver of the transatlantic slave trade. So she just smiles, nods, and hopes the irritating man will go away without giving her any extra work.

He doesn't.

The man stops pacing and turns to where the Skylark sits behind the desk, her perfectly arched eyebrows high with expectation. "I'm sending you and the rest of the Colored Auxiliary here in New York to deal with it directly."

The Skylark sighs. "What about the Chicago branch?"

He shakes his head. "The Egret already sent his team in, and . . . they've gone missing. Same with the Pittsburgh branch. There's something happening there. What, exactly, I'm not sure. It might just be that the Resonators have needed more tending to than usual and the Blight damage is keeping them from contacting us. But if it isn't, well . . . you're the only one I trust to figure out what the hell is going on."

The Skylark blinks, slowly. She doesn't need a psychic to know this is bad. "No."

The Hawk's face purples as he stares at the Skylark. "Come again?"

"Mr. Hawk, I am no longer a field agent."

"I understand that, Miss Skylark," he says, tone icy. "Which is why I transported here all the way from D.C. to give you this assignment. In person. If you had an apprentice, as we've discussed on *numerous occasions*, I would have set up an appointment on your calendar, but I see you still have not hired a replacement."

"I have been coordinating increased crop production within the tristate area like we discussed last time you were here," the Skylark calmly responds. "Plus, New Jersey has four Blights of various sizes, and the Department of the Interior has installed Resonators in only one of them. Have you read my reports?"

"Crop production?" the Hawk says, shaking his head. "Do you really think the bureau cares about crop yields?"

"Well, they should. With our oversight, blueberry yields in New Jersey have tripled in volume. And with Blights in a similar state across the Great Plains . . . the last thing we need is people starving to death." Because so many farmers had eschewed Floramancy in favor of Mechomantic contraptions in the late 1800s, crop yields took a nosedive in the Great Rust. The resulting food crisis had the government charging the Bureau of the Arcane with increasing growth of several key crops, and every single one of the Skylark's ten teams was stationed across the East Coast, helping farmers do their jobs a little better. "As for an apprentice, well, it is incredibly difficult to find good, motivated mages who want to work for the bureau."

"And yet, all of your colleagues seem to manage it." All the previous warmth has drained from his voice, and he gives the Skylark a murderous look. "Listen, I don't have to tell you that the Ohio Deep Blight is of utmost concern to the president himself. You are expected to be on-site by day after tomorrow. Coordinate with Onyx and Smoke and their teams here in New York before departing—you're to rendezvous with a contact at the Department of the Interior in Ohio day after tomorrow. Any further instructions will be relayed to you by carrier pigeon." The Hawk drops a too-thin file on the desk before he plops his hat on his head. "And bring your new apprentice."

"Sir?" the Skylark asks.

"The one you're going to hire before departing."

"I told you, the number of suitable candidates—"

"Dammit, Lark! Smoke and Onyx have each taken on four apprentices since the memo went out last year."

"Yes, and each has had one die on their watch," the Skylark points out.

"Yes, that is the chance people take when they join the Colored Auxiliary. Blight management can be dangerous work. But if there are enough Elementalists and Illusionists to fill the ranks, surely you can find one more promising Floramancer in this city."

"And if I refuse to go?" the Skylark asks, her voice low. She can't help but glance at the folder, too thin to be worth much. The bureau is sending them in blind. "I could quit, you know. No having to find a new apprentice, no traveling to fix this mess in Ohio . . ."

"Oh, sure," the Hawk says, smirking. "And if you no longer work here, then I suppose you can consider our previous bargain null and void. I don't know what would happen if the disciplinary council were to catch wind of your previous activities, but I doubt you would come out the other side of the investigation a free woman." There is a long pause, and the Hawk sighs. "I mean it, Estelle. You know that this is bigger than either of us. Stop being difficult."

The Skylark says nothing for a long time, and the rage that surges through her never makes it to her face, her expression remaining pleasant. She won't let the Hawk know how much his threat has rattled her, but she also will not be blackmailed. "Fine, I'll clean up your mess. Again. But don't go thinking that this means you can hold Tennessee over my head forever, *Brian*."

The emphasis she puts on his proper name makes him flinch a bit, but he smiles nonetheless. "Tennessee is exactly why I'm sending you, Lark. Get out there and find our missing mages." He pulls a piece of quartz from his pocket, placing it where the strange floor design converges in the center of the office, and a blue-green portal swirls into being. Before he steps through, he gives the Skylark a meaningful look over his shoulder. "And play nice."

With that, he is gone.

The Skylark takes a deep breath and stares at nothing for a long moment.

The mention of Tennessee has left her shaken. It's not as if she's not used to tending to Blights, even some outside her jurisdiction. But the most she usually has to worry about is a ruined set of clothes. If Ohio is anything like Tennessee . . . She eyes the report folder the Hawk left her. She'd rather not think on that right now.

Instead, she thinks about the matter of her apprentice. She knows why the Hawk is on her about it, just like he is on everyone about filling out the Colored Auxiliary's ranks and codifying the division of mystical workings. To this point, she's been able to avoid the mandate. But it appears that that time is up. Unfortunately, there is only one place she can think of where she can find a willing Floramancer on short notice.

She just hopes this one won't get herself killed.

Woe finds mages wherever they go.

FIVE

Simone, the girl I knew back at the boardinghouse, told me once what happened when a mage got nicked. She'd been caught up in some pretty bad stuff, bootlegging hexes and the like, but she said no matter what they brought someone in for, the process was the same.

"The flatfoots, they got this system, right? They're gonna ask you if you have a license knowing full well you don't, because hardly anyone can get a sponsorship these days unless you're rich and white. Sponsorship is a lie anyway, just another way to make us work for nothing. So you're gonna say no, and then they're going to offer you the opportunity to work for a Mechomancer, who's going to burn you out powering constructs and then kick you to the breadline before the cutoff for your license. If you say no to their generous offer of indenture, they take you to Rikers until a judge can sentence you; if you say yes, then you're gonna sell away your life and end up a husk with no options. They'll make it sound like a better deal taking the indenture, but trust me, go with the jail time. If it's your first offense, you'll get a week in the big house, probably. And those indentures? They last a year, minimum."

It had seemed like great advice at the time, but as I sit in the holding cell at the One-Three, the closest precinct to the Flatiron, where the portal decided to dump me out, I'm not so sure. No one said hardly anything to me; they just threw me into a holding cell in the basement, and no amount of yelling or demanding answers yielded any results. And I tried everything from asking nicely to screaming bloody murder. Predictably, they just threatened to knock my teeth loose if I didn't pipe down, so here I sit, cooling my heels, no options and a whole bunch of questions.

Either way, I know one thing before anyone has even said boo to me: I wouldn't hack a long stint in the slammer. I've already been here long enough to go stir crazy, and when I ask the spider in the corner near the ceiling how long I've been locked up, she graciously answers, *Only half a web's time, dear girl.*

In spider talk, that is about an hour.

So I find a corner, hunker down, and do what I've been doing this whole time in New York when I've been out of choices and life didn't see fit to throw me a bone: I avoid the problem, try not to think about what Pigeon will say when she inevitably finds out, and treat myself to some shut-eye.

At least I finally have a mostly rat-free place to sleep.

●●●

I had given up on anyone coming to tell me what was going to happen and was starting to wonder if I was going to shrivel up and die in prison when the clatter of an outside door startles me out of my funk. I clamber to my feet, straightening my even-more-rumpled dress, and fold my hands in front of me like I am a good girl who would never, ever manipulate the Possibilities without a license.

The cop who collared me is now unlocking the iron door to my cell, and someone else is approaching, the clack of high heels echoing on the stone floor.

It's the woman who kicked me out of the Flatiron. All of my best intentions evaporate, and I cross my arms.

"Say, what's this about?" I demand. The copper says nothing, just swings open the cell door before taking a step back, allowing the fine-looking colored woman to saunter in.

"Here," she says, thrusting a walnut at me. I take it, and the woman continues, "You told me you raveled a unicorn an apple. So show me what you can do." The woman—the Sparrow? The Swallow? —looks a tad bit more disheveled compared with the last time I saw her, her hat askew and lipstick a bit smeared, like she'd run down to the police station. Interesting.

I take a moment to evaluate the lay of the land. I might've been born at night, but it wasn't last night. Simone had warned me that the police have all kinds of tricks up their sleeves, and I'm already in it deep enough on account of raveling a few beers for an old white man. I'm not about to get wrapped up in whatever con these two are running. You can't hustle a hustler.

I hold out the walnut. "Lady, I've never seen you before. I'm a good girl, and I know that unlicensed raveling is illegal. I'm afraid I don't know what you're talking about."

The woman's eyes widen, and then her nostrils flare as she huffs in irritation. "*As you know*, I am the director of the New York office of the Bureau of the Arcane, Floramancy Division. All cases of illicit Floramancy performed by unlicensed mages are processed by my office, you ridiculous girl. Now ravel me a damn apple; I won't ask you again."

I roll the walnut in my hand and consider my options, which reside on the corner of Slim and None. But her fit of pique has the ring of truth, and the unicorn had said this woman was the most powerful mage in the Big Apple. Unicorns are pills, make no mistake, but falsehoods and riddles aren't their cup of tea. They leave those sorts of things for sphinxes.

"This is too much potential for an apple," I say, finally.

The copper shifts his weight uncomfortably, hand on his baton. But then the finely dressed colored woman tilts her head the slightest bit, and a hint of a smile ghosts around her lips. "Frugal. That's good. Make yourself some lunch, then. I know these boys in blue haven't fed you."

I snort. "And end up eating something poisonous? No thanks. You know as well as I do that I'm in for a bit of blowback if I ravel it for myself."

"You aren't nearly as clueless as you look either," she says. "Good."

"Hey!" My temper begins to flare again, and I'm half tempted to flip the walnut at the woman, but I don't. Because a tiny tendril of hope has unfurled deep in my heart. This is the closest I've gotten to any kind of job prospect in the past three months. I want to see where it goes. I cannot help but to hope that all of this is on the up-and-up. Plus, I'm not exactly keen at spending another moment in lockup. Indenture was starting to look good, but the Colored Auxiliary would be a far cry better.

"So, then, my dear, what do you suggest you do with all of that potential?" the woman continues, some of the tension draining away from her. Whatever lit a fire under her is burning out, leaving behind a stylish woman who is as cool as the backside of the pillow. For a moment I forget about her smug attitude and prickly demeanor, and I desperately wish I were her, looking like something out of a fashion magazine and as self-possessed as a starlet. But I very quickly push the yearning aside. Wishes have a way of messing up things, and I have raveling to focus on.

I roll the walnut around in my hand, getting cozy with the grooves of the shell. "How about I make Johnny Law over there some chow?"

The woman looks at the officer, who appears amused at being brought into whatever this is. "Are you okay with her raveling something for you?" she asks.

The copper shrugs. "Sure, sweetheart, whatever floats your boat."

I close my eyes and feel through the Possibilities. The police officer is easy to spot. His feet hurt, and his wife is on his case again because she found out that he's still betting money on the ponies. He also doesn't know it, but part of the reason she's so uptight is because she's got a bun in the oven and she's excited but worried about having another mouth to feed in this busted economy. I push aside those entanglements. He hasn't eaten, and his hunger stands out in shades of orange and blue.

And now I know exactly what to ravel.

I reach into the Possibilities and tug, using the walnut as fuel for the working. Blands always expect sparks or smoke when mages get to raveling, but that's just Hollywood adding a bit of the old razzle-dazzle. When I ravel the walnut, manifesting its potential as something else entirely, there's a popping sound, like opening an ice-cold bottle of Coca-Cola.

The walnut is no more. Now it's a honey-ham sandwich on rye bread with all the fixings and extra mustard, a beautiful pickle balanced on top.

The woman nods once, and her smirk melts into a beatific smile. "Marvelous. Well, I suppose you will do after all. Come along now."

The woman turns back toward the exit and begins walking off with quick steps. The officer and I just look at each other, blinking in confusion.

"Well, do not just stand there looking like a twit," she says, looking back over her shoulder. "Give him the sandwich and let us be on our way."

I hastily hand the man the ham on rye, and he takes it with a smile. Then I jog to catch up with the woman—The Skylark! That's her name—and an exclamation of dismay echoes down the hall just as we reach the stairs.

The Skylark looks at me with a raised eyebrow, and I shrug. "He just discovered there's swiss cheese on the sandwich."

"And?"

"He hates swiss cheese. Reminds him of his older sister." I cannot quite keep the grin of triumph off my face, even though it pulls painfully at my busted lip.

The Skylark stops and considers me, pausing perhaps a moment longer than she should. She looks like she's about to ask me something, then shakes her head. "Come on. We haven't a moment to waste if you're going to be ready for your first assignment."

I say nothing, just follow the Skylark out of the police station, grinning the whole way. The hot late afternoon sun hits me full force, burning away my relief. It strikes me that I have no idea what the Colored Auxiliary of the Conservation Corps actually does. "Hey, um, so what did I win? Did I just get a job?"

The Skylark gives me an incredulous look but doesn't stop walking. I'm forced to run to keep up with her quick stride.

"Why, you silly creature, you have just won the pleasure of being my apprentice. Now get home and pack your bags. You'll need to be moved into the rooming house before we leave. Where are you residing at the moment?"

"Not important," I say. "Won't be a problem."

"Good. We'll be heading to Ohio on Thursday."

"Ohio! But there's nothing there."

"You're not wrong, unfortunately. But take heart; we have other matters to attend to before we leave. Tomorrow we'll head over to New Jersey at nine a.m., sharp."

"New Jersey?" I say, trying to fight the feeling that I have made a very, very bad bargain. "That's even worse than Ohio."

"What, you thought working for the government was going to be all chatting with unicorns in park gardens?" the Skylark says, her tone dismissive. "Welcome to the Bureau of the Arcane. Now we need to get back to the office to do your intake paperwork before it gets late. So hurry up."

I sigh and try to match her pace, and I have the sneaking suspicion that this is a very bad idea.

Should've known better than to listen to that blasted unicorn.

The Mystical Arts
Encyclopedia Arcana, 1932 Edition

All the mystical arts function in a similar way, using a layer of global, interlocking power known as the Dynamism (see: DYNAMISM, page 26) to influence construction of materials and manipulate their most basic properties. This should not be confused with Mechomancy, which uses distilled energy to power manmade constructs and more closely falls under the umbrella of scientific manipulation (see: MECHOMANCY, page 234). The traditional mystical arts are often referred to as "lower arts," a colloquialism that has become more widely accepted in the wake of the proliferation of Mechomancy and its increased global influence in the nineteenth century.

Cerebromancy: Predominantly empathy, precognition, and mind reading. An area of study involved with utilizing the mind as a direct conduit to the Dynamism.

Faunomancy: The control of living creatures, including mythical beasts. Faunomancers were hunted during the Great Purge (see: WESTERN RECLAMATION, page 503), and Faunomancy is considered a threat to good law and order in most civilized nations. It is highly regulated in most Western nations.

Floramancy: The use of nature, most especially seeds and pods, to cast a variety of basic spells. The most basic form of mysticism, practiced by mages called Floramancers.

Illusion: Once thought to be a subset of Cerebromancy, because of the necessary mental component, Illusion has grown to become its own category since the invention of the motion picture, which proved Illusion used more than just the perception of living creatures. Even Mechomantic creations are susceptible to the workings of Illusionists.

Pavomancy: An ancient practice that uses stars, leylines, and magnetic fields to create pathways from one point to another, navigated by mages called Wayfarers.

Petramancy: The raising of stones or crystals from the ground to ravel or create new structures. One of the oldest known mystical disciplines (see: GOLEMS, page 134). Practitioners today are often referred to as Elementalists.

Sanamancy: The use of the Dynamism to repair damage to living organisms. More commonly known as healing. An extremely complex and dangerous art to learn.

Forbidden Disciplines

Figuramancy: More commonly known as shape-shifting. A weaker form of Cerebromancy, it can nevertheless be dangerous to the Illusionist if a form is held for too long (see: LOUP-GAROU, page 212).

Necromancy: The manipulation and permutation of dead matter. Includes reanimating the dead as well as synthesizing their remains into undead creatures. Illegal in most countries because of the high cost of spellweaving (on both the Necromancer and the Dynamism), as well as the historical uses of its energies (see: THE AFRIKAN GENOCIDE, page 13).

Wytchcraft: Also known in mystical circles simply as Craft. The combination of several of the low or forbidden arts without the proper respect for their distinct mystical boundaries, leading to a high probability of blowback. Its widespread and unregulated practice throughout the early twentieth century is considered a likely cause of a destructive phenomenon known as a reversion wave (see: REVERSION WAVE, page 426; THE GREAT RUST, page 157; WYTCHES, page 522).

The view from the roof of the rooming house.
Now you can see why I wasn't all that anxious to pay my rent.

Chapter

SIX

There's nothing interesting about paperwork, and that goes triple for government paperwork. It takes me an hour to fill out my personal information and family history.

The questionnaire about my abilities, however, is much simpler. I just have to check a box.

"Just one?" I ask, looking down the list. *Cerebromancy, Floramancy, Pavomancy, Petramancy, Sanamancy.* There's also a line for anything that doesn't fall under those larger categories.

"Naturally," the Skylark says. "I'm sure I don't need to tell you that the practice of Craft is strictly prohibited by the Bureau of the Arcane."

I roll my eyes inwardly but don't say anything. No need to make any trouble on my first day. "How am I supposed to do . . . whatever it is we do, if I'm not yet licensed?

"You'll have an apprentice's provision, allowing you to work the Dynamism while supervised by a licensed agent like myself," she replies. "And what do you mean, *whatever it is we do?*"

"Just . . . I'm not entirely sure what our whole purpose is?" I say as I tick the box for *Floramancy*. "The Conservation Corps,' Colored Auxiliary?"

The Skylark blinks at me. "You applied for the job and don't know what the corps does?"

"I, uh . . . I know that it has something to do with President Roosevelt? His plan to fix the Great Rust?"

She puts a hand on her hip. "And what about all that business about serving your country? Your interest in Mechomancy?"

I grimace. "To be honest, ma'am, I just said that bit because I thought that was what you wanted to hear."

There is a subtle shift in the Skylark's expression. "I see. Well, yes, as you said, the Conservation Corps was created by the Bureau of the Arcane under the first Roosevelt administration to deal with the various effects of the Great Rust. I likely don't need to tell you that the government didn't seem to have much of a need for mages by the midtwenties; Mechomancy was the foundation of the country's economy, used to create everything from household appliances to farm equipment to bridges and dams. When the Blights appeared, however, anything that ran on or had been built by Mechomancy stopped working, the light artistry holding the machines and structures together evaporating in a blink. I'm sure you've seen images of Blighted zones?"

I nod. Shrinesville isn't all that far from the Scranton Blight, and I saw what it had done: collapsed bridges, buildings reduced to rubble. It was like that everywhere. There was one famous photograph that the papers loved to reprint: a white farmer in Omaha looking over his land, dozens of rusted tractors and harvesters dotting his withering fields like cattle that had just lain down to die.

"The Conservation Corps was created to assist Mechomancers in rebuilding this infrastructure so the country can recover," the Skylark went on. "A job that, more often than not, requires us mages to use our abilities to beat back the effects of the Blights, and come up with new techniques to make Mechomantic machinery resilient to these effects while the mages at the bureau work on a more permanent fix for the Blights, which has eluded us to this point. But that's not all. The Great Rust has affected crop yields, coal and oil supplies, rivers and lakes, you name it. That's where the Colored Auxiliary comes in. The vast majority of the work in these areas needs to be performed by Elementalists and Floramancers, since our abilities still work in Blighted zones. And as you well know, most of the folks who are still actively training in the traditional mystical arts are colored."

I nod, but a strange feeling starts to fester in my middle. Why is it that we're supposed to fix all these things that someone else broke? It doesn't seem fair. But I need the work, so I say nothing as the Skylark continues.

"The Colored Auxiliary's primary purpose is to mitigate the effects of the Blights, whatever they are," the Skylark continues. "While our abilities aren't hindered by the Blights, and the damage to the Dynamism for the most part doesn't have any direct effects on people or animals, there have been exceptions to this. We tend to crops and livestock, strengthen the ravels for roads and levees, address medical ailments that have struck some folks within Blighted zones; just about anything that needs doing, that's us. We're also asked to address any other . . . peculiar phenomena that arise in Blighted zones. You've heard of Blight Beasts, yes?"

I nod again. Everyone had heard of them, though photographic evidence was nonexistent. The beasts supposedly took shape only within the Blights, and they apparently resisted being photographed.

"I know the way the country regards the Colored Auxiliary—like glorified janitors—but the truth is that the work we do can be dangerous, and our tasks are many and varied. For the last year, for instance, most of what we've been doing is Resonator management."

"You mean those Mechomancer contraptions," I say. It's not a question. I'd heard that the Blights nearest to the cities had started getting these things—machines that, when charged by a mage, could dissipate the effects of the Blights for miles around. When we first heard about them on the radio, I thought it sounded like a bunch of Mechomancer nonsense. They'd probably do the Blighted areas more harm than good. But Pigeon said we didn't have anything to worry about in Shrinesville. She said they likely wouldn't be installing any fancy machines anywhere near a dinky little town that's mostly farmers and Negro mages anyhow.

The Skylark nods. "That's right. The Resonators are designed to lessen the impacts of Blights on the local population. We keep the Resonators charged, and they can suppress the Blights' effects for weeks or months at a time. That's the theory, anyway. In practice, these things need constant charging, and they break down more often than they're supposed to. Hence, us getting sent all over creation to fix them. But they tell us the newest Resonators should be able to run smoothly for years, without a charge, even."

"Golly," I say. "Pretty soon, they won't need us mages at all, huh?"

I mean it as a joke, but either the Skylark doesn't find it funny or she doesn't have any sense of humor whatsoever. I'm thinking it might be the latter. Whatever the truth is, though, her face remains blank as she continues.

"I am sorry to say it, but it looks like you're going to be learning what we do on the job. There's something going on with the Ohio Deep Blight—multiple Resonators on the fritz there, more than the Colored Auxiliary in the area can handle, so we've been called in to assist." There's the smallest twitch in her expression, but it's gone just as quickly. "First, however, we're going to make that trip to New Jersey that I mentioned, where I will show you how we go about charging up the Resonators. That way, you'll be at least a little prepared for when we make the trek to Ohio."

I nod and return to my paperwork. All apprentices get a room, board, and twenty-five bucks a month, which is more than I've seen in ages. After I've finished the questions and smeared ink across the piece of paper, the Skylark has me raise my hand to swear my allegiance to working for the betterment of the United States.

"I assume from your dodging of my question earlier that you do not have your own lodgings for this evening?" the Skylark says as she gathers my paperwork.

I nod sheepishly.

She sighs. "I'll have to make some arrangements to get your space ready in our rooming house, but the quartermaster has most likely left for the day. For tonight, you can stay in the office and sleep on the sofa. Tomorrow, after we are finished with our tasks, we'll get you squared away."

I nod, suddenly homesick again. My last two sleeps have been spent in a rat-infested tenement and a jail cell, and now this one will be in a government office.

I'm not sure if the Skylark notices, but her voice softens. "Rest up, and I'll meet you at nine a.m., sharp, tomorrow at Penn Station."

"Where are you going?" I ask.

She gives me a tight smile. "I'm afraid I have matters of my own to attend to. There's some cold chicken in the icebox if you get hungry, and some dime novels on the wall over there. Try not to destroy anything—the wards get rather nasty if you do."

The Skylark leaves, and I am left alone in the office in the Flatiron. The lights flicker on automatically as I enter a small kitchenette off the main office, and I root through the icebox and find not only the chicken but a few strawberries. Strawberry seeds are usually too small to have much potential, but I run my hands over the fruit just in case. A good mage never wastes Possibility.

After I eat, I find a romance tucked back in the corner of the shelf, and I read until I feel sleepy. The couch is comfortable, and although there's no blanket, the office is warm enough that I don't mind.

I'm so happy to finally have secured employment, I drift off easily, my dreams filled with the fabulous creations I will one day ravel for Hollywood stars.

Though it hardly seemed possible when today started, I can't help but wonder if I'm one step closer to my impossible dream.

●●●

I manage to wake up well before nine a.m., and the morning is mercifully cool. By the time I arrive at Penn Station, I admit, I'm actually feeling pretty good about the impression I'll make this time.

That feeling should have been my first sign that I was in trouble.

When I meet the Skylark at the eastern side of the station, she halts me before I've climbed even partway up the impressive steps that lead to the entrance.

"What are you wearing?" she asks.

My bindle, dropped when the cop collared me, was by some stroke of luck still sitting on the ground by the entrance to the Flatiron when I'd accompanied the Skylark back to the building yesterday, so I was able to switch out my blue dress for my yellow dress, which is no more fashionable or attractive but does fit a little better, draping in at least a somewhat flattering way over what Linus Colby had once called my "prodigious curves." I hadn't thought much of Linus, but that compliment stuck. Inspired by the sight of the Skylark the day before, and intimidated by the idea of working with someone so very fashionable, I had wrestled my curls into a low bun, which while messy is more professional and sophisticated than the girlish braids I had yesterday.

At least, that's what I thought.

But there is no way I am in the same league as the Skylark; we aren't even playing the same sport. She wears a black-and-white-checkered traveling suit, complete with matching heels. Today's hat is a bright red fascinator that accents the ensemble, and the effect is something straight out of a fashion rag.

I take a deep breath and square my shoulders, forcefully pushing aside my insecurities. We're going to New Jersey, after all, and chances are more people will be dressed like me than the Skylark. "This is my traveling dress," I say.

"How many *dresses* do you *have*?" the Skylark asks, the words punctuated like she is trying to find the rumored patience of Jesus and failing.

"Two. I like to keep my look, uh, spartan," I say with what I hope is a wry smile. It seems like a better answer than to just declare that I'm broke.

"You should've mentioned you needed clothes." The Skylark picks up her valise and sighs as she begins to descend the stairs again. I run to follow her. "We are going to have to outfit you before we go anywhere. I thought we could do it later, but this"— she gestures in my general direction—"needs rectifying."

Curiously, she seems less annoyed than she does resigned, as though she was expecting this turn of events. Which I suppose she should have been. It's not as if any rich and successful mages were champing at the bit to join the Conservation Corps. If there were even any left.

We reach the bottom of the stairs, and the Skylark hails a cab. "You cannot go around fulfilling your role as an agent of the US government looking like an orphan begging for bread crusts," she says. Her tone is mild, but the words still sting. "We're Negroes; the locals are already going to suspect we're running some kind of hustle when we show up to help, Bureau of the Arcane credentials or no. Looking needy will only make them more suspicious. How old are you, by the way?"

I blink. "Seventeen."

"Seventeen. Nearly a woman. Even more of a reason we need to get you a proper wardrobe."

"Why don't we just take the portals?" I ask, gesturing to the entrance nearby, desperate to change the subject. This woman reminds me too much of Pigeon, and a jab of homesickness threatens sudden tears. I guess I just have a soft spot for henpeckery.

"Because where we are going, the portals do not."

A man stops his construct at the curb, the Mechomancy stinking of oil and combustion. The rubber smell of the tires nauseates me, and climbing inside is the last thing I want to do. He eyes us before sticking his head out of the vehicle. "Double for darkies," he says, matter-of-factly. There's a nonchalance to his voice as the slur rolls off his tongue that makes it feel even more terrible than usual.

"Fine," the Skylark says, unbothered. I want to point out that her fancy clothes didn't make the cabbie any less of a heel, but I wisely keep my mouth shut.

The cab takes the Skylark and me across the river, and I press my face to the glass to look for krakens or water dragons. There's a chance you'll see some of the tinier ones sunbathing on such a warm day. But there's nothing but dirty water and a momentary view of the Manhattan skyline before we're swallowed by buildings on the other side.

The man pulls his metal monster over to the first curb he sees, in the middle of a neighborhood without any kind of storefront. "This is as far as I go," he says.

The Skylark is visibly annoyed but again does not seem surprised. "Fine, but don't go expecting a tip," she says, handing the man a quarter before getting out. I follow, much less gracefully.

"Where are we?" I ask, taking in the neat rows of houses. I've never been to this part of the city.

"Brooklyn. Bedford-Stuyvesant, to be specific. It's not much to look at just yet, but as soon as the portal station is finished this will be a bustling neighborhood. Come, the tailor is just a bit farther."

We walk along the wide sidewalk, lined with brownstones that are impressive but have an air of moderate neglect, like an apple left a little too long on the counter. Across the street a cadre of mages—Elementalists, presumably—raise massive pillars of amethyst from the ground. Most of the work crew is white men, but I note the telltale curls of a few Jewish men, a number of whom wave at the Skylark as we pass. She returns their jaunty waves, a rare smile bending her red lips.

"Do you know what they're doing?" she asks.

I watch as the men strain, and the scent of fresh earth and iron tickles my nose. "Raising pillars?"

"Yes, but why?" she asks.

"Those crystals anchor a Wayfarer's portal, right?"

She gives me an approving smile, and I almost stumble in shock. "Indeed. Once the pillars have been raised and the ravel is set, a single Wayfarer will be able to activate a portal directly to the Manhattan network, which can send people to whichever stop they need. It'll be much faster than the old method of opening a Wayfarer's gate, and people in neighborhoods like this one, and even ones farther out into Brooklyn and Queens, will be able to get to Manhattan in a blink." She casts a look across the street, and what she says next is quieter. "Despite what most folks say about Mechomancy, the mystical arts can still do things more efficiently."

"Do you know them?" I ask, giving the workmen one last glance as we continue walking.

"I know just about every mage in the five boroughs."

"You didn't know me," I say.

"All of the *licensed* mages." She gives me a sharp look, her penciled eyebrows a cool slash of judgment, and it's another opportunity for me to study her face. She's really pretty, and the sudden realization knocks me for a loop. It's weird to think that someone so prickly could also be pretty. I usually don't do well with pretty women. I tend to fall all over myself to make them happy, and that seems like a recipe for disaster with someone as curt as the Skylark. Trying to make this woman happy would be a fool's errand. But that doesn't mean I won't try. There's a license in it for me if I play my cards right, but I'm beginning to wonder if working for the Skylark might not be so bad in itself. Besides, twenty-five dollars a month is a whole bunch of cheddar.

"Here we are," she says. We've stopped in front of a redbrick storefront with a candy-striped awning and wide, clear windows. Madame Alistair's Coterie Extraordinaire, proclaims the gold lettering etched onto the glass. And then, smaller: By Appointment Only.

"I don't suppose you made an appointment?" I ask.

The Skylark rings the bell next to the door. "You needn't worry; they know we're coming. Barb will have seen it."

There's the sound of approaching footsteps, and a light-skinned Negro woman opens the door. She wears a pink silk robe, and her hair is in rag curlers. My mouth goes dry. She's too pretty by half, the kind of girl that belongs in a pinup calendar, not answering the bell at a tailor. Upturned nose, rosebud lips, and a heart-shaped face.

It is a morning full of insecurities for me, and I dislike it greatly. I haven't felt this peculiar since the day Willie Farnsworth asked me to go walking with him in the woods and tried to kiss me. It would've been the worst day of my life, but it happened under a black walnut tree, so I at least had a bounty of bits to show for my troubles. I still sometimes have nightmares about that boy's lips coming for me, all puckered and ridiculous. I'm the same kind of nervous now, completely unprepared for whatever I'm about to walk into.

"You aren't supposed to be here until tomorrow," the beauty mumbles, leaning against the doorframe while smothering a yawn. Her robe slips down, giving me a tantalizing glimpse of her shoulder. She notices me noticing and gives me a wink, and my heart fairly leaps out of my chest like I'm an extra in a Betty Boop short.

The Skylark, thankfully, doesn't take note of it. "Barbara, have you been in the gin again? You know it futzes with your perception."

The finest thing I have ever seen in all five boroughs heaves a dramatic sigh and rubs her eyes with the back of her hand. "It's not my fault. It's all Alistair brought back from her last trip to London. I keep telling her I have to stick to whiskey or it's going to be nothing but confusion in the shop, but . . ." She trails off. "Anyhow, come on in; she's awake, as usual."

Barbara steps backward, disappearing into the gloom of the shop, and the Skylark follows. I trail behind, wards tickling my skin as I pass through the doorway. Just beyond is an empty room with a wood floor, the boards immaculate. It takes a moment for my eyes to adjust, and once they do, Barbara gestures the Skylark and me over to a low brocade settee.

"I'll get Alistair and be right back," she says with a slow smile. Her hips are like a metronome as she leaves.

I am in love.

I take in my surroundings, because this is the first time I've ever been somewhere like this and I want to do it justice when I finally write Pigeon about it. The walls are papered in a design reminiscent of paisley, focusing signs woven into the flocked paper. There are no electric lights to be seen, the space lit by stone sconces, crystals raveled to emit light. A bowl of walnuts—a fortune's worth—sits in the middle of a coffee table atop a frilly lace doily. There's no fabric, no baskets of notions like one might find in the shop of the seamstress back in Shrinesville. Whatever kind of tailor Alistair is, she's using the mystical arts for her creations. I want to take a picture of it all, but I feel like that would annoy the Skylark, so I leave the camera in my oversize skirt pocket.

It's funny; this was the kind of life I'd imagined when I'd packed up my bindle and lit out for the Big Apple, and now that it's finally happening, I'm not entirely sure what to do with myself.

"Skylark! What an unexpected surprise." A woman with a deep voice, a plummy British accent, and blue-black skin walks through the back of the room, the decorative wall concealing the doorway she uses to enter, a different door than Barbara used to leave. Her hair is slicked down in a conk, and she wears fitted trousers with a white dress shirt and suspenders, which only lengthen her wiry frame. Her wing tips are shined within an inch of their life, and her smile is wide and welcoming, despite the slight censure in her words.

If I had thought myself in love before, I am absolutely gob-smacked now.

"Alistair, stop giving Barbara gin. We've discussed this," the Skylark says, sighing. I'm starting to think the Skylark has a whole retinue of sighs. This one is less exasperated and more amused while also being a little irked.

"You're Alistair?" I ask after a moment, feeling a little off balance. The women in this city, my goodness. I have always yearned to wear a well-tailored suit, and Alistair does it effortlessly.

"Yes, it's an old family name. And you must be the new apprentice. Stars help you," she says with a hearty laugh.

"No tales out of school," the Skylark says, standing. "We were supposed to get an early jump to Trenton so the girl here and I can meet Onyx and balance that latest Blight."

"The Resonator's failed again?" Alistair asks.

"Naturally," the Skylark replies. "As you can see, however, this one needs something to wear. Onyx is going to give me an earful for being late, but I cannot have an apprentice who looks like she just got off the breadline." Skylark gives me an arch look, but I say nothing. What can I say? She's right.

"I think we can do something about that," Alistair says with a smile.

"I thought you might agree," the Skylark replies. "Also: she needs a name."

I blink stupidly at that last bit. Names are a big deal, and pricey here in New York; I figured taking a name would be something that I wouldn't get to do until I'd been a licensed mage for a while. Even paying for a bootleg name is a huge expense. My sister had to save for three whole years before the local seer dubbed her Pigeon. Though it was certainly worth it. A huge improvement over *Dorothy*, though I would never tell her or my mama that.

"You're a medium?" I ask Alistair, since those are the folks who usually do namings. Alistair shakes her head.

"No, Barb's the farseer. I am an . . . expert in exploiting the Possibilities," she says.

"The *Dynamism*," the Skylark corrects with a scowl. Alistair just gives a liquid shrug. "But she is being modest. She is the best tailor in three states. If she can't dress you properly, it can't be done."

Alistair gives another of her musical laughs. "Always so complimentary. She's right, of course. Let me get my kit. Make yourself at home."

"Thank you," I manage, still rather stunned.

"If you'd truly like to thank me, we haven't eaten breakfast yet," she says, gesturing at the bowl of walnuts with long fingers. I figure that means I'm supposed to ravel them up something to eat. A ravel like that wouldn't come close to covering a new outfit nor a name, but at least it's something I can do.

I glance at the Skylark for her okay, and she nods. I reach for the bowl, picking the two nuts that call to me the loudest. And then I close my eyes and reach.

Just like with the copper, I look to where Barbara and Alistair touch the Possibilities. It takes no more than a couple of heartbeats to see Alistair's yearning: an old-fashioned English breakfast complete with beans and a slice of tomato. Barbara is just wishing her headache would go away, so I make her an extra spicy Red Snapper, a drink I read about in one of my favorite magazines. One nut ravels into a deep red beverage in an ice-cold glass and looks more appetizing than I'm expecting. I personally can't understand why anyone would want to drink tomato juice and vodka loaded with olives, but the article claimed it was the best cure for an evening of excess.

Alistair returns, Barbara in tow—the younger woman has

taken out the rag curlers and slipped into a blue dress with an embroidered hemline of birds in flight. Her eyes light up as she sees what I've done. "Say, that's swell! I had one last time I was in France. Didn't realize these were finally catching on here in the States." She picks up the glass and drinks deeply, draining it before using the straw to fish out the olives at the bottom.

"You even got the toast just right," Alistair says, looking at her breakfast with a bit of contemplative surprise. Barbara begins to eye the food, and Alistair slides the plate across the table. She grins as she plops down next to me and digs into the plate of eggs, beans, toast, and sausage with sliced tomatoes. She smells like lavender and sunshine, and my palms get a little sweaty just sitting this close to her.

"How is it that you choose a person's name?" I ask, to distract myself from her effortless beauty. Naming is a closely guarded secret, one of the few rituals that psychics do not talk about. Even Pigeon had refused to tell me anything about the day she got her bootleg name.

Barbara swallows and wipes at the corner of her mouth. "I can't tell you all that, silly! But don't worry; it doesn't hurt a lick."

"I wasn't worried. . . ."

"Buttercup, you look like you just saw the ghost of Robert E. Lee coming to enslave your soul," she says with a laugh. She drops the fork onto the plate and slides it over to Alistair to finish before she twists so that she's facing me. "Here, give me your hands."

I hold them out, and she takes them in hers. She closes her eyes and purses her lips, and when she does I completely forget about

Alistair and the Skylark sitting nearby. There's a tug, and I can feel Barbara reaching into the Possibilities and doing . . . something. If I closed my eyes and focused I could probably see, but I'm enjoying the view in front of me too much to try.

Barbara suddenly stiffens, and her eyes fly open. Her pupils and irises are gone, her eyes white like they've been covered by a thick film. Alistair makes a move toward Barbara, but the Skylark puts a hand on her arm, gently restraining her.

"Is this normal?" I croak just as Barbara's hands grip mine tightly enough to hurt. I try to yank my hands back, but she's got them fast. Barbara's lips begin to move, but the sounds she makes are no language I know. It's guttural and strange, like she's having a conversation with someone else.

"You said it wouldn't hurt," I yelp, and try to pull my hands back once more, but there's no getting loose. I cry out in pain and shoot to my feet, trying to pull myself free. "A little help?" I ask, my question coming out less as words and more as a whine of agony.

"I've never seen this happen before," Alistair says, her face twisted with concern. "Estelle, you have to stop her."

"I can't and I won't; this is Barbara's ability. Do not remove your hands," the Skylark says sharply, directing that last bit at me. She is completely unbothered by the strange turn of events, but then again she's not having her hands turned into ground chuck. "Let her ride out the vision."

I moan, hot tears tracking down my cheeks as Barbara continues to grip my hands painfully, but eventually I take a couple of deep breaths and sink back down on the settee. I once heard a woman talk about childbirth as an inescapable misery followed by a reward unlike any other. Whatever my prize is after this torture, I really hope it doesn't require the use of my hands.

Several heartbeats later, Barbara relaxes, her eyes clearing up as she stares into mine. "For speed and ruthlessness and the ties that bind, you are Peregrine," she says, her voice deep and filled with some power that raises goose bumps up and down my arms. "You are patient, but only because you wait for the perfect moment to strike. This will not be the only name you have, but it is the name you will carry for now."

As Barbara drops my hands, I give a nervous laugh. I'm mostly relieved that I can flex my fingers and get the blood flowing back into them. "Peregrine. That sounds like an okay name."

"It is a very good name," the Skylark says, giving me that curious look once more.

"You have a great task ahead of you," Barbara says, blinking owlishly after her strange fit. I don't ask her to clarify. Everyone knows it's bad luck to ask a psychic about the future. Nothing good can ever come of knowing the many possible paths through time, so I just nod in acknowledgment of the words.

Alistair looks from me to Barbara and clears her throat. "Well, let us find you a suitable ensemble, now that you have a name."

I nod, wanting leave this episode behind as quickly as possible. But I can't help but feel like the friendly, jovial mood is all but gone. The tone now is downright *ominous*. The Skylark continues to study me like I'm a new lab specimen. Barbara has sort of folded in on herself, as though the naming took more from her than she'd expected. And Alistair seems much less self-assured, her hands smoothing and rearranging her clothes like she can tailor the awkward right out of the situation.

Alistair gestures for me to follow her, and I do, standing to go. My hands still hurt, half-moon indentations visible on my palms from Barbara's murderous grip, and as we leave, the Skylark murmurs to Barbara in a low voice, although I can't hear what she's asking.

"Was your name always Alistair?" I ask, trying to change the subject, and she laughs.

"I've had a number of names; this is just my most recent."

"What kind of bird is an Alistair?" I ask. I've only ever heard folks take bird names. Not sure why, though. Figured it was just common practice.

"No bird at all. I told you, it's a family name. Now, no more questions. I need to focus."

I want to ask Alistair what her discipline is, but that feels rude, so I just button it. We step through the doorway into another room, and I sense a tug and push of some kind. It feels a bit like a Wayfarer's ravel, and I wonder if we stepped through that doorway into a place much deeper in the building than I think—or perhaps someplace else entirely.

But even though I try to distract myself, my attention is still on the strange moment that I just experienced in the sitting room. I've never had a psychic do a reading before, not even to read the stars when I was born. Ma was firmly against such nonsense and always said looking into the future was just borrowing trouble. Better to just pay it when it came due. And now I understand why.

Just because I'm not supposed to ask about the future doesn't mean I won't wonder.

Much has been made about my apprentice and the abilities she demonstrated while tackling the Ohio Deep Blight. The truth is that I had no demonstrable knowledge that the girl was anything more than she was, not even during our visit to licensed mages 23190, Barbara Calder, and 16798, ███████ ████████.

Chapter

SEVEN

While Laura gets the once-over from Alistair, the Skylark remains in the sitting room with Barbara. Despite her reassurances to Alistair, who dotes on her partner a bit too much, the Skylark has never witnessed such a scene. She has heard tales—the Bureau of the Arcane is full of such war stories, with mages relating all manner of strange and unpredictable occurrences within the Dynamism. But this? Barbara's channeling was more strange and unpredictable than most.

That makes the Skylark wonder any number of things—most of all, who her new apprentice really is.

"Barb? Are you still with me?"

The woman turns to the Skylark, her eyes wide. "Yes. Bit fuzzy, though. She's strong. Much stronger than she looks. I'm glad you finally found an apprentice who uses Craft as effortlessly as you do, though. Knowing I wanted something cool and refreshing for this headache? Genius. I know a couple pubs here in Brooklyn that would hire her on the spot, license or no."

The Skylark chuckles. "Yes, well, the girl almost didn't get the position. She came in blathering about Mechomancy and 'serving her country,' sounding like the ghost of Booker T. Washington. But her facility with the Dynamism has been . . . surprising. Still, with the governmental line on the Great Rust still being that it was the result of Wytchcraft, I don't need her getting us into hot water. I will have to speak with her."

The Skylark pulls a walnut from the bowl in the middle of table, bouncing it off the surface. As it flies through the air, it ravels into another one of the tomato-juice concoctions the Peregrine created. It lands softly on the tabletop, the ice in the glass rising slowly to the top.

"Show-off," Barbara chides with a smile. But she picks up the glass and drinks deeply.

"She's not . . . like me, is she?" the Skylark asks, phrasing the question carefully.

Barbara shakes her head. "She's one hundred percent red-blooded human being, as far as I can tell. Though I've never met anyone like you, and who knows what I would have seen if I'd known you before Tennessee?"

The Skylark cannot help but wonder as well, but she says nothing.

Barbara takes another sip of her cocktail, then puts it down, her expression pensive. "You should know her trepidation is earnest, and she hasn't lied about anything she's told you thus far. She is hiding something, but I daresay it could be something even she herself doesn't know about." She thinks for a moment, then smiles. "She looks up to you, you know."

The bark of laughter that erupts from the Skylark is genuine. "The girl doesn't even know me." She leans back into the seat cushions, relaxing for the first time that morning. With her fledgling apprentice otherwise occupied, she takes a moment to decompress before the upcoming storm. She stayed up until early morning perusing the latest reports coming back from the Ohio Deep Blight, and they were worse than she had thought. Not only was the Blight now growing at the rate of a square mile a week, but the initial reports by the teams sent in to mitigate the damage were not good. There were notes about strange sightings, as well as a growing tally of missing mages across a number of disciplines. At first it had been just a couple here and there. Now it was whole teams. All colored mages that no one seemed inclined to go searching for, of course.

Barbara finishes her drink and appears to make up her mind about something. "Look, it's bad form for me to tell you what I saw when I pulled down the girl's name, but you should know, because it's going to impact you as much as it will her. She's about to go through a change. A shifting of fortunes."

The Skylark blinks, momentarily taken aback by the tone in her voice. "Well, of course she is. She's just joined the Bureau of the Arcane."

Barbara shakes her head, her curls swishing with the forcefulness of her response. "No, you don't understand. It's more than that. You're about to embark on a mission, yes? It's going to end up being more than you think."

The Skylark's mirth fades away. "We're going to the Ohio Deep Blight."

Barbara's eyes widen. "Estelle, are you certain that's a good idea? What about your . . . condition?"

The Skylark rolls her eyes and decides to ignore the woman's use of her true name. "I don't need to remind you I've been working Blights since before you were in pigtails. And I've dealt with much worse, besides."

"I know, but . . . why don't you just give me your hands—"

"No," the Skylark says abruptly, drawing away, then catches herself. "I'm sorry, Barb. I appreciate it; really, I do. But I'll be fine—*we'll* be fine. Besides," she says as she stands, "it's not as if a reading did me any good before Tennessee."

Barb appears to want to say something else, then thinks better of it and nods.

The Skylark straightens her jacket and looks to the passage to Alistair's rooms, wondering when she and the girl—Peregrine now—will emerge. She is not afraid of what awaits them, not in that moment. She can't be. For a woman like the Skylark, nothing is ever simple. What is one more thing added to the list?

I admit I am fond of the unpredictability of the Big Apple.
A marching band, for no reason at all!

EIGHT

Alistair is a genius.

I leave the tailor in a flattering houndstooth skirt with a matching jacket, the blouse underneath a buttery yellow. Over it all is a dark cloak with the insignia of the Bureau of the Arcane embroidered on the front. It is too warm for the cloak, let alone houndstooth, but I'm not at all uncomfortable as the Skylark and I walk toward the end of the block to find a taxi back to Manhattan. And that's not all. Alistair also gave me a raveled valise with three more outfits: a day dress in sky blue, another in green, and what Alistair called an "expeditionary ensemble," which contains a split-sided skirt, leggings for modesty, and a long-sleeved blouse, all made of a sturdy material that I don't recognize. There are also underthings and nightclothes in gingham, and as long as I throw a handful of seeds into the valise every few days, the clothes will always be clean when I need them. Alistair also mentioned something about the valise changing the color of the garments if I wish, so that I could "refresh my wardrobe," and once I'm settled for the day I fully intend to take that bit of raveling for a spin. I have half a mind to unravel the valise just a bit to see the workings of the whole thing, but it would be my luck that I'd be left with a handful of leaves and regrets, so I leave the binding as is.

"This getup really is magical," I say, giving a twirl as I dance along the sidewalk. Alistair had even managed to give the skirt a pocket with a bit of raveling done to it so that I can fit everything I have with me inside, including the Brownie camera. I'm so excited that I've nearly forgotten the brutalization of my hands. "I usually hate when people use that word, *magic*, ugh, but—"

"You shouldn't use it," the Skylark says. "It's offensive. And your new attire better be utterly life changing, considering the price we paid." She pulls a pocket watch from her suit jacket, checking the time with a flick of her wrist. "We haven't had breakfast, and it's dangerously close to lunchtime. Let's find someplace to eat, and we can hail a car after. Onyx and his apprentice will still be raising pillars, so we have some time still."

"What do you mean, 'raising pillars'? Is Onyx an Elementalist?"

"Yes. It's about charging the Resonators. Elementalists raise pillars, which we Floramancers then imbue with life, and the Resonators are supposed to redistribute that energy. I'll explain a bit more when we get to Trenton. For now, let's focus on other things."

I nod. I am famished, and it's been only the excitement of the day that's kept me from paying attention to my contentious belly and the sounds it makes as we walk along.

I follow the Skylark as she enters a sketchy-looking diner

and blazes a path to a booth not far from the door. The diner is forgettable. There's nothing to distinguish it from every other establishment just like it, but there's a smell in the air that tickles my nose in a familiar way, a scent of roses and burnt sugar that raises my hackles. A white waitress eyes us as we sit down but continues on her way toward a table of flatfoots with her coffeepot. I half wonder if we'll even get served. New York might not have Jim Crow like the South, but there are dozens of ways to make a body feel unwelcome.

"Maybe we should pick another place," I say, but the Skylark waves her hand dismissively.

"I've eaten here before. It'll be fine, especially once they see we are part of the Bureau of the Arcane." She opens her valise and pulls out a cloak that is similar to mine, putting it on and settling back against the booth.

"Why is your cloak green?" I say.

"Licensed Floramancer," she says, pointing at it. "Unlicensed apprentice," she says, pointing to mine. "Anyone wearing dark blue is an apprentice, but the licensed mages have different colors based on their disciplines. Elementalists wear dark gray, Illusionists purple, Wayfarers brown, and Floramancers green."

"Am I going to meet the other apprentices soon?" I ask. Probably not the point the Skylark was trying to make, but it would be nice to have a chance to make New York friends. There'd been Simone before she got nicked, but no one since. I don't think about it too much, but I am pretty lonely. New York is a city that begs to be explored with an accomplice, and even after a couple of months living in Gotham I still haven't seen everything.

Plus, it would be nice to meet some mages who weren't so . . . prickly.

The waitress appears at my elbow, ending the conversation. The name tag on her stained blouse reads *Nancy*. "Today's special is corned beef hash. It comes with two eggs, toast, and a cup of joe for a quarter."

"We'll both have the special, thank you. Eggs over medium," the Skylark says without even a look in my direction. I decide to remain silent—the Skylark doesn't strike me as someone who would care about details like what I was hungry for. Only when the waitress walks away does she turn to me. "So, tell me why you want to be a licensed mage."

I open my mouth to tell her about my bakery plans, but I realize it's not something I'm quite ready to share. Pigeon's mocking laughter still haunts me, and things are finally going well. I don't want to ruin it with the Skylark stomping on my dreams, silly or not. "Because once you're licensed, you can ravel wherever, whenever, and whatever you want."

She leans back in the booth and tilts her head as she studies me. "Such as?" she asks.

"Golly, anything! Prohibition has made it illegal for us to work the Possibilities in any meaningful way, but to me, that's like telling a body they can't breathe, no matter their perfectly good set of lungs. Raveling is part of who I am. Why wouldn't I want a license?"

The Skylark frowns and opens her mouth to answer, but the

waitress returns with two steaming mugs of coffee. I pick mine up, but it's only a few inches from my nose when I put the cup back down.

"Don't drink it," I say, pointing to the steaming mug in front of me.

The Skylark has the cup halfway to her mouth, and she pauses. "Why not?"

"Because it isn't what it pretends to be. Hold up a minute until the waitress returns."

The Skylark sets her cup down and stares into her mug for a long moment before turning back to me. "Listen here. If you're going to be my apprentice, we need to be honest with one another."

"I *am* being honest. You asked what I wanted, and I told you the truth. The opportunity and the freedom to be my best self," I say, stressing the last word. "Isn't that the American dream?"

"You honestly think that I believe that? I'm no seer, but I know there's something you're not telling me."

"I . . . don't know what you're asking."

"Okay, we'll start with this," the Skylark says. "Which of the arts can you work? And don't try to pretend it's only Floramancy."

"You told me I could only write down one discipline," I say carefully, "and I chose Floramancy." My heart begins to pound in my chest, too hard and too fast. I feel like a cornered rabbit. I might've been raised a rootworker in Pennsylvania, but I'm not so green that I don't know what this fancy New York mage is angling at.

Wytchcraft.

Craft, as people usually call it, isn't a big deal. Really. All it means is the use of more than one discipline of the mystical arts, and if you were raised like I was, that isn't anything unusual. In fact, it was encouraged. How were you supposed to ravel something for someone without looking at how they touched the Possibilities, to see what they desired? The government would say doing something as innocent as that *constitutes an unlawful combination of Cerebromancy and Floramancy*. For my ma, well, that was just providing folks a quality ravel.

That's not to say Craft can't be dangerous. When used improperly, the blowback can be devastating. Like what happened in the Triangle Shirtwaist Fire, when a Mechomancer hired a bunch of mages to combine multiple disciplines with his machines. The destruction was catastrophic. But that wasn't because of Craft—that was poor raveling. Every rootworker worth their salt knows that as long you follow the most important rule—raveling must always be done in the service of others—everything is dandy.

Then came the Great Rust and everyone saying the world went to hell because of mages working Craft recklessly. Why else would it be Mechomancy that fell to ruin, while the mystical arts still work just fine? they asked. That's just a bunch of ignorant hogwash. But Craft was an easy scapegoat. By the twenties, hardly any white folks were still practicing the mystical arts, what with so many Mechomancer constructs available in the Sears catalog. Why share a ravel with a neighbor when you could spend a little coin and buy a construct that would wash clothes or till a garden just for yourself?

Most country Negroes like me and mine stuck with the old ways. After all, there's something nice about raveling for a neighbor and having them return the favor with some eggs or a jar of jam or the like. And that's why Craft is such a big deal. There is fear when a colored person is doing the raveling and getting all mixy-mixy with the mystical arts, but not so much when white folks do it, should they choose. So as far as I'm concerned, the prohibition on Craft is just the same old prejudices and suspicions dressed up in the latest fashion.

Still, Prohibition is the law of the land, and the Skylark is an agent of the Bureau of the Arcane. Which is why I'm more than a little surprised when she says, softly, "Everyone has a little something extra."

I've heard that saying before. And I'm not entirely sure how to respond.

The next thing she says, however, comes out sharper. "So I'm going to ask again: What else can you do?"

"Okay, okay, fine," I say, voice low. "I suppose I can do a bit of Cerebromancy. But I only use it to reach into folks' minds when I'm raveling; I don't channel anything greater than that. Nothing like Barbara."

"All right. What else?"

I pause. "Faunomancy. But I won't use it! I promise."

"That's right," the Skylark says, putting her hands over her face and rubbing her eyes. "You told me you talked to one of the unicorns in Central Park."

"Hey, that *unicorn* talked to *me*," I say, holding my hands up.

The Skylark sighs. I can tell this conversation has taken a turn for the worse, and I start to panic a bit. The woman might be prickly, but she is my best chance to get a license. I can't give up, not when I'm this close.

"Look, Miss Skylark—"

"It's just Skylark."

"Okay, Skylark, please listen to me. I came to apply for a job at the Bureau of the Arcane because . . . I have no other options. I came to this city four months ago with sixty dollars and a dream, and now they're both almost gone. All I want is a license. That's it. Nothing nefarious. You can tell me whatever you'd like—that I need to keep my disciplines strictly separated, that I can only work Floramancy, that I have to keep my trap shut and do nothing more than ravel you a cup of coffee every morning—I'll do it. As long as there's a paycheck and a license in it for me, you have my word, I won't work any Craft whatsoever."

"That's not the point—" But whatever the Skylark is about to say has to wait as the waitress drops off two plates of corned beef hash topped with beautiful sunshiny eggs. I hate hash, and even have to admit that this looks like the most delicious plate of food I've maybe ever seen.

"What are you staring at?" the Skylark asks me.

"This isn't hash," I murmur, loud enough for the Skylark to hear, but not the cops sitting a few booths behind her, and definitely not the waitress, who has retreated behind the counter and hasn't spared us a look since.

"I don't believe this establishment has a license. . . ."

"No, I'm not saying it's been raveled by a Floramancer," I clarify. "I'm saying it's an Illusion. It's probably not even edible."

The Skylark looks at the plate before her and frowns.

"Look at this," I continue. "Our dishes are dang-near carbon copies of each other. Hash usually looks like something a cat might throw up—when have you ever seen diner hash look so scrumptious?"

The Skylark says nothing for a long time while I poke and prod at the food. To anyone who doesn't practice the mystical arts I'd look like a picky eater, pushing my food around the plate, but what I am really doing is looking for the edge of the ravel. The burnt sugar and fresh-flowers scent overwhelms, proving my suspicions true. A good Illusionist wouldn't make the ravel so easy to spot—much less so easy to break.

"Ah, got it," I say. The Skylark sits up a little in her seat as I snag the edge of the design and tug, unspooling it into its true form.

A pile of mud, leaf debris, and something that looks like a half-eaten sandwich sits on the plate, smelly enough to make the Skylark pull a handkerchief from a hidden pocket and hold it to her nose. Everything appears to be organic—it wouldn't kill anyone to eat it—but this gunk is definitely not the kind of thing anybody wants to put in their mouth.

"How did you . . ." The Skylark trails off, giving me what a detective in a pulp novel could only describe as an arch look, and I take a deep breath and let it out.

"Look, you got all kinds of questions about what kind of

abilities I have. I don't want to get in trouble, but I suppose you should know that my skill set is . . . rather unorthodox. You know what you just said? That everyone's got a little something extra? My ma used to say the same thing. Except, she would tell me I had maybe *more* than a little."

"If someone were to try to defraud the Bureau of the Arcane—" the Skylark begins, and I hold my hands up in surrender.

"You think I'd sign up with the Conservation Corps if I was out to run a grift?" I say, as quietly and calmly as I can. "I'm not out to con anyone. I'm just looking for a license. That's it. It's not my fault that I can do things that I can't share on your employment forms. Like being able to unravel lots of different kinds of workings." I shrug and gesture toward the Skylark's plate. Now that I know what the ravel looks like, it's no problem to unspool it, revealing a similar pile of trash. "You can't pretend talents like mine aren't useful. Heck, you think Alistair doesn't use Craft?" I tug at the fine herringbone jacket I wear.

"Alistair isn't a member of the Bureau of the Arcane," she says, "and you're not hearing me. I'm not asking you these questions because I'm trying to suss out whether you work Craft. You think I don't know what the laws outlawing Wytchcraft are about? Or how the mages in our families have been working it since long before white folks slapped that word on it?"

Her words are as sharp and as quiet as ever. I don't respond, but she doesn't appear to have been expecting me to, and goes on.

"I'm asking these questions because I need to know whether I can trust you. You might have walked into my office looking for nothing more than a license, but you need to understand, working for the Colored Auxiliary is not some temp job. It's 1937. The mystical arts, and those who practice them, are under threat from all sides, and we're the only thing standing in the middle. And this *unorthodox skill set* you're talking about? I don't know what that means, Barbara didn't know what that means, and I don't think even *you* know what, exactly, that means."

I don't say anything, because this isn't how I'm expecting this conversation to go. She seems like she's okay with Craft, but how does that jibe with her being an established member of the Bureau of the Arcane?

It doesn't. And I need a moment to realign my thinking.

"Like it or not, you and I are a team," she continues, "and we're going to be depending on each other quite a bit while you're my apprentice. Our lives may be in each other's hands. And I'm not just talking about what we find in the Blights—I'm talking about what we'll find outside of them as well. So you need to hear me when I tell you that the bureau has rules about how the arts are practiced, and you must be very, *very* aware about how you carry yourself now. No more keeping secrets from me, no more eye-rolling—yes, I've noticed—and no more of this ravel-first-ask-questions-later attitude whenever you're working the Dynamism." She locks me with a steely glare. "Do you hear me?"

I nod dumbly. This could be a gift or a curse, and I'm not sure just where it will land for the moment. So I very wisely keep my trap shut. I can play by her rules for now. Maybe.

She nods in return. "All right. To be clear, that does not mean that I won't ask you to use these abilities of yours—when the time calls for it."

"What do you mean?" I ask.

"Well, let's start with our breakfast." She puts up her hand to signal the waitress. The white woman returns, her disinterested expression melting into one of horror when she sees the plates.

The Skylark gives the woman a winning smile, flashes the Bureau of the Arcane insignia on her cloak. When she speaks, her voice is cool as a cucumber, without a hint of anger or annoyance. "Could you, perhaps, bring us food that is actually food?"

The waitress opens and closes her mouth a few times, but before she can respond, the Skylark turns to me. "Apprentice Peregrine, while Nancy here locates her tongue, would you kindly go show the officers over there what it is they're eating?"

I have to work to keep the grin off my face, because I like the way the Skylark thinks. I clamber out of the booth and walk over to the two police officers sitting at the other end of the diner, their half-eaten plates still on the table in front of them. They've been giving the Skylark and me the hairy eyeball since we walked in. The coppers in New York have a look that can be described only as grim-faced, and these two men are utterly indistinguishable from every other one I've seen during my time in the city. It reminds me that I'm still irked at my run-in with the police yesterday. It seems only fair to give these flatfoots some real work to do instead of harassing simple, hardworking mages just trying to help folks out.

At my approach they straighten in their seats, their hands going for the silver nightsticks hanging from their belts. I give them a friendly wave, making sure the bureau symbol on my cloak is visible, and point to their plates.

"Hello, Officers," I say. They only scowl at me. "I was wondering what the two of you are eating this morning?"

The front door jangles as it opens and closes, and I turn to catch a glimpse of the backside of the waitress as she beats feet right out of the joint. The police don't notice; they're still glaring at me.

"What are you talking about?" one of the men growls.

"May I?" I ask, not waiting for a response before I unravel the plates in front of them. When the reality of what they've been eating is revealed, they erupt to their feet, their stony mugs replaced by twin expressions of revulsion.

The Skylark appears behind me. "I'm certain the culprit is still in the kitchen, should you men wish to make an arrest," she says.

The two officers, however, are too busy dry heaving at the sight of the "food" they'd been enjoying. It's too fun, and I grin at them as I remember my rough treatment from the day before.

Perhaps I do have a bit of a mean streak. Huh. I'm learning more about myself daily.

When it becomes clear that the officers aren't going to be of any use, the Skylark sighs and makes her way into the kitchen, returning with a pale-skinned, spindly kid who looks no more than twelve or thirteen. "Never mind, gentlemen. This is the culprit, such as he is."

"I'm sorry! Miss Nancy, she promised me a meal if I just covered the kitchen until the food delivery could get here," the boy says, close to tears. He shakes with fear and looks at the cops with terror in his wide blue eyes, the color shifting from shades of cornflower to cerulean. Illusionists always have weird eyes.

I feel a little bad for him, truthfully. But only a little. A talented white kid like him will get plucked right out of the reformatory and sent to one of the better schools to hone his abilities. If he was colored, there would be a police wagon and a portal with his name on it.

The Skylark, deciding her work is done, moves toward the door of the diner. I follow, stopping only long enough to grab my valise from where it sits in the booth.

Outside in the hot morning sun, the Skylark says nothing for a long moment as we stand on the sidewalk, as though she is working through something. Then she stands a few inches taller, adjusting her fascinator so that it rests perfectly on her head. "Well, I must say that was enlightening," she says. "Now, to New Jersey."

New Jersey, and one of the Resonators there.
I'm still not certain how they work, or if they even do.
The people in the nearby houses must be constantly ill
from the stink of the Mechomancy.

Chapter

NINE

We do not return to Penn Station to catch a Wayfarer's beam to Trenton. Instead we go to Grand Central, which, according to the Skylark, has far more local routes than Penn Station.

"We're already a few hours behind," she says sharply, "and we cannot be waiting to make our way through the line there. We'll have a better chance of catching a beam at Grand Central. So let us make haste."

That is how I find myself running after the Skylark, weaving between people on their way to the cashier's window. As we wait in line, I tug on her sleeve.

"I know I've said this more than once already, but since you just paid for my whole new wardrobe, I think it's a pressing issue: I'm pretty much busted flat. How am I supposed to pay for all of this? Can I get an advance on my pay?"

"That's not necessary. I'll bill everything to the bureau, including your clothing. Any other questions?"

I've got more questions than a math test, especially after Skylark's whole thing about the danger we might be facing. But this does not seem like the time to indulge them, since the Skylark has told me how late we're going to be at least three times. (Which is funny, because it was her idea to stop at that disastrous diner. And my belly is still empty, I might add, which is honestly its own kind of tragedy.) I take a deep breath and remember I just have to keep my eye on the prize. Twenty-five dollars a month. Room and board. A mage's license. A life of my own. Whatever danger lies ahead, I can't turn back now.

The Wayfarers in Grand Central, all of whom are white, know the Skylark, waving us though without even a glance at our cloaks. We hit the platform and the line moves quickly. I'm itching for a chance to ask one of the Wayfarers about their work, but this isn't the time. One moment I'm descending the steps to the platform; the next I am stepping onto the sending circle behind the Skylark. There is a moment of weightlessness as the beam catches me up, and a sensation like submerging in a perfectly warm bath before I am spit out in New Jersey. I can never understand why someone would want to take a Mechomancer's construct when Wayfaring is so much better.

The terminal in Trenton is little more than a Wayfarer's circle with a colored man standing in a makeshift hut nearby. He gives the Skylark a half-hearted wave.

"He's in the Colored Auxiliary as well," the Skylark says before I can ask. "We maintain this particular endpoint just to service this Blight." That is something. Negroes aren't usually given licenses to practice Pavomancy, because it's supposed to be too complex for colored folks to understand, even if it is still one of the lower arts. There's something both exciting and unnerving in seeing firsthand how the old excuses are no more real than the corned beef hash in that Brooklyn diner was.

The Blight is immediately apparent, the colors of the world getting a little bit dimmer at a spot only a few hundred feet ahead of us, like a gray cloud has settled over the land. The air also smells strange, metallic and thick—though I quickly realize that's not the Blight. Off to our right, a mile away, a dozen or more factories send plumes of black smoke into the atmosphere on the horizon. Mechomancy.

The Skylark looks around, shielding her eyes against the mid-afternoon sun. "Looks like Onyx and his apprentice have raised their pillars here and moved on. So we'll get started and meet up with them farther inside the Blight." She gives me a curt nod. "Okay. See that place on the horizon where everything looks like someone forgot to clean a window? That's the edge of the Blight. As you may already know, Blights have traditionally been mitigated with mystical constructs called beacons. They're like anchors for the Dynamism—precisely crafted crystal pillars raised by an Elementalist, empowered by Floramancy. Onyx and his apprentice are raising and repairing the pillars; now it's our turn to work our art. Once we do that, the beacons will dispel the negative effects of the Blight enough that people will be safe and the Dynamism can gather and function as normal. Any questions?"

"Yes, actually. Where do the Resonators come in? I read an article about them, but they never seem to explain just what it is they are."

The Skylark purses her lips. "Well, Resonators are placed at the center of Blights and amplify the effects of the individual beacons, supposedly increasing their effectiveness and longevity. Trenton is a manufacturing town, as you can see, and a Resonator was installed here last year. Fortunately the Resonator here is still functioning just fine. We don't need to worry about the Mechomancy; we're just focusing on our beacons today."

The Skylark opens her valise to reveal an entire arsenal of bits: walnuts, tiny twigs of jacaranda, a few pecans—extremely rare—and most important of all, okra seeds. I reach for a few of them, pulling my hand back at the last moment.

"Um, how many am I allowed to have?" I ask. It wouldn't do to look greedy, but I've never seen such a bounty of potential, not since the day I wandered into the mage's market in Chelsea. It was there for only a single day, and I didn't have enough coin to buy much of anything, but seeing all of what the Skylark has makes me yearn to ravel up something impressive.

"Well, we need jacaranda for the beacons, and the okra seeds definitely for the Blight Beasts. Anything beyond that is just about how much you're comfortable wielding."

That's right. Blight Beasts. The mention of them makes this feel real to me in a way it maybe hadn't before, and I take a handful of okra seeds and the jacaranda, as well as a couple of walnuts. I don't much care for pecans—the nut can be too finicky to get a decent construct—so I leave those be.

"When we get back to the barracks for the night, we'll get you fitted with a bandolier to carry your bits," the Skylark says. "For now, we can leave our bags here. We'll want to make sure we can move quickly in the Blight."

"Will they be safe?" These tough times have made felons out of just about everyone. My first day in New York, I was bowled over by a man fleeing a shopkeeper after stealing a loaf of bread.

"I'll ward them, so, yes," the Skylark says.

I settle my brand-new valise next to the Skylark's and watch as she scribbles a few glyphs into the ground.

"What are those?" I say.

"Runic symbols. They can create wards but without using any bits. You don't know your runes?"

I shrug, but the answer is that this isn't any kind of raveling I've ever seen. I make a note to look into it on my own later.

We walk toward the Blight, the silence anything but comfortable, and then we're passing through its diffuse edge, into a world in gray scale.

For everything I'd read about Blights, none of it could have quite prepared me for walking into one. I shiver as the Possibilities become muddled. Not gone, it's all still there, all around me, but it's . . . foggy, like there is a film between me and the Possibilities. If the undamaged world is an ocean of possibility, this place feels more like a thick fog. I understand the big deal now—it's awful, ten times worse than the stink of the Mechomancer factories.

"Let yourself adjust before you try to ravel anything," the Skylark says. "The Dynamism is there to draw on, same as always, but when you start to work, it's going to be like stretching to find something on a high shelf. You have to work through the Blight, and that can take some practice."

I nod. This is not going to be a fun afternoon. Especially

since all I can think about is eating, my stomach gurgling sadly. Maybe I should've grabbed a handful of pecans from the Skylark's valise—not to ravel, but to eat.

"See those?" the Skylark says, pointing to a set of quartz pillars at four nearby street corners. They're positioned right next to the light poles, some of the stones shinier than others. "Those are the beacons. Once they have enough stored energy, they'll revitalize the area, the Resonators circulating the trapped potential. Have you ever charged an object before?"

I shake my head. The Skylark pulls a bit of jacaranda from her bandolier and lets it begin to grow in her hand. "All you have to do is take a bit of jacaranda and coax it to grow around the pillar, pouring in energy from the Dynamism to create a feedback loop between your ravel and that of the Elementalists."

I watch her work, noting how the jacaranda is tied to the Possibilities. Normally, once you've raveled something, you seal it off so that it stops channeling energy and it can exist without drawing off the Possibilities. In this case, the ravel is left open and looped back into the Possibilities, same as the Elementalists' ravel that it's connected to.

"Leaving the ravel open doesn't thin out the Possibil—the Dynamism even more?" I ask.

The Skylark shakes her head. "No, it actually forces the energy to level itself out, so that ambient potential is pulled in from other parts of the Dynamism. And then the Resonators are supposed to increase this feedback tenfold."

"'Supposed to'?" I say.

The Skylark raises an eyebrow. "The energy that does the work is the same that we've been using since the Colored Auxiliary was formed a decade ago. The Resonators do increase that effect, but they also seem to tap the pillars' energy much more quickly. Whether the increased effect is worth the extra work . . . Well, that's not for me to decide."

I purse my lips, then walk over to another obelisk, pull a bit of jacaranda from the pile in my pocket, and make quick work of raveling it onto the pillar. Once I'm finished, I step to the side to present my handiwork with a bit of a soft shoe and a "Ta-da!"

"Nicely done," the Skylark says "Now: Do you think one can create a beacon with any kind of ravel aside from an Elementalist's crystal pillar?"

I blink. She's trying to teach me. I've never much cared for school, mostly because I don't like when someone asks a question they already know the answer to. Just tell a body what you want them to know!

"Well," I say, "I can't see why not. As long as it's in a similar part of the spectrum."

The Skylark's spring-loaded eyebrow goes into action. "And what do you know about the energetic spectrum?"

"Well, I know that each of the mystical disciplines draws on the Dynamic energy present in living things, but to different degrees," I say. "Floramancy is the purest form of Life, deriving its power from things that grow. The rest of the arts work with energies on different points in the spectrum. This distinguishes the mystical arts from Mechomancy, which draws its power from Death."

"Precisely. Elementalism is right in the middle of the spectrum, which makes for a solid anchor for our Floramancy to do its work within a Blight. It's also the reason, we believe, that the Resonators have been so difficult to work with. Even if the Mechomancy within them is able to amplify the energy of the beacons for a while, it can't help but devour that energy at the same time. This is the paradox that Mechomancers are currently trying to solve with their newest Resonators."

"Yeah, good luck with that," I say, and the Skylark, if I'm not mistaken, gives me the smallest approving smile. "So, is that why Mechomancers worked with Necromancers for so long? Because their powers resonated with each other, like ours do with the ravels of Elementalists and Illusionists and such?"

The Skylark's expression goes stormy. "It's better if we don't speak of forbidden arts. Let's get to work."

I want to push the point, but the Skylark's demeanor makes it clear that's not a good idea. So I simply follow her down the road, and when we arrive at the next set of pillars, we each take a side of the street, raveling the jacaranda vines so that they grow and bloom in a riot of purple flowers. I've never been so close to freshly raised quartz; it tingles when I touch it, and just being near to the pillars makes me feel a tiny bit better. Especially since the air smells of chemical death, the nearby factories billowing noxious smoke in the background.

Mechomancers mostly power their machines with an alchemical compound made of buried Death that they call diesel. But it wasn't always this way. For hundreds of years, all the way up until the end of the Afrikan Genocide in the 1860s, Mechomancers had huge factories and compounds filled with enslaved colored folks. The Necromancers they employed would draw the life out of them, using their souls to power their constructs. The slave trade and the power of white Necromancers made Mechomancy what it is today, and this country was built smack dab on that foundation. It's not a thing most folks like to talk about, all those millions of Negroes that died during slavery, but I can't sniff out a Mechomancer construct without thinking about it. It puts me in a bit of a funk, knowing that all the work the Skylark and I are doing, as well as the Elementalists who raised the beacons, will be for naught, consumed by the Resonators. All so that the factories I'm looking at now get to merrily chug along forever.

After the conflicts that ended the Afrikan Genocide and slavery with it, many wondered if Mechomancy would survive. But the country's Mechomancers, shrewd as ever, helped the government to capture the outlawed Necromancers and worked with all sorts of powerful mages to find new sources of power. That's when they discovered the Death buried in the earth, the material left over from dead life millions of years old—first coal and crude oil, the latter of which was eventually refined through alchemical processes into diesel. Wherever you look, there's always more Death.

Now their factories are still filled with people, even if they're technically not enslaved. Inside those nightmarish constructs a mile away, folks are making sure everything is well oiled and functional, doing the grunt work that pays their wages. It seems like such an awful way to live. I know that economic collapse after the Great Rust made work hard to come by for many, and the Prohibition just made things tougher, but just thinking about slaving away in a factory, stinking of oil and metal, makes me feel a bit nauseated. The government maintains that the Blights were caused by reckless experimentation with Craft. But standing where I am now, it's impossible not to believe that the poison the Mechomancers dump into the air all around us had something to do with it. And I'm not the only one who thinks so. Not that anyone cares what a bunch of Negro mages think. Mechomancy is quick, cheap, and easy, and everyone is convinced it can fix everything.

What no one seems to consider, though, is that the Possibilities always win out. The bill will come due eventually. As I lay the ravel for my tenth beacon, I think of the photograph from the papers, the farmer with all his dead machines and withered fields. Maybe the bill's already come due.

I don't see any more beacons for another couple of blocks, and I am starting to wonder how I might go about asking the Skylark about supper since I'm now hungry enough to eat a horse, when a disturbance violently grabs my attention. One moment I'm putting the finishing touches on my last jacaranda root; the next I'm in the middle of the street, looking toward the horizon.

"Ah, you can feel it," the Skylark says. "Good. That'll make this easier." She leaves her pillar blooming in shades of purple as the jacaranda takes hold. "How are you with defensive tactics?"

I open my mouth to answer, but I am cut off by an agonized roar. The sound sends chills down my arms despite the heat, and

I'm suddenly more worried about my bladder than my stomach. I do not think wetting my new clothes is going to win me any more favor with the Skylark.

At the end of the avenue stand three hulking shadows, massive and indistinct. They begin to move toward us, and I'm terrified when they fail to take shape—as they come into focus, they appear to me to be part black smoke and part rotting flesh, the wounds seeping and raw like someone decided to make a sculpture out of a butcher's wares. They close in on us, and amid their visage I see flashes of terrifying forms: a bear, a horse, a series of human faces screaming in agony. I never much understood what folks meant when they said their blood turned to ice, but I do now. My entire being feels chiseled from a glacier.

"Blight Beasts," the Skylark says, reaching into the bandolier she wears. "Some say they're echoes of what could have been, or once was."

"Are they deadly?" I ask.

"They can be," the Skylark says. "You and I are ready for them, so I don't suspect we need to worry about anyone dying today. But if they get ahold of you, it won't be pleasant."

Reading sketchy accounts of Blight Beasts and seeing them in the flesh are two entirely different things. My heart pounds and my hands slick with sweat. I want to run, but if I do the Skylark will leave me as she found me, broke and hopeless, albeit with a slightly better wardrobe than when we met. I have no doubt she doesn't give second chances to cowards.

I reach into my pocket and pull forth the generous handful of okra seeds I snagged earlier.

The Skylark notes this and nods. "Follow my lead, Peregrine."

I'm hoping her lead is to turn tail and run, but no such luck. The Skylark throws a handful of okra seeds, which scatter across the ground, each one growing and twisting into waist-high constructs. The ravels look like tiny warriors—figures of raveling roots with wicked, sharp thorn swords and tiny shields.

I've made living constructs a number of times—small beings with limited autonomy that maintain a connection to my will and work at my behest. I once raveled a tiny army of ant-like creatures out of grass seed to harass Pigeon after she ate the last piece of icebox cake, the throbbing headache of backlash entirely worth it. But I've never used them to fight.

The okra warriors run forward on quiet, leafy feet, the wide hibiscus blooms that dot their forms opening once they get closer to the beasts rushing toward them. That's when they spring into action, their darting movements as swift as they are surgical. Wherever they cut the creatures, the inky blackness rips away, wisps and tufts being torn off until the fleshy constructs seem to simply unravel, large chunks of formless matter falling away, as if the broken power holding them together is failing. Within a minute, the Blight Beasts are no more.

"See? Easy peasy," the Skylark says. "Now you get the next group."

I swallow even though my mouth is too dry. "Next group?"

"Of course. That was just the expeditionary force. They're really going to come after us now that we've unmade their friends."

That's when I see it—a billowing mass running toward us, dusty and ominous. It grows as it nears, and every fiber of my being is screaming at me to run away and never look back.

"All right, Peregrine," says the Skylark. Is that amusement in her voice? "Time to earn your keep."

My first official task with the girl was during a routine refresh of the Trenton Industrial Blight Resonator. The girl displayed uncommon ability, but I must stress that there was nothing about this encounter that would lead me to believe she was anything other than a traditional Floramancer.

Chapter

TEN

The Skylark stands motionless as she watches the Blight Beasts rush toward them. She will remain so. The Peregrine—such a big name for a small girl—stares wide-eyed at the approaching horde. The Skylark can almost see her shaking, and for a moment she wonders which of her apprentice's impulses will win out. Will the girl turn tail and run?

That was, truth be told, exactly what the Skylark had done during her first contact with a Blight Beast.

But then the Peregrine straightens, squares her shoulders, and tosses a handful of okra seeds at the clouds of damaged Dynamism that hurtle toward them.

The okra seeds quickly spin out into the same sort of warriors she just showed the girl, and the Skylark is relieved. The Peregrine's fear is obvious, her eyes comically wide in her dark face, but it hasn't kept her from using her abilities. That's good. She'll do better if she can keep her wits about her.

The girl throws another handful of okra seeds, and these spool into even larger warriors, their blooms brighter, their thorn swords sharper. The Skylark opens her mouth to warn the girl not to over-exert herself, but then the entire platoon of okra warriors, nearly twenty-five in all, is rushing toward the Blight Beasts.

The okra warriors carve into the dust cloud of energy and pollution, but the Skylark finds herself watching her apprentice instead. The girl stands with her hands on her hips, watching the okra warriors slash and tear, and despite the efficiency of their movements, she frowns, as though there's something bothering her. A moment later, she gives a slight nod and reaches back into her pocket.

"Say, Skylark. Do you have . . . three more okra seeds?"

The Skylark looks to the battle before them, the okra warriors hacking away at the group of Blight Beasts, but that's when she notices that the beasts are growing in size, their engorgement outpacing the efforts of the okra. This is concerning. Perhaps it was time to recalibrate these beacons with a different stone. Onyx swore by the resonating properties of rose quartz, and it did create a pretty beacon, but another stone might resonate more power-fully. Trenton was a pit, and by her estimation, the Resonators were draining the beacons more quickly each time. But even by New Jersey standards, this is worrying.

"Three seeds," she says, finally answering the Peregrine. "Yes."

The girl jogs over, and the Skylark drops the seeds into the girl's hand, careful not to touch her. The Skylark already knows the girl has a knack for Cerebromancy, and the last thing she needs is the girl probing her connection to the Dynamism, accidentally or otherwise. Those were secrets best kept hidden.

The Skylark watches as the younger mage turns and elegantly tosses the seeds at the rest of her platoon. Within moments, they shoot out quick tendrils, each of them wrapping around one of the okra warriors in the midst of their losing battle. Then each is pulled back, the mass of the constructs connecting to one another in a chaos of roots and vines.

"What are you doing?" the Skylark says.

"Well, those little fellas weren't doing much in the way of taking out the Blight Beasts, so I'm improvising." She gives the Skylark a wide grin. She's *enjoying* this.

Barbara's questions about the girl come back to the Skylark. But she's too curious about what the Peregrine is doing to pay them much mind.

The new construct snaps into place, and the Skylark nearly gasps. The okra warriors are gone, and in their place is now a dragon, equal in size to the buildings that line the block around it. The construct gives a deafening roar, its open mouth releasing a cloud of thorns and yellow-purple okra blossoms, and charges toward the Blight Beasts. With another roar, it locks its jaw on the things and tears them to pieces.

The Skylark's mouth is still hanging open, and she closes it with an audible snap. She has seen only one other person wield such raw power, long ago, and watching the Peregrine work makes clear how she came by her name. She's indeed quick, direct, deadly. Dangerous. But how dangerous, exactly . . .

The Skylark realizes her heart is pounding. Or perhaps it's not her own. She can't help herself; she reaches out to where the Peregrine's emotions touch the Dynamism—

But then, with a final violent cry, the Blight Beasts are gone.

The Skylark blinks and draws back into herself. "Well, my dear, that was—"

"Sorry, just one moment," the Peregrine responds. Before the Skylark can react, the okra dragon rears back, the sinuous plants that make up its body winding and slithering, and roars in the direction of the rest of the beacons down the street, okra seeds lodging into each one, huge hibiscus-style flowers blooming, the beacons powering up as the Floramancy takes hold. The Skylark takes a deep, restoring breath, the Dynamism opening up and the day brightening just a bit. The film between her and her abilities is gone. It's like a fresh breeze in a room full of stale air. Delightful.

Nearby, the Peregrine bounces. "How did I do?" she asks. "I know we were using jacaranda for the beacons, but I didn't want to waste the rest of the okra seeds' potential."

The girl is barely breathing heavily. A ravel of that power and complexity would likely have put the Skylark on her back. The Peregrine might not be orthodox, but she was brutally efficient.

The Skylark wants to be jealous, but she's just impressed. She likes to think that she left behind petty things like envy in her previous life, but the truth is that the Skylark has never been able to ravel so quickly or easily. There was nothing wrong with that, but it does make her wonder just how long it would take the Peregrine to understand the ability she has.

Not long, most likely.

"Skylark?" the girl says, her pride melting into concern. "Did I do okay?"

"You did fine," the Skylark says, taking a deep breath and letting it out. The weight that had been pressing on her all morning—the worry that she might soon be watching another colored mage die on her watch—dissipates. She gives the girl a smile. Perhaps this would work out after all.

"I think we're done here," the Skylark says. There is a loud gurgling sound, the girl's belly complaining piteously. That is one of the problems with the Skylark's body. She rarely needed food, so she would have to remind herself that the girl still had physical needs. "You must be starving. Let's find something to eat."

This is Melvin. He works the Wayfaring station in Trenton. He said he learned Wayfaring from Lewis and Clark themselves, but I'm certain he was just teasing me.

Chapter

ELEVEN

We find a diner in the colored part of town, and the food is delicious. I get smothered pork chops with a side of mashed potatoes and an ice-cold Coca-Cola, and the food is real and hot and just about the best thing I've eaten in weeks. After all the work I did in the Blight, I feel like I more than earned it.

The Skylark does as well, judging from her suddenly sunny disposition. She doesn't eat, just sips a cup of coffee. "I'm afraid I don't have much of an appetite," she tells me with a smile, and seems to have relaxed quite a bit after my display. I suppose it's not every day that she gets to see a mage as young as me ravel a dragon construct out of okra seeds, and there's a part of me that is glad I've managed to impress her.

Another part worries about the fact that she now knows just what I can do. I dislike expectations.

"Do we need to meet up with that fella you mentioned?" I ask around a mouthful of pork. "Onyx?"

"I know today's activity must have left you famished, Peregrine, but please chew and swallow before you speak," she says, and I'm reminded that no matter what my abilities, I've got a ways to go before I win her respect. "And no, there's no need to rush. He will have finished raising the pillars by now and is likely heading back to New York. We'll finish our work when you're through and then head back ourselves."

It's midafternoon by the time I finish eating, the summer sun shining high in the sky. We return to the Blight, and in less than a quarter hour we come upon the second set of beacons that Onyx and his apprentice raised. The charging comes naturally to me now, and drawing on the Possibilities is easier with each ravel. It's not long before the beacons are fully charged, and I'm able to breathe easier—even if I'm more exhausted than I've been in as long as I can remember.

We collect our things from where we left them at the edge of the Blight and stroll back to the Wayfarer's post, the old colored man tipping his hat at us as we approach. "You want me to send you right to the Flatiron?" he asks. "Onyx and his apprentice left a little while ago, and he asked for a direct route to the bureau offices, since the day is pert near done."

"Yes, if the path is still open," the Skylark replies. "Thank you, Melvin. I know the man can be difficult."

"Bah! It's no problem. But I will say that seeing your pretty face, Miss Skylark, more than makes up for that jackass."

The Skylark laughs, the sound pure and clear. Melvin winks at me, and I smile. I'm itching to ask him more about Wayfaring, as it's a discipline about which I know next to nothing, but it'll have to wait for another trip out here, when I can keep my eyes open and give his words the full attention they deserve. After such a big day of raveling, all I want is to figure out where I'm sleeping and snuggle into bed.

The Wayfarer circle is a stone slab surrounded by a ring of sand. Most Wayfarer paths are permanent, the locations fixed. The one near Shrinesville that I used to travel to New York had engravings etched in a metallic script, symbols I didn't know or recognize, similar to what the Skylark used to ward our belongings. It's exciting to think I still have more to learn. There is apparently a whole mystical alphabet that I have never seen. Melvin uses a long stick to make additional notations in the sand, and as he draws each sigil, it glows for a moment before settling into place, the sand taking on a sedate blue hue where he's made the marks. It doesn't take him long to set the path, his movements swift and sure.

"All right, who's first?" he asks.

"Peregrine," the Skylark says, stepping aside for me. "The beam will drop you right in the lobby of the Flatiron. I'll be right behind you."

I nod, shift my valise in front of me, and when Melvin gives me the signal, I step into the circle.

And that's when everything goes wrong.

One moment I'm standing on Melvin's platform; the next I am ripped from my body and sent hurtling through darkness. This is not like any sort of Wayfaring I've done before. It's a long moment of pain, spinning in what feels like some kind of vortex, before I come back to myself.

I'm looking at a house, but it's as if I'm viewing it through a distorted glass, the vision twisted and warped. An elderly colored woman looks back at me, and a crawling sensation erupts inside of and all around me. The feeling, I know, is the Possibilities—my mind trying to make sense of where I am as I realize my physical form is elsewhere.

I've heard tell of powerful Necromancers who can rip a spirit from the flesh as easily as one would pick an apple off a tree, and for a moment I think that is what is happening. But there aren't Necromancers anymore, the only good side effect of the Prohibition, finally rooting them and the rest of the Klan out of society, and I have no idea what this woman wants with me.

The old woman peers at me, leaning in close so that nearly the entirety of my field of vision is taken up by her wizened old face. "You hear me?" the old woman barks.

I try to speak, but the only sound I can make is a low moan, and so I try to nod instead, hoping she can see me. This couldn't have anything to do with Melvin's circle—whatever this old woman is doing is agonizing, not unlike the vice grip Barbara put on my hands earlier.

Here's hoping this isn't going to be a trend.

The old woman gives a short nod back. "Okay. I beg your pardon—I'd meant to waylay the Skylark. Thought you were her, truth be told; your auras are darn near a match for each other. Although there's something a bit more to yours." The old woman frowns at me. "Hmm, there's indeed something more."

She stands and moves through the room she's in, pulling me along with her like I am a balloon on a string. She's muttering to herself, some nonsense about a geas and the limits of obedience, so I focus on the details of the room we're in, as I have no idea what is happening and I imagine I might have to explain it to someone later. It's a plain house, modestly appointed, similar to the one I grew up in. Unusual, however, is the woman's choice of pet. There's a giant yellow hunting cat—a puma, from the look of it—grooming itself on the floor, and when the thing looks up, its eyes meet mine. There's a sense of recognition in the cat's gaze, as though it sees me and knows me. But my view whips around and the old woman fills it, blocking out her surroundings.

"When you see that girl, you tell her there's a problem in Ohio. She needs to go there and see to it. I've tried getting in myself, but something there is blocking me. I suppose whatever is there must know of me, heh."

I moan in response, because trying to speak is agony. Is this what it's like to be a ghost?

"Oh, and one more thing. She needs to be more prompt in answering my summons. Tell her Miss Fox has had about enough of being ignored."

With that, the power that holds me is suddenly released, and in a fraction of a blink I'm back in my body, standing in the middle of Central Park.

It's still a beautiful sunny day, and many people are out and about, strolling along around me. It takes a long moment for me to come back to myself and realize that the old woman has dumped me by the entrance to the unicorn enclosure. None of the cryptids are out and about, which is good because as soon as I have processed where I am, I fall over onto the grass and writhe about as all my bits and pieces react to whatever it is I just went through.

"Someone call the police!" comes a voice somewhere above me. "This colored girl is having a fit!"

I stumble to my feet, mumbling excuses about the sun and not enough to drink on such a hot day. I walk a little way, toward the park exit, waving a few concerned bystanders away when I stop. I'm missing something.

As if on cue, my valise comes hurtling out of thin air. I try to catch it, but it's like a rocket; the suitcase slams painfully into my chest, knocking me ass over teakettle. When I sit up, a white woman and her little boy are staring at me, the boy's face sticky from the all-day lollipop he's eating, the nicely dressed woman looking not a little scandalized.

"Wayfaring, am I right?" I wheeze. And then I fall back flat into the grass and try not to puke.

These fellas were nice enough to make sure I was
okay and even offered me a bite to eat.
I gave them a couple of walnuts in thanks.
Hope they put them to good use!

Chapter

TWELVE

Once I've regained my senses, I drag myself over to a nearby tree and have a nice long think. In a single day I have had my hands mashed by a beautiful dame, nearly eaten trash-pile hash, faced down *monsters*, and been ripped apart within the Possibilities by someone who calls herself Fox. And it's not even suppertime yet. I am beginning to think that twenty-five dollars a month is not enough dough for all this hoopla.

There is something terribly upsetting about the fact that once I've finally gotten the only thing I wanted—a chance at a license and an apprenticeship to a legitimate mage—everything has gone wrong. Because I dare not consider that perhaps this is exactly what life working for the Bureau of the Arcane is like. If I were still back in Shrinesville, I would think perhaps Pigeon hexed me, but there's no way she could work a curse from that far away. Nope, the only curse in my life is me.

Though, perhaps I should find some brick dust and silver. Just in case.

I breathe deeply and replay the scene in my mind. Any old

woman who can interrupt a Wayfaring beam is powerful indeed, and it was clear she knew the Skylark. So what could this Miss Fox want with her? She didn't exactly look like she worked for the bureau. She had no cloak, and I cannot imagine someone associated with the bureau would need to interrupt a beam to pass on a cryptic message.

Which means this is a mystery that only the Skylark can solve.

"Peregrine! Yoo-hoo! Hello!"

I turn at the sound of my new name to see a colored girl running toward me, her numerous bracelets and bangles jingling as she moves. Her hair has been pulled back into a low, neat ponytail, and her hair holder sparkles with a variety of colored stones. She wears a blue cloak just like mine, the Bureau of the Arcane seal picked out in silver thread.

Elementalists. They do love their rocks.

The girl leans on her knees after skidding to a stop before me, huffing and puffing as though she has been running for miles. She's reed thin and tall enough that even after I scramble to my feet I'm barely as tall as she is hunched over.

"I'm the Peregrine," I say, the new name feeling strange in my mouth.

"I'm Crystal," the sparkling girl says. She grins, showing nearly every one of her teeth, like she's trying to hawk tooth powder. I have never seen someone smile that way, and she reminds me of an overeager puppy. "Well, that's not my real name; it's my mage name. Just as I'm sure the Peregrine is not your real name, because what mother would name her baby after a predatory bird?

Anyway, Onyx and the Skylark sent me to find you."

"How *did* you find me?" I ask, because it seems strange that she could track me in a big city like New York.

"Oh, all of our cloaks have a tracking feature built into the ravel," she says, still grinning. She taps the Bureau of the Arcane insignia over my heart. "And it works, because here I am and here you are!"

"Here I am indeed," I say. "Does the bureau, ah, lose a lot of people in the middle of a beam?" And how often are they tracking us? That's an alarming fact, to know that my fancy robe lets the government find me so easily.

The girl laughs, the sound high and loud. "Oh, no! You're the first I've ever heard of going wayward. Aren't you lucky?"

Lucky indeed. Like a four-leaf clover in the middle of a forest fire.

Maybe it's the terrifying out-of-body experience I just had, but it crosses my mind that I could just bolt. Drop the cloak in a dustbin, take my nice clothes and the few bits I have left in my pocket, and run back to Shrinesville. Or anywhere, really. I'd be lying if I said that the day hadn't been interesting, but this job has given me much more than I'd bargained for already. Blight Beasts and condescending bosses were one thing, but the episode with Barbara, and the old lady . . . it all seemed to make good on the Skylark's ominous warning from this morning. What had I gotten myself into?

No, Laura. Think. Twenty-five dollars a month. Room and board. A mage's license.

For a moment the world dissolves away, and standing before me is Shirley Temple, all dimples and curls. She eats a puffy pink confection and is all smiles as she does a bit of a soft shoe. "Oh boy, this sure is the best cream puff I ever did eat!" she chirps.

The daydream fades and I sigh. "Lead on, Macduff," I say to Crystal.

"Okay, but we're going to have to hurry or else we'll be late to supper. Onyx made his famous roast beef; we don't want to miss that!"

"Supper?" I say, looking at the sky. "What time is it?"

"Oh, Onyx likes to eat at five. He says it gives him time to digest before going to bed. We are very early risers," Crystal explains.

I'm not sure what that means, but I am certain I'm not going to like it.

We leave Central Park and take a nearby portal to the Flatiron, since Crystal explains how the same insignia that she used to track me also gets us free fare. As we walk toward the closest portal a few blocks away, Crystal keeps up a steady stream of conversation.

"I really like your clothes; did you go to Mr. Medici?"

"Uh, no, we went to see someone named Alistair. It was honestly the highlight of my day," I say, still in a bit of a funk.

"Oh! Onyx prefers Mr. Medici; he says all the best tailors are men."

"He apparently hasn't seen what Alistair can do," I say. Melvin was right; this Onyx sounds like a bit of an ass. "Anyone who can tailor something to my curves is a genius."

"Hmm, that's true, you're quite busty, and I'm sure that adds an element of difficulty." I open my mouth to object that I'm not *that* curvy, but she just keeps on talking. "So you and the Skylark are coming with all of us to Ohio tomorrow, yeah?"

"That sounds about right."

"Heck of an assignment, huh?" Crystal says, laughing. "At least you'll have one night to get to know everyone. All of the apprentices, I mean. Sam and Nell and Malik, and the young'uns, Sophie and Gary. They're only twelve! Can you imagine being an apprentice that age? They'll be licensed mages by the time they're sixteen."

"Today's my first day," I say when she pauses. The girl can gab, that's for sure.

"Wait, is this your *first day*? And you got to work a Blight? I didn't get to go on a call until I'd been here for six months! And, my goodness, you got all catawampus on a Wayfarer's path. . . . That really beats my first day." She looks pensive for a moment and then laughs. "I took a train to come to New York, the first time I'd ever ridden one, and I thought I would die. Those Mechomancers, golly, they sure know how to make something as normal as traveling up the coast feel terrifying. And I read an article that J. Paul Getty thinks those Mechomancer constructs are going to replace Wayfaring entirely. They can carry loads more people than can travel by beam in a day, and they're apparently much cheaper than what it costs to deal with the Wayfarer's guild. Plus they have to maintain all the paths, untangle all the shifting leylines. . . . Hey, did you know he and Howard Hughes are working on a construct that can fly? To take people all over the world? They say it's even better than traveling by beam, but flying up that high, in some big metal monstrosity, it all seems so much less safe than a beam. Well, most of the time," she says, looking over at me, still disheveled from my latest Wayfaring experience. "Sorry. But you'd still rather take a beam than a construct, right?"

I just nod. I'm only half following the flow of her words. Today has been a lot, and all I want is to collapse into bed.

The sidewalk portal we take beams us right to an intersection near the Flatiron. There was no pain this time fortunately, only the familiar warm-bathwater sensation of shooting the leylines. Still, it's going to be a while before I can take a beam without tensing for disaster.

We do not walk up to the front door of the building. Instead, Crystal leads me to what looks to be a different kind of portal grate. The strange things are located around the city, and I nearly tripped over them daily when I first arrived until I figured out what they were. One of the wonders of New York is the local Wayfaring lines that crisscross the city, which, if you have a portal pass, means you can zip all across the city anytime you'd like. It's the nature of the ravel that makes it so special. See, it's impractical to expect Wayfarers to service them all, at all hours of the day, and so they devised a way to automate the process, using the stars for both navigation and power. But the portals have to have access to starshine at all times—hence, sidewalk grates. It seems strange to think about starshine during the daylight hours, but the stars are still there whether we can see them or not.

I could never afford my own portal pass, but that apparently doesn't matter now that I'm working in the bureau. The crystal plate Crystal leads me to is intricately carved with a crosshatched pattern, the earthy scent of an Elemental ravel emanating from the spot.

"This is the employee entrance. Also the colored entrance. We can use it, even though we're just apprentices. Can you believe that one day we might be real agents, like Onyx and Skylark? Isn't that exciting? Oh, I cannot wait until I get my license as well. I'm something of an inventor on the side, you know. I have had an idea for a construct that can do hair. Wouldn't that be handy?"

I give Crystal a polite smile. I saw an Elementalist construct once—an eight-foot-tall golem that one of the farmers near our house back in Shrinesville purchased to protect his home from unwanted pests. It was terrifying, and the way it caught a mouse—splitting into smaller versions of itself, chasing the poor creature down and devouring it—was the most terrifying thing I have ever seen. I cannot imagine letting an eight-foot-tall man made of clay give me an updo every morning.

All I say, though, is: "That sounds like something."

Crystal beams. "Onyx said so too! I've already got a proto-type, but it doesn't know how to braid, and to be honest it nearly snatched me bald the one time I tried to use it. But I'm positive I know what the problem is now. I'm going to give it another try soon—if you want, you can be the first to use it!"

I just nod. There's no reason to discourage Crystal. Everyone is entitled to a dream, and Crystal's seems much more reasonable than my own.

She gestures to the grate in the sidewalk. "Okay, here's how this works. Just stand on the star sigil," Crystal says, pointing to the back corner of the plate. I'd thought it was all a single piece, but I can see now that it's actually made up of four different plates, each bearing their own symbol. "Say your name aloud and it should let you in. I'll go first so you can see how it works."

Crystal doesn't wait for me to say anything; she just stands on the star shape and murmurs. And just like that, she disappears. I make to follow her, but my feet won't move. I am rooted to my spot.

Again, though I can't be sure why, I find myself entertaining my options again. I can turn heel and take off, go anywhere I'd like. My better instinct is telling me to leave the Bureau of the Arcane and all of the nonsense behind. But that's not who I am. I made a promise to myself when I left home, and it's one I've made again and again every single day I've been in New York: I'll be a great mage, or I'll be nothing.

It's my own damn fault I never considered what becoming a "great mage" would entail.

"Aw, hell," I say, after enough time has passed that it's possible someone will come looking for me. I take a deep breath and let it out. And then I stand on the star and say, "Laura Ann Langston."

Nothing happens.

I take a deep breath. I am going to have to get used to this, even if it requires a bit of teeth gritting. "Peregrine," I say.

There's a sudden feeling, like the universe is inhaling, and then I am somewhere else. No agony, no pain, and all my body parts seem to be where they're supposed to be. Neat. I'm two for two.

I am standing in an unfamiliar and strangely spacious hallway. Crystal stands a few feet away, looking a bit nervous. Her expression melts into one of relief when she sees me.

"Oh, good! I was worried you somehow ended up somewhere else again! That would have been some luck, huh?"

"Yeah," I say. "Some luck."

MECHOMANCY AND THE MYSTICAL ARTS

WORKING TOGETHER FOR A BRIGHTER TOMORROW!

Chapter

THIRTEEN

I follow Crystal down the hallway as she chatters on like a magpie, mostly just ruminations on the confusing nature of Wayfaring, but I'm not really paying attention. Instead I'm taking in the place that will be my new home.

The part of the building we're in now looks nothing like the decorative and professional main office where I slept. There's a more utilitarian look to it, the walls a flat white that offers little in the way of cheer, with a corkboard located at regular intervals. On the boards are government posters not wholly unlike the sort I've seen all around the city proclaiming the various pieces of old FDR's New Deal—though with a different sort of message. "Get Tested! Halt Syphilis in Its Tracks!" shouts one, showing Uncle Sam holding up his hand to halt a Mechomancer construct labeled "pestilence." Another shows a cityscape; "Good Health Starts with YOU!" it says, showing a line of smiling people who I guess are happy because they're clean and white.

I get the impression whoever put the posters up thinks the members of the Conservation Corps are dirty and diseased. Not exactly a ringing endorsement.

"Are these rooms where everyone in the New York branch of the bureau lives?" I ask.

"Not everyone, just some of the Colored Auxiliary," Crystal says. "And we aren't actually in New York, but in a pocket dimension maintained by the Bureau of the Arcane. It's really complicated, but I think one of the Wayfarers can explain it?"

I shake my head. "No, I get it," I say. "Are there mages from other cities here, then?"

"We used to share this floor with a few of the Chicago folks, but we haven't seen them in a while." It sounds like there's more to that story, but whatever it is I won't know, because she moves on. "The other New York apprentices are here, though—you'll meet them later since they're most likely still out in the field. I told you about Sam and Nell—they're Sanamancers. You know, healers? We're lucky to have them here instead of off somewhere with the army. And there's Malik, but he's only here sometimes. He's an Illusionist. Sophie and Gary are still too young for real work and go to a school out in Pittsburgh, the Elementalist Academy. You'll meet them when they come home on their school break in a couple of weeks. And that's all of us right now."

"That's it?" I would have figured a big city like New York would have a larger membership, but seeing how hard it was for me to get a job here, maybe not.

"Well, and now you!" Crystal gives me a wide grin and continues to talk. The girl is a first-class chatterbox, and I find it delightful. Even if I am only half listening. "I'm glad you're here. Maybe now Master Onyx will stop fuming over the Skylark being named head of the New York branch over him, when she hadn't even taken an apprentice for nearly a year."

That makes my ears perk right up. "Onyx isn't a fan of the Skylark?"

Crystal's eyes go wide, as though she said too much. "Oh, no, that's not it at all. The Skylark's not exactly in agreement with the bureau's priorities where Mechomancy is concerned, so that's awkward, for one. Plus, it's just that, well, Onyx thinks that Elementalists tend to make the best managers when dealing with multiple disciplines, and men besides. Floramancy is such a soft, feminine working when compared with the Elemental disciplines, and . . . well, you know. You typically play a support role in complex ravelings and such."

In that moment, I wish I could do the one-eyebrow-at-a-time thing that the Skylark has perfected so that Crystal could feel my full disdain. I've not even met this Onyx, and I already despise him.

I'm guessing my attempt at a chilly look doesn't come through, because Crystal just shrugs. We continue to walk, until she stops suddenly before an unmarked door and raps loudly three times. The door looks like every other one in the hallway, and when it opens a man in differently colored, bejeweled version of the Skylark's cloak—deep gray instead of dark green—stands on the other side. Spectacles balance on his nose, and although he's colored, his skin has a dry, gray, ashen look to it. Like no one's told him the good news about cocoa butter. Or, you know, the sun.

"It's about time," he says. His nasally voice is a bit higher-pitched than I expected. There's a trace of an accent, British maybe. He scowls at both Crystal and me, and while she ducks her head and murmurs apologies, I grin widely and give the man a shrug.

"Yeah, I reckoned that rather than come straight back here, it'd be more fun to waste my entire afternoon by dropping right into the middle of Central Park." No, I am not over the fact that some creepy old woman plucked me from the æther and held me hostage and everyone seems to be treating it like some trivial inconvenience. And I won't be in this lifetime.

The man, who must be Onyx, scowls at me but says nothing. He just steps back from the doorway so we can enter.

The room is not the office I was expecting, more of a sitting room, and I wonder if this is some sort of social area or perhaps part of his personal lodgings. There are a couple of low couches and a fancy kitchen area, which contains an icebox, a stove, and a table large enough to seat six. The Skylark sits on one of the low couches, and her expression is somewhere between relieved and irked when she sees me. I give her a big wave.

"Hey there, Miss Skylark."

"Welcome back, Peregrine. I am sorry about your troubled path back to us, an anomaly, surely. I trust you are unharmed?" The warmth from earlier is once more gone and the familiar brusqueness back in its place, but when she raises that eyebrow of hers at me, I get the sense that she perhaps wants me to save my questions about what happened to me for later. So I nod in answer to her question. "Excellent. And I see you have met Crystal, very good. This here is Onyx. As I've told you, he is a skilled

Elementalist; he is also the second-in-command here at the New York branch."

"Welcome to the Bureau of the Arcane," Onyx says with perhaps a bit more congeniality than he greeted me with a moment ago. "The country's premier organization for practice and preservation of the mystical arts. At a fraught time for our disciplines in this nation's history, the bureau believes in the value of mages, and in our ability to pave the way for a bright American future hand in hand with Mechomancy. With our assistance, Mechomancy will flourish once more."

I blink. "Ah. Yes. Of course." Crystal's words about the party line come back to me.

And lucky for me, Onyx is ready to educate me about the party line, pretty much ignoring my response and barreling on ahead. "The Bureau of the Arcane has a long and storied history of working to find ways to advance Mechomancy, since it is so much more efficient than the mystical arts. As mages, especially *colored* mages, we are very lucky to get to witness the advances science and technology are making, and help them continue their march forward. It might not seem like it, but the work we do is vital in supporting this country and building back Mechomancy even better than before!"

"You don't say." I give him a solemn nod. "Well, I look forward to fixing Mechomancy."

Onyx scowls. "No, that's not really what I meant . . . ," he says, trailing off. I know what he meant, but I chose to purposely misunderstand him just to be irksome.

Lucky for me, the Skylark makes a choked sound that I think is laughter, but when I look her expression is one of polite disinterest.

"Anyway," Onyx says, regaining his composure, "let us eat before the food I prepared grows cold."

We all sit at the table, and Onyx pulls a delicious-looking beef dish from the oven along with a pan of roast potatoes and a steaming pile of broccoli. Plates are handed around, and I take liberally from each of the dishes. It's a lot of food for only four people, and I pause before taking a second helping of potatoes.

"Um, is it just us or are we expecting others?" I ask.

"The healers and the Illusionists return tomorrow morning, and the Grimalkin is at her daughter's helping with the children and will be joining us at some point along the way. And those are the only other mages here," Onyx says. But his words make me wonder more how a major city like New York could have so few colored mages. Especially when I've seen people getting arrested for unlicensed ravels. Myself included. How come more folks haven't made their way to the Colored Auxiliary? Shouldn't there be more working mages in such a large city? It's baffling.

The Skylark gives me a kind smile. "Eat your fill. It's part of your compensation."

So, I do. Everything is a bit bland and underseasoned, but it's not the worst thing I've ever eaten. We eat in silence for a few minutes, until Onyx puts his fork down and looks at me across the table. "Peregrine. Tell me about yourself."

I shrug. "Well, Onyx, what do you want to know?"

"You may address me as Master Onyx. I was trained in the

English alchemical traditions, and I'm afraid I am rather devoted to them."

"And I'm afraid that as a colored woman in a country where folks like me used to be property, I won't be calling anyone master, if you catch my drift." I say it with a smile, no heat to my words. From the corner of my eye, I catch the Skylark's gaze across the table, half expecting to be on the receiving end of yet another one of those judgmental brow tilts. Instead her expression is amused, which makes me relax.

I can do this. Despite the unexpected trials of this day, I am a damn fine mage, and I just have to remind myself of that whenever I begin to have doubts.

Onyx, clearly put off by my cheeky response, clears his throat, dragging my attention back to him. He picks up his fork once more. "Well, then, you must tell me about your people."

I close my eyes and pray for some patience. What is it with folks always wondering about your people, as though parentage is any indication of success? Just because my family has no desire to ravel amazing things doesn't mean I can't be a great mage. At this point I know exactly what this man is about, and I just want to finish my food and sleep for about a thousand years. "I'm from a small town in Pennsylvania, and my people are all hedge witches and mud weavers. And that is that."

He looks at me for a long moment, and I think perhaps he doesn't know when to leave well enough alone. But after shaking his head and muttering something about backward American Negroes, he says something along the lines of "That's nice" and nothing more.

The rest of the dinner passes in blessed silence, and that is a relief after the very contentious day I have had. Once dinner is over, Crystal and I take care of tidying up. I'm placing the leftover food in the icebox when Crystal taps me on the shoulder. "I can show you to your room," she offers.

The Skylark has wandered off to who knows where, so I grab my valise and follow her down the hall.

"Sorry I didn't get a chance to clean," Crystal says as we enter a room only a few doors down from the room where we ate. There is a nameplate next to the door that reads "The Albatross," and I take a moment to consider how much worse my naming could have gone.

"Nice to get a room that's already furnished," I say dryly, noting the pinups taped to a wall next to one of the bunks as I set my valise down next to the door. Not that I don't appreciate the scantily clad girls wearing skirts short enough to show off their garters.

"Oh!" Crystal says, her hands going to her face. She stares at the pinups for a moment before running over to remove them. Her embarrassment is nearly palpable, and she doesn't notice my amusement. I have seen far, far worse. "This room belonged to one of the boys from the Chicago branch who went into the Blight. He was from North Carolina. He was, uh, very friendly."

I pull the sheet off the pillow, and it lifts, revealing a black-and-white photo tucked beneath. In it, a laughing Crystal hangs on the arm of a dark-skinned boy, the both of them dressed in the ostentatious manner that I've come to know is typical of Elementalists. "Were you sweet on him?" I ask.

"A bit. Maybe. I don't know." Crystal, who had pert near talked my ear off on the trip from the station to the compound, now seems at a loss for words.

"He was the Albatross?" I ask. At Crystal's confused look, I point to the hallway. "The name on the door?"

"Oh! Uh, no. We haven't had anyone in to change the name-plates for the past year or so. The Albatross was a Faunomancer. He was gone before I came on as an apprentice."

"How many people have you seen come and go since you got here?" I ask, a sinking feeling hollowing out my middle. There's a lot about the Conversation Corps that seems odd, and not just the great pay. The Skylark's reluctance to take me on, her apparent relief when I raveled the okra-seed dragon, and just a feeling that the building we're in, wherever it may exist in space and time, should be a whole lot fuller.

Where are all the colored mages? The government services are starting to look less like an opportunity and more like a meat grinder. And I am not about to be sausage.

"A few," Crystal says, staring at the picture of her sweetheart with a strange expression. "But it's just because of the Ohio Deep Blight. It's . . . well, they haven't been able to figure out how to fix it just yet, so there is that. The Chicago team went out there last week and hasn't returned yet, and that's unusual."

"But you were in the Trenton Blight today, right?"

Crystal nods. "Yeah. But people are saying that Ohio is nothing like Trenton. It's worse."

"But not dangerous? I mean, no more than usual." The mystical arts always came with a risk. Overextend yourself and you might have a stroke and die. Ravel selfishly, and the Possibilities could take a tooth or some other body part to teach you a lesson. But as long as everyone played fair, things were usually okay. Taking care of the Blight Beasts, for example, had improved the quality of life and strengthened the Possibilities. And even though stepping into them was unpleasant, like walking through slime, they couldn't really hurt a mage.

Crystal shrugs. "I don't know. I don't think so? But Onyx has been acting strangely ever since he found out that the Hawk, that's the Skylark's boss, was sending us to the Ohio Deep Blight. I've never seen him so fidgety. And that has me worried."

I restrain myself from making a derisive noise. If that's what she's basing her concern on, then there probably is absolutely nothing to worry about. After all, Onyx seems like the kind of fellow to get bent out of shape about water spots on a glass. I've known him for only a few hours, and even I can see he's not the best barometer for such a thing.

But I know who is.

I drop the subject and go about cleaning the room with Crystal's help, the work going quickly. By the time we've put fresh sheets and blankets on the bunk and taken out the last of the previous occupant's trash, excepting a particularly spicy pinup that I pocket when Crystal isn't looking, it's getting late. Crystal yawns widely.

"Well, I'll leave you to your rest. I mean, it's still sort of early, but we're going to head out at first light, so I think you'll want some time to prepare. The Mechomancers Union has agreed to give us a ride to the edge of the Blight, and you'll get to meet the rest of the Colored Auxiliary in the morning. Dream of diamonds!" she says, before hurrying out of the room, the door closing behind her with a soft click.

"If a team just went into the Blight, why do we need to go as well?" I wonder aloud, talking to no one but myself and the chipped white paint on the walls. I flop onto the bed and stretch out, sighing. It feels so nice to lie down. Especially after the day I've had.

"Are you really going to bed so early?"

I sit up at the Skylark's question, startling awake. I rub my eyes. I must've dozed off, and now my mentor is giving me an arch look from the doorway, a manila folder in her arms.

"I have had a very eventful day, and I have earned my rest. But I'm glad you're here. Are you going to tell me about the old lady who waylaid my beam?"

The Skylark gives me an enigmatic smile. "That depends. What would you like to know?"

I frown. "Is this a test? Obviously I want to know who she is and why she thought it would be a good idea to snatch a body out of a Wayfarer's path! Who does that?"

The Skylark laughs. "Miss Fox, that's who. That old woman you met is my former mentor. And whatever she said is not important at the moment. So don't worry about her."

I snort. "'Beware of Ohio'? That's not important?"

The Skylark's mirth dissipates and she frowns. "She said that?"

"Something of the sort, along with a bit about how something is blocking her from contacting you." There's a story here, and I hunger for it. The Skylark is such a puzzle; surely learning about this Fox person will tell me more about her. "Is she family?"

"Miss Fox is not family, per se. But consider the message passed along, and as for the rest, it is none of your business. An apprentice should be discreet about their teacher's dealings, so you're going to forget you ever heard of the Fox," the Skylark says.

"So then, the Ohio Deep Blight isn't dangerous?" I say, unwilling to let it go entirely. I want a mage's license, but I spoke with the Skylark's Fox. She was concerned enough to interrupt a beam. That's a considerable manipulation of the Possibilities, and no one does a ravel that big just to catch up. That's what postcards are for. "Crystal said that Onyx was concerned about the whole endeavor."

"Onyx is always overly concerned, especially when it comes to decisions I've made," the Skylark says, her tone icy when she speaks about the man. "But the Ohio Deep Blight is odd, which is why I brought you some light reading to get yourself acquainted with the anomalies that have been reported." She hands me the manila folder she holds, the thing surprisingly light. "That is all we know about the Ohio Deep Blight. You saw how quickly things can change within such a space, and you'll need to be ready for anything. Please read that before we set out in the morning. But as to your earlier question: I do not expect it will be any more dangerous than the mystical arts usually are. You raveled in a Blight earlier today, so you know it can be difficult to utilize the Dynamism in such a space."

The Skylark walks to the door but pauses at the last moment, turning around dramatically. Or perhaps it's my own anxious brain that makes the moment feel more weighty than it is. "If you're regretting joining the Colored Auxiliary after today, that is perfectly fine. I won't hold you to anything if you decide this isn't for you. We usually introduce apprentices to the way the bureau works slowly so they can learn our processes, but because of the plans to head to Ohio, I've tossed you right into deep waters. If you decide that you'd rather not accompany me into the Ohio Deep Blight tomorrow, you can take the clothing and leave. I'll even give you a small severance of five dollars."

I frown, immediately bristling. "Are you trying to get rid of me?"

The Skylark laughs. "No, child, I am simply giving you an opportunity no one ever gave me. The Bureau of the Arcane downplays the danger of serving in the Conservation Corps, most especially where the Colored Auxiliary is concerned. Surely you can see that? Yes, there are opportunities here, but they are not without hazards, the likes of which you probably have not encountered before. Bigger ravels mean more risk, and while you're exhausted from our work in the Blight today, I can assure you there will be days where you can feel the work in your bones. The mystical arts extract their cost, and the more you work your ravels the more you will realize that. It can be dangerous, especially if you don't know your limits. Continuing means you're accepting that risk. That is all."

She turns to go, and then hesitates and turns back around.

"Also, the Bureau has stated that the demands of the Ohio Blight go above and beyond that of our regular work, so there will be an additional hazard pay."

"How much?"

"Twenty dollars."

I blink. "Well. Not bad for janitorial work."

The Skylark considers my words. "Huh. I suppose you're right."

The Skylark bids me good night and takes her leave, the door closing with a click behind her. I sit there for a long moment, considering the conversation. It was one thing when the Skylark was curt and a bit brusque with me. I grew up with Pigeon, and I could've tolerated that for a long while. But her kindness and honesty are, well, unsettling.

Does she think maybe I won't cut the mustard? Because if so, I aim to prove her wrong. I raveled a dragon today. A *dragon*! Surely she doesn't think I'm too weak to accompany her and the rest of the mages to Ohio?

The whole conversation has left me feeling off balance, my earlier sleepiness gone. I pick up the pages and leaf through them. The background in the report is mostly just stuff I've read in the papers. Nothing shocking there. But then I come to a report of an interview with a healer who was the only one to return from a bureau expedition to Ohio, a woman named Beatrice. When Beatrice originally returned from the Blight, she'd told her superiors that her expedition was attacked by Blight Beasts while trying to repair the beacons, and she was the only one who survived.

However, another interview was conducted later by someone known as the Grimalkin, in which she told a very different story. There's a note that everything was dictated to the Grimalkin because Beatrice does not read or write. I frown. Didn't Onyx mention a Grimalkin when discussing the other New York mages?

I read through the report. Once, and then again. I put it to the side and change into my nightclothes and wash my face at the small sink in the room. Then I pick the report up and read it again.

It's no better the fourth or fifth time.

The gist of it is this: Beatrice entered the Blight with her team, but they weren't set upon by Blight Beasts as she originally said. Instead, she claimed that they had stumbled upon Mechomancers trying to remake old Klan machinery, mangled creations in the shape of trees constructed out of dead matter. They were the ones who killed her team, and she was only able to escape them because they thought she was dead. When mages from the bureau went to check out her claims, however, they found nothing. And Beatrice, curiously enough, died the next day. The report notes that it was later discovered that Beatrice's family are seers with a history of hysteria and madness.

I take a deep breath and let it out, and for some reason my mind turns to my sister. When I was younger Pigeon used to chase after me. Not as a game, but just to keep an eye on me. I found it frustrating, constantly having her right over my shoulder, chirping about this and that, and most of my day was spent trying to give her the slip. I was rarely successful.

Always, at the end of the day, after I'd had some grand adventure with her dogging my heels, she'd tell me all the many ways things could have gone horribly. But I never worried about the future because I was always more focused on the fun of the moment.

Now, after reading the information on the Ohio Deep Blight, I wonder what Pigeon would do. She always called me impulsive, though Pigeon mulls over decisions so long that by the time she has to make a choice, someone else has already decided her future.

I laugh at myself and put the report aside. Why am I wondering what Pigeon would do in this situation? She never even wanted to leave Shrinesville. She would never find herself facing such a decision for a number of reasons. Most especially because she lacks a sense of adventure, but also because even small ravels terrify her. She loves her small life. But I want more.

I lean back and close my eyes, and consider for a moment what I would do if I left. I'd head right on back to Shrinesville. Tell everyone how exciting New York was, how close I came to being a big deal, make my one day of being an apprentice seem bigger than it was. I'd be like those old men who went to fight the German Necromancers in the Great War and returned talking about great lumbering beasts that belched poisonous gas. We could all sit on the porch out in front of the general store and spin our tales for anyone who cared to listen.

More importantly I would be right back where I was before I left, living in my ma's house and raveling bits in exchange for eggs and the occasional jar of jam.

Stuff. That.

I'm a damn good mage, and I'll show everyone exactly that. I'm going to make some money and get my mage's license and show everyone just what Laura Ann Langston, aka the Peregrine, can do.

The Ohio Deep Blight won't know what hit it.

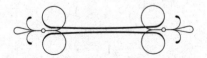

Part 2

INTO THE
DEEP

Took this out in front of the local general store before I left.
Never thought I'd miss Shrinesville.

FOURTEEN

I wake the next morning groggy and out of sorts. My dreams were plagued with visions of deformed livestock and Mechomancer constructs like twisted trees, Beatrice's ramblings from the report given life by my sleeping mind. The report had been a whole waste of time, but my brain was happy to spin a terrifying cocktail out of the speculation within.

But despite that, I'm not worried. I handled myself well in the Trenton Blight, and I will do the same in the Ohio Deep Blight.

I sit up and yawn. The room is filled with the weak sunlight of the very early morning, which is strange because I'm not even sure where in the world we are. I can't remember if Crystal told me or not, and my attention the day before was more for the weird old woman who interrupted my beam than portal geography. Portals are different than Wayfaring stations in that, once opened, they have a fixed destination, whereas a Wayfarer can tailor the endpoints of their gates to wherever they'd like to send someone. Either way, though, I could theoretically be anywhere from upstate New York to Timbuktu.

Putting the question to the side, I hurriedly wash my face and use my finger as a makeshift toothbrush in the room's humble lavatory before tucking my camera into another impossibly big pocket and grabbing my valise.

The hallway is no more crowded than it was yesterday, and I wonder once more just why that is. Shouldn't there be more mages working for the bureau? The first floor contains at least twenty rooms, not counting the kitchenette where we ate dinner and the room where I slept, and the day before Crystal and I passed a stairway, which means the building has other floors. It's still so odd that more people haven't signed up for government work, especially when things are hard for everyone, everywhere.

I'm walking down the hall, lost in thought, but snap out of it when I realize something's off. The hallway is much longer than it was last night. In fact, I've passed the same bulletin board three times already. I look closely at the set of posters I remember from yesterday, then turn my head up toward the electric light set in the ceiling. I tilt my head, listening, and take another step.

This is not the hallway I was in last night.

Before I can think about what I'm doing, I reach out into the Possibilities, find the seam, and pull. The Illusion woven around me falls away with a pop and a rush of sweet-smelling air.

"Damn! I thought we'd at least get her to walk another hundred feet," says a voice. A golden-skinned boy wearing a dove-gray derby and a matching double-breasted suit steps into view as the false hallway dissipates into the Possibilities. There is a mean look to him despite his attire, as though he doesn't mind making a little trouble every now and then. He's flanked by a couple more people my age whom I don't recognize. A little ways off to his right sits a large, golden cat, the puma's yellow eyes meeting mine as though to say, "Good for you, not falling for this mess."

I recognize the cat. It's the same one I saw keeping time with the old lady who interrupted my beam.

"Malik, don't be mean," says Crystal, pushing aside a girl and another boy so that she stands between Malik and me. The expression on my face must be pure murder, because that's how I honestly feel. Who is this clown? Are all Illusionists such chuckle-heads?

Crystal turns puppy eyes on me, her lower lip jutting out in a near pout. "Please don't be mad. They just wanted to have a bit of fun, and you figured it out, anyway."

"How did you do that?" I ask, because the ravel hadn't felt any kind of way. While Mechomancy feels oily and Wayfaring feels like rushing wind, this felt like cool glass against my skin, and the scent of it was almost nonexistent until I'd broken it. If it hadn't been so obvious that the hallway wasn't the same length it had been last night, I don't know how long it would have taken me to figure it out. That sort of thing *never* happens to me. But then, I've never been in an Illusionist's pocket space before.

Doesn't mean I can't duplicate it, though. I have learned a fair amount by taking things apart and seeing how they work.

Everyone is just kind of looking at me and Malik, waiting for what's going to happen next. When the awkward has gone on long beyond even my tolerance for such things, I sigh. "I'm the Peregrine. Nice to meet you."

Malik studies me, his full lips twisted a bit in disgust, and I settle fully into dislike for the boy. I've never been able to tolerate pretty men, and after what happened with Onyx last night, I am even less in the mood than usual.

"I'm Sam," the other colored boy says, shouldering past Malik with a smile. The boy is dark-skinned, tall and muscular, like he would be right at home driving a plow. If Pigeon saw him, she would immediately go into a swoon. "I'm a healer, so no power names for me, I'm afraid."

"And I'm Nell; I'm also a healer," says the girl. When the hallway falls silent, she adds, "And Malik here is an Illusionist, though I'm sure you already guessed that." She is tall and lanky, her skin lighter than mine but nowhere near as light as Malik's. He has striking gray eyes that seem ludicrously out of place in his golden face.

Thank goodness he's a boy. That's what got me into hot water with the preacher's daughter, after all. Those damnable eyes. There has yet to be a set of pretty eyes that I haven't fallen for, and if he were a girl, I would be all kinds of distracted. The last thing I need going into this Ohio Blight is a crush, getting me all twisted into knots.

"And the puma?" I ask, pointing to the golden cat.

Nell and Sam exchange a look while Malik laughs. "Good try, but we aren't going to fall for that."

"What are you talking about?"

"You want us to believe there's a giant hunting cat behind us?" Nell asks.

I frown, and look again, ready to protest—but the cat is gone.

Is this Malik, messing with me again?

I don't have time to think about it, though, as Crystal grabs my hand and pulls me along with her. "We came to fetch you for breakfast," she says. "We always try to get there first, before Master Onyx and the rest of them show up and take all the best pastries."

When we arrive to the same break room where we ate dinner the night before, there is a full breakfast spread laid out near a back wall. I make a beeline for the food, my belly grumbling loudly, and while I fix my plate, Crystal keeps up a constant stream of chatter. But I don't hear any of it, because I glance back to where we entered the room, and there's the puma again, sitting next to the doorway, watching me unnervingly. No one else seems to be paying the animal any mind, as if they can't even see it.

Honestly, this is not the sort of thing I want to deal with first thing in the morning. But I never can ignore an animal in need.

After piling my plate full of fruit and pastries and then grabbing a separate plate and piling it full of ham, I tell Crystal I'll be back in a minute, then walk just outside the room, the puma following me. I set the plate of ham down in the hallway and gesture toward it.

"I don't think you're anyone's familiar, because no one else seems to be able to see you. But I can see where your soul touches the Possibilities, and I know you're hungry. So here."

The puma sniffs the plate, then looks up at me.

"Well, it's yours if you want it. Now, time to come clean. I remember seeing you with the old woman who snatched me out of my beam yesterday. Whatever you're about, I hope it's not mischief, because I do not have time to deal with any nonsense right now."

A moment's pause, and then the puma, lightning quick, gulps down the ham. I flinch at the quick, hungry movement, but before I can say anything else, the puma turns down the hallway and disappears, like it just walked through a portal of some sort.

"Hey, what are you doing?" Crystal asks, suddenly behind me.

"Oh, uh, nothing . . . ," I say, trailing off, watching where the puma vanished. I have a feeling it'll let me know what it wants when it wants. Isn't that just like a cat? "Is there somewhere we're supposed to sit?"

Crystal leads me to a table with the other apprentices. Malik gives me a dark look when I sit down, especially when Sam scoots his chair to the side to give me space to sit.

"You have to eat fast so that you're ready to go when the mages are," Nell says around a mouthful of scrambled eggs. "No one ever waits for apprentices."

"Gotcha," I say, and set into my plate of fruit, ignoring Malik's whole demeanor. Seems like something I'm going to be doing a lot, so I might as well get some practice in. "So where are you all from?" I ask. "And how'd you get to work at the Bureau of the Arcane?"

"I'm from Pittsburgh," Sam says. "Nell is too. We joined because our mentor back home, Frederick, was recruited by the Colored Auxiliary, and he got in touch with us when the bureau needed Sanamancer apprentices. What about you?"

"I'm from Shrinesville." By the looks on their faces, they've never heard of it. I'm not surprised. "It's out near Harrisburg. Lots of PA folks here, huh?"

"A few, yeah," Nell says. "Crystal is from North Carolina. You can tell because when she gets excited, the country drips right into her words, no matter how much she's been practicing her diction."

"Rude," Crystal says. But she smiles and gives Nell a light shove.

Malik hasn't said anything, so I turn to him. "How about you, fella?"

The boy places his fork on his plate with annoyed precision. "I'm from D.C. You should eat more and talk less. This is the last good food we'll get for a while."

Nell gasps. "Malik! What has gotten into you this morning?"

"What, he doesn't always act like someone's put a tack in his shoe?" I ask, and everyone laughs. Everyone but Malik.

"Only most of the time," Sam says, giving Malik a soft look and bumping his shoulder against the other boy's.

Malik's cheeks pinken, and he stuffs his mouth full of eggs and chews furiously. "What's your discipline, again?" he asks.

"Me? I'm just a Floramancer. Plants and the like, you know?" I take a bite of a flaky half-moon pastry I grabbed from the spread. It melts like butter in my mouth. It isn't a ravel, and I cannot believe something like this could have come out of the oven I saw here. "What is this pastry? It's amazing."

"You've never had a croissant before?" Crystal exclaims.

"As if you'd ever had one before you came to work for the

bureau, Crys," Sam says with a laugh. If Malik is all storm clouds and scowls, Sam is all sunshine and smiles. "She's still new. This is your what, third day?"

"Second," I say.

"Fair warning," Sam says, smiling as ever. "Try not to die. I've only been an apprentice for a month, I am no good at resurrection."

I frown. "Wouldn't that be Necromancy?" I ask, before I consider my words too carefully.

The table falls silent.

"We don't talk about Necromancy," Crystal murmurs.

"It's bad luck," Nell says.

"Sorry. I was actually wondering because I've never met a real life Sanamancer." Healing is a rare and delicate art, and a Sanamancer can accidentally kill a person just as easily as heal them. Bodies don't like being manipulated through the Possibilities, and Sanamancy was the first art rendered nearly obsolete by the Mechomancers and their scientific procedures. Turns out it's all-around safer to just stitch a body back together than to rely on the Possibilities to correct the injury.

But the way everyone is looking at me, it's like I insulted their moms, not brought up the most forbidden of the forbidden arts. It's a strange reaction when we're all attempting to be mages. I'd expect that kind of reaction from a bland who rejected the power of the mystical arts altogether.

"I won't bring it up again," I say, and turn my attention to my plate. No one says anything, and I hate that I undid all my goodwill with a flippant remark. I stuff the rest of the croissant into my mouth so I can't say anything else. Pastries seems like a safer endeavor than small talk.

Turns out making friends is still hard.

Did you know that Pittsburgh is a city of Elementalists?
True, or at least what the rock polishers wanted me to believe.
Impressive town; I only wish I would've had time to enjoy it.

Chapter

FIFTEEN

A sharp laugh grabs my attention, and I look up from my food to see the rest of our group enter, the adults each wearing their robe, the Bureau of the Arcane insignia plainly visible. There are a couple of faces I don't recognize. A wizened old man, shuffling in toward the nearest chair, eyes hooded and sleepy; an older woman with a passel of animals, including a wolf, all of them snugged up around her like she's one of them.

There are familiar faces as well. Melvin leans against a wall, eating an apple, and he tips his hat when his gaze meets mine. Onyx stands at the front of the room with a scowl on his face, his clothing entirely different from the day before. He wears a khaki shirt and cargo shorts, clothing better suited to a jungle expedition than a trip to Ohio. Or maybe not, I immediately think—I've seen the monsters in America's Blights, such as they are.

The Skylark stands off to the side, drinking delicately from a cup of coffee. She surveys the room, and I wonder why Onyx is addressing the group instead of her.

"I hope you all slept well and are ready for whatever awaits us in the Ohio Deep Blight, anomaly number zero-zero-three. Today's briefing will be courtesy of our liaison from the national branch of the Colored Auxiliary, the Smoke, freshly arrived from the main office in Washington, D.C."

A tall, slender colored man with bronze skin and pure white hair smiles at the group. I glance from him to Malik and wonder if they're related. There's a similar look about the two, even as Malik scowls at the man now standing before us.

Ah, definitely a story there. Maybe this is the reason he's such a pill. Daddy issues.

"Thank you, Onyx. It's good to be back here in the New York office once again, and it was with true excitement that I volunteered to accompany all of you when the Hawk told me about the challenges in Ohio. Not that you aren't all capable," he says with a nod toward the Skylark, whose mild expression would make a dedicated poker player proud, "but I have missed fieldwork, and this seemed like a ripe opportunity to get back into it. It was also a good chance to check on the progress of my own apprentice, my son, Malik." Everyone twists to look back at our table, and Malik wilts into his chair in embarrassment.

The Smoke doesn't seem to notice; he just continues talking. "I'm told you've all been briefed about this mission, and why Bureau Director Hawk has tasked some of our most talented mages with it," he says with a wide smile, revealing a missing tooth on the left side of his face. "The Colored Auxiliary has long undertaken jobs too difficult for our pale cousins," he says with a low chuckle, "and it would seem we're being called on yet again.

Before we take our leave, I just wanted to say a few words about what the bureau knows so far, a few things that haven't yet made it into any of our reports.

"Last year, after the ODB Resonator was installed, the bureau placed nearly a hundred additional beacons in the Ohio Deep Blight to mitigate its effects on the land and population and control its spread. Two weeks ago, it was discovered that the majority of those beacons were gone, tapped at a rate that we've never seen before, even when Resonator degradation is taken into account.

"We sent a sizable group of mages from the Chicago branch into the Blight to repair the beacons, but all save one of them never returned. A response team of bureau mages discovered nothing out of the ordinary, but they were unable to locate the missing mages. Our job now is simple: we're to go in, rebuild the beacons, and find the missing team. The area where the Resonator resides is a town close to the center of the Blight called Myersville, and it's possible we'll need to travel that far in order to complete our task. As we don't know exactly what we'll find inside the ODB, we'll be taking healers with us. We've also requested a bureau Faunomancer accompany us; while unlikely, it's possible that a basilisk or some other cryptid might be responsible for the damage to the area, and the reason our team went missing."

The Smoke continues. "We will beam from here to a bureau-controlled Wayfaring station just outside of Pittsburgh; this is the closest one to the edge of the Blight, though we'll still be about twelve miles from where the damage to the Dynamism has spread. Fortunately, a liaison from the Mechomancers Union has agreed to drive us from there to the edge of the Blight."

The Smoke asks for questions, and the woman surrounded by a menagerie raises her hand, dislodging a chickadee who complains about the lack of warning in whistles and chirps. This, I realize, must be the Faunomancer the Smoke mentioned. She is a dark-skinned woman with a snow-white bob wearing a fashionable dress of green. "What about the reports of twisted beasts preying on farms in the area? Do you have any confirmation of such a thing?" Her animals shift as she speaks and chime in their own opinions in a noisy, distracting chorus that apparently none of the other mages, beyond the Grimalkin and me, can understand.

Crystal leans forward. "That's the Grimalkin. She's the only Faunomancer in the Colored Auxiliary."

"Just one?" I whisper back.

Crystal shrugs. "They don't have much business in Blight repair; the Grimalkin is only on staff for when we need to use animals to relay messages fast. What few Faunomancers are employed by the bureau work in the Department of Cryptid Control. It's not as if there are many licensed Faunomancers these days."

I nod. Faunomancy is a rare discipline to specialize in, highly regulated even before Prohibition. In the late 1800s, a group of Faunomancers led a series of increasingly militant protests against the meat industry. Upton Sinclair was one of the most prominent, and his writings on the topic helped pass the Humane Farming Act. But many farmers, opposed to the act, have been working for years to silence Faunomancers and have the whole art outlawed. There aren't many people out there defending them. Most folks don't care about where their food comes from, I suppose. And they certainly don't want to hear from people who can tell them what the animals themselves think of the meat industry's practices.

"The Grimalkin's weird, though," Nell continues with a grimace. "It always feels like she's not really paying attention to you, like she's distracted, but it's not that. It's just that the bird or wolf is talking to her at the same time."

"Faunomancers," Malik says, shaking his head. "Talking to beasts all the time. Useless art. What a waste of the Dynamism."

"Be careful, fella. White folks might say the same thing about you," Sam jokes. I watch as he touches the back of Malik's hand. Another small bit of affection. When Malik catches me watching, I quickly look away and back to the Smoke, who is trying to answer the Grimalkin's question.

"I'm sure there has been all kinds of speculation; the Ohio Deep Blight is the country's largest and nastiest. The Chicago branch has dedicated almost all resources to it for years now. I think it's safe to say that the land has been affected in ways we likely don't fully understand." The Smoke falls silent for a moment, his gaze roving so that his eyes land on every mage in the room. It's a nonanswer, but one that feels like something more. "A Blight is a Blight, but that's no reason to let your guard down. Be careful, and trust in your skills. And one another. You have your team assignments, so let's load up the constructs and head out."

People begin to stand and clear their plates, and I make my way over to the Skylark. She gives me a long look. "Did you sleep?"

I shrug. "Not especially. Bad dreams."

"Same. I suppose the unknown tends to have that effect," she says, even though her expression is pensive, like she wants to tell me something more. Before she can say anything else, the Faunomancer appears next to us.

"I don't know you," she says to me. I'm guessing that etiquette classes are not part of the bureau's offerings to the Colored Auxiliary.

I smile like I'm a magazine ad for toothpaste. "I'm the Peregrine, apprentice to the Skylark," I say, holding out my hand to shake. The Grimalkin ignores it, but one of her tiny birds takes flight and lands atop my finger.

You smell of many delicious things, the chickadee chirps at me, and I can't help but smile, for real this time.

I open my mouth to respond, but the older woman is watching me too closely. I'm determined to follow the Skylark's warnings now, so I just reach into the pocket of my skirt and pull out a bit of croissant.

"I was saving this for later, but I think you might like it more, friend," I say in what I hope is the tone of someone who can't speak directly to animals.

She takes the crumb and flies back to her perch on the Grimalkin's hat. The older woman decides something and turns back to the Skylark.

"The Peregrine. That's a powerful name."

The Skylark smiles politely. "Let's hope we don't find anything in the Blight that forces her to live up to it. I'm surprised to see you here, Grimalkin. I figured you'd have your hands full with the Oklahoma Blight."

The older woman swats at the Skylark's comment like it's a fly.

"Oklahoma is nowhere near as bad as Ohio. The kids back there have that one all locked up, not that anyone cares about that dusty place. Maybe if they hadn't decided to massacre those mages in Tulsa all those years ago, they'd be able to grow more than disappointment there. This Ohio Deep Blight is all hands on deck, my dear. Which is why I wanted a word with you." The Grimalkin looks over at where Smoke and Onyx are engaged in conversation with another well-dressed man. It's the man I didn't know, and he wears the white robes of a Sanamancer.

"Why don't you accompany me to the storeroom for provisions," the Skylark says, before turning to me. "Peregrine, wait here for a moment. I'll be right back."

I stand awkwardly by myself as the rest of the apprentices find their mentors. I'm wondering just how long the Skylark is going to be when Crystal approaches me. "What are you doing, standing there?" she asks.

"Waiting for the Skylark to get back from the supply room."

"But where's your bandolier?" she says, pointing to a curious contraption she wears across her torso. It looks like the sash a beauty pageant contestant might sport. I shrug, and Crystal lets out what can only be described as a squeak of alarm. "Oh no, I think I was supposed to take you to the storeroom last night to get one, but I forgot! It's how you carry your bits when you're walking around. You're going to need one."

"No sweat," I say, hefting my valise. "I'll see to it myself."

I head out into the hallway, the same way the Skylark and the Grimalkin went, looking for the puma as I go. He's nowhere to be found, but I discover the Grimalkin and the Skylark speaking in hushed tones in the middle of the hallway. And even though I know I shouldn't eavesdrop, I can't resist pausing a moment out of sight before approaching them.

"The fool is as hardheaded as ever. Being down at the main office just made him even worse," the older woman mutters, her voice low. "He's refused to listen to any of my warnings, or those of my animals."

"What do they say?" the Skylark asks.

"The birds are all telling me how many have fled. And that something terrible befell the ones who didn't. I tried to convince the Hawk to delay a day so I could scout ahead in the Blight, but he thinks it's too dangerous. You know how he feels about procrastination," she says with an eye roll, and the Skylark sighs.

I decide to finally clear my throat, and both women turn around, the Grimalkin giving me an arch look. "We should put a bell on you."

"Sorry to interrupt, but Crystal was in a bit of a panic about me getting a bandolier before we go? And some bits?"

The Skylark nods. "Right she is. We're headed that way. Let's go."

We make our way down the hallway, and we've gone only a short distance when we stop in front of a door marked SUPPLIES in bold, golden letters.

"This . . . this wasn't here last night," I say, feeling a bit unmoored. I've heard stories of buildings with complicated portals woven into the architecture, but this is my first time witnessing it firsthand.

"No, the bureau only lifts the ward on the supply area after a formal request," the Skylark says. There's a tone in her voice, but I'm not quite sure what it is.

"You'd better believe those white mages don't have to submit paperwork for the tools to do their job," the Grimalkin says, her wolf letting out a yip of agreement.

"That's only because most of them couldn't knit a proper construct if their lives depended on it," the Skylark mutters, and the Grimalkin laughs bitterly.

"Separate but equal," she replies, nodding at me over her shoulder. "You'll get used to it. Despite the daily injustices, there are comparatively more opportunities for women in the Colored Auxiliary. Such as they are, I suppose."

"Compared to what?" I ask.

She laughs, the sound genuine. "Good question. It's hard times right now, which means it's twice as bad for colored folks, and twice as bad as that for colored women. Just never think that the bureau sees you as more than you are."

"And never show them what we can do?" I say, and this time, the Skylark doesn't give me a reproachful look.

The Grimalkin taps her nose. "Exactly. Smart cookie. As long you remember to color inside of the lines, you'll be fine."

Here it is, yet another warning about the difference between what we mages can do and what the Bureau of the Arcane expects from us. Skylark's warning from the day before, how the mixing of disciplines is frowned upon, as well as Onyx's impassioned speech about the onset of a golden age of Mechomancy during dinner the night before, are still fresh in my mind. The Grimalkin seems to think more along the lines of the Skylark than Onyx, and I file that fact away for later. I am definitely getting the sense there are two kinds of mages in the Colored Auxiliary: those who truly believe blindly supporting Mechomancy is a good thing, and those who know better.

Then we are through the supply room door, and I am distracted by the wealth that surrounds me.

The room is much deeper and wider than the door led me to believe and contains dozens of shelves, each numbered and ordered in a way that makes me recall the time I sneaked into the New York Public Library to gawk at all the books. The shelf beside me as I enter is full of pre-worked Wayfaring stones, their end locations written in a neat hand below each box. Next to that is another shelf of precious stones, these unraveled and glimmering dully, reflecting the room's overhead light bulbs. But it's the Floramancy shelves that draw my attention, and I gasp as I look at the bounty before me.

There is so much, all just waiting to be raveled. An entire world of potential. Walnuts and dried okra pods and dried jacaranda vines. Almonds and black-eyed peas and pecans, even teeny tiny collard green seeds. Everything a Floramancer could want, all of it just whispering for me to make something happen.

"This might be the most beautiful thing I have ever seen," I say.

"Take as much as you can carry," the Skylark says, handing me a burlap sash like Crystal's that I drape across my body. There are a number of pockets stitched to the rough material. It isn't as nice as the Skylark's—hers appears to be denim—but I'm glad to have the extra storage. It's also raveled to contain more space than it should, so I take my Brownie from the pocket on my hip and put it into one of the more accessible pouches in the sash.

"You have a sense now of how unpredictable Blights can be," the Skylark says. "You also know that the one discipline that always seems to function well despite the clouding of the Dynamism is Floramancy."

"And yet Smoke is leading the expedition," the Grimalkin mutters, picking up a Wayfaring stone and dropping it into a pocket.

"He isn't leading it, per se. But he does have seniority since he's attached to the main office in D.C.," the Skylark explains to me with a sidelong glance at the older woman.

"Bah," the Grimalkin says. "You know how those men are. Give them an inch and they'll take a mile." The Skylark ignores the comment, but I watch the older woman as she moves through the storeroom, picking up bits that would not be of any help to a Faunomancer.

I smile. Everyone has a little something extra.

"You have five minutes to grab whatever you think will be useful," the Skylark says. She doesn't need any extra herself to sense my urge to do a little exploring of my own.

I turn my attention back to what's before me, digging through the bins to select the seeds that call to me most strongly, dropping handfuls into the many pockets of my bandolier. I fill them with all kinds of items, giant handfuls of quartz and okra seeds and star-shaped seedpods that I have never seen before. The Skylark and the Grimalkin resume their earlier conversation, this time just departmental gossip, as I snatch up a few bits that are not used in Floramancy: Wayfaring stones—even though I have no idea how to use them—as well as a few pretty crystals that seem to sing. I'm debating whether to cram a chunk of striated tigereye crystal into an already very full pocket of the bandolier when there's a golden flash out of the corner of my eye.

The puma is back.

This time I don't hesitate. I follow the big cat as it weaves between shelves, stopping before a caged-off area, a sign on the outside of the metal door inscribed in runes. I can't read these wards—runic spells are notoriously finicky and Ma never taught us "uncertain art," as she had always called it. But the hunting cat seems to really want me to have something in the cage.

"Just what do you think you are doing?" the Skylark says, appearing behind me like a restless haint.

I jump, startled by her sudden appearance. I consider blaming my natural curiosity—goodness knows she'd believe it—but I have a feeling she might actually believe the truth and decide that is the way to go. "There's a puma, a great big golden hunting cat, that I've been seeing all morning."

The Skylark scowls. "How long have you been seeing this puma?"

I shrug. "Not long. It appeared in the hallway on my way to breakfast. Oh, and it was with the old lady who interrupted my beam. Your old mentor."

The Skylark's spring-loaded eyebrow snaps into action, and she looks around the small area before the shelf. "And is it here right now?"

I point to a spot on the floor a few feet to the Skylark's right. "It led me to this cage."

She purses her lips. "I can't see it, but there is something amiss with the Dynamism in this area. You think there's something in this cage it wants you to have?"

I nod. The great big cat hasn't moved, and its liquid-gold eyes give me a strange feeling as I lock onto them.

The Skylark considers this for a moment, but then she touches the cage and murmurs something in a low voice. The door springs open, and a purple glass bottle no bigger than my hand leaps from the shelf on the far wall and into the lone empty pouch on my bandolier, a pouch that I am pretty sure was not there five minutes ago.

"What the heck is that?" I ask. I'm talking to the puma, but it just walks off, which is the most catlike thing the creature has done.

"That is a soul jar," the Skylark says.

"A what?" I open up the pocket and am going to remove the object when the Skylark stops me.

"Take the vessel. There's a reason the cat wants you to have it. If it's an agent of Miss Fox, it's doing her bidding, and she has a way of knowing how things will turn out. So keep the bottle for now."

I swallow dryly. I have no idea what a soul jar is, and I'm not sure I want to know. But I'm clearly out of my depth here.

She pats me on the arm, her expression sympathetic. "We'll talk about this later. Finish up so Melvin can get us to Pittsburgh to meet our ride."

The Skylark waits until I leave the secured area before closing the door and locking it, so I don't get a chance to see what else the space contains, but I get the sense they are things that might be a bit more dangerous than a few okra seeds. The bottle is heavy in my bandolier, and only made heavier by what the bottle leaping into my pocket might mean.

I follow the Skylark out of the supply room. The Grimalkin's already taken her leave. The Skylark is pensive as we walk to grab our packs, and she halts me with a cool hand on my arm.

"I know this seems strange," she says. "But you can trust me. It's my job to train you, and my methods might seem unorthodox at times, but I promise I will always have your best interest in the forefront of my decisions."

"I know," I say, but my mouth is dry. I give what I hope is a reassuring smile and tell myself that I am not freaked out by having a Necromancer's vessel in my bandolier.

Even if my sweaty palms say otherwise.

The first inkling I had that the girl may have been more than she appeared was on our way into the Ohio Deep Blight. She was curious about things that had little to do with Floramancy, and even went so far as to investigate the secure area within the supply closet. To this day I have no idea how she managed to open the cage or obtain a vessel. . . .

Chapter
SIXTEEN

The Skylark watches her apprentice and tries to push aside the misgivings that burble in her middle. There are five of them in the back of a Mechomancer construct, the rest of their expedition in another vehicle, and as it bumps along the dusty road, the apprehension the Skylark feels grows exponentially.

Something bad waits for them within the Blight. But the Skylark does not know what it is; she isn't even certain the danger is imminent.

You could call it a gut feeling. That is, if she had any guts.

The Skylark tries to close her eyes and rest like the Peregrine and Crystal, both of whom are fast asleep. Skylark is glad to see it—she knows the girl can't stand the feel of Mechomancy, and being in this contraption must feel like a sort of punishment. Onyx is stringing tiny stones onto a length of cord he brought with him and muttering while he works, and the Grimalkin murmurs with her critters, the oversize wolf at her feet whining in response to something she tells him. The Faunomancer tried to persuade her one last time to postpone the mission, to wait until she could try gathering more information through her animals' networks, but the Skylark knows there's no chance the Hawk would have agreed to it. Besides, she knows in her heart—though she doesn't have one of those either—that the only way to truly understand what is happening in the ODB is to head in there herself.

Plus, the Fox is somehow interested in the whole mess. That's an excellent sign that the Ohio Deep Blight is more than it seems. The Hawk's bureaucratic concern is one thing, but when the Fox deigns to get involved, it's another matter entirely.

They hit a pothole, the jostling motion making the Grimalkin swear. "Is that bastard trying for every crack in the damn road?"

"Seems like," Onyx says, tying his finished string of beads to one of the many buttons on his bejeweled cloak. He still wears his expeditionary garb underneath, and in the early morning heat he sweats from his many layers, the vainglorious fool.

The Skylark glances at her apprentice. The Peregrine. The Grimalkin said it right: such a strong name for a young girl. The Skylark really wished she could have remained behind. Especially after the Necromancer's vessel leaped into her bandolier. The girl was horrified, even though she tried to hide it. Being able to claim the vessel must mean the girl has some talent for Necromancy, even though she clearly doesn't know it. It worries the Skylark, just a bit. Why did the Fox's Ligahoo, the hunting cat that only the Peregrine could see, see fit to have the girl claim it? What did the Fox know?

The Skylark takes a deep breath and releases it. Everything will be fine. The girl is capable, despite her fear in Trenton. Not to mention as cool as a cucumber after the Fox hijacked her beam.

Maybe the girl is exactly what they need to get the Blight under control once and for all. Either way, the Skylark's conscience is clear. She gave the girl options, choices made with all the relevant information, all truth, no lies.

It was something she'd never had.

"Estelle? Are you listening?" the Grimalkin barks, her wolf letting out a sharp yip of agitation.

"No," the Skylark says. "And you know better than to go around throwing out my proper name like that, Pearl."

"Bah, you Floramancers and your superstitions," the Grimalkin says, but there's a look of contrition on her face. Her cat jumps into her lap, tail twitching at the minor disagreement. "Have you told Onyx about what your girl told you?"

Onyx frowns. "She has not told me anything."

The Skylark shoots the Grimalkin a hard look, but the older woman is now hiding her face in the fur of her cat.

The Skylark sighs heavily. "Miss Fox is the reason my apprentice strayed from the Wayfarer's path on the way back from Trenton. It seems that the Fox wanted to give me some kind of warning, and she delivered it to her instead of me."

"And what did she say?" Onyx asks.

The Skylark shrugs. "Her usual cryptic mumblings." It was bad enough the Grimalkin had brought Onyx into their earlier conversation. No sense in adding any fuel to the man's fire.

"I wasn't aware that you were still in contact with your mentor," Onyx says, trying to sound casual and failing.

"She is not my mentor, and I am not in contact with her, which is why she had to interrupt a Wayfarer's beam just to get a message to me. Either way, I think you would agree that there is something odd about this assignment. I hope we get to the bottom of it sooner rather than later."

"You are seeing shadows and calling them constructs," Onyx says smoothly, before picking invisible lint off his sleeve. "Honestly, Skylark, I think sometimes you let your emotions overrun your good sense."

The Skylark says nothing, just bites her lip. They have work to do. This is no time to get into yet another bickering match with the Elementalist.

The construct slows to a stop, the braking mechanism screaming from the effort, and the apprentices rub their eyes and sit up with jaw-cracking yawns. One of the Grimalkin's birds flies out the open back of the vehicle before returning.

"It seems as though we are here," the older woman says.

"Well, then," the Skylark says, clapping her hands. "Despite my disdain for this infernal contraption, we made decent time. Whatever awaits us will soon be revealed."

The Peregrine blinks owlishly. "Do you think it will be something bad?"

"It's a Blight," Crystal says, rubbing her hand across her face. "Of course it's going to be bad."

The Skylark says nothing, because the girl has the right of it. They are already starting off bad. The Skylark simply hopes that this will not be something worse, like another Tennessee Valley.

Because she does not think she will survive dying twice.

The first place we stopped was completely abandoned.
That should've been our first sign.

Chapter

SEVENTEEN

The Ohio Deep Blight is gross.

I climb out of the construct, my stomach burbling unhappily at the stink of the Mechomancy. Smoke billows out of the back of the vehicle, the exhaust of spent alchemy, and the white driver watches us with hooded eyes as we disembark. A few hundred feet ahead in the road is a barricade, with glowing emergency beacons and painted red signs warning that a Blighted area lies beyond. Just beyond the barricade the world is painted in shades of gray and ash, a stark contrast to the bright summer greenery around us where we stand. It's nothing like the Trenton Blight, which just made the world look a little muted. This place looks dead. Dead grass, dead trees, dead earth. The bleakness makes me shift from foot to foot, adjusting the weight of the pack on my back nervously. Before leaving, I changed into the most functional outfit Alistair raveled me—a button-down shirt and trousers tucked into sturdy boots. The Skylark and I also exchanged our valises for backpacks and wore our bandoliers strung across our chests. We would have to travel on foot, since the work itself was bound to be tedious. Now I understood what the Skylark meant by taking whatever I was comfortable with. All this gear is heavy, and I am half tempted to ravel an okra construct to carry it all for me, blowback be damned.

"Still feeling good about accepting this job?" the Skylark asks as she draws even with me.

"This is exactly the sort of glamorous work I envisioned when I first walked into the bureau," I say with a wink, trying to hide the uncertainty roiling inside me. The voice of doubt in my brain always sounds like Pigeon, which is fine because I'm great at ignoring my sister. This feeling is not in my brain, but in my gut. There is something deeply foul about the land before us, like an animal carcass that has gone putrid in the summer sun. This makes the Trenton Blight feel like a walk through Central Park.

The Skylark gives me a curt nod. "Make sure you stick with me, understood? As your mentor I am responsible for your safety, and if anything happens to you, the paperwork would be considerable."

"Your concern for my well-being is, frankly, a bit embarrassing," I deadpan, but the Skylark ignores the humor and walks off to confer with Onyx and the Grimalkin.

"It's creepy, right?" Crystal arrives beside me, speaking in a rush, her eyes wide in her dark face so that she looks much younger. "I mean, I read the reports, but they really don't do justice to this. Look at the sky! What kinds of things have gone wrong when the sky isn't even blue anymore?"

I nod. The more I stare at the place beyond the barricade where the Possibilities wither to nearly nothing, just a wisp of their usual glory, the more my anxiousness grows. Plus, there's the smell, of death and decay but also the iron and offal smell of birth. It's a strange scent, overwhelming in its strength. "Do you smell that?" I ask Crystal.

She wrinkles her nose and sniffs loudly. "Smell what?" she asks.

I shake my head. Maybe I just need to get used to the normal scents within a Blight. Yesterday I didn't notice any kind of odd smell, but then again I was powerful nervous about letting the Skylark down. Trenton probably smelled just as awful.

"Where's everyone else?" I ask, looking back down the road from whence we came. There is no other vehicle, and that strikes me as odd.

"Gone on ahead," Onyx says, stomping over to where Crystal and I stand. "They're mostly just here as support, since we'll be doing the real work of charging the beacons. They'll meet us later on at the rendezvous point."

"What if we need a healer before then?" I ask, and Onyx gives half a laugh.

"Girl, it's a Blight, not a war. What do you think you're going to run up against that's going to require healing?"

I say nothing. Because I don't know. There is just something about this place that makes me nervous in a big way.

That's the moment my fear rears up, savage and unreasonable. It's a strange thing, a new thing, the fear of the unknown, and I do not like it. Not even the possibility of life in New York City filled me with this much dread, and I cannot fathom what it is that has me so upset. I could die, sure, but I could walk outside and get murdered any day of the week. But the Ohio Deep Blight is so very wrong, like seeing a person with their skin turned inside out. The way the Possibilities fade away into a profound emptiness? The barren trees, leafless and brown? The utter stillness? There are no clouds in the sky, no birds, only a slate-gray nothingness that is like nothing I have ever seen.

But I have to enter it. Everything I have ever wanted lies on the other side of this task, and so I will not falter. I will not fail.

"It reminds me of winter," Crystal says, but nothing more, as though, like me, she is overwhelmed by the maelstrom of her emotions.

"Even winter has a few birds here and there. My chickadees are telling me that they can't sense a single creature for leagues around," the Grimalkin says, her tiny black-capped birds chittering in agitation as they fly around her head. I have never heard so many swear words from such small creatures. Who would've thought birds would be so foul-mouthed?

"Are we ready?" Onyx says. "We have quite a bit of ground to cover before we rest tonight."

No one objects, so Onyx steps out ahead, leading the way past the barricade, knapsack strapped high on his back. Crystal follows him, and the Grimalkin gestures for me to go next.

"The Skylark and I will bring up the rear," she says. "Just in case."

I swallow the lump in my throat and nod, walking after Crystal and pushing down all my misgivings. The moment we cross into the Blight, I take a deep breath and let it out. I'm expecting to get a wallop of . . . something. An ominous warning, or maybe even a bit static from where the Possibilities fall away.

But there is absolutely nothing, just a sense of unease, no different than when I crossed into the Blight back in New Jersey. Although the scent of decay and rot nearly overwhelms me.

"All right, then," says the Skylark, adjusting her gloves. "Let's get to work."

●●●

Less than an hour into our journey into the Blight, things start to go wrong.

The task of repairing this Blight is no different than what we practiced in Trenton the day before. Along either side of the road, Onyx and Crystal raise pillars of quartz, new and sparkling. The Skylark and I follow behind with our bandoliers full of bits, tying the stone back to the Possibilities, however thin they might be. The ravel feels a bit like tying off a bit of knitting—if the yarn were made of slime and foul air. I'm hoping that I'll get used to it as we go along.

But after charging the handful of beacons along the north side of the road, Onyx and Crystal stop short.

"Where'd the anchors go?" Crystal asks with a frown. "We haven't even gone a mile. Surely they aren't all completely gone?"

Onyx unfolds the map he tucked into the breast pocket of his shirt and looks at it. "We've been using the roots of the pillars that were here before to anchor our new pillars. This indicates that the beacons should continue for at least another five miles, and yet there are no anchors left here. I admit it is . . . curious."

"It's not only that," Crystal says. "We've charged a dozen beacons already, and maybe it's just me, but the Dynamism doesn't feel any different to me than it did before we started."

She's right. Reaching for the Possibilities here is even harder than it was in Trenton. If gathering energy there was like reaching for something on a high shelf, as the Skylark put it, this is like groping through a pitch-black room, trying to grasp something that feels familiar.

"I wonder if it's possible there's some sort of malfunction with the Resonator?" the Skylark suggests. Her expression is serene, as though she is untroubled by the oddness of the place. But there's a twitch under her left eye that belies her demeanor.

"Are we sure . . . ," I begin, and hesitate. I don't aim to sound insane, or worse, cowardly. But something is deeply wrong here, and so before I can reconsider, I continue. "Are we sure this is even a Blight at all?"

Everyone turns to stare at me, and Onyx raises an eyebrow in a way too like the Skylark. "Young lady, if this isn't a Blight, then what is it?"

"Let's turn back," the Skylark says, ignoring him, and I let out a silent sigh of relief. Perhaps she feels the same thing I do. "We can send a message to Smoke and the rest of his team that we've left to regroup. They can meet us outside of the barrier."

"I agree," the Grimalkin says. She digs out a nub of pencil and a slender strip of paper. A few scribbles and a murmur to a chickadee perched on her shoulder, and the bird takes off, the scrap of paper in his beak. The message is on its way. "We aren't that far from the boundary yet. If we're going to turn back, the time is now."

That's when the sound of an animal in pain comes to us, a screaming sound the likes of which I have never heard before. I instinctively reach for my bandolier, and there is a handful of okra seeds in my hand as the Skylark and Onyx turn toward the sound.

Something lumbers toward us on the road, the creature making a squealing noise like a stuck pig. It walks like a drunken thing, weaving this way and that, and by the time I figure out what it is my stomach has gone sour.

At some point the creature was a dog, maybe someone's beloved pet. But that was a while ago, and now the thing looks like it's been to hell and back. Open sores ooze along the canine's coat, and a huge seeping injury marks its left hindquarters. It doesn't speak, at least not like a regular dog; instead there's just an odd-pitched scream coming from it, the sound rising and falling as it gets closer.

"My god," the Grimalkin says, but she doesn't say anything else before a pillar shoots up out of the ground, impaling the dog where it stands. It's a mercy, and Onyx lowers his hand, the pillar remaining in place.

"What kind of Blight can do that to a dog?" Crystal wonders aloud, the horror lacing her voice an echo of what I'm feeling.

"One that we must repair," Onyx says, standing a little straighter. "Skylark. Surely you don't think we can leave after seeing *that*?"

"That . . . that . . . abomination is exactly why we should leave," the Grimalkin says, a tremor in her voice. "When have you ever known a Blight to twist a living creature so? To steal its voice? The poor thing couldn't even beg to be put out of its misery." Tears flood her eyes, and she sniffs hard to maintain her composure.

"Grimalkin is right," the Skylark says, her gaze locked on the body of the dog. In its death it seems to have somehow deflated, as though whatever was keeping it going has escaped as well. Stomach acid burbles in my middle, and I have to swallow hard to keep from puking. The awful smell has gotten worse, and Crystal pinches her nose.

"Let's discuss this first," Onyx says.

"There is nothing to discuss," the Skylark says, her voice low. "We are in over our heads here."

"Now, that is no way to assess the situation. We are the best the Colored Auxiliary has to offer," Onyx says. "Are we truly going to turn tail the moment we encounter something unusual?"

"Yes," the Skylark says. She spins and walks back the way we came, ignoring Onyx, which is exactly the right thing to do. I might be new to Blights, but a dying, diseased dog seems like all the warning a sane body needs to change the trajectory of their day.

"Are we certain this is the best course of action? I feel like you aren't weighing the facts," Onyx tries to interject, but we've already turned on our heels and headed back to the entrance to the Blight. We've come only a short ways, no more than a quarter of a mile, and the walk back out of the Blight is a grim, silent one.

Only, we never get back to the threshold of the Blight.

"Didn't we just pass that marker?" Crystal asks after we've been walking for nearly twenty minutes without finding the boundary. I blink, because she's right. I recognize the jacaranda raveled to the quartz pillar, because I just did the working. The purple flowers are already wilting and dropping off into the dirt, the fragile petals dried and brown.

"What's going on?" I ask, pointing to the pillar as everyone gathers around.

Skylark kneels and picks up one of the petals, sniffing it. "I've not seen a beacon fail this quickly."

"Hmm," Onyx says, adjusting his stones. "I can't be sure, but if I were to venture a guess based on what I see here, it seems as though this particular Blight is bending its edges in on itself. This is why we cannot find its edge."

"Blights can do that?" I ask.

"Lord," the Grimalkin grumbles. She drops her pack and roots around in it, pulling out a notepad. "This should be documented."

"It seems like someone should've known this was happening," Crystal says, her voice small. I cannot help but agree. "Don't people live here, within the Blight?"

"Some, still, yes," says the Skylark. The expression on her face is one of concern.

"So we're trapped here?" I say, an edge of panic in my voice.

"Not at all," Onyx says. "There is a Wayfarer's gate in Mercersburg. If we can get there, we can beam out of here."

"You mean we turn head further *into* the Blight?" Crystal asks.

The memory of the dying dog sends icy fingers down my spine.

"That is only a few miles past Steubenville, where we were going to meet up with Smoke and his group anyway," the Grimalkin says. "I can send them another message. Tell them to stay where they are."

"That, I think, is currently our only course of action," the Skylark says with a nod. "Onyx, how far is Steubenville from here?"

"Approximately five miles," he says, pointing back deeper into the Blight.

"Well, let us be on our way," the Skylark says. She doesn't look any more happy about the idea than I feel.

And so, with hesitant feet, we begin to walk.

It was not immediately obvious upon entering the Blight that the Peregrine was interacting with it in a way that was different than the rest of us. To understand the ODB, you have to know how a typical Blight feels: a difficulty in executing the most mundane tasks and the muting of the senses, like a haze has fallen between you and the rest of the world. The ODB was like a blanket falling over one's head: we couldn't sense anything and we couldn't see things in the way we usually did. It was like being blindfolded and bound, and we were all trying to compensate the best we could.

Truthfully, we were all too concerned with ourselves to notice the Peregrine much at all. • • •

EIGHTEEN

As they walk, the niggle of apprehension that the Skylark felt when the Hawk landed in her office to give her the details blossoms into full-blown anxiety. The landscape, the strange scent in the air, the disappearance of all the animals and the mutations in those that remained . . .

It is just like the Tennessee Valley.

An abandoned cabin. Blood soaked into the wood of a doorway. A whispered warning.

For a moment the Skylark is back in that place, back in those moments when the creature ripped into her, tearing into her chest, devouring her heart. She lies there in the dead grass and dirt, bleeding out her last, as the white man running the work crew stares down at her.

"We lost a darky. Get another out of the truck."

That was the last thing the Skylark remembered. The next thing she knew, she was sitting in the living room of a very old Negro woman wearing a brightly colored headscarf.

"Do you want to die?" the old woman asked. "Or do you want to live?"

"I'd like to live," the Skylark, simply Estelle back then, had replied. "I . . . I'm not finished."

The old woman nodded. "I can fix you, but you'll do something for me in return. Help me keep the balance. That might not sound like much, but it's hard work."

"I can do that," she said, even though she really had no idea what the old lady meant. All she knew was that she wasn't fond of the idea of death. The old woman across from her, the old woman she'd later come to know as Miss Fox, had given her a toothless smile.

And then Estelle had fallen asleep once more.

When she awoke it was to find herself back in Tennessee, buried under the bodies of her companions, their chests rent just like hers had been. The supervisor stood nearby, eating a human heart, and the bloody smile he gave Estelle snapped her into action.

It was the first time she used the full measure of her abilities, raveling a creature of considerable power from the bits left in her pocket. A few moments later, the man was dead.

While it wasn't a joyous occasion—she lost a number of friends who had signed up for the Conservation Corps work crew with her—she felt more alive in that moment than ever before.

After the overseer's death, it was discovered that he had been working with a Necromancer who had promised him a measure of wealth in exchange for the hearts of mages. The man had used the cover of the Bureau of the Arcane, whose initiatives had been funding the work in the Tennessee Valley, to recruit and slaughter the colored mages he needed. But the man had been a powerful one, the brother of a Tennessee senator. And that meant an investigation.

The Hawk was responsible for said investigation, and it wasn't long before Estelle was sitting before him in his office. She decided to tell him the truth—what did she have to lose? When she was finished, he did not say he was going to prosecute her. On the contrary, he offered Estelle a job with the bureau—but not one without conditions. She agreed to keep quiet about what had happened in Tennessee, and he agreed to keep quiet about this young mage's unauthorized use of the mystical arts.

Not many would care about a passel of dead colored folks, and for all his kindness to her, Estelle didn't know if the Hawk was truly one of them. But taking the job wasn't about him.

Estelle knew there was nothing she could do to bring back the people who had died with her. But she could make sure that no one else died going forward.

And for the past five years she had done just that. She had worked tirelessly for the Bureau of the Arcane as a low-paid journeyman, and when the Colored Auxiliary was formed last summer she'd accepted a position there. She'd run her part of the Colored Auxiliary in the manner she saw fit: going to places where colored mages, and their way of life, were under threat. She never found any other evidence of Necromancy in the regions that were under her purview, but that wasn't the only threat facing her people. And the Skylark had done a lot of good in her time. But most of it had been at Miss Fox's urging. The woman would frequently appear to her in dreams or a quiet moment of contemplation, pushing her toward this incident or that. It seemed to the Skylark that keeping the balance felt a lot like looking out for colored folks, which suited her just fine. Every Negro knew that white folks wouldn't save them, so better to save themselves.

But now the Skylark knows that she's made a terrible mistake. Not in the work she has done, but in ignoring Miss Fox. The old woman had been trying to reach out to her for months, and the Skylark had been very good at ignoring the repeated warnings about something festering in Ohio.

But the strangeness of the Blight and Miss Fox waylaying the Peregrine has the Skylark reassessing things. Because if Miss Fox is involved, then this Blight hides a far greater secret, and the Skylark has no idea what it could be. Well, that is not true. She worries that it could be a threat that is too familiar by half.

Necromancers.

As they walk a little ways down the road, the light fading too quickly as a sudden dusk settles in, the Skylark realizes she is going to have to tell the rest of the mages her suspicions. It's not a welcome prospect. But if she's right, and they're facing something much more dangerous than a Blight—if, somehow, a Necromancer is involved—it's best to be prepared.

Even if it will mean revealing secrets she has promised to take to her grave.

The church outside Steubenville.
Nothing to make you lose your faith like an abandoned church.

Chapter
NINETEEN

By the time we arrive to the road that will take us to the rendez-vous point, the sun is setting, or at least the light is fading since I'm not really sure where the sun is even supposed to be, that familiar orb nowhere to be seen in the ash-gray sky. Onyx and Crystal set to raveling everyone a light stone so we can continue. The day was much shorter than it should have been, and I dislike how the natural order of the world seems to have been upended. But I am powerless to do anything but hope that the sudden nightfall is not a sign of something more dire.

I watch as the two mages slowly work the Possibilities. The Blight, or whatever this is, is taking a toll on us. I distract myself by watching them ravel the stones, picking up rocks from the side of the road and changing them subtly so they cast a bright glow. I could probably reproduce the effect if I tried, maybe with an okra seed. But I don't try. I just accept a stone from Crystal.

We walk, everyone too exhausted speak. I feel like I've been awake for days, my feet dragging, and at first I think it's just because I'm not used to carrying so much weight and walking so far. But I don't think that's it at all. Fine lines of pain bracket the Skylark's mouth, and the Grimalkin has to stop to calm her animals every quarter of a mile or so. Crystal and Onyx look like they couldn't ravel another light stone if they needed to.

A mile or so later we find ourselves on the outskirts of the place we're set to rendezvous with Smoke's team, Steubenville. It becomes clear, even from here, that the place has been abandoned for some time.

"Did everyone evacuate?" I ask, trying not to think about the disfigured dog and failing. I don't want to consider the alternative.

"They must have," the Skylark says. She glances around at the dark buildings on the outskirts, ramshackle houses with windows that look like ominous eyes, doors hanging open to an unrelenting darkness beyond. "I don't see any bodies, nor any sign of violence. It's not unusual for folks to flee a Blighted zone when the beacons start to fail, though rarely do entire communities leave. According to the report, the Blight has only been this bad for a couple weeks."

"They're gone, all right," the Grimalkin says, coming to a stop beside her. "And considering what we've seen here, I can't say I'm surprised."

As we stand there, warily regarding the town, night fully descends, and we are in a dark so unrelenting that I find myself waiting for things to leap out at me from behind every tree. The stones we carry are the only source of light: there are no stars and no moon, not that we can see, anyway. There are no night sounds either: no footsteps of critters scurrying through leaf litter, no calls of owls or other nocturnal birds. Instead there is only a thick, unnatural silence that becomes more oppressive with each passing moment. Even the Grimalkin's wolf is upset by the landscape, the creature letting out a soft whine when we finally turn down the road that leads into the center of Steubenville.

"Take heart," Onyx announces, his exhaustion creeping into his words. "The town square is just ahead. If Smoke received our message, they should be close."

The town's lights are unlit; whether they're mage lights or Mechomancy lamps, I cannot tell. As we continue on, I notice there's debris in the streets: a shoe, a child's doll, a pile of silverware. "Why is it so cold?" I ask. The temperature has dropped precipitously since it got dark; it feels more like November than June.

Crystal bumps into me, and a glance at her face reveals her worry. "Sorry," she says, her voice low. "This place is giving me the heebie-jeebies."

"Same," I say. I try to summon a smile for her, when an ear-splitting scream beside us shatters the ominous silence.

I whip around, only to see the Grimalkin's cat diving down the front of her dress while the old woman swears.

"Dammit, Fyodor, mind your claws!"

The cat replies with an equally salty retort, and my face heats. How does a cat get such a foul mouth?

Onyx marches to the front of our group, his mage light held aloft. "Look, there's the sheriff's office. If Smoke and the rest of our colleagues have made it here, I suspect they'll be in there. Come along."

We make haste to the swinging door of the sheriff's office. I shiver as we enter.

"Hello?" the Skylark says, loudly and clearly. "Smoke?"

No one answers. The sheriff's office is quite empty, though it appears there was a group of people here within the last week. There are blankets piled in a corner, a few empty cans of beans, the remnants of a recent fire in the hearth.

"Smoke and the rest of them should be here by now," the Skylark murmurs as she walks the perimeter of the office.

There is another scream—but this one from somewhere outside.

Everyone freezes. "Someone is in trouble," I say.

"You're right—" says the Grimalkin, but I'm already out of the sheriff's office.

"Peregrine!" the Skylark yells after me.

The Grimalkin says something as well, but I'm already thundering down the steps and out into the lane. I run in the direction of the sound, light stone held high, my heart pounding. Somewhere in my brain I realize this is stupid; I should have stayed put or run in the other direction. But all I can think is that I recognized the scream.

I turn a corner and skid to a stop. There, in the middle of the street, fighting what can be described only as living darkness, is the rest of our group. A fire blazes in the center, where it appears a number of torches have been dropped. Sam and Nell are bent over a prone form all in white, a Mechomancer's lantern held aloft, and Malik and the Smoke are trying to ravel something. Judging by the ferocity of the dark, smokelike form in the face of their exertion, they have not been successful.

I don't hesitate. I reach into my bandolier and pull forth a handful of okra seeds, their power waking slowly when I call to them. The Possibilities feel miles away, and it takes everything I have to draw enough power for a ravel. It is painful, but there are lives at stake. I inhale quickly, focus, and throw the seeds.

They fly through the air toward the inky blot of a creature. In the dark it's hard to discern it, more emptiness than anything else, and I sense it shifting and moving more than I can see it. Contemplating the thing for too long might make me go mad, so I turn my attention away from the beast and instead toward my creations. As each okra seed hits the ground, it transforms into a waist-high construct armed with a sharp thorn in one hand, bright flower-shaped projectiles in the other. They are sloppy, not as tightly raveled as my warriors from the day before: leaves drooping, the vines pulling this way and that so that they are slow and a bit misshapen. Still, they rush with purpose toward the shadow beast, driving it backward as they tear into what form it has. I leave them to their task and rush to assist Sam and Nell where they kneel next to the older colored man I saw earlier in the day. In the light of the fire, Nell's face is tear streaked, and Sam's expression is grim.

"We have to get him to the sheriff's office!" I say.

"It's too late," Sam replies "He's already gone."

"We can't just leave him here," Nell says, crying prettily.

"I think we have to if we want to live," I say urgently. A glance over at my constructs reveals that they are grossly overmatched, the tide turning in favor of the formless creature.

Malik and Smoke hurry to our side. "We need to move," the younger one says, with a wide-eyed glance over his shoulder. "Those constructs are weak."

"There's nothing to draw on here," I snap. "Do you have any better ideas?"

Smoke shakes his head dismissively. "There's not enough starshine here to weave a decent Illusion."

A headache pounds behind my eyes from my raveling, but that doesn't keep a fine indignation from welling up. As frightened as I am, I'm still irked that they've so easily dismissed my efforts, especially when they've got absolutely nothing to show for theirs.

"All we can do is run and hope the thing doesn't follow," I say, my tone sharp. "The rest of the team is in the sheriff's office around the corner."

Sam and Nell stand, and I hazard another glance over my shoulder. Where there were previously more than a dozen of my okra warriors, there are now only three, and I hastily grab another few okra seeds out of the pocket of my bandolier and toss them at the beast, this time grunting at the pain that zings through me. There's a tickling sensation under my nose and I swipe at it, hoping the wetness I feel isn't blood. That would be very, very bad.

"Come on!" There's a shout from behind us, and I turn, the effort momentous. Onyx and Crystal are in the middle of the street raising a barrier of crystals while the Skylark coaxes jacaranda vines to grow around the things.

I don't need any other prodding. I turn and run back down the street, Sam's and Nell's footfalls echoing behind me, Smoke's and Malik's behind theirs. Guess they aren't as dumb as they look.

"Get inside," the Skylark says as we run past.

When I slam through the sheriff's door, the Grimalkin is painting strange symbols on the walls in a dark, thick liquid. I can only imagine it's blood, and for a moment I fear the worst, counting the Grimalkin's companions. But then I notice the seeping cut on the older woman's arm.

"These barriers should keep us safe," the older woman says, collapsing into a rickety old chair and wrapping a length of fabric over her wound. It's already brighter in the building with the Grimalkin's wards in place, the light stones seemingly stronger, as though they don't have to work quite as hard to hold the dark at bay. "That took more out of me than I thought it would."

"Peregrine, you're bleeding too," Nell says.

I swipe the back of my hand under my nose. Dammit. Guess all those okra constructs did take a bit too much out of me.

Nell scrubs her face, wiping away the last of her tearstains. "I can help with that."

I shake my head. "I'll be fine once I get something to eat. But the Grimalkin appears to have cut herself deeper than she intended, likely so maybe there's something you can do for her."

Nell nods, but before she can move toward the older woman, the door bursts open once more. The Skylark, Onyx, Crystal, and the Illusionists enter in a mad dash, the door slamming behind them.

"I don't suppose you managed to find some starlight so you could Illusion that thing to death—" I want to throw some shade Malik's way, but my words dissolve into a coughing fit. Hard to be cool when you're choking on your own blood.

The Skylark gives me a sharp look. "No, but Onyx, Crystal, and I managed to dispense with the creature for the time being. We can deal with it properly in the morning, when we've hopefully gathered our strength and the beacon we raised has gathered whatever of the Dynamism it can. In the meantime, Peregrine, see to that nosebleed of yours. It is a sight."

Sam pulls out a handkerchief and hands it to me. I use the cloth to pinch my nose before dropping the knapsack I still wear on the floor and leaning back against it. If I were at home and I'd pushed myself like this, my ma would have given me a cool cloth for the back of my neck and a nice glass of sugared tea, and I would have been back together before I knew it. I try to remember the last time I felt this poorly after raveling, and I can't. Not even the time when I was six and decided to ravel a mess of friends to play tag with after finding a pine cone full of evergreen seeds. It had been an amazing afternoon, but the selfish expenditure of the Possibilities had left me ill for nearly a week after. Still, what I'm feeling now makes any blowback I've ever felt from a self-ravel seem like a picnic in comparison.

I suddenly wonder if I'll perhaps not ever see my ma again. But I push the dark thought away as quickly as it comes; I need to pay attention to the conversation happening before me. The Skylark has her arms crossed, and Smoke is muttering something about her and the Grimalkin overreacting.

"There is no way that was a Blight Beast. Frederick has dealt with dozens of them before," Nell says, voice low as she uses her arts to stitch the Grimalkin's wound closed. As she works, she whimpers, blood dripping from her nose as well. "I'm sorry. That's all I can do, Grimalkin. Any more and I fear I'm going to pass out."

"More than enough," the old woman says gruffly, patting Nell on the shoulder. "Save your energy."

I consider Nell's words. Whatever that thing was out there, it was much more powerful than the beasts the Skylark and I fought in Trenton. But if it wasn't a Blight Beast, then what was it?

"That is a good question," the Grimalkin says, her eyes meeting mine. Did I say that last part out loud? I'm feeling more than a little addled, so it could be I've been keeping up a running dialogue, which is unsettling. Most of my thoughts are not fit for polite company.

Onyx holds up his hand. "Arguing isn't going to help us here, and I think we can all agree that this Blight is like no other we've encountered before." Onyx's voice has gotten even plummier, his overenunciation of vowels becoming much more noticeable. "Perhaps this is an advanced stage of Blight that we haven't yet seen."

Crystal nods. "Or . . . Master Onyx, is it possible it's not something new, but rather something ancient? The Ohio Deep Blight was one of the first that manifested, and it has always been the most problematic. Is it possible this land had Dynamistic issues even before the Great Rust?"

"It's an interesting question," Onyx replies, "though there is no record of anything like what you're describing."

"What about the records of the First Nations?" Sam asks. "They were here for millennia before the European Mechomancers."

Smoke waves away Sam's suggestion. "The First Nations practice nothing but unrefined Wytchcraft."

"The First Nations have talented mages who have much to teach us," the Skylark says gently but with an edge of authority. "But in this case, I doubt they have ever seen anything like this. Gentlemen, correct me if I'm wrong, but the Ohio Deep Blight was the first one to receive a Resonator last year, was it not?"

Onyx nods thoughtfully, but it's Smoke that speaks. "What are you suggesting, Skylark?"

"I'm not suggesting anything," my mentor replies coolly. "I'm merely observing that this Blight has one of the oldest Resonators—one that had been malfunctioning with frequency of late, even if we didn't encounter this sort of behavior until now."

"Do you think perhaps the Mechomancy in it has broken down?" Sam asks. "Done some sort of further damage?"

Smoke scoffs. "What is there within a Resonator that could have this sort of effect on the Dynamism? It's all metal and oil—dead, inert substances. And the alchemy in the diesel that powers it hardly has enough energy to—"

"I don't think we should rule any theory out," Onyx says, breaking in once more. "Whatever the cause, it is our charge to reckon a solution. We are all top mages in our fields; that's why we were sent here. We will figure out a way to fix this and find our lost cousins from the Chicago branch. For now, let us do what we can to get comfortable here. We'll eat, sleep, and come up with a plan in the morning."

"We have to see to Frederick's body first," Nell says. Like me, she reclines against a pack, a handkerchief still pinched around her nose.

"No," the Skylark says, the single word landing heavily. "No one leaves the safety of the wards until the morning. While we were able to dispel the creature that killed Frederick long enough to get ourselves to safety and have barred the immediate area against its intrusion, I have no doubt it is still out there. We can put his remains to rest before we continue on our way tomorrow."

Nell drops her hand, eyes set. "But—"

"No," the Skylark cuts her off again. "Frederick is dead. There is nothing we can do for him now that will change that. We need to think about those of us who are still alive. Our obligations are to one another, and to any members of the Colored Auxiliary who may still be out there. That is our job."

Her words cast a pall over the room, and after a long moment everyone breaks off to see to their needs. There is a washroom, thankfully. I quickly use the commode before rinsing out Sam's handkerchief. Thirst parches my throat, but the water smells weird and has a silty, slimy look to it. I still have my canteen, but what about when our supplies run out? I don't trust anything in this place to be uncorrupted, and I hardly have the energy to work a purification ravel.

I make my way back to my knapsack and fish out the canteen,

drinking as much as I will allow myself. The water tastes a bit metallic but is delicious all the same. As soon as I twist the lid back on, the Skylark appears next to me, her expression hard.

"You didn't drink the water from the sink, did you?"

I shake my head, the movement igniting a fresh wave of agony from the pounding behind my eyes. "I don't feel right," I say, voice low. "And it's more than just the difficulty raveling." The skittering feeling across my skin has subsided now, but I still feel like I'm missing some vital part of me, like I woke up missing a hand or something.

"I feel it too. I wanted to ask, you haven't seen your friend, have you? Since we left the storeroom?"

I frown before I realize she's talking about the puma. It is strange that only just occurred this morning. I feel like I've lived a whole month since then. "Nope. Haven't seen him. Do you think he's got anything to do with this?"

"No," says the Skylark, certain, but she frowns in thought. "It seems strange that only you were able to see him. Not to mention the vessel he gave you. I want to try something in the morning. I will wake you before I do the others. Try and get some rest."

The Skylark moves off to confer with the rest of the adults. Crystal comes out of the washroom and plops down near me. I can't quite see her expression in the dim light. After a moment, she sniffs and swipes away a tear.

"Did you know him?" I ask her.

She looks at me now, her expression unmoving. "Know who?"

"Frederick," I say, keeping my voice low so that my words won't travel to where Sam and Nell lean against one another, speaking in low voices, their grief clear.

"No, I didn't know him," Crystal says, sniffing again. Her voice is flat, none of her usual cheeriness to be found. "I'm just . . . I don't want to die. And I can't shake this feeling."

"What feeling?"

"That everything dies here. And we're going to be next."

After the loss of the healer Frederick it first occurred to me that we had potentially walked into a trap. I did not know or suspect that the person who laid the trap was a member of our party, nor did I have any suspicion at the time that the bureau had Necromancers in its midst. The council may find me naive for such an oversight, but I must stress that events were unfolding quite quickly and we were all hard pressed to do what we could to keep our wits about us. . . .

Chapter

TWENTY

The Skylark always wakes early. She has ever since she was little. Her mama worked in a bakery, and it was normal to see her rise before the first rays of dawn pinkened the sky, her capable hands coaxing the yeast, flour, and sugar to do their thing. Not with the mystical arts, but with good old-fashioned elbow grease. No one else in the Skylark's family was able to ravel a lick—at least, not anyone she was aware of. If any of her grandparents or great-grandparents or anyone further back than that had natural abilities, they were destroyed by Necromancers during the Afrikan Genocide. It had been her aunt Clem, no blood relation but a cherished family member all the same, who taught her how to find wonder and meaning in the swamps of Georgia.

"Follow your instincts, child. Your talent knows more about this world than your brain. You got to learn to listen to it." Clem had been raised a rootworker, and though her ability to work the Dynamism had been so weak as to be nearly nonexistent, she was the one to teach Estelle—how to use spiderwebs to bind wounds and a bit of redbrick dust to unravel a hex.

She taught Estelle how to embrace her gifts no matter what anyone else might say.

The Skylark is thinking about Aunt Clem as she wakes. There was no way Clem would have found herself in the middle of this mess in Ohio. She would've walked right up to the edge, felt the strange wrongness of the place, turned on her heel, and left.

The Skylark is beginning to wish she'd done exactly that.

There is no sense delaying the inevitable, so the Skylark climbs off her bedroll, the raveled item barely visible in the early morning gloom. Next to her the Grimalkin and her brood still snooze, the wolf lifting his head to whine a sleepy good morning to the Skylark. She gives the beast a nod of acknowledgment before going to find her apprentice, where she slumbers with the rest of the girl apprentices, the men having found a side room for themselves to sleep in.

The Peregrine sits up after a small touch on her foot, standing and kicking herself free of her bedroll. The Skylark gestures for quiet and then beckons the girl to follow her, noting that she slept in her bandolier, same as the Skylark did. The girl has good instincts. She was the first of them to run toward the danger, and just like back in Trenton, she knew exactly what to do to slow the creature down, even if it was nothing like the ones they'd faced before. The Skylark still has doubts about the Peregrine, but the girl is quickly putting each one to bed.

It doesn't hurt that the Fox, evidently, trusts her. Though the Skylark suspects even the Fox likely doesn't know what the Peregrine is truly capable of.

The Skylark edges the door open to peek and see if the creature still lurks beyond the threshold. The creature was like nothing she'd ever faced before, not even back in the Tennessee Valley, and she will approach it now with not a small amount of caution, and fear.

Through the crack in the door, the world is painted in shades of gray, the sun is not quite risen, but the strange ashen sky is light enough to discern the street outside. The great inky blot from the night before is gone, and the Skylark steps boldly out onto the porch.

The Peregrine joins her, and the girl's face scrunches as she takes in the town. "This place seemed bigger in the dark," she says.

The Skylark agrees. Last night the walk from the road to the town proper seemed to take hours, but from their vantage point on the porch, the main road is clearly visible through the spindly, leafless trees. Even the barrier that she and Onyx worked to erect seems much closer, the beacon stones no more than a hundred feet away.

The Skylark frowns at the sight of the stones, stepping off the porch to inspect the crystalline pillars more closely. The obelisks were ten feet tall the night before; now they are no more than waist high, and the surface of the quartz is no longer icy and smooth, but black and pitted. The jacaranda vines she painstakingly grew around the pillars to lend them warding power are shriveled and dead, a brown powdery substance the only sign that there was ever anything growing on the crystals.

"What happened to them?" The Peregrine frowns at the spots, running her own fingers across the remnants of the vines on another pillar. She looks so young in the early morning gloom that the Skylark has a brief moment of regret. Why did she give in and take an apprentice? What will she do if she has sentenced the poor girl to death?

"They look . . . burned up," the girl continues, brushing her hands off on her clothes. "Is that to be expected?"

"I'm not sure," the Skylark says, opting for truth. "Nothing about this place is . . . normal."

"I wouldn't say that," the Peregrine replies, and, with a wry smile, echoes the Skylark's earlier lesson. "It's as normal as a Blight can be, right?"

The Peregrine puts her hands on her hips. There's a wariness in her expression that wasn't there the day before, and the Skylark realizes that no matter what happens next, none of them will leave the Blight the same as they entered it.

She's just hoping that they *will* get to leave.

"I wanted to try something, since we are having so much trouble drawing on the Dynamism. Do you still have that bottle the cat led you to?"

"Of course." The Peregrine pulls the vessel forth from one of her bandolier pockets, and the purple glass seems to glow in her hand. "Are you finally going to tell me what it is?"

The girl holds it out, but the Skylark doesn't reach for the thing—the cat clearly intended it for the younger mage, and it wouldn't work for the Skylark, anyhow. She doesn't have a lick of Necromantic ability.

But maybe this strange girl from a backwater town in Pennsylvania does.

The Skylark pulls a handful of okra seeds from one of the pockets of her bandolier and gestures for the Peregrine to follow her. The Skylark squares her shoulders and reveals none of the nervousness she now feels, her middle churning over the memory of the night before. Every instinct she has screams for them to run back the way they came, to hide out right there, behind the Grimalkin's wards, until someone else is sent to come find *them*, just as they were sent to find the team from Chicago. But the Skylark has to approach this matter like an adult, not a frightened child.

The adult thing to do is rarely easy.

Once they step beyond the defensive barrier, the abomination coalesces quickly, strange puffs of that inky darkness appearing from all corners of the town: from under the eaves of the abandoned houses, out of the windows of empty storefronts, out of strange holes in the ground that they had missed in the darkness. The Skylark tosses the handful of okra seeds before her, each one popping into a similar version of the constructs she created the day before. They run forward and start hacking at the creature, their tiny thorn swords mostly useless.

"Okay, here's what you're going to do. You won't have much time," the Skylark says, a glance over her shoulder at the sheriff's office behind them. She isn't quite sure how soon the rest of their group will wake, and the last thing she wants is for anyone to see what she thinks is about to happen. "As soon as the last of my constructs are destroyed, you're going to open that bottle."

"This?" the girl says, looking at the bottle. The Skylark's constructs were already being torn to pieces by the violent movements of the writhing, smoky monster. "What's that going to do?"

"Honestly . . . I'm not sure," the Skylark says. "So be ready to run if it doesn't do anything. But if I'm right, it's going to buy us some time. Okay, steady, steady . . . now!"

The last of the okra-seed constructs is thrown to the side, unraveling into bits of green that quickly dry into brown nothingness. The Peregrine twists the tiny cork stopper out of the bottle and points the open end toward the creature now bearing down on them.

There is a momentary pause, and then the world shivers, like someone decided to give reality a good shake. The Peregrine gasps, but her expression isn't one of anguish, but of exhilaration. Before them, the shadowy monster freezes before beginning to spin, rotating around an unseen axis. The creature lets loose a haunting moan that the Skylark can feel in her bones. And then the creature is spinning like a cyclone and is sucked into the bottle, leaving nothing behind.

Once the entirety of the dark miasma has been captured, the Peregrine quickly puts the lid on, a look of distaste on her face.

"This smells," she says, sticking out her tongue in disgust. "I'm asking again: What is this bottle?"

"It's . . ." The Skylark considers lying but quickly decides against it. She told the young Peregrine that she would be truthful with her. Trust goes both ways. Plus, the girl has been more than patient, waiting until now to press about the item. "It's a soul jar."

The girl's eyes go wide. When she speaks, her words are filled with terror. "You really got me out here doing Necromancy?"

The Skylark shushes her. "In a way, yes. Let me—"

"Necromancy is evil," the Peregrine says, her voice rising in the quiet of the early morning. "You *told* me Necromancy was evil."

"Keep your voice down," the Skylark says. "I never said anything of the sort. I simply said we wouldn't speak of it."

"Because it's bad!"

The Skylark takes a breath. The girl is not prepared for this moment. Which the Skylark understands. She wasn't either, and she was older and more experienced than the Peregrine then. "Answer me this: Why is Necromancy evil?"

"Because . . ." Her face twists with distaste. "Where do I start? Necromancers killed thousands of people. Ripped their souls from their bodies. Used those souls to experiment, to power Mechomantic machines. Why are we even having this conversation? Everyone knows the Klan, what they did, the Afrikan Genocide. . . ." She trails off.

The Skylark understands why the Peregrine is so skittish about the idea of Necromancy. The legacy of that dark art is fraught for colored folks. After all, it was the Necromancers who brought Afrikans to North America during the slave trade, using colored mages to power constructs created by Mechomancers. That was back before people considered the Klan to be a bad thing, when Necromancers were just another guild of mages. People began decrying the Klan and its peculiar kind of Necromancy only when overseers began to ravel the souls of colored folks right into constructs. By the time the Afrikan Genocide came to an end, millions of Negroes had been murdered to further Mechomancy.

It was a bleak time for Negroes, and many found speaking of such a thing to be ill luck.

"You're not wrong about any of that," the Skylark replies calmly. "But you're talking about Necromancers. Not Necromancy."

The young girl throws up her hands. "Is there a difference?"

"The difference is everything. The Klan uses bedsheets, right? They stitch them into robes and cowls to hide their identity."

"And?"

"And," the Skylark says, "are bedsheets evil just because the Klan uses them to terrorize colored folks?"

The Peregrine is quiet for a moment. "Fine," she says, less sure of herself, perhaps, but not much. "Necromancy is Death art. Our abilities draw on Life." She kneels, picks up the withered remnants of leaf and vine that moments ago were the Skylark's constructs. "Necromancy is the opposite of everything we do. Of everything I know."

"Ah, but is it?" the Skylark asks. "Necromancy manipulates the energies present in living things, or things once living. Its power can be used to work unspeakable evil, yes. But the art is not derived from Death. No matter what anyone has told you."

She instinctively touches her chest, and the long scar that bisects the center of her body beneath her shirt, her fingers trembling. The Skylark owes her life to a bit of Necromancy, and she's done naught but good with her extra time. But how can she impress that upon her apprentice without vomiting out the whole sordid story?

And does she even want to? In her time working with mages,

the Skylark has found that it is best to let folks come to their own conclusions. Browbeating and rhetoric got a body only so far, but laying out the facts and hoping that someone chose the better path? That was usually a safer route.

If the Peregrine notices her mentor's distress, she doesn't let on. The girl still examines the bottle in her hand uneasily. "I know there's a lot I can do that I don't understand, but I'm telling you, Skylark, I don't have anything in common with those murder mages."

The Skylark regards the Peregrine. She chooses her next words carefully. "I won't claim to know everything about Necromancy. I have no aptitude for it, and the practice of it has been outlawed for as long as I've been alive. But I can tell you that I've seen enough of the mystical arts to know what most people in this country don't want to admit. That it's not what you can do; it's what you do with it."

The Peregrine raises her eyes. The Skylark can't say what the girl is feeling, but it seems her fear is tempered, for the moment.

"I told you back in New York that you needed to be careful about how you use all of the tools at your disposal—but that you'd also need them," the Skylark continues, collecting herself. "Necromancy seems to be one of those tools. And you've just saved the rest of us from the fate that befell Frederick. If we'd left that creature be, it would've stalked us and just waited until we were exhausted before devouring us as well. Now come with me; we need to see about something."

The Peregrine follows her as they walk briskly down the street and turn the corner to where last night's battle took place. As they draw even with the spot where Frederick fell, the Skylark's suspicions are confirmed.

Lying in a heap next to the road is a pile of leaves and other detritus, and not much else.

"Where did his body go?" the Peregrine asks. Her grip tightens on the glass bottle, and the Skylark takes a moment to gather her thoughts before she answers.

"He's gone." She touches her chest again. The emptiness inside her feels the same as usual, but what will happen to her as they remain in the Blight? When she next speaks, her words are soft. "And if we aren't careful, we'll be next."

Hard to believe that less than a year ago,
this was a popular general store.
This place is cursed.
That's all there is to it.

TWENTY-ONE

The Skylark can't be as calm as she seems. How can a person's body just be gone, leaving behind nothing but dead leaves and a few loose threads? That sounds like a fairy story. But then, the Skylark is not prone to emotional displays. As for me, I don't know what to do with this information, nor what I've just learned about my abilities. Cry? Fall to pieces? Run back home to Shrinesville and swear off the Possibilities forever?

All of those options seem better than the path I'm on, but of course I do none of them. Not because I'm loyal to the bureau; they can go suck an egg for what they've let us walk into. But because there are still things to be learned here. And if I didn't know before that the Skylark was the one to teach them to me, I suppose I do now.

The bottle—the soul jar—feels entirely different with the inky monster contained inside. Heavier than it should be. And charged. Just touching the glass makes my skin thrum. I place the bottle back in the pocket where it was before.

"What could make a dead body turn into this?" I ask, gesturing to the piles of dried dead leaves.

"Nothing we want to deal with, I can assure you of that. Come on, let us return to the others and tell them what we saw."

"And about the bottle?" I ask, a tendril of panic zinging through me.

The Skylark puts her hands on my shoulders and looks me dead in the eyes. "Absolutely not. The Grimalkin might be counted on to hold her tongue, but the rest of that lot back there will not understand. And more than one of them would sell you out in a moment if they think it will gain them some clout with the bureau. We keep this to ourselves."

For once, the Skylark and I are in complete agreement. Despite the Skylark's words, I still think Necromancy is the foulest of the mystical arts, an ability mired in death and destruction. I don't know why the bottle works or even how, but I sure as hell am not about to start embracing it. No need to let anyone know about the little something extra I seem to have.

The walk back to the sheriff's office is a quick one, and when we open the door it's to find our companions awake—and an argument brewing. The Grimalkin and her animals stand on one side of the room, with Smoke and Onyx on the opposite side of the space, the apprentices standing against a back wall, looking on with apprehension.

"There you are!" shouts the Grimalkin, and her cat lets out a yowl before launching itself through the air at me.

You're alive, Fyodor says as I catch the feline awkwardly. I didn't even know the cat liked me.

"Yes, I very much am, thank you for your concern," I whisper, burying my face in the animal's fur, the cat's warm weight providing a comfort I didn't know I needed. There is just something so nice about cats. Maybe it's their utter disdain for everything.

I knew you could hear me, the cat purrs. *Although, it is rude to pretend you cannot.*

The Grimalkin gives me a quizzical look, but before she can say anything, Onyx chimes in. "Thank the heavens that you're both all right! We thought some evil had befallen you, since the wards failed."

"I've no clue how they could have failed," the Grimalkin says. "I've worked those runes dozens of times, and they were raveled from fresh blood. I'm telling you, there's something wrong with this place."

"I agree," Smoke says with a nod. "But we need more information about what is happening here. The Grimalkin here has already told us of your plan to leave. But to turn back before we've reckoned the cause of these disturbances and found the other team would not only be cowardly, but a dereliction of duty."

"We can't turn back, anyway," the Skylark says. "We tried that yesterday and just got rerouted back on our path toward the center of the Blight."

"You didn't tell us that," Smoke says, censure in his voice.

"What are you talking about? We sent along Kevin," the Grimalkin says, her expression pensive. "He never got to you?"

"No, he did not," Smoke replies, and the Grimalkin's face falls, as does my heart. Frederick isn't the only ally we've lost.

"Staying will mean our death," the Grimalkin says, when she

finds her words. "My animals can sense workings far beyond anything any of us can, and they all warn me that there is something dangerous at the heart of the Blight. They woke this morning speaking of . . . well, I can't say it made much sense, but I can say that we are not prepared for whatever is happening here."

"Nonsense," Smoke says dismissively. "They're beasts, not seers."

The Grimalkin is not offended, nor is she deterred. "Whatever happened to the other team—and I am beginning to think the worst—it's going to happen to us as well. We told you last night about the sickly dog we had to put down. This is way over our heads. We need to regroup with the bureau, come back with more provisions, a bigger force—"

"I agree with Smoke." It's Onyx, who had been deep in thought until now. "The town of Mercersburg is mere miles down the road, another opportunity to gather information about what's happening here, if there is anyone left there. There, we can decide whether to continue on to the center of the Blight and complete our mission, or Wayfare out. Whatever we are going to do, there's only one way forward."

"We'll never make it," the Skylark says, and relief floods through me at hearing her speak.

"What do you mean?" Smoke asks, turning his gaze upon the Skylark.

"Our beacons from last night have almost been devoured. The thing that did that is all around us now. Eating away at our bodies, at our abilities."

Onyx starts to gather his bags. "All the more reason to press on—"

"I'm not finished," the Skylark says. "I believe I know what we're dealing with here. We are trapped in a Necromancer's summoning."

"Necromancy!" Onyx says, drawing back a bit. "What makes you say that?"

The Skylark's gaze doesn't meet mine. "What's happening here is more than just a corruption of the Dynamism. This place is draining the life force of everything in the area. Any abilities we use are being devoured as well. It's why the wards failed; it's why we didn't find any beacons from the previous teams; it's why we feel so horrible performing basic ravels. And look," she says, holding out her hat. The edge is frayed. "Even the basic constructs we have with us are coming unworked. If we stay in here too long, we'll meet the same fate."

"People can come unraveled?" Malik asks. He and Sam sit so close to one another, their hands touching lightly. Malik catches me watching them and pulls away subtly. He scowls, but the expression can't hide the fear in his eyes.

"Yes," the Skylark says, dragging my attention back. "Which is why we need to find another way out of here. Now."

"Impractical," says the Smoke. "If what you say happened to you yesterday is true, then there probably is some kind of linked pathway within the Blight. And if that is the case, then Wayfaring is our best bet."

"I snagged some Wayfarer's stones from the storeroom," I say.

"Can we use them to head back to New York?"

Everyone turns to me. "Why did you take Wayfarer's stones?" the Smoke asks, his tone icy.

I blink and shrug. "Why not? Everyone needs an exit plan."

The man's nostrils flare, and I cannot be the only who sees the way he clenches and unclenches his hands, like he is trying to keep from hitting me. "Those stones are not useless trinkets. If you were to have fallen last night, do you have any idea how much—"

"Good thinking, kiddo," the Grimalkin interrupts. "Let me see what you have?"

I fish out the Wayfaring stones and drop them into her palm. The Grimalkin looks over the stones and sighs. "Unfortunately these have the same problem the ones I grabbed do," she says, digging out a handful of similar stones from another pocket. The Smoke throws his hands up in the air in exasperation. "It seems like this place has already stripped the ravel from them. They're nothing more than fancy rocks now."

Just as quickly as my hope rose, it withers and dies, one more victim of the Blight.

"Well, at least I don't have to worry about filing an unauthorized usage report," the Smoke says, clearing his throat. "We already know backtracking is useless. I say we push hard to get to the center of the Blight. If this is like the Skylark says, and there's Necromancy at work here, it is even more urgent that we find the person responsible and stop them."

"You think this is a rogue practitioner?" Onyx asks, stroking the stubble on his face that sprang up overnight. "Like the Tennessee

Valley incident? If so, we would have a responsibility to—"

"Enough," the Skylark says quickly, shutting down further conversation. It's a subtle but unmistakable reminder that she is actually the one in charge of this expedition. Smoke might be from the D.C. office, but it's the Skylark who is running the show. "We'll table this discussion until we get to the Wayfaring station. Ready yourselves; we leave in ten minutes."

From the scowl the Smoke gives her, I have a feeling that persuading him to leave won't be easy. And if he insists on continuing on, what will everyone else do?

As far as I'm concerned, first chance I get I'm going to leave the Smoke, Onyx, and whomever else behind, along with their death wishes. There isn't anything worth dying over. Especially not in Ohio.

This family was fleeing the Blight and looked pretty rough.
I wonder if they managed to make it out.

Chapter

TWENTY-TWO

When we finally leave the sheriff's office, the sun is high, but it is weak and ineffectual. The day is much cooler than it should be, and I sip at my water sparingly. I had half hoped there would be some kind of mutiny when it came time to go, the Smoke and Onyx splitting off to be heroes and leaving the rest of us behind to find another way out of here, but there is none of that.

Instead, we all set out sullen and grim-faced. Even with the dread of what lies in front of us, though, I have to admit there's a sense of relief when we reach Steubenville town limits. None of us want to be here, and in the light of the dim, flat disk in the sky, even the Smoke and Onyx seem to be reconsidering their brave words from just a half hour earlier.

"Your mentor know you can chat with beasts?" asks the Grimalkin, falling into step next to me and banishing my sour thoughts about men who don't have the sense God gave an earthworm.

I'm not surprised by the question—it's my own stupid fault for chatting up her cat—but I do look around to make sure no one else is within earshot. Onyx and the Smoke lead the way far up ahead, and Sam and Nell talk in lowered voices, Malik watching them with a look that can be described only as envious. Crystal trudges along next to the Skylark, talking the older woman's ear off even as she keeps stumbling over her own feet. It's possible this place is affecting her even more than the rest of us; I need to check in on her. Once I extricate myself from the Grimalkin's interrogation.

I hesitate. But the Skylark said she trusts the Grimalkin as much as she trusts anyone. That's something. And it's not like she'll believe me if I lie.

"Yes, I can talk to your friends all right. And yes, the Skylark knows. But she made me promise that I wouldn't go around using every discipline I can work all willy-nilly, since the bureau frowns on it and all that."

"Ha!" She lets out a laugh, and then lowers her voice again. "Yes, I remember telling the Skylark that myself once upon a time. She's not wrong, but mind this: when it comes time to try and get out of this place, you use every single trick you have at your disposal. We're going to need it."

Fresh anxiousness wells up, because there's a quaver in the Grimalkin's voice and her eyes have gone far away, like she's seeing someplace else. Which reminds me that there is a question I want to ask.

"Miss Grimalkin, Onyx mentioned something about the Tennessee Valley incident. What was that about?"

"Ah yes, I had a feeling one of you young ones might ask. . . ."

She trails off for a moment, and it's only the peeping of one of her chickadees that brings her back. "Petrie here has the right of it; there is something similar about what is happening to the land around us. Even though he wasn't there, his ma was my companion at the time. Either way, a while ago now, more than ten years, there was a mage in Tennessee who claimed that there was a water dragon nesting in one of the valley flood basins there. The idea was to build a series of dams to divert the additional flooding it would surely cause." The Grimalkin stops and peers at me out of the corner of her eye. "You know about dragons?"

"I've never met one, but yes'm, I know a bit about them."

That's not exactly true. I don't know a bit about dragons. I know everything there is to know about them. *Everything*.

They're just animals, I know, same as any other—well, any other that can work the Possibilities, like unicorns and griffins and such—but there is something so awesome and terrifying about dragons. A full-grown dragon has been known to be mistaken for a mountain, and there are sailors who will tell stories about waking dragons on their journeys, setting off cataclysmic storms. Even krakens, which are sort of the tough guys of the deep, are afraid of dragons. Can you imagine? So yeah, I know some things about dragons. Truth is that I learned to read just so I could read the big book of dragon lore my ma kept on the mantel. It was one of three books we owned: a big book of dragon lore written by Thomas Jefferson; a family Bible where we tracked marriages, births, and deaths; and a tiny encyclopedia on the mystical arts that was handwritten by my grandma who self-emancipated during the

Afrikan Genocide and moved herself up to Pennsylvania. I would say that last one was interesting—after all, the woman talked to a *river* to figure out her escape—but she once made me clean her whole house for nicking a few bits out of her box and raveling a cat construct to catch the mice eating up her cottage walls. I was never very fond of her after the fact. How was I supposed to know the mice took care of small tasks for her?

Anyway, for all I know about dragons, the Grimalkin gives me a look like she clearly doesn't believe me. "Dragons aren't quite as fierce as Mechomancers make them out to be. They were nearly hunted to extinction just because they aren't the type to eat a body first and ask questions later. A dragon is smart and reasonable and fair. And that's why the bureau called as many mages as it could to Tennessee to help reroute the waterways and give the dragon a nice, big, deep lake to sleep in, since that's just about all you can do with an older dragon once it makes up its mind. But when they got there, the dragon was the least of their worries. The mages discovered a group of resurgent Klan Necromancers in the state trying to raise a bunch of the Founding Fathers from the grave, and ripping out colored hearts to do it."

"But weren't the Founding Fathers all cremated?"

"All but Jefferson, that slave-owning bastard. Rumor is that he was convinced that one of his Negro alchemists would find a way to cheat death and use it to bring him back to life, as if they wouldn't all just run off the moment he was no longer there to work the chains of Necromancy."

"Wait, Jefferson was a slave owner?" I ask. I am having a hard time following her lecture. Thomas Jefferson owned people? How am I supposed to ever read that dragon book he wrote again knowing that? One more book ruined because the author was a terrible human being. Next thing you know someone's going to tell me Paul was a cold-blooded dragon hunter and the Bible will be right out of the window as well. I'm never going to get to enjoy a book again, at this rate.

She laughs. "Of course he was. The Founding Fathers were all a bit hypocritical, if you ask me. Telling that English king to go pound sand while they were living off of the backs of our kind, their Necromancers stealing our souls and our abilities to power their war machines, and for almost a century after."

I must have reacted in some way, because the Grimalkin cuts herself short. "Anyway, the Skylark had recently enlisted with a Conservation Corps work crew that had been sent to the Tennessee Valley. Her entire crew was captured by the Necromancers. They were tortured, killed . . . she was one of very few to survive. And there I was, on the other side of the state, trying to convince that dragon to take a nap in a brand-new lake. . . ." The Grimalkin trails off. "You know, now that I think about it, this is much closer to Tennessee than I like."

"The Skylark . . . was tortured by a Necromancer?" I say, hesitantly. "She watched people die?"

"That she did, young one."

I have so many questions but no way of articulating them; instead, I ask, "Do you think any of this could be caused by a dragon?" I hold my hands out to take in everything around us.

The Grimalkin shakes her head. "I had considered it for a moment when we found we couldn't escape from this Blight. It is possible to end up trapped in a dragon's dream—some of the old ones are powerful enough to create a pocket realm while unconscious, folding in time and space around them like a big old blanket. But dragons are Life Elementals. If we were in a dragon's dream, the colors would be vibrant and there would be animals and plants, more than you've ever seen. It would be dangerous and overwhelming, but nothing like this. You know the Garden of Eden?" At my nod the Grimalkin continues. "They say that was a dragon's dream, and when she woke and flew away the Sahara was what was left. I wish this was a dragon's dream," the Grimalkin says, her tone somber. "But I worry that whatever we find at the end of our journey will be nothing so terrible and beautiful."

We walk along in silence after that, the Grimalkin most likely worrying about the future, me mired in the sadness of a lost love. I cannot believe Thomas Jefferson was a slave owner. Is there a single hero from history who wasn't a monster?

With my mind preoccupied with something other than my impending doom, I lose myself in thought for a long while, not much noticing the effects of the land on me for once. We make much better time than the day before, and by the time the Skylark calls a halt to eat something, I am famished.

I quickly devour a handful of nuts and berries from my knapsack, a trail mix that has been dried and processed and wouldn't be much use for raveling. I sit and watch everyone else, since the repast is unusually quiet, everyone deep in their own musings. The more we walk, the better I feel, but the rest of the group looks terrible. The Grimalkin's skin has taken on an ashen hue, and Crystal doesn't look much better than she did earlier, when it seemed like she was having trouble walking. Onyx has a slouch, like his pack is filled with rocks—which, I realize, it probably is.

Even the Skylark looks a bit disheveled. The changes in her are noticeable, and we have been in this tortured landscape for less than a day. What would happen after another day, and then another . . . ?

How long until it doesn't matter?

The only one besides me who doesn't look haggard is Malik, and I am surprised to find him standing next to me.

"Don't mind me; I just came to ask you why the hell you keep staring at me," he says.

"Are you and Sam sweet on each other?" I say without missing a beat. Might as well get everything out into the open.

His expression shutters. "No. That's sinful." His voice is flat, like he's repeating a line he's practiced in the mirror dozens of times. His gaze slides away from mine but goes right to Sam, who twists around to watch our conversation. I give him a little wave, and he returns it hesitantly.

"That's too bad; he seems to actually find you tolerable," I say, tossing a bit of dried fruit into my mouth. "You aren't likely to find that anywhere else."

If he had a retort ready, I don't get to hear it, because at that moment there's a sound in the distance. We all turn toward it warily—it's been so long since we heard anything in this landscape aside from one another. From down the road comes the sound of hooves, and heading toward us on the road are two mules pulling a cart, a white family riding in the back.

"Oh, great, just what we need," Malik grouses.

"Where do you think they came from?" I ask.

"Probably a town just up the road. Lots of people live within Blighted zones, though I can't imagine anyone staying in this place."

"Are you going to tell them there's no way out of here?" I say wryly. "Or am I?"

Malik frowns in contemplation just as the people pull even with our group. There's a man, a woman, and two small children, all of them looking at us expectantly. I bite my lip.

"Sorry to bother you, folks, but would you happen to have any food or water you could spare?" says the man holding the reins. "Not for me, but for my wife and children." His eyes won't meet ours. His shame is nearly a physical presence. I'm not sure if it's because he's embarrassed to ask for help or because he's asking for help from colored folks.

"We have enough for all of you," the Skylark says. "It's just dried fruit and nuts, but you're welcome to it."

The woman's face breaks into an expression of relief. "You don't know how much we appreciate this," she says. "We've been hoping things would get back to normal, but they just get worse and worse."

Onyx walks forward to hand the man the bag of trail mix, careful not to look at the woman in the eyes lest her husband take offense.

"We slaughtered our hog last week," the man says with a nod of thanks. "But the meat was off, and we all got sick from it. We've been trying to eat whatever berries and the like that we could find, but there's not much, since summer never came."

"Why didn't you evacuate with everyone else?" I call.

"Wasn't no kind of evacuation or the like," the man says, shadows playing in the deep lines of weariness in his face. "One day we went to town and everything was normal, people complaining about the gray setting on the land, the fact that the Blight had gotten bad again. The next week I rode down, and everyone was just *gone*, like something had come through and blown them all away. The streets were full of debris, like no one had rode through in a while, piles of leaves here, there, and everywhere. Janesville had never been so quiet."

"Janesville?" the Skylark says, inquiring. "Isn't that a colored town?"

"We live outside city limits," the woman says, too quickly. I'm not sure if she's saying that so we won't think she's colored or because she's afraid we might look a little too closely at her features. Either way, not my business. I got enough on my plate to fret over.

"How long ago was this?" the Skylark asks, and the man shrugs.

"Two weeks, maybe? If everyone got an evacuation order, they didn't send any riders out to the farms. Because we heard nothing."

After another round of thanks, Onyx tells them that they should change course for Mercersburg and the nearest Wayfaring station to get a beam out of the Blight rather than trying to take the road. Then the mule continues along on its way, the family

255

slouching and drained behind him.

I wish we could have ridden with them, truth be told. But there was no room on the wagon, and who knows if they would have let us, even though we shared our food with them.

As we continue walking, I find the Skylark and pull her to the side.

"I got a question," I say, feeling all kinds of jittery after the conversation with the white family.

"I am certain you do, but I doubt I am equipped to answer it. Peregrine, we are as out of my depth as we are everyone else's."

I take moment to let that confession sink in before I continue. "I reckon so, but I think maybe you know quite a bit more than I do." I want to ask her about what the Grimalkin told me, but somehow I can't find the words. And so what I say is: "I want to ask you about the bottle. And what that monster might be that's inside."

"Putting things together, are we?" she says, amusement in her voice. "Why don't you tell me your thoughts?"

I swallow hard. "Well, just now that man described seeing piles of leaves when he found the town abandoned. And when we found the spot where poor Frederick died, he appeared to have turned into leaves as well. All the people in Janesville . . . ?"

The Skylark nods but doesn't say anything more. And I cannot stop myself as words keep tumbling out.

"So that monster that tried to kill us, the thing that definitely wasn't a Blight Beast, that got sucked into this soul jar of mine . . . ?"

"Yes," the Skylark says. "It is my suspicion that contained in that jar is the energy of whatever working claimed the lives of those townspeople. As well as their souls."

Revulsion swells in my middle. "Should I let them out?"

"Not here," the Skylark says. "They'll just go back to trying to kill us. I promise you, we will find a way to put them to rest. For now, keep this information to yourself and just keep walking."

My heart aches in my chest. I am even more eager to ask the Skylark about what happened to her in Tennessee, but I still can't figure out how, and I doubt she'd tell me anything now anyway, especially when her eyes flick toward the Smoke and Onyx, deep in conversation not too far away.

I fall silent, and the Skylark falls back to talk to the Grimalkin. At one point I turn to glance at them over my shoulder. They both watch me with a look that is far too interested. It makes me feel even more jittery.

Or perhaps that is just the effect of realizing I'm carrying around a town's worth of dead people in my bandolier.

Finding this place seemed like the first real bit of luck we had.
Should've known it was going to go south.

Chapter

TWENTY-THREE

We decide to stop slightly before dusk, on the outskirts of another town, Crofton, that looks to have been abandoned. It's clear we aren't going to make it to Mercersburg, whether because it's farther than it should be or because we're too tired to make good time is uncertain. What is certain is that it's a good idea to stop before the dark hides threats from us. After the events of the night before, we waste no time finding a fully defensible location—a two-story farmhouse perched on small hill at the edge of town.

The house is large and inviting, but that's not what catches our attention. In a land of death and decay, this place is alive and thriving. Birds flit around the trees in the back of the property, which bear rich green foliage, unlike every other tree we've seen. The grass is high and deep green, standing in stark contrast to the gray-hued straw that populates the rest of the landscape. Something about this place is keeping at bay the terrible nature of the deadlands, as I've started to call them, and it seems like it's more than the warding runes that the Grimalkin spots at the edge of the property. Whoever made their home here may have had some training in the mystical arts. It's a hopeful sign.

Inside, the house is nicely furnished and there are even a few cupboards full of canned goods. There also are more runes carved into the doorframes of the dwelling. I really need to find a book on what these runes do and how they might interact with Floramancy and the like. But that is a lesson for safer times.

After walking the house and spending more than a little time in a library with so many books that I gasp when I see them, I turn my attention to the woodpile out back. It's large and dry. The nights are far colder than I was expecting—it's June, for the love of bits—and I spent the night before snuggled up to Crystal. But I would much prefer the warmth of a roaring fire. The girl has sharp elbows, and I am pretty sure I have the bruises to prove it.

Smoke and Malik haul wood while Onyx and Crystal raise pillars for additional defensive warding, just in case this new town has its own souls lurking about. Sam and Nell volunteer to inspect a well we spotted toward the back of the property. Turns out I'm not the only one feeling some kind of way about the water within the Blight, and the comments from the family in the wagon only reinforced that everything within the space should be considered dangerous until proved otherwise. Once Crystal and Onyx have finished their work, I head out to where the pillars have been freshly raised, ready to do my part. The Skylark works a bit of jacaranda around the first pillar, and I do the same around the next. Raveling is easier than it was yesterday. I wonder if it's due to the Possibilities being stronger in this strange pocket of normalcy. But then, in the pouch of my bandolier, I feel the soul jar shift a little, and I'm afraid I know where my fresh burst of energy has come from.

I try not to think about it.

Crystal leads me from pillar to pillar, continuing to raise them in front of me as I go. I have just twisted another bit of jacaranda vine around one of the last rose-quartz pillars when she goes down.

One moment, the girl is chatting away as usual; the next she's laid out. I let out a cry of alarm, and Sam and Nell race over to look after her. I finish twisting up my bit of vine to set the ravel and join them.

Sam helps Crystal sit up, and blood is flowing freely from her nose. "I think I overdid it," she says, her voice weak and whispery. She looks like she hasn't slept in weeks, and there's an ashen hue to her skin that is worrisome. It's clear that I'm the only one whose well-being is better today than it was yesterday, which seems to confirm my troubling thoughts about the vessel I carry.

"I think she's dehydrated," Nell says, holding her hands over Crystal. Sam hands Crystal a clean rag for her bloody nose—the boy apparently has a wealth of handkerchiefs in his pack—but her hands are slow in taking the scrap of cloth, so he holds it to her nose.

"Here, I have some clean water left," I say, pulling out my canteen. "Did you all check out that well? Does it need to be purified?"

Sam and Nell exchange a look.

"We hadn't had an occasion to learn yet, though Frederick said he would, well . . ." Nell trails off, her expression haunted. She's been quiet all day as we walked, and I don't know the girl well enough to know if that's just how she is or if this is her working through her grief. She just lost her mentor the night before, so a little grieving is more than understandable. I tried to speak to her, to apologize for her loss, but everything I said felt hollow and empty, so I just kept smiling at the girl instead, hoping to comfort her a bit.

But this is somewhere I can actually help. Especially considering the ease with which I'm drawing on the Possibilities here. "I can show you. How to purify a well, I mean."

"Really?" Sam says. "You know how?"

"I used to do it for folks back home in Shrinesville all the time," I say. They are staring at me suspiciously, and I hold out my hands. "Why are you looking at me like that?"

"Purification rituals are Sanamancy," Nell says, her voice barely above a whisper. "But you're a Floramancer. Are you going to work . . . Craft?"

"Look, I was raised by rootworkers who used many different disciplines," I say, too annoyed to spin some lie to cover what I'm suggesting. Being reported to the bureau once we're back in New York is the least of my worries at the moment. "Craft or no, what we need right now is clean water. Crystal is drinking the last of mine, and I suspect most of us are going to be tapped out soon. The only healer who knew how to purify is dead. So unless one of you has a hidden spring in your pocket, I think you're stuck with me showing you both what's what."

Nell and Sam nod, and I stand with a sigh and walk over to the nearby well, the two of them following me cautiously. These fools and their worries about who can do what and when. We are dying. This place is killing us. If there was ever a time to toss the rule book to the wind, it's now.

The well, aside from being rather large—at least ten feet in diameter—is nothing special. By the state of the stones, it looks to have fallen a bit to disrepair. There's a large wooden cover for the top that Sam and Nell have pulled to the side. Moss and ferns mound up over the stones that ring the mouth of the well, another indication that the thing hasn't been used much in recent years. That said, everything *around* the well is lush and verdant, a sign that whatever force is protecting this place has been keeping the water clean, too.

There's something strange about the well. It isn't the scent; in fact, I don't smell much of anything at all. I lean over to look down at the water—I can see a shimmer, but it's hard to tell exactly how far below me the water begins. I lean farther, and that's when it happens—an overwhelming pulse in the Possibilities that washes over me, and before I can regain myself, I am falling.

A moment of weightlessness ends with my shoulder slamming into the rock wall, pain exploding on my left side moments before I hit the water. But then I continue to fall, sinking into the inky darkness, too fast, unnaturally fast, past the point where I should begin to float.

Something is pulling me down.

Hungryhungryhungryhungryhungryhungry

The voice slithers through my mind as my lungs begin to yearn for fresh air. I kick out, half-panicked, catching the creature, which is solid and sinuous. But the kick is enough to get the thing to let me go, so that I can bob to the surface and grab a couple of breaths.

"You are not eating me," I say.

Food does not speak or fight, the thing says, and a head lifts slightly out of the water. I gasp.

I am face-to-face with a wyvern. A distant cousin to the dragons that slumber across this land. I swim backward away from the thing, fingers gripping the stone wall, brain racing through my options. Wyverns aren't known for eating people, but these are extreme times. And the creature is obviously hungry.

"No, food does not speak or fight, and if you know that then you must have been someone's companion." It was always one of the first things a mage imparted when training their bond beasts. No eating people.

I am not a companion. The thing's voice winds through my mind, wet and slippery. *I am a well-vern. I keep this well safe and clean.*

I nod, understanding now. Whoever owned this house knew their way around the mystical arts. If I were building my own house, and it had a well, finding a well-vern to live in it is the first thing I would've done as well. Not just because I love dragons and everything dragon adjacent, but because having an uncorruptible source of fresh water on a property is always handy. Well-verns, a domesticated breed of wyvern, had once been mainstays of homes in places like this—many families would build intricate wells in the hopes a well-vern would take up residence there, as they are far more efficient than purification ravels. But well-verns are rare in the days of indoor plumbing, when people have been content to let Mechomancy water pumps take care of their water needs. "You seem well cared for," I say.

I am. I keep the well clean for Betty.

"Where is Betty?" I say, assuming she's the mage who owns the house.

Gone gone gone. Baldur took her.

"Baldur? Who is Baldur?"

Bad bad bad.

The mere mention of the name sends the well-vern into a frenzy, the animal swirling and swimming through the water so that I have to grip the bricks along the wall to not be pulled under once again.

"Wait, wait, maybe I can help," I say. If I don't calm this massive beast, it could accidentally drown me.

"Peregrine! What is going on? How did you end up in the well?"

I look up to see the Grimalkin, peering down at me. Sam and Nell must have gotten her once I fell in.

"There's a wyvern down here! And it's hungry!"

"I'll go look in the house and see if there's anything to feed it," the Grimalkin says. "Sam, Nell, the Peregrine doesn't appear to be in immediate danger, but I'm sure she'd appreciate a hand out of there all the same."

"I'll find a rope," Sam says as the older woman hurries away.

No rope, no rope, I will help.

The well-vern seems to have gotten itself under control enough to raise its head out of the water. It swims over to me, and I cannot help but draw an awestruck breath. In the gloom I can make out the beast's giant eyes, spiky facial scales, and set of wickedly curved horns. It's beautiful and terrifying, and I'm stuck between ecstasy at being this close and apprehension at seeing a creature so ancient and powerful. I clear my throat nervously. "I would be much obliged if you could help me," I say.

The well-vern swims so that the back of its head is right before me, and I figure that means I'm supposed to grab onto the horns. The moment I do, the serpent explodes up and out of the well, its muscles flexing and bunching with the effort.

It is the most terrifying and exhilarating thing I've ever done.

The creature rests its head lightly on the edge of the well. I take a breath, try to swallow my heart back down from where it seems to have lodged in the base of my throat, and then awkwardly grab the edge and heft myself over the low stone wall. My left shoulder screams in agony to remind me that I injured myself in the fall.

"Let me look at that," Sam says. He doesn't wait for me to agree before he starts poking at the injury through the Possibilities, as though he can sense the place where it causes me the most pain. "Seems like you just bruised it really well. Nothing for it, but I'll do what I can to ease the pain."

"Save your energy," I say, wincing as I move my arm about. Sam's face has already taken on a gray hue of fatigue, and while the shoulder twinges, it isn't a life-or-death matter. "As long nothing's broken, I can deal. We don't know what else we might run up against."

The Grimalkin comes rushing from the house, her chickadees flying all around her, a bag in her hand. "I found a bag of dried fish inside; I suspect this was for the well-vern."

The Grimalkin hands it to me, and the well-vern watches the bag with shining eyes. It holds on to the edge of the well with its stubby arms, the claws at the end webbed, and as terrifying as it was in the dimly lit well, it's not at all so now. There's something charming about the beast, and I love it so. Is this what it's like for the Grimalkin and her companions? Did they feel that way when they first met?

"Does this smell familiar?" I ask the well-vern, holding out the dried fish.

The serpent's tongue reaches out and snags the fish as an answer, and I am so surprised that I laugh.

"Look at you. You're a natural," the Grimalkin says with a smile. Like everyone else, she has dark circles around her eyes.

"I'll let you handle this," I say, since Sam watches me with a peculiar look. No need to give him any reason to add "unlicensed Faunomancy" to whatever report he's going to write about me later. Besides, there's more than enough to be done before the sun sets and true darkness finds the land. Plus, I am soaking wet and starting to catch a chill. I need to change.

I say farewell to the well-vern, who watches me go with large liquid eyes, before heading to the house. It is surrounded by oak trees, not surprising since there was obviously someone with some experience in the mystical arts living in the house—the trees would be a plentiful source of bits for much of the year. But what is surprising, as I study them more closely, are the keys hanging from them. Rusted iron keys, silver keys with a strange patina, keys made of bone, keys with ornate, bejeweled decoration. They hang from every branch, and around the base of the trees is a thick red band of brick dust.

All of this is for protection.

When I was younger my mama made me wear an iron key around my neck. It was on a long string and hung down my back. She told me the key had many purposes. For one, it helped hide and manage some of my more powerful talents until I was old enough to control them. It also let my mother find me wherever I was, the trinket somehow hexed. When I got my menses, the key was put away, hung on a tree outside my ma's house until it was needed again. Keys like that tend to stay in families, since so much of the mystical disciplines are inherited.

But I have never seen so many keys, not like this, and I have a feeling that there is something about this place, more than it just being a nice place to stop for a night. A powerful family lived in the house, tending to the well-vern and warding the lands.

And yet, it seems they fell victim to whatever is poisoning the place. It's a powerful reminder that despite the safety of this oasis, we are far from saved.

I head for the room on the first floor that I claimed as my own. As I walk, I ponder the well-vern's words. Who is Baldur? Is it possible that's the name of a Necromancer? But how could a Necromancer manage to set up shop in the middle of the country's most famous Blight without anyone noticing? Is it because they were smart enough to set their ravel within the Blight, where no one—except maybe the Bureau of the Arcane—would notice? It is definitely something to bring up to the Skylark the next time I can get some time alone with her.

The thought makes me trip a little over the floorboards, even though they are smooth and evenly spaced, and I come to a stop in the great room in the front of the house. If Pigeon heard me talking about Necromancy being alive and well now, in 1937, she would mock me for seeing bogeys around every corner. It's been more than seventy years since the end of the Afrikan Genocide, since the war that finally ended the unholy union between the Necromancers and Mechomancers who settled this fine land, the former stealing colored folks from the Afrikan continent and bringing them to North America to power the constructs of the latter. Seventy years since the last time Mechomancers used the souls of colored folks to power their machines. What scattered remnants of the Klan that still existed were outcasts, like the one the Grimalkin spoke about in Tennessee. But that was always the problem with Pigeon: when you thought you knew everything, there was no room for possibility.

No matter what my sister would have said, it's looking clear to me that the active practice of Necromancy isn't just a relic from a time long gone, as some would have us believe. After all, the Bureau of the Arcane keeps a few Necromantic vessels lying about.

I sigh and continue walking to my room. I don't have any answers. All I've got are suppositions and guesses. That and a dime will get me a cup of coffee.

I enter the room I selected and head straight for my pack in the corner. I've been wearing the same clothes for two days, and I want nothing more than to put on something clean. But when open it, I realize that my options are going to be very, very limited.

Every single piece of clothing, raveled so expertly by Alistair, has been undone, my pack left full of nothing but what look to be old leaves.

On our second day in the ODB, we realized that someone on our team was working against our better interests. I did not want to think it was my young apprentice. Who wants to believe that a Negro girl could be responsible for such malice against her own kind? But her ramblings soon became unhinged, and it was at that point that I began to worry in earnest about the Peregrine.

TWENTY-FOUR

"I daresay you are overreacting," the Skylark says as she watches the Peregrine sitting morosely on the floor. "It's not . . . unattractive."

The girl wears a dated nightgown they managed to find in an old box. She sniffles and dashes away a few more tears. "That's easy for you to say. You aren't wearing a stranger's nightshirt." The Peregrine plucks at the flannel material. "Besides, it's not this that I'm in fits over. It's losing all those wonderful clothes you bought for me."

"Yes, well, that I do understand." The Skylark would also mourn losing an entire wardrobe created by Alistair.

All the Peregrine's new clothing, down to her underthings, are gone, unraveled by the toxicity of the Blight. *No, not a Blight*, the Skylark mentally corrects herself. *Something far more dangerous.*

The Peregrine sighs and gestures at the Skylark. "Why are your clothes still intact?"

"I suppose it's because I bought these from a Woolworth's," the Skylark says, looking down at her traveling clothes, which are dusty and a bit sweat stained, but otherwise no worse for wear. "Although I fear my hat is already doomed," she says, removing the thing and tossing it into a corner of the room. As soon as it hits the floor, it goes to pieces, as though sitting on the Skylark's head was the only thing holding it together. "Department-store clothing is not my preferred attire, but I was hard pressed to find something suitable while Alistair was overseas. It was just my luck that Mechomancer fabric was all the rage last season."

They are alone in one of the many bedrooms within the house, which the Skylark discovered had a Wayfarer's ravel upon it—the room was much larger than the footprint it apparently occupied. She continues to wonder what kind of people lived in this house, because the place gives her a sense of calm and well-being that she has definitely been missing since they entered the Blight. Hell, she hasn't felt this serene ever. The house is raveled in ways that would likely still be revealing its secrets after months of study.

"All right, if the loss of Alistair's fine clothing has been properly observed," the Skylark says, "I'd like you to tell me everything the well-vern told you."

The Peregrine recounts what she remembers, and when she is finished the Skylark frowns in confusion. "Odd."

"That's one way to put it," the Peregrine says. The storm of emotion has passed, and the girl paces through the room, arms crossed. While the other apprentices had fallen into a sort of funk, wearily seeing to their jobs and otherwise keeping to themselves, the Peregrine seems to have only come alive since arriving here. And the Skylark would be lying if she said she didn't suspect it was the danger they were in. Some people thrived under pressure, and the Peregrine, she could see, was one of them.

The girl taps her lips. "So, I guess the questions are: Who is this Baldur fella, and why did he take Betty, the mage who lives here?"

"Yes. And I am afraid I have no good answers to either of those questions." The Skylark sighs. An ache has developed in her chest, right in the spot where her heart would if she still had one. It's worrisome. "The Grimalkin couldn't get anything further out of the well-vern. Once it had eaten its fill, it went back to hiding in the depths of the water and refused to come back out."

"You said before that you thought this was a Necromancer's working. Would that account for my clothes coming unraveled?"

The Skylark worries the top button of her shirt. "Perhaps. I was pondering that question, as well as the mystery of why everyone is feeling so poorly. Keep in mind, my knowledge of Necromancy is rudimentary at best. . . . All right, Necromancy, like any other art, involves the collection and focusing of natural energies. The release of energy produced upon death is considerable, much more than that of even the most powerful bits we use to ravel. Remember when we talked about the Life-and-Death spectrum of the mystical arts?" The Peregrine nods, and the Skylark continues. "Necromancy, like Floramancy, exists firmly in the Life end of the spectrum; it simply uses a different aspect of Life to ravel."

The Peregrine's expression is uneasy. "So, Necromancy is corrupted Floramancy?"

"More that they're two sides of the same coin, if that makes sense. However, the sheer power of Necromancy, and the terrible acts required to draw on those energies, have, in our nation's history, attracted the worst kinds of people. The sort who desire that kind of power, and who find the cost acceptable. Though it wasn't always that way."

The Peregrine ponders that, and as she does, she gently twirls the soul jar between her fingers. The Skylark doesn't know much about the objects, but she does know that the vessel would take a toll on her if she were to hold it for an hour. The Peregrine plays with it like a walnut. The Skylark can feel it, can sense the girl's true abilities moving beyond her knowledge and experience.

When the Skylark was little, Aunt Clem once took her to the beach, to see the edge of the world, as she called it. Estelle was thrilled with the waves, the ebb and flow of the water, like the earth was breathing. But while she wasn't paying attention, an especially large wave knocked her off her feet, the current pulling her out into deeper water, where the creatures whispered things about the meaning of life and death. She managed to regain her footing when her aunt grabbed her by the upper arm and hauled her back into the waist-deep water, but she had never forgotten how quickly wonder could turn into fear and anxiety.

She is having a similar feeling the more she speaks with the Peregrine.

"I was thinking," the younger mage says after a long moment. "Everyone in the bureau, everyone I've met, anyway, had been relatively certain before we arrived that what was going on here in Ohio was your typical Blight repair job. Is it possible the higher-ups at the bureau—your boss, maybe—actually knew what was happening?"

"Why do you ask that?"

"Well . . ." The girl seems nervous in a highly uncharacteristic way, and it's a moment before she speaks. "Were you captured by a Necromancer in the Tennessee Valley?"

The Skylark goes still. "What do you know about Tennessee?" she asks, unable to keep the iciness from her voice.

"The Grimalkin mentioned it, and that you had been there." The girl tries to look her in the eye. "She said it was, uh, really bad."

"What happened in Tennessee was nothing like this, if that's what you're wondering," she says. "My crew and I were set upon by a coven of Klansmen who were working with some Mechomancers to create a power grid to provide electricity to a large swath of the mid-South. They thought the Conservation Corps wouldn't miss a few dozen Negro work crews, and under other circumstances, they might have been right. The bureau broke things up and couldn't find any evidence of other covens. But regardless, the ravel the 'mancers were working, as powerful as it was, didn't do anything like this to the land there."

The girl nods slowly. "I'm sorry you went through that, and I hope you don't mind me prying too much. But that's not what I was getting at. I asked because, well, the bureau clearly knew that Necromancy was alive and well after what happened in Tennessee, right? And, heck, they were keeping Necromantic objects in their storeroom." She holds up the vessel. "Is it that far-fetched to think that someone might have known something was happening here that was more than your typical Blight? Your boss, whoever gave you this mission, he didn't mention anything, did he?"

The Skylark shakes her head, deep in thought, and the girl continues.

"So if they had even the smallest suspicion that a Necromancer was at work here, why wouldn't they say anything to you about it?"

"Are you suggesting that the Bureau of the Arcane is in league with whatever Necromancer is at work here?"

"Well . . . no," the Peregrine says, seeming to be working through her thoughts as she speaks. "That wouldn't make any sense. Because if they were aware of some plot involving the Blight and Necromancers, and they were working with them, why send a team of their best mages to uncover the plot? I suppose the most logical explanation is that they didn't know. Or, perhaps, that they didn't care."

The Skylark nods. The girl's instincts are not wrong. But her speculation has opened a more terrifying possibility in the Skylark's mind. One to which she's not ready to give voice. Or even belief. Not yet.

"These questions are worth pondering," the Skylark finally says. "But they won't help us escape this place. We only have ourselves to rely on now. And for all you have yet to learn, you have more skill than you know. A natural talent that many have to work for."

"Some talent," she mutters. "If this whole thing happening here is not degradation from the Blight but rather the result of a Necromancer's ravel, it's too bad I can't just undo it. What's the point of having a skill if you aren't sure how to use it?"

The Skylark laughs, the sound hollow, just as there is a knock on the door. After a slight hesitation it opens and the Grimalkin enters, her expression grim.

"I have something to say and it won't wait," the Grimalkin says once she's shut the door. "I came here because I just wanted to let you know this is as far as I go. I won't be continuing on with you tomorrow."

"What? Why?" the Peregrine says.

"This place is too much for my companions. They've refused to go any deeper into the Blight, not even to search for the missing mages. They warned me that nothing can live in this place. They are certain that the team from the Chicago branch is gone, lost to the ravel. There's also something about what the well-vern said that's given them a powerful fright. And what kind of Fauno-mancer would I be if I didn't mind my companions? We'll stay here and establish this place as a sort of base of operations. The wardings are intact, and if you encounter an impasse before you get to the Wayfaring point, you'll have somewhere to fall back to."

"Have you spoken with Smoke and Onyx?" the Skylark asks.

"No, I wanted to tell you first. But I also wanted to draw on your . . . previous experience. Can we talk in private?"

The Peregrine rises, perhaps to leave, but the Skylark halts her with a gesture. "Whatever you want to say, you can say in front of my apprentice. We have no secrets about Tennessee. Especially as you decided to take it upon yourself to inform her of said previous experience."

The Grimalkin smirks. "Fair enough. I wanted to see if you

had any idea who this Baldur is. Ever heard the name?"

The Skylark shakes her head. "The Peregrine mentioned the words of the well-vern. I was equally flummoxed."

The Grimalkin sighs. "Well, looks like we're going to have to tell those fool men what we discovered and see if they can be of any help. Though I doubt it."

As they leave the room and make their way back to the great room, the Skylark finds herself watching her apprentice a bit more closely than before. There is absolutely nothing about the girl that should make the Skylark nervous, but for some reason she thinks how much the Peregrine reminds her of Miss Fox.

She isn't sure whether that is a good thing or not.

The more I see of this land, the more I wonder what it looked like before the badness began.

Chapter

TWENTY-FIVE

The Grimalkin, the Skylark, and I make our way to the great room that dominates the front half of the house. A fire in the hearth warms the room and chases away the chill that's sunk into my bones since I came out of the well.

"There you are," Crystal says, sitting up from where she reclines against a nest made of pillows next to the fire. "I wondered what was taking you so long. We saved you some stew and a biscuit."

"Lower your expectations," Malik says with a frown. "There's no meat." He leans against the wall looking unbothered, his gaze on me in a way that for the first time doesn't seem so loathsome. Maybe because I know what he's about and don't care? I hope so.

I take the bowl, the dry biscuit soaking up most of the gravy. I dig into my food and it's delicious, the beans and spices a nice change of pace from the dried-fruit-and-nut mixture in my pack. After the first couple of bites, I sink down next to Crystal and take advantage of her nest. "How do you feel?"

"I drank a whole bunch of the water from the well, and I feel a lot better. There's a nice mineral content. The well-vern takes its work seriously."

Crystal hands me my canteen, which she has refilled for me. She's not wrong about the well water, and I drain the canteen. I didn't feel bad before drinking the water, but I definitely feel better after drinking it.

"Is this everyone?" the Grimalkin asks, as Onyx, Sam, and Nell file in from another room.

"Where's Smoke?" the Skylark asks.

"Should we go look for him?" Sam says, eyes filled with worry.

"He told me he intended to check the house from top to bottom for any more clues as to who lived here or what happened to them," the Grimalkin says. "And he can take care of himself. I think it's best if we don't split up now that we're all together."

While the Skylark, Onyx, and the Grimalkin speak in low voices, I relax with the other apprentices. Well, as much as I can. Crystal lays her head on my shoulder, and I pat her hand. We don't know each other that well, but there's something about being constantly afraid that allows you to take your comfort where you can. And she isn't the only one who needs a little physical reassurance. Sam and Nell stand close together, shoulders nearly touching, as though they are two elderly oaks supporting one another. All through the walk they've kept close to one another and have been nearly inseparable since arriving to the house. The loss of their mentor seems to have bruised something in them, and everyone on the team is giving the two space to grieve.

Except Malik, that is. He watches Sam and Nell with a grim expression. It must be hard for him to suddenly be the odd man out. But this isn't the time for romance, so I hope he can keep it together until we get to safety.

The moment drags on, no Smoke to be found. Outside, the landscape has grown dark, and in the spaces between the quiet come what sounds to be wild animals, the screams and yips eerily similar to the noise the dog in the road made yesterday. But judging from the Grimalkin's earlier conclusions, it must be something far more terrifying. I am certain the sounds are nothing anyone wants to tangle with.

"Well, what do we have here?" the Smoke says, sweeping in with his usual pompous air.

"Where have you been?" the Grimalkin demands, crossing her arms. At her feet, Fyodor puffs up. That cat knows what's what.

"I was simply inspecting the generous library." His cheer seems forced, and even though he's looked good for most of the day the illusion has started to slip, revealing dark circles under his eyes, deeper than they were before.

The Grimalkin clears her throat and turns toward the group, even though her words really seem to be directed at Onyx and Smoke. "I wanted to let all of you know that I won't be continuing on. My companions have warned me against going any further, saying it isn't safe. And I have to respect their wishes."

"What's this, now?" Onyx demands, the Grimalkin's declaration causing him to stand a bit straighter. "There is a discussion to be had about our next course of action, but I must insist that whatever is decided, we do not allow the team to be split. We need to stick together."

"And I need to stick with my companions. I think it's time we acknowledge the possibility that the lost team is no longer alive. That they were devoured, as we are even now being consumed. Can't you feel it?"

"Yes," Sam says, voice clogged with emotion. "Frederick said the same thing as soon as we crossed the barrier. He said the land was hungry."

"But we can't go back, because the only way to get out of here is Wayfaring. And we need a circle for that? Right?" Nell says. There are a few solemn nods, but nothing more than that. It's sorta funny the way we refuse to reckon with our own mortality and rapidly approaching end, preferring to leave it unspoken instead of spelling it out.

There's a heavy silence in the room before Crystal speaks. "So that's why we're so weak, why everything is so hard. I've been raising crystals since I was in diapers, but I thought I was powering a several-ton construct the way I felt today."

"This is the question I was hoping to find the answer to," Smoke says with an easy smile. The expression is meant to be reassuring, but it just feels a little bit hollow in light of the horror of the land slowly digesting us. "And from the look of the library, someone else was searching for the answer as well. But neither they nor I found it."

"We think the answer to what is happening lies in the conversation the Grimalkin had with the well-vern out back," the

Skylark says, deftly omitting my part in the exchange. The smile she directs at Smoke is genuine, and my stomach sinks. The man gives me the creeps. Not because of anything obvious, but there is something about him that I find off-putting. It feels . . . like he's only a shadow of a person.

"Is that so?" Smoke says.

"Yes. I didn't get much out of the creature, but it did say that its companion, Betty, disappeared and that Baldur took her."

"What's a Baldur? Or is it a who?" Crystal asks, and no one seems to be able to answer the question.

"Well, at least we now know there is some kind of entity at work here," the Smoke says.

"Yes, which means this must be a Necromantic working, just as the Skylark suggested," Onyx says, stroking his chin.

"So what are they working on?" the Skylark asks. "This is a big undertaking. Perhaps they sought to use the Blight to cover their destruction, but why now? What's brought them to Ohio?" It's a good question, but no one seems to have any ideas. Either that, or they're keeping them to themselves.

"Perhaps we should approach this another way. We might not be able to stop what is happening here, but we can stop the people responsible. I may be mistaken," Onyx begins, "but there are few ways to neutralize a working, aside from a few forms of Necromantic conjuring or blood ravels."

I sit up a little straighter. If there's a way someone with Necromantic abilities can stop this, I want to know. I don't like knowing this about myself, that I can tap into the Possibilities that surround manipulating the energy of Life, but if I can save us then I will dress myself in all white and start marching with the Klan. Not that they'd have me, but the intent is just about the same.

I open my mouth to say something, but a slight head shake from the Skylark has me leaning back against the pillows of Crystal's nest without bringing up the bottle full of nastiness that remains in my bandolier.

"Be that as it may," the Skylark says, "It doesn't help us in the short term, nor the long term. We are far better served with a few of us scouting on ahead and seeing if we can find a working Wayfarer's gate and going to fetch help."

"That is cowardice," Onyx sniffs.

"That's survival," the Grimalkin shoots back.

The conversation devolves into a full-blown argument, with the mages going back and forth on the best way forward while we apprentices look on with horror.

I have never seen adults bicker like children, and I will be frank when I say it does not inspire confidence in our odds of survival.

"Look," Smoke finally says, voice pitched to carry over the dispute. "I've been reluctant to do this, but I can see now that it is necessary. Skylark, I am relieving you of your leadership position."

The silence that falls over the room is thick, so that the only sound for a long moment is everyone breathing.

The Skylark recovers first. "What? On what grounds?"

Smoke adjusts his cuffs and gives her a shrug. "It's clear that your past trauma has eroded your sense of duty and completely undermined your bravery, and as a member of the D.C. office, I am now relieving you of your responsibility for this mission."

"You can't do that," the Grimalkin interjects, and Smoke holds up a silencing hand.

"I can, and I just did. The Hawk asked to have this mission sent to the New York teams because of the Skylark's previous experience, and failure, in Tennessee, and it is now clear that was a miscalculation on his part."

The Skylark's eyebrow twitches, and I half believe that she just might throw a hex at Smoke. Her expression is pure murder. "My experience in Tennessee is how I know this isn't a battle we can win. That ravel was nothing on the scale of what is happening here, and still dozens of mages died."

"And in the same manner dozens of mages have died here as well," Onyx says with a theatrical sigh. "I didn't want to tell you this, Estelle, but I think I must. The Hawk was not completely truthful with you."

The Skylark turns her attention on Onyx, still steely eyed. "Explain."

Onyx swallows and nods. "He came to see me after he spoke with you. He said that there was something wrong here in Ohio, that the bureau had sent in three mage teams and not a single one had returned. He wanted me to ensure our team got to the center of the Blight and figured out what was going on, but that he was worried you would lose your nerve long before that." Onyx straightens, standing taller even as shock is writ large on the Skylark's face. "He said he knew it was something I could get done, even if you were technically in charge because of your position. I'm sorry I didn't tell you sooner."

"That doesn't change anything," the Grimalkin says. "We can still find a Wayfaring station and beam out of here."

Onyx shakes his head. "Hawk told me he and the rest of the bureau didn't think the Wayfaring stations would work, since the Resonator was faulty. The only way to get out of here is to press on, to stop the renegade mage creating this treacherous ravel."

"And that is what we shall do," the Smoke announces. "Rest up, my friends. We leave first thing in the morning. This Necromancy will not last long against some of the best mages the Colored Auxiliary has to offer."

The Smoke takes his leave, in conference with Onyx, the Grimalkin vexed and the Skylark flattened. It's clear she hadn't expected this betrayal, not from either the Hawk nor Onyx.

"You're not going to leave this alone, are you?" the Grimalkin asks. Fyodor is all puffed, clearly also spoiling for a fight.

The Skylark shakes her head. "No. This isn't over."

They leave the room, their steps heavy, after Onyx and Smoke. An awkward silence descends upon the room, and Crystal grabs my hand.

"Hey, are you okay?" Crystal asks.

"Do you think we'll make it out of here?" I say, the words tumbling out. I thought I had my emotions in check, but it turns out I'm just as terrified as everyone else, an edge of hysteria creeping into my words. I might trust the Skylark, but I don't trust Onyx or the Smoke, and I have no doubt that a zealot like Onyx would march us right into the maw of death. His little speech from the first night is too fresh in my mind, and a man who believes that Mechomancy is of the utmost importance is not someone I want to follow into battle. I'm not sure where Smoke falls on the matter, but I'm willing to bet it's closer to Onyx than the Skylark. And it's just my luck that the room's sudden quiet makes my question louder than I would've liked.

"Of course we will," Malik says, but his words lack his usual dismissive tone, as though he can't even muster a lie for himself.

"We need a plan," Sam says, standing from where he huddles with Nell. "Marching toward the center of whatever this place is won't work. Nell and I are at the limits of our abilities. Healing requires Life to work, and we're running on fumes at this point."

"We have nothing left," Nell says. "We're so weak we didn't even realize there was a well-vern keeping the water clean. It didn't feel like a well-vern. It felt normal."

"A typical well like that would feel like spring, like an abundance of Life surging forth," Sam explains. "But this place is dead. All of it. We can't keep walking, hoping to find a Necromancer to kill. And why didn't Onyx tell us before about the Wayfaring station? We should still try to Wayfare before we go fighting anyone. I think the Skylark is right: some of us should stay here and the rest should try to go for help."

"We'll be dead, too, if we stay here," Nell says, her voice low. Her eyes take on a faraway look. "Three times the shining one will rise from the dead, living and dying in an endless loop. But on the third rising he will be not as he was, but as the god of death. His life will mean the end of all we know."

Nell's voice is strange as she speaks, and chills run down my arms, the fire's warmth disappearing in the wake of Nell's words. A glance around the room shows that everyone else in the group has been similarly struck by the pronouncement, and Crystal is the first to snap into action.

"What else do you see?" she asks, but Nell just shakes her head before dissolving into tears, Sam comforting her.

"Is Nell psychic?" I whisper, leaning in close to Crystal to ask the question. I've always disliked the random burblings of seers, but now I'm thankful for whatever it was she saw. Maybe it'll give us a way to survive.

The other girl shrugs. "Maybe? Not sure. Definitely seems like with that pronouncement."

I sigh. "All of us have a little something extra."

"Yeah," Crystal says, her expression troubled. "That's what my mama says." She sniffs a little, and I pat her leg, not wanting to say anything more in case it causes her to lose her composure. I think we're all having a hard time realizing how bleak things are. We're safe for now, but the future seems insurmountable.

It seems impossible that just yesterday we were walking into this place with our heads held high, ready to fix a problem we only half understood. What fools we were.

"I know we are all frightened and out of our depth," Malik says, "but my father is right. If this is a Necromantic working, we should find our way to the epicenter and eliminate the cause."

"Mal. We won't make it that far," Sam says, his voice gentle. "The bureau needs to be called in. This is too big for us to handle. I can't heal a paper cut right now, and Crystal passed out trying to raise a few simple pillars. This place is killing us, and marching along like good boys and girls is not the answer," he says, muttering this last bit. Oof. Now I get what Malik sees in the boy.

"It definitely feels like the energy drain has gotten worse the closer we get to the point of origination," Crystal says with a yawn. "But that may be a function of the space, to attempt to drain us before we can get to the mage behind this."

The silence weighs on us, and lethargy makes my limbs heavy; I stand with a sigh. From down the hall comes the sounds of raised voices, the adults continuing their discussion, it seems like. "We should rest and prepare ourselves for the worst."

"The Peregrine is right," Crystal says. "I'm exhausted, and who knows what we'll face tomorrow." Any sign of the bubbly girl I met a couple of days ago has evaporated. Crystal's face is ashen, and her eyes are noticeably sunken, despite her claims to feeling better. In the low light cast by the flames I study her, and a sharp realization slices through me as I take in the fresh hollows in her cheeks and the way her dress seems to be a bit looser.

This place really is eating everyone alive. Not just unraveling clothing and sapping reserves, but actually devouring folks where they stand. The only thing keeping me from being supper right along with everyone else is the jar of living death I've been carrying around.

There is nothing good about that thought, and I wish I could pluck it from my mind the moment it comes to me. But all I can think is that I'd better figure out how to stop this ravel before everyone else is destroyed by it.

No pressure.

A nice family photo I found.
Hope they left before everything went south.

Chapter
TWENTY-SIX

"We should settle this first," Malik says, even as I yawn widely.

"What's the point? Are you going to tell your father he's wrong?" Sam asks, a hint of something in his voice. Bitterness?

Malik rears back, as though slapped. "What's that supposed to mean?" he asks, eyes narrowed.

"Nothing," Sam says, but it's clear that whatever he was referring to, it wasn't the problem of how to survive this awful, Blighted land. "Look, I just think we need to come up with our own plan," Sam says. "We've all known the bureau just sees us as a bunch of janitors for the mystical arts, but I never thought they'd willingly send us into a situation like this. Forget the bureau; we need to think of ourselves."

"And what would you have us do?" Malik asks, his anger and frustration evident. "You heard Onyx and the Smoke. It doesn't matter how we got here; what matters is that we're not getting out unless we deal with whatever is at the heart of the Blight. I for one am not going to sit here, hiding, hoping the protection doesn't give out. Onyx is right. We've got a job to do."

"I don't know," I say, standing and stretching. "I didn't sign up to fight Necromancers."

Out of the corner of my eye I spot a flash of golden fur. Somehow, the puma is back.

It stares at me from across the room, its golden eyes locking on mine once more. Then it turns and walks back down the hallway. It feels like an invitation, and before I can think too hard about what I'm doing I'm up and out of the room, leaving the ongoing argument and following the puma as it stalks the house. Voices come from behind one of the closed doors, Smoke and Onyx, and the puma hesitates only to make sure that I am following before continuing on its path.

The big cat stops before the door to the room that I claimed earlier, and when I enter the space is the same way I left it. As I close the door behind me the puma stares at me for a moment.

"Well? What now?" I say. I'm so tired, and I just want to sleep and hope that the problem sorts itself out.

The big hunting cat's skin begins to ripple, the undulating fur nauseating. I take a step back and the fur splits, opening to reveal a boy with golden skin and strange eyes, his hair a mass of ropey locks. He looks like a lion made human, and a shiver of reverence runs along my skin.

"What the hell?" I shout, fumbling at the bandolier I still wear for a handful of bits to defend myself. How the heck did he get through the wards on the house? Unless he's friendly, in which case the wards wouldn't have stopped him. But shape-shifters tend to be a dangerous lot, so I keep a tight grip on my bits.

"My name is Louis," he says with a smile. He's shirtless, his only concession to modesty a pair of trousers hanging low on his hips. Even in his human form there is still a bit of the cat about him, his high cheekbones and molten gold eyes giving his broad face a feline aspect. "The Wily Fox sent me. I'm here to help."

The Wily Fox. The old woman who waylaid my beam is named Miss Fox. Are they the same person? It seems like.

I put the bits back in my bandolier and relax a bit. The Fox was the Skylark's mentor, so I figure he's probably okay. "You led me to that soul jar before I left the bureau."

His expression is one of intrigue. "So you used it?"

"I did. Not that the Skylark nor I had any idea what we were doing. Why would you give me such a thing?"

"Wily Fox told me to. She said you had uncommon ability, and when the time came, you'd know what to do with it."

"But I didn't even know I could work Necromancy." The word still feels foul in my mouth, no matter what the Skylark told me about it. I take the soul jar from my bandolier and show it to him. "And even if I had, what made you think I would want to carry around the souls of those poor people lost to whatever's happening here?"

He blinks. "Because you can."

I cross my arms. "You know, just because you can take the form of a cat, doesn't mean you need to act like one."

He gives me a toothy grin. "Necromancy is not an evil art. It didn't originate with the colonizers and slaveholders who corrupted this land. Like everything else they came to call theirs, they stole the power, from the same mages they exploited and killed. Mages like you. That power is yours by birthright. So, to answer your question, what you *want* has nothing to do with it. You *have* this ability." He points at the bottle in my hand. "And the responsibility that comes with it."

"Okay. So then what do I do with this power? What do I do with the souls in this thing? How do I fix what's happening here?"

He shrugs. "No idea."

I sigh. A headache has started behind my eyes, and the boy scuttles closer, every movement more feline than human. "Don't despair, Peregrine."

"I'm not despairing—I'm desperate. This place is devouring me and the rest of the mages here. I don't have time for a history lesson! We need to either escape or stop this ravel that's killing the land. So unless you have something that can help us to get out of here, or to start fighting back, you should feel free to take yourself back to wherever you came from. And while you're there, put on a shirt. Because this"—I gesture in his general direction—"is highly inappropriate."

Louis smiles, the grin predatory. "You like me."

"No, I don't," I say, letting my temper get the better of me. "I like girls. Sorry."

I blink, and between one moment and the next Louis is gone, replaced by a feline girl wearing a tattered dress.

"Wha—?" I say, eloquent as usual.

"Now that you mention it, I actually like this better," she says, looking down at her body.

I blink, and it takes me a few heartbeats to find my voice. "You're a shifter. Like, a *true* shape-shifter."

She grins, and my stupid heart gives a little flippity flop. "Not quite. I'm Ligahoo," she says, coming even closer. "You aren't afraid?"

"Well, no," I say. I desperately want to ask what a Ligahoo is, especially since I think I remember the Skylark mentioning the word before, but I even more desperately don't want to appear ignorant in front of her. She's too pretty, and I can already feel those golden eyes eroding my common sense. "Should I call you Louise now?"

"If you like. I'm Louis and Louise. Sometimes both, sometimes neither, but either one is fine. I'm here to help you, so you should like me." She walks over to me and gives me a hearty sniff, burying her face in the space between my neck and my shoulder. "You smell like Wily Fox. But younger. I like it."

My mouth goes dry, and my middle is doing all kind of acrobatics, and I'm pretty sure there is not a worse time for this sort of thing. "How exactly are you here?"

"Projection," Louise says. "I'm here and I'm not here."

"That is very confusing."

She shrugs elegantly. "I'm Ligahoo."

"So if you're not here, I'm going to assume that means you can't get us out of here."

She shakes her head. "No."

"Can that Fox woman you know?"

Louise frowns. "Even if she could, she won't. She wants you to find Gnarled Fox's cabin first."

I sigh. "This is not the time for quests, Merlin."

Louise gives me a sharp-toothed smile. "That's funny."

"We're in the middle of a Necromancer's construct, it is currently devouring us, and you want to give me another task."

"The answer to how to fix everything here is there," she says. She suddenly straightens, cat ears appearing on the top of her head and she listens to some far-off noise. "I have to go. Wily Fox is summoning me."

"Wait, how am I supposed to let you know when I find this place?"

She leans in and quickly nuzzles the side of my head, her grin feral as she leans back. "Don't worry. I've got the scent of you. I'll find you anywhere you go."

"Well, that is reassuring," I mutter to cover my embarrassment. I'm not sure if I'm being wooed, mocked, or a combination of the two.

"Don't die," Louise says, and then she is gone just as suddenly as she appeared. I collapse onto the floor, leaning back against the wall with a weighty sigh.

"What in the seven hells is a Ligahoo?" I mutter to myself. Louise's appearance has created for me more questions than answers. Who exactly is the Wily Fox, and what does she have to do with whatever is happening here in Ohio? And who is the Gnarled Fox? A relative of some sort? How many of these Foxes are there?

And what does my mentor have to do with any of it?

I smack my hand against the wooden floorboards in frustration. I have no real answers, only questions. But even so, Louise has given me a much-needed lifeline. If she's real and not just some fever dream created by my brain, finding this cabin might be the key to unraveling this whole nightmare place. I know for damn sure it's better than whatever plan Onyx and the Smoke are cooking up.

But I feel like I might go mad before we get that far. I'm scared, and I don't think I can talk about my new friend with any of the other apprentices, not without bringing up my newfound abilities. . . .

I need to talk to the Skylark. If anyone can make sense of this, she can.

At that moment, a scream echoes through the house, halting my thoughts and sending me running down the hall in the direction of the cry.

Malik, Sam, Nell, and Crystal stand in the hallway, tension in the lines of their bodies.

"Was that you?" Malik asks, and I shake my head.

"Where did it come from?" I ask, heart pounding. The sound of the scream, pain filled and terrified, still echoes in my ears. Nothing good can be on the other end of that sound.

"Down the hall," Nell says, her voice small.

There isn't much light in this part of the house, and I pull an okra seed from my bandolier, raveling it into a lantern, something a little more fancy than the lit stones Crystal and Onyx created the day before. I hand the lantern to Sam, since he's the tallest of us, and he leads the way toward the back of the house.

"What happened to the lights back here?" Crystal wonders aloud. The house had a fine series of raveled lights along the wall, quartz crystals that had long ago been set to cast a warm yellow glow, and now every single one is dark.

"I don't know," I say, just as a foul scent assaults my nostrils. "But I think we should be ready for whatever."

I pull out a few okra seeds, keeping them handy in case we need more than a lantern, and we make our way down the long dark hallway.

There are rooms on either side of the hall, but the doors are shut tight, either locked or raveled so that we are forced down the hallway, back toward where I suspect the library might be. We've gone only a short ways when we all pause, Nell's whimper turning my blood cold.

There is a woman's body lying in the hallway.

Sam strides ahead and I follow him, pushing past a stunned Malik to see who it is. For a heart-stopping moment I think it's the Skylark, but when Sam rolls the body over it's the Grimalkin, her face twisted in a rictus of agony even in death.

I glance at Sam, but he just shakes his head morosely. "She's gone," he says.

"Oh no," I say, a jab of emotion stabbing my heart. Part of me is hoping that it's all an Illusion, a tasteless joke we can laugh about later. But when I lean in the Grimalkin is clearly gone, her eyes open and staring straight ahead. Sorrow blooms in me, and I blink at the unexpected tears. I reach out to close the woman's eyes, and a zinging spark runs down my arm from the contact. I jerk my hand back.

"What?" Malik demands.

"Nothing," I say, feeling strange. I feel overly full somehow, like my skin has grown too small, and the sensation is weird. I breathe shallowly as my vision swims just a bit. I once drank a Coca-Cola too quickly, swallowing more air than pop, and it feels like something similar. I take a deep breath, worried that maybe I'm going to faint like a lady from a movie, but the wooziness settles down and I feel mostly normal.

"It's just like with Frederick," Nell whispers, tears sliding down her cheeks.

"Wait, I thought Frederick was killed by the Blight Beast," I say. My voice sounds far away. What is happening?

"He died of a heart attack. We thought it was fear because of the Blight Beast," Sam says. "But I suppose we should assume nothing."

"Hearts are usually the first part of the body to give out," Nell says. "It could be that it was the ravel here that killed Frederick. He was the oldest of us. It could've just sapped him until his heart quit."

"Did the Grimalkin die of a heart attack?" I ask Sam, but he shakes his head.

"I can't tell. But from her expression," he says, raising the lantern so that the light picks out the hollows of the Grimalkin's face and transforms it into a terrifying mask, "it wasn't an easy death."

I kneel next to the Grimalkin, opposite Sam, who is on the other side of the body, and take her hand. And suddenly, there's a pulse of energy and I'm ripped from my body.

I can see the Grimalkin talking to someone I can't make out, her worry and fear writ large on the moment. But then there is a flash of energy, purple in hue and lilac scented before the Grimalkin is struck down.

The vision passes, and I'm back next to the body, still gripping her hand. Is this Necromancy? Or something else?

"Did anyone check the wards?" I ask once I catch my breath.

"I will," Crystal says.

"Go with her," I say to Sam, and he nods and gets up to follow. I ravel another okra-seed lantern and hand it to Malik. He looms over me, his expression hard.

"You know something," he says. It isn't a question.

"Someone did something that ripped her from her physical form before killing her," I say without thinking.

"How do you know that?" Nell asks, voice low.

"Ah, my mom was a seer of a sort," I lie. "I sometimes have flashes of things, but it's not usually worth much."

"We've all got a little something extra," Nell murmurs, her gaze meeting mine.

Then, silence. Even Malik can't find the words to continue interrogating me; he just bends down next to the Grimalkin and folds her arms on her chest. I should have thought of doing that, but I am too scared to do much more than remind myself to breathe.

"The wards are all messed up," Crystal says, running back into the parlor, Sam right behind her. "All the ones we could see, on all the doorways, the cornerstones . . . someone's taken a knife to them."

"Where are Onyx, Skylark, Smoke . . . ?" Nell asks. "And what about the Grimalkin's companions?"

I hadn't even thought of them. I haven't heard the cry of a bird nor the whimper of a wolf in the house. There's no way they would have left the Grimalkin's side willingly.

We all stand, looking down the hallway before us. As one, we continue walking, our steps slow and deliberate. With the runes ruined, we still have the boundary we set up when we arrived, but that's nothing compared with the protective spell tied into the foundations of this house. Death could be waiting for us in the library, and I roll the okra seeds in my hand, just to remind myself I have options if I need them.

We turn a corner and the light stones set into the wall flicker, as though the ravel is struggling to cast light. But a brightly lit doorway beckons at the end of the hall. The shelves are easy to see, and we make our way to the library, a tense procession.

Inside is a mess. Books have been tossed around like a tornado ransacked the place, and torn pages littering the floor. There is a lump in the middle of the room, the fur unmistakable. It's the Grimalkin's wolf, his side staved in and his neck twisted viciously.

"Oh no," Crystal says, her eyes flooding with tears.

Sam shakes his head. "My God," he whispers, his soft words more prayer than exclamation.

There's a screeching sound, and the Grimalkin's cat, Fyodor, comes bounding out, launching itself at me. The cat's claws dig into my shoulders, the pain jarring, and the thing climbs me like a damn tree until I manage to grab him and hold him in my arms.

A fission of energy runs across my skin, and there's a pulling sensation, like something has just pushed through me to the tabby, which looks at me with strange, swirling eyes. I blink and my vision clears.

"Can you ask Fyodor what happened?" Crystal asks, looking right at me.

"What?" I ask, my surprise genuine.

"Peregrine, we all know you can work some Faunomancy," Nell says. "I think the time for lies is past us."

I don't bother trying; I just turn to Fyodor. "What happened?"

The cat's response is nearly unintelligible, a string of violent hisses and mews. *Bad things, bad, bad things.*

"Does he know?" Nell asks.

I shake my head. "Something bad, but at this point that could be any of a dozen things."

"Well, let's try to see what we can learn from this mess," Sam says, gesturing at the debris within the library.

"Do we have to?" Nell murmurs, and Sam puts a strong arm around her and squeezes.

"Don't worry, it'll be fine," he says. Malik watches them enviously, and I have to agree with the sentiment. I'd like a hug right about now as well.

We search the room. Smoke, the Skylark, and Onyx are nowhere to be found, but a large puddle of blood, sticky and soaked into the wood floor, is an ominous sign. There are a handful of feathers in one corner, but no bodies of birds. Still, I prefer not to consider what that could mean.

"We should search for them," I say, but before anyone can reply, Fyodor bites my arm, hard, and launches himself out of my arms and dashes off.

"Fyodor!" Crystal yells.

"He's probably scared," Nell says, wrapping her arms around herself. "I don't blame him."

"Me either," I say, rubbing my arm.

"We all should be," Sam says, crossing his arms across his massive chest. "I had been afraid that this place was slowly killing us. There wasn't anything in my healer training to tell me how to deal with the pain and exhaustion we've all been feeling. But now I feel like that's the least of our worries."

"What do you mean?" Malik asks.

Sam looks at his boyfriend with despair. "Can't you sense it? We're being *hunted*."

It was at this point that I lost consciousness for a long period of time. While the cause is unknown, I am left to assume I was attacked by the Peregrine, afflicted by a Necromantic curse from which I am still recovering. I cannot account for the days I was unconscious, but it is one of my greatest regrets that I was not there to prevent the Peregrine from doing what she did next.

The loss of Sam, Nell, Crystal, and Malik will always haunt me.

Chapter
TWENTY-SEVEN

I am dead. Again.

That is the Skylark's first thought as she slowly wakes. Death, to her mind, is the only way to explain the soft bed she lies upon, the sweet scent of lilac filling her nostrils, and the voice of her mama, dead some years ago after the flu swept through their holler, singing a song about raising up the okra and fighting to freedom.

Only, there is no nose to smell. No skin to feel, no ears to hear.

This is death, the Skylark thinks, because that is all she can do.

"You ain't dead," comes a voice, one the Skylark was hoping she wouldn't hear. "But it was a near thing. You're lucky you still got a debt to me, else they would've snatched your soul first. Of course, you ain't got a body. They made sure to destroy that nice and final-like, so that's a problem. But at least you ain't dead."

The Skylark tries to turn her head, and the world spins around quite alarmingly and goes dark.

"Would you wait a minute, you damn fool? I just told you that you ain't got a body. How you think that works? Not well, I can tell you. Now settle down and wait until I can find—ah! There it is. This should help."

There's a cool sensation, and the Skylark has the strange feeling of being lifted and set down again, but this time it's less like lying on a soft bed and more like sitting in a chair. Slowly she comes back to herself, her body tingling as though the circulation has been cut off to her entire being.

"Speak!" the voice says. "Wait, what was that incantation? I know Louis wrote it down somewhere after I forgot it last time. Let's see. . . . Speak, spirit, open thine eyes and look upon the world once more!"

It's like a curtain is pulled back. The Skylark blinks, and the scene around her comes into view. She is in a small room. The walls are freshly whitewashed, the furniture is hewn out of driftwood and knobby branches, and a wizened old colored woman peers at her curiously.

"Miss Fox?" the Skylark says, the sound froggy and strange, like she hasn't spoken in years.

"Good, looks like I got you before any part of you was devoured. Any part you'd miss, anyway." She takes a step back. "Well, this is quite a pickle you put yourself in. Been trying to reach you, but it's a powerful veil they got in place. None of the Foxes could get through, though Louis did manage to speak to your girl. I don't know what she said, but I think she knocked him for a loop. Or *her*, I suppose, since Louis is now calling herself Louise. Those Ligahoo. They can never settle into a form for long. Though, in this case, I think it's because she's a little sweet on your girl."

It's been years since the Skylark has seen Miss Fox in person, rather than through strange portents and the like. Being in a room with the woman once again brings their first meeting crashing back through her memory. "Am I alive?"

"Well, you were dead before I even met you, so you've been dead, but if I didn't have a geas on your soul, you surely would be dead again. Just how did you get yourself mixed up in such nasty business, anyway?"

The Skylark has to think, which is becoming harder by the second. She was speaking with Smoke, asking him to show her the research he'd done since he was convinced they could challenge a Necromancer. Onyx was there as well, along with the Grimalkin. Smoke peeled open the book, and there was a flash, and pain—

"The Grimalkin! She's dead!" The Skylark feels the shock of the memory, but within a moment, it's dim and far away. "The Ohio Blight. There are Necromancers there, Klansmen, surely. And someone, or something, named Baldur."

"I reckon all your companions have been devoured, then. It's messy business raising a dead god."

"A dead god?"

"Child, ain't you ever heard of Baldur? Louise didn't know who he was either. But she's just a young thing. What are they teaching you children these days?" She just shakes her head. As always, Miss Fox is entirely unhelpful, and the Skylark doesn't yet have the energy to roll her eyes. Or, you know, eyes at all. "Anyway, you're going to find yourself powerful tired in a few moments when the enchantment winds down and your soul gets to drifting again, so stop worrying about all that mess. It's going to take me a while to build you a new form, and until I do you need to save your strength."

"But my apprentice . . . ," the Skylark says. Speech is hard, and she can feel her wits already beginning to scatter.

"Louise gave your girl a tasking. She is more than she seems, but I expect you already know that. And if your apprentice has a lick of common sense to go with all that ability, she will be along shortly."

The Skylark groans, the sound less like her living voice and more like that of a spirit haunting a stately manor. She can sense her consciousness splintering, the way it did when she drifted off into sleep, back when she slept. Only this sensation is much more powerful, like being drunk on absinthe. Her wits flee, but not before she utters one last thought.

"A lick of sense might be hoping for too much."

Sorta funny how regular things seem ominous when you know you got a target on your back.

Chapter
TWENTY-EIGHT

We apprentices, on our own now after the sudden disappearance of the elders and the death of the Grimalkin, decide that the best course of action is for everyone to sleep in the same room and keep watch in shifts of two. I usually wouldn't be one to advocate for a sleepover, especially with the boys, but I'm feeling rightly unsettled after the scene in the library and my encounter with Fyodor. I still haven't told everyone about Louise, or what I learned of what our next steps should be, trying to find the home of this Gnarled Fox. Mostly because I'm not entirely sure how to do that without revealing too much about myself. That, I've decided, will be tomorrow-Peregrine's problem. Tonight-Peregrine has enough to deal with.

We place the Grimalkin's body in the library with that of her wolf and say a few words over her before covering them both with a sheet. It's sorely lacking as funerals go, but it's not as if we have many options, and we have our own hides to worry about. No one has said anything about the conspicuous puddle of blood in the middle of the room, but I keep looking at it, unable to tear my gaze away. When I look up, I find Malik doing the same, his face ashen. Does he truly think his father is dead? Or is this just an act? It's hard to know who to trust when danger is everywhere.

With everyone feeling more than a little skittish, we bunk down in the room I chose for my own. Malik carves a few runes into the door with a penknife, and I watch him intently.

Nell lays a gentle hand on my arm. "They're for protection," she says.

My face must have given away my worry. After the loss of the Skylark, I'm short on trust and even shorter on bravery, and if I'm being honest, the man who was Malik's father is near the top of a very short list of suspects for who destroyed the original set of runes. Though, at this point, I can't know if it was him, or if he was in control of himself even if he did do it. If a nefarious mage is indeed at work in Ohio, who knows what's possible?

"You recognize the runes?" I ask.

"Yes," she says simply.

"I recognize them too," Crystal says from where she tends to the fire in the hearth. The space is warm, at least, even if it no longer feels as safe as it did earlier in the day. The room has a single bed, and the plank floor is covered with a threadbare, but clean, carpet. We all agree that Crystal should get the bed since she's the worst off. Even despite her constantly drinking the water from the well—Sam and Malik went outside to quickly fill everyone's canteens—she still seems sick and run down.

Sam and Nell agree to take the first watch, with me and Malik set to the take the second. I don't think I'm going to be able to sleep, even if it is already well past midnight, but my body has other ideas. One moment I'm replaying the moment with Louise in my brain, picking it apart to try to see what I might have missed the first time through, and the next I'm rolling over, stiff and groggy, as Crystal wakes me for my shift.

A weak light filters in through the curtainless window as I sit up. The sky is gray and watery, the barest bit of sun well beyond the horizon just beginning to lighten this cursed land.

I am never going to take the sunshine for granted again.

I sense movement around me; Malik must be getting up as well. I snooze for another couple of minutes, but before I can fall asleep again, I pull myself to my feet.

Malik is indeed already up, but I'm surprised to see Crystal is still up as well. They are standing next to the door and discussing something in low voices.

"What's going on?" I ask, making my way over on tired legs.

"You tell us," Malik says, expression hard. He holds up a too familiar purple glass bottle, the cork stopper still in place. "I know what a soul jar is—my father has a collection of relics from the Afrikan Genocide. But why do *you* have a Necromancer's bottle in your bandolier?"

I go to snatch it back from him, but he pulls his hand away deftly. "Why were *you* going through my things?"

Crystal is the next to speak, her expression soft but serious. "Don't dodge the question, Peregrine. I told him you'd have an explanation. Tell us what's going on, or we're waking the others."

When I hesitate, Malik steps intimidatingly close to me. His

315

whispered words have an edge to them. "You're the only one on this expedition we hadn't met before. We're in the midst of a Necromancer's ravel, people are dying, my father is missing, and you turn up with a soul jar. Tell us what's going on, *now*."

I sigh. Even I have to admit, this looks bad. I guess I'm going to be telling them all my secrets even earlier than I'd planned. I take a breath and then tell them everything: about the Fox waylaying me on my way back to New York, the puma visiting me in the storeroom, everything the Skylark told me about Necromancy, my experience with the creature in the soul jar and how it seems to be protecting me from the worst effects of this place, and last night's encounter with Louise.

"So that's what we're apparently supposed to do," I finish. "Find the cabin of someone called the Gnarled Fox."

Malik and Crystal are speechless for a moment. I don't know if they're trying to puzzle out if I'm making this up or if I have indeed lost each and every one of my marbles.

"This is all true?" Crystal finally says.

I nod. "Of course, I have to acknowledge the possibility it's all a hallucination brought on by the land to torture me, to give us hope and thereby make all of our deaths more delicious. Who knows?"

"Okay, let's say you can do . . . Necromancy," Malik says tentatively. "Why can't you do anything about the situation we're in? I mean, you caught that thing, whatever it was, in this jar. Can't you, I don't know, figure out what's poisoning the land? Keep it from eating us alive? Bring my father and the others back?"

There's so much hope in his eyes that my heart aches. I don't like Malik all that much, but the look on his face is more than even I can bear. "If I could do any of that, I would," I say, my words gentle. I'm feeling bone tired without the vessel on me. Is this what this cursed place feels like to everyone else? "But I don't know anything about this ability I apparently have. Even that stupid bottle wasn't my idea." I close my eyes, the reality of the situation washing over me. "I don't know why I'm like this. Trust me, I've been wondering the same thing. As far as I know I'm just a mage like you. And I'm sorry I didn't tell you all this sooner, but I'm out of my depth here. That's not a position I'm used to being in. The Skylark was trying to help me to understand Necromancy as much as she was able . . . now she's gone. I don't know where she is, I don't know where everyone has gone, I barely know where we're going. I'm no better off than the rest of you. I'm terrified that we're all going to die and that, despite whatever power I have, I'm not going to be able to do anything to stop it."

Both Malik and Crystal stare at me for a heartbeat. Then Crystal starts laughing. "So that's why you put that plate of ham in the hallway during breakfast?"

"I couldn't understand why none of you could see the puma," I say with a shrug.

Malik pauses, then narrows his eyes. "You said you joined the bureau so that you could get a license, right? What were you trying to do with it?"

I give a half-hearted smile. "Honestly? I want to be a baker."

Now it's apparently his turn to laugh. It's the first time I've ever seen him smile, and I maybe understand why Sam is smitten with him. He holds the Necromancer's bottle aloft. "Don't know how much baking you're going to get up to now that we know what you can really do."

"Yeah, I'm amazing. Right up there with Jesse Owens." I hold my hand out for the soul jar. "Can I have it back?"

Suddenly the vessel jumps out of Malik's hand and back into mine, crossing the distance between us in an instant. Creepy. I put it back in my bandolier without meeting either of their eyes.

"I think it's probably best if we go along with what this shape-shifter told you," Crystal says. "It's really the only idea we have other than sitting here and hoping to survive whatever killed the Grimalkin and took everyone else." She sniffs. Crystal still believes Onyx, the Smoke, and the Skylark to be alive, and even if she's not a seer, it gives me a little more hope it's true as well.

"Louise isn't a shape-shifter," I say. "She's a Ligahoo, if any of you know what that is."

"I do," Malik says. "When I was younger my grandmother used to tell me that if I misused my abilities the Ligahoo would come for me. She said it would appear as a man carrying a coffin with three candles. Each candle represented one of the chances I'd get."

"Did you ever see one?" I ask.

Malik nodded. "When I was younger I cast an Illusion to make myself appear white. I just wanted to see what it would be like, you know? Anyway, the blowback was terrible, and I ended up sick for nearly a week. While I was in bed, I had a dream that an old man came to visit me and blew out a candle and said, 'That's one, young buck. Straighten up and fly right.'"

Any other time I would think that perhaps Malik was having a go at me, but there's something about his face that leaves no doubt that he is being honest. I shiver, even though the room is still warm from the embers in the fireplace.

"What happens when the candles all go out?" Crystal asks.

Malik levels a gaze at her. "The Ligahoo takes your abilities and eats you right up."

We all fall silent in the wake of Malik's words. That's when a loud and terrifying noise comes from the other side of the door. It sounds like something big and heavy being dragged across the floor.

"Maybe it's Fyodor," Crystal whispers.

Malik and I exchange a look. "Does that sound like a cat to you?" I say.

Behind us, in the center of the room, Sam and Nell are still asleep. "We should wake them," Malik says. The dragging sounds are now accompanied by the stomping of large feet.

"We're up," Sam calls back, voice low. In an instant he and Nell are on their feet, their packs secured.

The thing, whatever it is, is now outside the door. The knob rattles violently, and then comes a pounding, but the door stays shut. The runes that Malik carved into the doorframe the night before glow red hot as the thing in the hallway tries to bash its way into the room.

I fall backward, scrambling across the floor and bumping into Crystal just as the door bends inward, the wood unnaturally flexible. The warding is the only thing keeping the door from exploding toward us. Malik turns, his eyes wide with fear.

"Window," he mouths, and we rush for the only access we have to the outside.

I'm the second one out, right behind Crystal, and I grab a couple of spindly lengths of jacaranda vine growing on the verge while everyone else slips through. Thank goodness we picked a room on the first floor. I don't want to think about what that escape might have looked like if we'd had to climb.

As everyone else makes for the property line, I fling the jacaranda vines back at the window, and just in time. There's a creaking and then an explosion from inside the room, and the vines find their purchase on the outside of the house, roots flowing over the window casing in thick ropes, just in time to keep whatever wanted into the room from following us.

"Go, go!" Sam yells as we take off down the road, running as though our lives depend on it. Because they do.

I hazard a glance over my shoulder, but there's nothing behind us. I worry about the well-vern, how it will survive whatever is in the house if it comes after it, but I can't think about that now. It was safe before our arrival. I can only hope it remains safe.

We run down the road, dirt kicking up around us in a cloud. We slow our pace when we realize we're not being chased, our extreme exhaustion overcoming the adrenaline. By this time, we're close to the heart of the nearby town, and we make our way silently and warily through abandoned buildings. They look decrepit and unused, like the residents fled decades ago rather than weeks.

"What do you think that was?" Nell finally asks after a long, loaded silence.

"I don't want to know," Malik says, his tone sharp. I have to agree with him. Any hope that I had that the Skylark is still alive feels like it was smashed along with the door to the room. I refuse to mourn her—goodness knows that if anyone could get out of trouble with a beast like that, it's the Skylark—but my throat clogs with worry as the reality of the situation hits me. The Skylark was the first person in a long time who seemed to think I might become something grand. And it's looking pretty likely that she's dead.

I swipe at my face, even though my cheeks are dry and my eyes gritty with exhaustion. I can deal with these thoughts later. For now, I very much do not want to meet the thumping, slithering thing inside the house. I just want to get the hell out of this place.

"It's getting worse," Crystal says, pointing to a building that is little more than a pile of sticks. The wood looks like it may have been swarmed over by termites, the grain eaten away into a powdery dust.

"It's because we're getting closer to the center," I say, and as soon as the words are out I sense the rightness of them. "The closer we get, the harder it will be to continue on."

We walk, the silence weighty, until we reach the edge of town. I pause before an old billboard for Wrigley's Doublemint gum, and everyone sort of shuffles to a stop with me. The twins in the full-color ad are now gray, and the paint is peeling in great curls. But that isn't what grabs my attention.

Burned into the billboard in large black capital letters is:

BALDUR WAKES!

We all exchange glances, look back the way we came, and then put our heads down and continue forward, into the unknown.

●●●

We walk on in silence, each of us swallowed by our thoughts, as the light grows brighter, the sun still hidden beyond the gray cloud barrier but the day progressing all the same. I'm trying to figure out just how I'm supposed to find this Gnarled Fox's cabin. I keep looking for Louise, hoping maybe she'll reappear and guide us there. But no such luck.

Crystal's steps are heavy and plodding, and it's only the frequent sips from her canteen that seems to keep her going, the minerals from the well-vern's water providing her a measure of strength. Sam and Nell wobble, and we're only a couple of miles outside of town, the landscape changing slightly as we find ourselves on a path between the trees of a sparse but looming forest, when they both stop.

"What's wrong?" Malik asks.

"I need a break," Nell says, her breathing labored. "This place, can you feel it? There's nothing here. No life at all."

Sam nods in agreement. "We need a better plan than to just keep walking."

"Especially since we don't have a map," I say. "I guess it's too much to hope we'll pass a sign that reads 'Gnarled Fox's House, one mile.'" At their confused looks, I hold my hands up in surrender. "Okay, I get it, bad time for a joke."

"Is she well?" Sam asks, turning to Malik. He shakes his head.

"Peregrine. What are you talking about?" Crystal asks.

I blink. "The Gnarled Fox. The Ligahoo said we should find them? Sorry, I know the story I told back at the house was a doozy."

They're all still looking at me, and I realize they have no clue what I am talking about. Could they have completely forgotten?

I get my answer when Nell says, "Maybe we should turn back now? Maybe it's best if we stay with the Grimalkin at the house after all, where it's safe."

"No," Malik says, tone hard. "You heard what Onyx and the Smoke said last night: the best course of action is to try and get to the center and stop the Necromancer who raveled this in the first place. It's the only chance we have of surviving."

I blink and open and close my mouth a few times, struggling for words that never come.

They've forgotten everything.

I reach into my bandolier and remove the soul jar, holding it close. Is this the only thing keeping my memories together? There is something stealing away the minds of my companions— something, or someone.

It reminds me of a story my mama told me once, long ago. I had asked her about the Afrikan Genocide and why more colored folks hadn't self-emancipated. My ma had given me such a look that my insides had nearly turned to dust. "You think they didn't?" she said. "Those Necromancers just found a way to cloud their minds. Day after day, row after row, they harvested bits in a cursed stupor, raveling to feed the Necromancers' power without understanding what was happening to them, until the day they were plucked from the fields to have their souls extracted. It was only when the most powerful rootworkers forced their way through the curse that they were able to fight back. Don't you dare judge something you've never experienced." I had never seen my ma that angry, and I still haven't since.

I hope I get another chance to vex her mightily. Even with the jar in my hand I can sense the pull of the space, dragging at me, trying to find purchase so that it can devour me like everything else. It's like invisible fingers prodding and poking at me, looking for a soft spot to dig in.

"Do we even have a map?" Crystal asks, tilting her head as she studies Malik.

The boy's lips compress. "No. Onyx and Smoke have the maps."

"Well, I'm sure they're just a little bit ahead of us," I say, deciding that all I can do is play along and look for any sign of the Gnarled Fox myself.

Nell nods in agreement before suddenly straightening. "Wait, do you hear that?"

"Hear what?" I say, but Nell is turning toward the trees that line either side of the road.

"It sounds like . . . singing. . . ." Her gaze goes glassy, and then, without another word, she turns on her heel and runs off into the woods.

"Nell!" Sam shouts, chasing after her. He's no sooner hit the tree line than I'm running after him.

"Stay here!" I yell over my shoulder to Crystal and Malik as I chase after the healers, hoping they remember my order long enough to heed it until I get back. I can't afford to lose anyone now, and there is no doubt that any music Nell is hearing is a trap.

As I run after them through the woods, hurdling deadfall and skirting unnerving lumps that rise between the roots of the trees, I reach into my bandolier for a few okra seeds. There are precious few bits left, but I grip them in my fist as I give chase. No point in being frugal when we could all be dead by dusk.

The trees open up suddenly into a clearing, and I nearly barrel into Sam's back where he's come to a halt. He catches me with a single strong arm, holding me until I regain my balance. Nell stands in the midst of a field of flowers, the shapes twisted and strange. The blooms, which in a better time could have been saf-flowers or marigolds, are no higher than her thigh and are dry and dead.

"Nell, what are you doing?" Sam shouts. There's a curious buzzing. It vibrates through my chest, like a swarm of angry bees has lodged somewhere near my heart. When I take a step toward Nell the sensation grows stronger, driving me backward.

"There's something wrong with this place," I say. "Can you feel it?"

"Yes," Sam says, a whole range of emotions packed into the single word. "We have to help her."

"Nell!" I yell. The girl is oblivious to the sound. It's like she's locked in a waking dream of some sort. She gestures and mutters, and it's only after another moment that I realize she is talking to someone.

I swallow dryly and reach out for the nearest flowering plant.

I can ravel almost anything—fresh plant matter ravels the best, the potential for it to become something else already there, but I can ravel even from material long since scattered, its life small and dormant. A quick look at the flowers around me, though, and I know that trying to ravel from them would be a wasted effort.

Still, I reach out for them, just to be sure. There is a pinch and I yank my hand back, the tip of my finger bloody like I pricked it on a thorn.

The flowers, for all they appear dead and gray, are *hungry*.

Sam has tried to walk toward Nell and immediately dances back. "They feel like they're biting me," he says, despair in his voice.

"You both run entirely too fast." It's Crystal, huffing and puffing as she appears beside me.

"Why didn't you stay on the road?" I say.

"Malik didn't think it was a good idea to split up," she says.

"Where's Malik?" I ask, looking back the way we came. I'm trying not to panic, but this might be the thing that breaks me. How am I supposed to keep them safe if they have no idea of the danger?

Crystal turns slowly and looks behind her, giving me an exaggerated shrug. It reminds me of the time Pigeon got into Ma's blackberry brandy and drank herself silly. "I don't know; he was right behind me," she says after a long moment. She finally appears to sense where she is. "This field feels wrong. Well, more wrong than usual, I guess."

"Can you raze a path through the flowers to Nell?" Sam asks

me. At least he seems to be holding on to his wits for the time being.

"I can try." I toss a few okra seeds, and they ravel into a trio of waist-high warriors. I send one of them into the field to bring back Nell, but the construct unravels after only a few steps.

Crystal sits on the ground and flops out on her back. Sam and I give each other alarmed looks, but her eyes are still open, and she appears to be all right.

"Leave it to me," she says, woozily.

A few feet away, a stone rises up into the air amid the twisted stalks of the dried blooms, and then another.

Sam doesn't hesitate. He jumps forward and begins making his slow way to Nell upon the rocks rising before him. He's gone only a few feet when Malik comes stumbling out of the trees.

"We have to run," he says, winded. "There's something coming. I tried to slow it down, but I can barely ravel a damn thing."

There's a crashing sound headed toward us from far away in the trees, the ruckus steadily approaching. I turn toward the threat, heart pounding and my palms slicking with sweat.

"I got this," I say, pushing aside my fear. "Help Sam get Nell out of that field so we can run."

I send the okra warriors toward the wood line, the constructs marching forward doggedly, and pull the last of the okra seeds from my bandolier to ravel a few more. I remember back in New Jersey, when my first set of constructs were destroyed by the Blight Beast. Now I have no hesitation about sending them forward to their doom. I wish I had stronger access to the Possibilities like I did back then; I would ravel a platoon of okra-seed dragons and let them tear this place to pieces. But I have to work with what I have.

The creature that comes crashing through the woods isn't one of the shadow creatures we faced our first night here, the kind that now resides in my soul jar. It looks like the beast was once a cow, but somehow that cow got mixed up with a dog and a chicken. The body of the creature is bovine, with the spurred feet of a rooster and the head of a canine. Numerous sores cover its body, the pustules erupting into bloody lesions. It stinks of death and decay, and I'm not sure whether the smell is the rotting corpse of the animal itself or the Necromancy that is powering it.

"Stars and stripes," Malik breathes from behind me, his voice part horror and part awe, but I'm not paying attention. I have to slow the thing down so we can get Nell out of the field.

Even with the additional constructs I raveled, it quickly becomes clear that this monster is much too powerful for them. The dog's head snaps at my soldiers, shredding them with ease.

I dig through my near-empty bandolier and come up with three walnuts. I grip them in my hand, letting them wake together. I am about to ravel the biggest, most powerful construct I can reckon when there is a scream from behind me.

I turn to see Nell sinking into the field. The land is swallowing her.

"Peregrine!" Malik shouts, and I turn back toward the wood line to see the last of my okra warriors being trampled by the cow-dog-chicken monster. Without hesitation I pull on what Possibilities I can and throw the walnuts at the ground before me.

They erupt, and standing where they hit the dirt is a ten-foot-tall warrior, complete with a sword and a shield. The creature steps forward, and I take a step back to keep from falling over. I put more of myself into the raveling than I wanted to, and now I'm light-headed and unsteady and can feel blood on my lip.

But my creation is worth it. It's a goddamn masterpiece.

The knight steps forward, meeting the monster from the woods with its sword, the walnut's hard shell lending strength to the weapon. It cleaves through the side of the cow beast, and the thing lets out a sound somewhere between a bark and a bellow.

With the monster occupied, I turn back toward the rest of the group. Crystal still lies on the ground, and her path of stones is now complete. Sam has almost reached Nell.

"You have to hurry," Crystal says, sobbing a little. "I can't hold them for long."

"Malik, can you carry Crystal?" I say, an idea suddenly coming to me.

"Can I . . . yeah, I can," he says as my intent becomes clear. He leans over her, and they exchange a few words before she climbs onto his back. Malik begins to follow Sam's trajectory, using the stones to walk through the field without touching the flowers.

"Peregrine, I can't keep the path open for you!" Crystal calls, her voice filled with pain.

"You don't have to! Just get Nell!"

I turn back to the walnut warrior, who is doing a fine job of hacking the cow beast to pieces. But no matter how many times the construct tears into the pustulant flesh of the monster, the thing won't die. I have to wonder if that's the point of these wretched creations. Just one more thing to wear us down.

My strength is fading, even with the jar of souls in my bandolier. I realize that there's no use fighting the beast; it'll just regenerate endlessly, most likely pulling death from the landscape around us. So I turn my construct toward the field, sending it lumbering into the treacherous crop after Malik and Crystal. I leap onto its back as it walks past, altering its shape just a bit so that I can grab a handhold and climb aboard it, well above the tops of the flowers. It's not as easy as I thought it would be; my arms are about as strong as egg noodles, and the hard shell exterior is surprisingly slick. It's only my desperation that keeps me from losing my grip and falling to the ground.

Malik and Crystal are nearly to where Sam stands next to Nell. His big arms pull at the girl, but despite his efforts she continues to sink into the earth, all the way up to her chest.

"Come on, you can't give up. Come on, Nell!" Sam bellows.

But Nell doesn't say anything. Her mouth hangs slightly agape and her gaze is far away. White lines have threaded their way across her dark skin, the cracks widening as huge swaths of it begin to flake away.

"It's okay," Nell says, her voice small. "I'm fine. I can see him! Oh, he is bright."

"Sam, you have to let her go," Malik says, grunting as he adjusts Crystal's weight. Blood pours from her nose, and she coughs wetly.

"Crystal, you can let go of the path," I say. Even standing in the middle of the deadly flower field, the walnut construct is strong, and I absorb the sword and the shield into the warrior's form so that it has its hands free to pick up Crystal and Malik. Crystal, exhausted from her efforts, immediately passes out while Malik scrambles up onto the walnut warrior as I shape him handholds to grip.

"Impressive," he says. It's the nicest thing he has ever said to me. I hope he remembers it an hour from now.

"Sam, you have to come on," I say, leaning over to hold my hand out to him. A crashing sound comes from behind us, the cow beast following, its dog head growling viciously. Its progress is slow; the field is no friend to anyone, but that's not the only problem. As I watch, the flowers have begun to wrap themselves around the legs of my walnut construct, devouring it like they are devouring Nell.

Nothing is left of Nell now but her head. She closes her eyes and mumbles something, and then she is gone, the ground swallowing her up.

Walk toward the split oak. That is where you will find the Fox.

It is Nell's voice, in my head and all around me, and I am so startled that I almost lose my grip and end up in the field as well.

"Nell," Sam says, the sound raw, pain and agony packed into the single syllable. He is trapped within his own misery, oblivious to what's around him. The walnut warrior scoops the large boy up, and we make our way rapidly across the field toward the road in the distance.

Toward the split oak. Where the hell is that?

I twist and look behind us as we go, watching as the corrupt creature falls to its knees among the flowers, the field consuming it just as it did Nell. By the time the walnut warrior exits the field, the beast behind us is no longer a threat. I don't feel any kind of joy, just a numb and hollow emptiness.

As we climb down from the walnut warrior, it begins to crumble, the ravel completely spent. Sam grabs Crystal, cradling her in his big arms like she weighs nothing. Which she may now. Crystal is in a bad way, and who knows how much of her burned up raveling those stepping-stones.

As the walnut construct crumbles into dust, my gaze is drawn back to the murderous field. We've survived yet another attack.

But not sweet, quiet Nell.

As Sam and Malik kneel nearby, I watch the field, unable to move. I try to swallow past the lump in my throat. Despair hollows out my chest, and I don't know what to do with the feeling. This can't be happening.

I'm half hoping to see Nell chasing after us, yelling that we walk too fast.

There is nothing but the disconcerting swaying of the flower stalks.

Seeing abandoned houses now fills me with a fine terror. What happened to all these souls?

TWENTY-NINE

I have never been a crier. I've never found it soothing, therapeutic, or useful. Sometimes, when the arguments with Pigeon got really bad, I would burst into angry tears. But I've never sobbed quietly from a broken heart or sadness, not like Pigeon or Ma sometimes did.

"A good cry is cleansing for the soul," Ma used to say, one of the bits of advice she freely doled out. Ma was a strong advocate of letting go of bad feelings, and for her that meant putting on a kettle, making a cup of mint tea, and crying out all those terrible emotions.

There's a lot to cry about now. Our friends and mentors are dead. Our rations are gone, our packs lost in in the madness of the devouring field, and we each carry a single canteen slung across our torsos, most near empty. I watch the sides of the road for oncoming threats, a few bits in my hand in case I need to do a quick ravel for protection. There aren't many left, and I worry what will happen when my last walnut is gone. Crystal hasn't awoken, and Malik and Sam take turns carrying her as we make our way down the dusty road. I'm not even sure what they remember at this point as they both walk along quietly. Do they know that we just lost Nell, and are they near a breakdown, as I am? Or has that tragedy now been scrubbed from their memories? I'm not sure what answer I fear more.

More than anything else I wish the Skylark were here. She would know what to do. But she's dead like everyone else, so it's up to me to try to get us out of this place, to keep us from being devoured by the machinations of a Necromancer, four more victims in the endless tragedy of the American Negro.

I have never, ever been friendly with failure, and this is not the moment where I will start. And that's when I see a giant, lightning-split oak a little ways in the distance.

Nell's final words are going to save us.

I wonder who the Gnarled Fox is, and what their cabin might look like. If it's somewhere protected by warding, like the last house we stayed in was, it might be intact. I want to think that maybe the place will call to me when I find it, that it's somewhere we can rest and regroup, as I'm not sure what time it is and I know we for certain do not want to be wandering down the lane when full dark comes. Plus, there's Crystal to think about. We tried stopping and waking her a handful of times, but she is still unconscious. I'm hoping we can find this cabin soon, so we can tend to her.

We pass a couple of homesteads that look likely, but each time I approach the houses I find the wood rotted and fragile, the doors coming off the hinges when I try to open them, in one case my foot going straight through the porch step on my way to the front door. I'm guessing none of those are my destination.

Nor are the few houses that are still occupied, the families watching us with hollow eyes.

"How are they still alive?" Sam wonders aloud as we walk past a farm with a white man sitting on the porch, watching us warily. It's the first he's spoken since we lost Nell, and I'm hoping the question means that maybe he's retained some of his wits.

But then I notice his skin. There are white lines forming—faint, for now, but they look just like the ones under Nell's skin before she died. I swallow. We need to find this cabin, and fast.

We get an answer to Sam's question a little while later when we pass a farmhouse, a white boy of ten or eleven playing out front. He stares at us hatefully, and Sam raises a hand to wave at the kid. The boy picks up a rock and throws it at us, and I have to dance out of the way.

"Hey! What's your problem?" I call.

"Go to hell, you damn darkies! Baldur is coming, and once he gets here, you and all your dirty kin will be wiped off the map. Good riddance!" The boy spits in the dirt. His face is hungry, and his eyes are sunken into his head. A man appears on the front porch, a shotgun in hand, the threat clear.

We say nothing, just keep walking. Neither the boy nor his pa follows us, but his threat buries itself into my subconscious and niggles at me as we continue our death march. These people aren't like the other family we met on the road, trying to evacuate. These people know what's happening and are exactly where they want to be. There is something truly unsettling about watching people welcome their own death because of a little hate.

Just as I am beginning to lose hope, our luck turns. There is a small cabin, really little more than a shack, perched just beyond the wood line. It's made of stone with a wooden roof, and there are runes carved into the doorpost. It calls to me, like that feeling I used to get when I came home after a long day and knew that Ma would have a glass of lemonade and a plate of shortbread waiting.

"Wards of protection," Malik says, pointing to the runes. "It's kept the building intact."

And there, beautifully carved and burned into the gnarled wood, is the outline of a fox.

I could almost cry from the relief that washes over me. But my eyes are still dry and gritty, not a tear to be found.

"Should we knock?" Malik asks.

I shake my head and bound onto the porch. This place is expecting me.

We enter the house, tumbling in and finding a humble single room. It looks as though the cabin has been unoccupied for some time, but it's clean aside from an accumulation of dust. There is only one window, and it faces out toward the road. A woodstove squats in one corner, a generous stack of firewood next to it. It's inviting and warm, and my shoulders relax for the first time all day. For the moment, we are safe, and that is no small thing.

There is a rickety chair next to a small table and a lone bed that Sam gently puts Crystal in before collapsing onto the floor, sitting upright with his back against the wall. "I'm done," he says, wheezing a bit.

The statement doesn't require an answer, because the truth is we all feel the same. The hollows around Malik's eyes now look like bruises, and Crystal's breathing is ragged and irregular. The only reason that I feel somewhat okay is because of the jar of souls in my bandolier. But even that is a limited kind of protection. My head pounds, my mouth is filled with ashes, and every muscle in my body aches. We cannot keep running like this. Not even me.

The land is hungry, and we are what is on the menu.

"Rest, both of you. I'll make a fire," I say. The work of it is familiar and gives my brain something to focus on. By the time the flames are dancing in the grate, both Malik and Sam have fallen asleep, Sam on the floor next to Crystal and Malik in the chair, his arms folded on the table and his head lying atop.

I take the opportunity to search the cabin. There are a few containers here and there, but the canister of flour is full of dead beetles and the canister of sugar is empty. There are a couple of cans of beans, dusty and unopened, and I set them to the side to eat later if anyone feels like food. My appetite is nonexistent. The last time I ate was last night, but who can really think about food when death is breathing down one's neck?

I'm wondering if there might be a well nearby, and whether it's safe to step outside to look, when there's a noise, like a creature caught in a trap. At first I think maybe I'm imagining it—no one has been in this cabin in a long time—but as I listen I realize it's coming from under a baseboard next to the door.

I approach cautiously, pulling one of my last walnuts from my bandolier. There's a spot where the baseboard comes away from the wall, the wood cut in a way that a roughly six-inch panel opens up, and when I remove it, a book comes flopping out of the wall.

It hops toward me and stops at my feet.

Now, I have seen a number of incredible things in my life, including the time Timmy Johnson ate four whole apple pies in less than a quarter of an hour. But I have never, ever seen a book hopping around like a critter. I'm hesitant to touch it. I've heard tales of books, all kinds of books, that can talk and see and grant all kinds of powers, but at the end of every single one of those stories, the book's curse comes back to find the person in the end, leading to a gruesome death.

Unbidden, my mind flashes back to Nell, the strange white lines fracturing her face and her soft voice whispering, "It's okay," like some kind of prayer.

When you're already courting death, what's one more dance?

I pick the book up. If it is a cursed tome of immeasurable power, then maybe I can at least get Sam, Crystal, and Malik to safety. I open it, and the first page is blank. No warning, no words at all, just a blank page made of fine paper, ivory hued and clean and waiting for the kiss of a nib and ink.

"What's that?" a sleepy voice asks. Crystal struggles to sit up in the narrow bed. "Where are we?"

"A cabin we found after we left the field," I say, keeping my voice low. Relief floods through me, but I swallow it down so that Crystal won't panic. "Malik and Sam are sleeping. They carried you for a couple of miles."

"Nell is dead, right?" Crystal says, sniffling.

I nod, unsure if I'm glad she's able to remember or not.

"I want to cry, about everything, but I just feel so empty inside. Like someone sucked everything out of me and replaced it with straw."

"It's another effect of this place," I say. I too want cry for all we've lost, not just the people but also the pieces of our souls we've left out on that dusty road. But, like Crystal, I find my eyes dry.

"What is that?" she says after a long moment.

"A book. It was making noise in the wall. It appears to be blank."

"Does it have a protective rune on it?" Crystal asks.

I frown. "Maybe. How would I know?"

"Let me see it?"

"Take it easy," I say, handing it to her.

Crystal turns it in her hand. "Here it is—it looks like it's locked. This might be, um, a blood rune." Crystal points to a place along the spine where the leather is warped and a deep groove sits below a tiny spike.

"What does that mean?"

"It can only be opened through a blood price. And only by people with blood that has certain characteristics. There are stories that during the years of bondage, slave owners would lock their books just like this so that colored folks couldn't open their grimoires."

"I wish that surprised me."

Crystal sighs. "Yeah. Same. So, are you going to try it?"

I look at the book for a long moment. I didn't come this far to *not* try to use my blood to open a mysterious book in the home of a mage I've never met. Plus, Louise told me to find this place, and so far she's been pretty reliable. If it wasn't for her, I wouldn't have the soul jar, and who knows how bad things would be without that bit of noxious help.

So I press my index finger to the spot. There's a sharp sting, like a bite from a small animal, and I pick up my finger to see a small drop of blood there.

"Here's hoping it isn't hexed," Crystal says.

"Hexed? You're telling me this now?" I say. "Why would you let me open it if it might be cursed?"

We steel ourselves for some sort of doom, but it doesn't come. Instead, the book falls open in my hands, the pages filling with cramped handwriting. I step closer to the woodstove, as the light coming in through the window is pitiful, and begin to read.

"It's a journal," I say. I don't get a chance to say much more, because suddenly I am falling, tumbling head over heels into a world that is not our own.

January 23, 1896

They're back. I can smell them whenever I step outside.
Their foul workings waft through the countryside, and
we've taken to hiding behind our doors when dark falls.
The Johnsons have lost their cow, and there are rumors
that the Washingtons saw a group of white folks dancing
under the full moon.

The battle might be over, but I think our war is just
beginning.

Chapter
THIRTY

I blink once and then again. I am somewhere. But where, exactly, I don't know.

I turn slowly, the world around me resolving itself into a hallway full of windows. Above each one, a date flashes, the script the same cramped writing as the book I just opened.

"Ugh. Cursed after all," I mutter. I just cannot catch a break.

I've never been properly cursed before, although I saw Pigeon go through it twice, mostly on account of her poaching another girl's boy. It is a simple thing to unravel a curse—usually just takes some ritual with a frizzy hen or a long soak in a bath of redbrick dust and silver powder, depending on the kind of hex.

But it is immediately clear to me that if this is a curse, it's *not* that sort of kitchen-table hex. I'm so far out of my depth I can't even see the shore. And that scares me more than anything else.

The air before me wavers for a moment, and out of nothing comes something: a grizzled old colored man, stooped and twisted. He leans heavily on a cane made of a rough branch, and he stands before, studying me.

And finding me lacking, judging from his expression.

"Who're you?" he demands. "You're a little young to be a Fox, aren't you?"

I don't know how to answer the second question, so I go with the first. "I'm the Peregrine. I found your book. Or, your journal? And it apparently cursed me. I don't suppose you can lift the curse, please?" Closed mouths don't get fed, and I'm hoping asking nicely will get me out of yet another predicament.

"No curse here, Miss Peregrine. You're in the book. If you found my journal it means that you're a Fox, no doubt about it. Maybe not a proper one, just yet. But a Fox all the same."

I frown, taking my time and letting his words sink in. "You must be the Gnarled Fox. I was just in your cabin."

The old man gives a nod. "Sure enough. Before I departed this world, I sealed my journal away, leaving it and my cabin hidden in plain sight just in case those fools tried their nonsense again, so that whichever Fox had to deal with this mess would have a bit of a primer. The best way to learn is by looking to the past. Most happenings happened before, even if they wore different clothes the first time around."

"Okay . . . I'm sorry, can we back up a second? So, you're saying that there are lots of Foxes?"

He scowls at me. "Of course there are! How are we supposed to maintain the balance if there aren't a whole host of us? You ever seen just one bird? Or just one deer in the woods? No! You need a community to care for a place, even one as terrible as this cursed continent."

I have so many questions, mostly about just what kind of ravel he's got me twisted up in. It's much more sophisticated than anything I've ever seen or done, and I yearn to know the hows and whys of such a construct.

"Anyway, enough jawing," he says, as though I've been the one pontificating. "I need to get back to being dead, and you've got a lot to learn. The important passages are all here. Take a gander and then get back to saving the world."

"Wait, what am I supposed to do?" I say, but the man is already gone and I am left alone with my frustration.

I huff out a breath, because this is yet another thing in a whole laundry list of trials and tribulations. But as I turn around, I realize the space I'm in seems to be safe. I'm not in pain like when Miss Fox hijacked my beam, and there are lots of interesting things hanging on the walls. It's a bit like an art museum. I visited the Metropolitan Museum of Art during a special series to see the works of some dead white man from France. The colors had moved and swirled in a way I found nauseating, and all the white visitors kept looking at me like maybe I was lost.

I wonder just how I'm supposed to go about understanding my reason for being here—the Gnarled Fox was surprisingly unhelpful, even for a dead man—and so in the meantime I walk to the closest panel, and within seconds it pulls me in, showing me a life not my own.

February 28, 1896

The Washingtons are missing. As are the Johnsons. Two entire families just up and gone.

I went by their homesteads, and a creature came after me. A great swirling creature of darkness, made up of the pain and fear of many. The souls of colored folks. I captured them all in a soul jar gifted to me by the Fox of the East, but they were so corrupted that there was little to be done with them. I purified them and released them, but this settles the fact.

We got Necromancers. The Klan has found its way to Ohio.

March 3, 1896

Spoke with the other Foxes, asked them for advice. Wily Fox told me to find the source of the nonsense and unravel the working, but far as I can tell there's no working at all, just a bunch of twisted animals and missing colored families. Local mage council wants nothing to do with it, and I ain't much surprised.

Who wants to listen to an old man carry on about monsters in the dark?

March 4, 1896

They found Joshua Washington today. Skinny, haggard, mumbling of men stealing his life from him. I gave him a soak of redbrick dust and silver powder and got to work.

I'd expected a geas or a curse, but what I found when I began to examine him was like nothing I'd ever seen before. A bondage, not of soul, but of body. Every single cell of the boy's being was wrapped up, claimed by some name that I didn't know and couldn't fathom. And when I tried to unravel the binding . . .

. . . . the boy came unraveled as well. I can't even give his kin the ashes. They still haven't returned.

But Joshua's death is not all for naught. From his ramblings I gleaned where they had taken him: a tree draped in strange fruit over in Fulton County. I won't write down how he described the tree, because it's a bit much even for me, but I will say it sounded properly unnatural. There's a few workings that require such a thing, but only one that I can think of that could unravel a body so thoroughly. These damned fools are waking a dying god.

I have to stop them before it's too late.

April 4, 1896

This will be my final entry, as my time is short. I can feel the workings taking everything I have left, but with my death so goes the Klan and all its corrupt Necromancy and skullduggery. But just so that future Foxes can be prepared, here is my final testament:

Two weeks ago I made my way to the Deathstruck tree in Fulton County. There I discovered exactly what I had feared: strange fruit hanging from the tree. They pulsed as I approached. Inside I found the folks that had gone missing these past few weeks. When I tried to unravel the working, I discovered I was caught up as well. It seems the Klan is learning, figuring out how to use our own abilities against us, just as their forebears did with Necromancy in the age of colonization. There was Floramancy there that I missed. Still too hasty even in my old age.

So I used theirs against them. I bound all of their working to me, every last bit of it. I stole it from them! All of that life, all of that death, I took it for my own, starving that dying god of what it needed to wake.

The Klan appeared, and I bound them to me as well, every last one of them. I reckon at some point they will return, so I am leaving this for the next Fox that will come through this part of the country. The designs are laid for them to do it again, so whoever reads this journal will get the entirety of my knowledge, and a bit of theirs, I'm afraid. I'm locking this journal so that only a Fox can open it. It will be my last great working.

I know you're wondering: Just how did that girl get a picture
of the Gnarled Fox when he's dead? No idea.
But he was on film looking pensive all the same.

Chapter

THIRTY-ONE

"Quartz and peridot, I thought you were dead!"

I blink, my eyes hurting. I feel as though I was the one who purified the souls in the jar, who unraveled the workings of a group of Necromancers, who tied my own soul to the working to keep them from raising a dead god and saved the land. My head pounds and I am even more confused than before, too many thoughts in my brain that have no business being there.

"Peregrine? Can you hear me?" Crystal asks.

I shake off the remainder of the vision or ravel or whatever it might be and turn to Crystal, struggling to sit up. Both Malik and Sam are awake now, watching me from the places where I left them, exhaustion carving deep lines into their faces.

"How long was I out?" I shake my head, hoping to clear some of the fog. My head is full of things that are not mine, impossible ways to access the Possibilities and manipulate the world around us. Things that I was taught long ago were forbidden or dangerous, but now I know are methods that folks rely on. Folks like the Foxes, who have a whole litany of secrets. Some of which are now mine.

"Not long, but you kept muttering things, and when I tried to get close to you something, uh, pinched me?" Crystal smiles, relieved. "I thought for sure you were a goner." Her smile fades. "Just like Nell. And the Grimalkin."

I blink. "You remember."

Malik scowls. "How could we forget?"

I swallow my relief, because the cabin may have returned their memories but we are still in far too much danger to relax. I take a deep breath and let it out, enjoying the simple sensation of my lungs filling with air. "I know what we have to do."

"Oh, and what is that?" Malik asks, his voice quiet. There's no sarcasm there, which is just as alarming as Malik's sallow skin. It's another reminder we won't last much longer in this place.

"We have to get out of here," I say, standing, my muscles stretching painfully as I do. "The journal I read, it talked about raising a dead god. They've done this before."

"Who?" Sam asks, his voice barely more than a whisper.

"The Klan," I say, my voice low. "Or the Knights of the White Camelia? Is there a difference?" All this extra information in my brain has no reference point, so that I know things without understanding how they relate to the world around me. It's a disconcerting feeling, and it takes everything I have not to just sink into the corner and inventory things, separating them into fact and fiction. "Whoever it is, they're using Necromancy to raise a dead god."

"Why would they do that?" Malik asks, his tone sharp.

"I don't know," I say, feeling silly. "But there's someone who might. Miss Fox. Well, I'm hoping she knows."

"Are you sure you're okay?" Crystal asks. "Because you aren't making a lot of sense."

Who can argue with that? I feel like the time Patty—that was the preacher's daughter—and I stole a jar of apple pie moonshine and got zozzled. Everything is happening both too fast and too slow, and nothing makes much sense. "Let me heat up this can of beans I found and I'll explain while we eat."

The beans heat quickly and are, surprisingly, still good. By the time my belly is full, my brain feels a little more settled, and I try to explain everything I saw in the Gnarled Fox's journal, everything I know, and the like.

Malik clears his throat. "So, in this . . . vision you had—"

"It wasn't a vision. I was in the journal," I say, tossing it at Malik. He flips through the book, frowning.

"It's blank," he says.

"It requires a blood price," Crystal offers.

Malik looks at the journal, shrugs, and pricks his finger on the same spot as I did. For a long moment there's nothing. And then, without warning, the small, leather-bound notebook bursts into flames.

I grab the burning tome and throw it into the woodstove, since we have no water to douse the flames. Within the grate it burns in shades of purple, and I frown. "That's weird. I wonder why it didn't work for you?"

"Maybe it's not for Illusionists," Malik says despondently.

Sam has nodded off, his bowl of beans untouched beside him. He still sits in between the bed and the stove, and the faint white lines under his skin are growing thicker by the moment. I touch him gently to rouse him, and he moans.

"We need to get out of here," I say. Sam is going downhill much faster than the rest of us, and I wonder if there's something about healers that makes them more susceptible to the effects of Necromancy.

"And just how are we going to do that?" Malik says, his voice growing more intense.

I shake my head. "I don't know. I wish the Gnarled Fox was here to tell me."

A curious pressure starts in my chest, and a coughing fit seizes me. I reach for my canteen to get a sip of water, but before I can I begin to gag.

"Peregrine!" Crystal shouts. I bend over, stomach heaving. At first I think perhaps the beans were turned, but then I bring up what looks to be a tooth. A small white object that's surrounded by a bit of bile and a few beans, the vomit a nauseating splatter on the floor. I immediately feel better.

"What is that?" Malik demands, and I shake my head.

"I don't know," I say. I don't want to reach down and pick up the weird thing, but I do, wiping it on my clothes. When I hold it up to have a look it splits in half, releasing a billowing white smoke.

"Dammit, girl, I thought I told you I wanted to stay dead," says the old man suddenly standing before me.

It's the Gnarled Fox. Not alive, but definitely summoned from beyond the grave. Crystal lets out a cry of alarm, and both Sam and Malik shout in surprise.

"What is this?" I say, feeling more than scared. What the hell am I? The Gnarled Fox said I was a Fox, but this is far beyond any of the ravels I have ever done.

"It's just a bit of Necromancy, child," he says, his tone softening a bit. "Foxes can summon other Foxes when they need help. I figured the journal was enough, but apparently not."

"Can you tell us how to get out of here?" Crystal asks, but the Gnarled Fox doesn't seem to hear her. He just stands before me, all fading smoke, waving back and forth in a strange breeze.

"Better hurry before I go. You didn't pay much of a price, and the Possibilities are thin here," the Gnarled Fox says.

"How do I stop the Necromancer's ravel?" I ask.

"Unwind it, same as any other working. But you and I both know you'll never make it that far without being devoured."

"Fine, then how do I get out of here?" I say, trying not to let my frustration overwhelm me.

"You already have that information." He taps my head, and I can see it completely. And then before I can thank him, he is gone, back to æther.

I turn to Malik. "Do you have your penknife?"

Malik reaches into his pocket and pulls out the short blade. I use the blanket from the bed to wipe up the small pile of vomit before using the penknife to carve a series of circles into the floor, three of them, all connected to a larger circle in the middle. It's nothing like I've ever seen before, but the design is seared into my memory by the Gnarled Fox.

"What are you doing?" Crystal asks, her voice soft. I shake my head, because if I try to do anything but get us somewhere safe my attention is going to wander and I'll forget what I'm about. My thoughts are so scattered and panicked that it's all I can do to finish what the Gnarled Fox has put in my head.

When I finish there is a circle, about three feet in diameter, surrounded by three other circles of the same size. In the center of each circle is the rough cut of an animal. Nothing fancy, but I know what they are. The center circle holds a fox, the western circle an ant, the eastern circle a bird, and the northern circle a cat with a mane that I am certain is supposed to be a lion. There's no southern circle, but if there were, there would be a hyena there.

I have no idea what the circles mean, but I can feel the way they call to me. And the way they are anchored to the stars.

This is it. This is our ticket out of here.

That's when there's a scratching at the door. It's insistent and determined, and I pull a walnut from my bandolier. The rest of the apprentices are watching me like I've gone mad, and I don't blame them. I would think the same thing if our positions were reversed. I'm not actually sure that I haven't gone mad. Perhaps my sanity was the price I paid for raising the dead.

Behind me, Crystal and Malik are saying something, but I ignore them. Instead I open the door to find a pale tabby cat on the threshold. It struts in like it owns the place.

"Thank the stars I found you before they did," the cat says.

Crystal sits up straighter in the narrow bed while I close the door. "Why can I hear that cat talking?"

"Same," Malik says, his face deathly pale.

"You can hear him?" I say. I might be in a bit of a panic.

"Of course they can hear me, girl," the cat says, and at that, I realize it's not like when I'm working Faunomancy. "Do you have any idea of what you've done? I should be on the way to my final reward, but here I am riding Fyodor like some kind of parasite."

"Wait—Grimalkin?" Crystal says. We all exchange a look. But Crystal and Malik are only staring at me. The way a body looks at a Necromancer.

"I . . . put you in Fyodor's body?" I say, my voice quiet. My arms are chilled, and my beans feel like they're going to come up all over again. I just want to sit on the dusty floor and cry. It's all too much.

"There's no time for existential crises, Peregrine," the Grimalkin says. "We have to get out of here before the Necromancers find us."

She's right. Before anyone can say anything else, I pick up the Grimalkin and hand her to Crystal. Then I steer Crystal to the projection circle with the ant.

"What are you doing?" she asks.

"The Grimalkin can't anchor the circle by herself in this form," I mutter, "so you'll have to take her."

She starts to say something else, but I'm already moving toward Malik. He holds up his hands when I approach, taking up a defensive stance.

"I'm not going anywhere until you calm down. You look a mess," he says.

"We stay here any longer and Sam is dead. So either go and stand on the lion or kiss your beau goodbye."

Malik makes a choked noise and looks over at Crystal, alarmed.

She's unsteady on her feet, but she just shrugs. "We all knew about you two, Mal," she whispers. "We never cared."

He says nothing but moves to stand in the circle with the lion. He looks like he wants to hit me, but I'm too worried about Sam to pay him much mind. I walk over to the boy, who hasn't moved. When I point to the circle with the bird, he just shakes his head.

"I can't," he says, his voice far away.

"You have to. I won't leave you to die."

Sam just laughs, but I have a head full of all kinds of forbidden arts. I don't know if it came from the journal or from when the Gnarled Fox touched me, but it doesn't matter. We're running out of time. I consider my options for half a moment before I sigh.

"Okay, I'm going to do something. Don't fight it, okay?"

Sam makes a huffing sound that might be another laugh but also might be a sob. I still hold Malik's penknife, and I slice open my thumb, letting the blood well before pressing it to Sam's forehead.

"Hey! What are you doing?" Malik tries to leave the circle but goes nowhere. "What's happening?" He puts his hand up and pushes against the invisible barrier locking him in place.

"The ravel has already started," I reply, but my eyes are locked on Sam's. I give him a smile. "It's going to be fine." I can hear myself talking, but the words sound far away, like they're a memory. All my attention is on Sam, linking him to me.

I can sense the exact moment when it happens. He's an empty shell of a person, so much of him already devoured, but that's okay because I have entirely too much life in me at the moment, thanks to the Gnarled Fox. I push a little of that life, and of my life, into Sam, and then I force him to stand and enter the circle.

Everyone has decided that maybe I'm the monster in that moment. Malik is yelling and trying to pummel the invisible barrier that surrounds him, Crystal has buried her face in the Grimalkin's fur, and Sam cries silent tears as he steps onto the last circle, that with the bird of life.

I feel strange and floaty and euphoric. It's hard to focus. I'm Sam, standing in the circle, unsteady on my feet; I'm also me standing in the center of the fox circle, about to open a beam for the first time ever.

I will shoot the leylines like my people have done for generations.

Crystal and Malik are both yelling at me, trying to get my attention, and something approaches outside the cabin, lurching toward us. But everything is fine, and I am better than I have ever been.

I open the path and take us away.

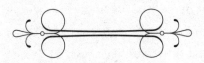

Part 3

THE ONCE AND FUTURE FOX

No matter how many pictures I took,
they always came out blurry. Strange.

Chapter
THIRTY-TWO

I wake. Slowly. My head pounds, and for a long moment I'm not quite sure where I am or what happened. I feel terrible, but when I crack open a single eye there's sunlight. Real sunlight, not the watery gray stuff from the Blight. That makes me sit up in a hurry. Which is a huge mistake.

Everything hurts. Even my teeth. I groan, and my muscles flex and pull, the aching soreness awful, and also welcome. The pain means I'm still alive.

But where the hell am I?

A glance around reveals I'm in a bedroom. Flocked wallpaper, a small writing desk, a chest of drawers with a pitcher and a wash-bowl, and the bed where I lie. Everything looks so calm and normal that I pinch myself to make sure it's real.

It's real. And better yet, the strange, dreamy, overly full sensation in my brain is gone, my mind settling once more into familiar grooves of thought.

"Don't worry, I saved it."

The words come from an old woman hobbling into the room,

leaning heavily on a gnarled cane. I sit up a bit straighter in the bed, and the scent of lilac and sunshine, cut grass and sea spray wafts around me. There's something here that fills me with happiness, with brightness and cheer. It's the opposite of the deep dread and foreboding of the ruined land in Ohio.

"Saved what?" I ask, the question only one of many I have. I recognize the old woman settling into the room's lone chair. It's Miss Fox. She wears a purple kerchief on her head today rather than the paisley one from our first meeting, when she waylaid my beam. But other than that, she looks exactly the same. Weathered face lined with age, dark skin, and what I can only describe as a bit of a mischievous expression, as though she knows all my secrets and finds them hilarious.

"All the knowledge the old Gnarled Fox gave you. It was all in your head, crowding out the things you already knew and the like. It's a wonder you survived absorbing it. That ravel was a mess of a working. What was he thinking, putting so much in there? Most of it won't even make sense to you for a few years."

"I summoned a ghost," I say, a bit stupidly.

"Of course you did," Miss Fox says without a lick of surprise. "You had everything the Gnarled Fox knew in your noggin."

I blink. It's a wonder I didn't go mad. "From the journal?"

"Of course, the journal, child. What other grimoires have you been ingesting?"

I shake my head. "None. Thankfully."

"Although if you summoned the Gnarled Fox to ask him a question, he probably tried to reorganize the information. There's a number of ways to work such a thing, but I'm guessing you all didn't have time to do it proper-like."

The old woman studies me, like she's trying to decide whether I might be fish or fowl. "You know, it seems to me that you might have said something the first time we met, about being a Fox. If you had, I would've been a bit more forthcoming with you about Ohio."

I shake my head. "I'm not a Fox. I'm the Peregrine."

"Hmmph, for now, maybe. But you opened old Gerald's journal, and only a Fox can open a Fox binding. You used the blood rune, right?"

I nod. Who are all these Foxes? I don't get a chance to ask, though, because old Miss Fox just keeps on talking.

"Gerald, he was the last Fox up North. I always wondered what happened to him. He was ornery, but it seems odd that he would've died rather than retreating to his own space until his replacement was trained. Suppose he didn't have a choice." The old woman pauses and looks a bit abashed. "I hope you don't mind me creeping a bit through your mind. I was curious just how you managed that Wayfarer's gate. Haven't seen a working like that since I was a little."

I need a moment, so I clear my throat noisily. "Can I get a glass of water?"

"Louise." The woman has barely uttered the word before the feline girl appears in the doorway. She gives me a toothy grin, like I look delicious. I'm not sure if that's a good thing or a bad thing. "Can you get the Peregrine something to drink? And maybe a bite to eat as well. She's gonna need the energy."

Louise gives a short nod and dashes off. Miss Fox leans in conspiratorially. "I should've known you were a Fox when Louise decided to shift her form. Only a Fox can ensnare a Ligahoo like that." She winks.

"Ligahoo," I say, my molasses-slow brain trying to remember where I know the word from. The headache pounding behind my eyes isn't making it any easier to think. "Louise told me she was a Ligahoo. That's a kind of shape-shifter, right?"

"It is, but don't you go pulling that face," Miss Fox said. "Those old stories about shifters, dead people carrying around their coffins and the like, are nonsense. The Ligahoo were the pets of the gods once upon a time. They carried messages between the great clans and were lovers to the most powerful mages, godlike themselves in their power. But that is ancient history, and there are very few Ligahoo left. Some were brought here during the genocide, just like our kin, and others found themselves at loose ends when the European Necromancers began to ravage the Afrikan continent. That's where all those bugaboo stories come from. Nothing but fear and loathing worked into half-truths, just like always."

I struggle into a sitting position as Louise returns with a tray. There's a sandwich and a big frosty bottle of Coca-Cola, both of them looking as pretty as a magazine ad. The first sip I take ignites a powerful hunger in my middle.

"You're going to be starving for the next few days. That's the Necromancy. And probably the Wayfaring as well." Miss Fox struggles to stand until Louise steps closer to give her a hand. "I'm going to leave you to your lunch, but you come find me when you're finished eating and we'll discuss this Ohio nonsense."

"I'm not sure what you expect me to do," I say around a mouthful of sandwich. It's ham with mustard and sharp cheese, my all-time favorite, and I chew quickly so that I can swallow. "That place is nothing but death."

"Of course it is. Someone needs to be able to unravel the working and put things to rights."

"And that's me?"

"Child, have you been listening to a word I said? Of course it is. Stopping things like the ravel being worked out there in Ohio is what a Fox does, and since you found your way into Gerald's journal, that means you're the new Northern Fox. You may not have earned the name yet, but you're it. We'll talk about this later. For now, rest."

She leaves the room, leaning heavily on Louise's arm as she does.

Her words, portentous and terrifying, put me off of the rest of the sandwich, but I down the soda, the sugar nice and bubbly in my middle. While I'm alone, I take a moment to gather my ragged thoughts and try to unravel Miss Fox's words.

How is it I'm the replacement for this Fox person? I just got my first real mage work less than a week ago! I want to be a baker! I am perhaps the person least qualified for such a job. If anyone should be the new Fox, it should be the Skylark. At least she knows things about the proper way to ravel, and how to get things moving without making everyone angry in the process.

That's when I remember the Skylark is dead, and the bottom falls out. Tears prickle my eyes, and I blink them away. At least I can maybe cry again.

Louise returns, this time with a big slice of lemon icebox pie.

"I thought maybe you'd like something sweet as well," she says, quietly. There's something subdued about her now, nothing like the girl I bantered with not too long ago.

"Thank you," I say. Louise watches me for a moment as I eat the pie, and the sandwich—turns out I'm too hungry to let it be—and I watch her right back. "What's that look for?"

"Are you really so lost at the thought of performing your duties?" Louise says, jumping onto the foot of the bed and crouching, more wild animal than girl.

"What duties? The old woman thinks I can unravel the working in Ohio. If I could do that, I would've done it when I was there. I can't even get to the ravel itself."

"But you're a Fox," Louise says with a confused frown. "It is your job. It's what the Foxes do."

I swallow the bite I'm working in my mouth and tilt my head. "You know what the Foxes are and what they do? Can you explain it to me?"

Louise shifts a little as she considers the question. "Okay. You know how the sun always shines every morning and always sets down at night? Or how, in the winter here, it gets cold, and in the summer it's nice and warm?"

"Of course." I take another bite of the icebox cake; it's absolutely delicious.

"That's what a Fox does."

I cough as I choke on my bite of food, and Louise deftly jumps off of the foot of the bed and comes around to give me a heavy thump on the back. Once I've recovered I look at her.

"You're joking, right?"

She shakes her head. "The Foxes maintain the balance. They protect the Possibilities and make sure that everyone is cared for. Once upon a time they united the clans. They are one of the few things standing between us and the end times. And sometimes that means they have to risk their lives for the greater good."

"You can't just expect me to agree to go back there and fix everything all by myself," I say. "Even if I did have some sense of what I was supposed to do, I'd probably die before I could do it."

Louise shrugs. "Everyone dies."

"Even a Ligahoo?" I shoot back.

"Even us," Louise says, her voice low and sort of sad. I can't tell if it's because she's disappointed in me or because there aren't many of her people left. "But I have always known I would die in the service of a Fox, just like my parents, and their parents before them. It's what our people do. So I suppose it is hard for you to understand. Your people take and do not give back. It's your nature."

Ouch. Now I feel like a heel.

I don't want to think about what Louise and Miss Fox are telling me. I don't even want to get out of this bed. I want to wake up at home, safe and sound and still dreaming of being a great mage. How am I supposed to ravel desserts for the likes of Clark

Gable and Shirley Temple when I'm worrying about dead gods in the middle of Ohio? Here I am, finally getting what I've always wanted, to be a great mage, and it's probably going to lead to my death. The Possibilities have a strange sense of humor.

I push the plates away and swing my legs over the side of the bed. I've just climbed to my feet, unsteady as all get-out, when Miss Fox returns. Her expression is no different than it was before, but somehow I think she's a bit disappointed in me as well. Well, maybe I'm a bit put out as well, seeing as how no one even asked me if I wanted to be a Fox. I was just trying to save the other apprentices.

"Your friends are getting restless," she says. "We don't have much time—the ravel is almost complete, and you've got work to do. If they do manage to finally wake that old god, you're gonna have a dickens of a time handling the problem."

"What happens if I don't stop the working in Ohio?" I ask.

"Well, the short answer?" Miss Fox says, giving me an arch look. "We all die. A ravel like that will keep growing and spreading until it covers the planet."

I close my eyes for a moment, savoring the headache pounding behind my eyes. Damned if I do, even more so if I don't. I can almost hear Pigeon laughing at me over this turn of events. "You always wanted to be important," she'd say, eyebrows risen nearly to her hairline. "To be a great mage, to ravel something unforgettable. Now you get to save the whole fool world. And you're telling me that once you've gotten everything you've ever wanted, you're not sure you want it?"

I take a deep breath and let it out. The phantom voice of my sister is right. How better to become a great mage than preventing a cataclysmic disaster of mystical proportions? So much for my dreams of desserts. In my mind's eye Shirley Temple giggles and waves goodbye before the dream fades away.

I suppose there are more important things than cake.

"Well, I suppose you'd better tell me just what I need to do, then."

●●●

The sleep shirt I still wear is long enough to cover all my bits, so I follow Miss Fox and Louise as they walk through the house. It feels familiar, not unlike the house with the well-vern. There's a Wayfaring charm upon it; the rooms shift and twist, taking us from the bedroom to the parlor without going down any stairs. Not that I couldn't have walked there. The initial pain I felt upon waking has subsided, and to be honest, I feel pretty good.

But the feeling that strikes me more than any other here is the way in which I sense the many ravelings in the house. The Wayfarer's charms branch and switch back on themselves, the energies harmonizing flawlessly. It's like hearing an orchestra for the first time, after spending my entire life listening to a single violin. It's beautiful and overwhelming, and there's a part of me that wants to weep at the wonder of it all. Is this what it means to be a Fox? What did I unlock when I opened the old Gnarled Fox's grimoire?

Malik and Crystal jump to their feet when I enter, Crystal bursting into tears. "We thought you were dead," she says, launching herself across the room, her arms wrapping me up.

"I'm going to suffocate if you keep squeezing me like that," I groan, before hugging her back. After a moment she releases me. "Where's Sam?" I ask.

"Resting," Malik says, voice low. "Look, I . . . owe you an apology."

I shrug. "Can't really blame you for not believing I'm twice the mage you'll ever be." He gapes, and I punch him lightly in the shoulder. "I'm kidding. It's fine. But now we have work to do."

"Indeed we do," says a familiar voice.

I turn to see the Skylark walk into the room.

My heart leaps, and a sudden lump forms in my throat. I have to cough to clear it. "I thought you were dead," I say.

She smiles, soft but genuine. Behind her, Fyodor—or the Grimalkin—appears and sits at her feet.

"Oh, she's been dead," says Miss Fox. "This is the second form I've had to build for her, and to tell the truth it's getting a bit tiresome. Is that everyone? Anybody else planning on joining in this conversation?"

Malik looks past the Skylark. "What about my father?" he asks.

"And Master Onyx?" Crystal adds.

"Ah," the Skylark says, her voice strained, as if she's still remembering how to speak. She coughs delicately. "I am afraid Onyx did not make it, nor did your father, Malik. I'm deeply sorry. There was a creature . . . a strange, terrible, corrupted thing. I'm not sure how it got past the wards, but before we could react, it was upon us. The four of us were still speaking after our conversation the other night; the creature tore into us all. Only the Grimalkin was able to escape the room."

"I still died," she says, grooming herself where she sits on the floor. "The creature didn't get me, but the encounter with it took its toll nevertheless. I'm just glad it didn't get you kids."

I can't believe the Skylark is actually alive. Once more I have an unreasonable number of questions and a deficit of time. More for later.

"Where is Nell?" the Skylark asks, after looking around among us.

"She . . . didn't make it," I say, remembering her sad, soft sound of surprise as the ground swallowed her whole.

The Skylark looks stricken by the news before she nods slowly. "I am so sorry we've lost so many to this cursed ravel."

Malik blinks rapidly, but still has to dash away a tear. He is stoic in his grief. "I thought he was gone, but hearing it . . ." he says. He collapses back into his chair, head held in his hands. I can only imagine how he must feel.

Crystal folds into herself a bit and falls onto the couch. I sink down beside her and put my arm around her shoulders. "I'm sorry," I murmur, the apology for her and Malik's loss, even though my gaze is on the Skylark, settling into another chair, moving strangely. Miss Fox had said that she built the Skylark's form. There is a conversation to be had there, and I mean to have it.

"All right, enough of this," Miss Fox says, clapping like a schoolteacher. "Save your mourning for when there isn't a dead god rising in Ohio."

Crystal hiccups a little but straightens, nodding in agreement.

"So you know who Baldur is?" I ask, and the old woman nods.

"Baldur is an ancient Norse god. The Shining One, they once

called him, or the White One, depending on the translation. Baldur ain't really the problem, though—it's what he represents. Every pantheon's got what we call the *dying and rising god*. Greeks got Dionysius. Egyptians got Osiris, Christians got Jesus himself, and so on and so forth. Their job is to die and either be reborn anew, or be reborn when something specific comes to pass, such as the changing seasons or the end of the world. Gods are complicated things, and with dying and rising gods there's a duality of Life and Death that makes things tricky."

"Because they exist on two ends of the mystical spectrum?" Crystal asks, and the Fox gives her a toothless smile.

"Sure enough. A dead god needs Life to be reborn. A living god needs Death to ascend. But to start the process requires a truly massive amount of energy, enough to power a raveling on a continental scale. In the past, when Necromancers have sought to do this, they have taken drastic steps—killing countless people, for instance, or corrupting hundreds of square miles of land, in order to create a sort of mystical feedback loop—an imbalance of power that builds on itself indefinitely. The ravel is already set in Ohio—you all have witnessed the effects of this ever-intensifying corruption. To stop this whole mess, you're going to have to unravel it."

"How did it even come to this?" Crystal asked. "The Klan, organized Necromancy, I thought it was all gone after the Afrikan Genocide?"

Miss Fox takes a seat, holding her cane in front of her. "The things people believe never really die. Ever they rise, and ever they need to be defeated anew. For centuries, Necromancers have been willing to destroy the world for what they believe, and those who have long benefited from the power they wield have given them all the political cover they need to do it. Now it seems that means providing them with a Blight in which to ravel without scrutiny. They knew that the most the bureau would do would be to send in teams from the Colored Auxiliary, and if one or two teams are killed there, well, it's not as if anyone would consider that much out of the ordinary."

Everyone is quiet for a long moment after, and the weight of what is happening finally hits me. While we were in Ohio I was focused on getting through the day, on just surviving. But now . . .

Now there is still work to do. And it's much bigger than anything I've ever tried to accomplish in my life. Pigeon's imagined words come back to me. I yearned to be a great mage—and what greater ravel could there be than stopping someone from destroying the world?

I swallow the stomach acid that burbles up in the back of my throat. If I think about more than one step at a time I'll be overwhelmed, so I take a deep breath and turn back to Miss Fox, since everyone seems to be waiting for me to say something.

"Okay, so the ravel has to be stopped, correct? Because if they raise the god, he'll just die again, giving them the power to resurrect him again and so on and so forth."

The Fox slaps her knee. "That exactly. The initial ravel will kill everything in the area by slowly draining it of Life and using that Death energy to raise the god. But a dying god can't stay alive, so when they die again that's another burst of energy, eventually working as a permanent battery to those summoning it, creating a powerful font of both Death and Life. Now, the Necromancers just care about raising their god, but there are others who can benefit from such a massive release of Death energy."

"Mechomancers," Malik says, and Miss Fox nods solemnly.

"Sure enough, just as it ever was," the Grimalkin says, jumping onto the arm of the couch where Crystal and I sit. "But what I cannot figure is what the Mechomancers need all of that energy for. What are they working toward?"

"There has been some talk within the bureau of the government continuing to try to find ways to limit the Possibilities," the Skylark says, her voice strange and gravelly. "Prohibition was only the first step. It only outlaws ravelings of a certain complexity, as even the government knew it would be nearly impossible to prohibit the use of the mystical arts in homes and small communities—the sort that typically fall to Negro mages across the country. But that doesn't mean they're not trying to find new ways to do it."

"The limiting of the Possibilities sounds like the sort of program politicians would undertake, yes," Miss Fox says. "But it's my experience the Mechomancers have more concern for their pockets than anything else. So the question is, what kind of mischief are they about to unleash that requires so much power?"

"Air travel," I say. As soon as the words are out of my mouth, I know my instincts are correct. "I read in the paper that Howard Hughes is trying to construct a flying machine, one that can go coast to coast in a matter of minutes, no Wayfaring needed. Maybe they need the power for that."

"That's preposterous. Why replace working the leylines with such a thing?" the Grimalkin says, before starting to groom herself. "Apologies," she says in the middle of licking her paw. "The instinct is strong."

"Don't worry, we'll have your Peregrine build you a new form," Miss Fox says. "It's indecent to leave a person in an animal."

I shoot the older woman a panicked look, but Malik chimes in, half lost in his own misery. "My father said there are Mechomancers who want to do away with the mystical arts entirely," he says, his voice low. "Leave nothing but science and alchemy, what they think are superior disciplines."

"Well, that is the dumbest thing I ever heard," I say. "Anyone can learn to ravel if they work at it."

Malik shrugs. "I didn't say it was a good reason."

"This has always been the problem," Miss Fox says with a heavy sigh. "Breakings of the Possibilities have happened on various scales throughout history, and are always caused by the refusal to let folks in a given area practice the arts as they were meant to be practiced. You don't actually think all this slicing and dicing of the mystical arts is the way it was meant to be, do you? Faunomancy, Floramancy, and such? Those ain't our words. That's the way of the colonizers. They divvied their arts up so much that they were left with nothing but ashes, and when even that started to fail, they combined alchemy and science into Mechomancy, hardly requiring any art at all. But the mystical arts have been around far longer than their machines and constructs. The Possibilities will always balance out, somehow, some way. And when the reaction is powerful enough—"

"You get the Great Rust," the Skylark says.

Miss Fox nods. "Or the Spanish flu. Or the Johnstown floods. Really, this land has been telling folks for a while to get their business in order, and we just keep on legislating nature, as if the Possibilities care what a bunch of men in some building in Washington have to say about them. And if those Necromancers raise this god of theirs, that too isn't going to go how folks think it will. The people living nearest to that birthing will be wiped clean off this planet, same as the low-level Necromancers doing the midwifing. The only people who will profit will be the same ones who always do: those powerful enough to not be anywhere near the damage."

"So how do we even get close enough to the ravel to do anything about it?" Crystal says.

"That is a good question," Miss Fox replies. "The Peregrine used some of the old ways to beam you out of there, but I daresay you won't be able to take that route back to a precise location in Ohio, especially as the Death ravel progresses. We need to figure out how to get you to the source of the ravel to unmake it."

"Do you think a dragon could help?" I say.

There's a long silence as everyone stares at me like I've just sprouted another head.

"I don't like dragons," Louise says, hissing a little. "They're bossy."

"Child, what makes you think a dragon would be any help?" Miss Fox wonders, giving me a look that can only be described as incredulous.

"We can't get anywhere close to the ravel itself, which we were thinking was in the center of the Blight," I say. "The closer we got, the worse the drain on our lives were. Which is also why we can't beam right to the center of the ravel. But we met a well-vern who seemed immune to the effects of the Necromancy. Dragons are pure Life, and even a dragon's dream is Life giving. If we can find a dragon to accompany us to the center of the Blight where the ravel is anchored, maybe I can unravel the whole mess." I clear my throat. "Personally, it seems better than the other option, which, according to the Gnarled Fox's journal, is tying the ravel to me and letting it kill me so the whole mess burns itself out, like he did."

There's a long moment of silence before Malik stands. "This is silly. Where would we even find a full-grown dragon, anyway?" He heads for the door to the room, saying over his shoulder, "I'm going to go check on Sam."

Crystal sighs. "I'll go after him," she begins, but I grab her wrist and pull her back down to the couch.

"No. Leave him be. It's a lot to process, and he just lost his father," I say. I don't know why I'm feeling charitable, but I do get that this is not Malik's sort of conversation. It seems like fairy stories, not the sort of work he and his father seem to think is the point of the bureau. But I've seen too much to not know there is far more to the mystical arts than what we are taught.

Crystal sighs and places a cool hand on my cheek. "I know. That's exactly why he shouldn't be alone. And Sam is far too ill to offer much in the way of comfort."

I watch her go, and something like admiration burbles up in my middle. It's clear that she is upset over Onyx being gone, but even now she thinks about others. Crystal is a stronger person than I thought.

"He might be a bit salty, but he's got a point," Miss Fox says. "Where are you going to find a dragon willing to help?"

"Well, I know a place," the Grimalkin says. "How do all of you feel about a trip to Tennessee?"

I wanted to include a few more pictures, but Miss Fox was quick to snatch up my Brownie camera for her own amusement. So you'll just have to accept my words from here on out.

THIRTY-THREE

I brace my hands on my knees and retch into the tall grass at the edge of Norris Lake while everyone else pretends not to watch. My second time using the Gnarled Fox's Wayfaring ravel actually went better than expected, despite all the heaving. I didn't lose consciousness, at least.

After the Grimalkin announced that she knew where to find a dragon, we didn't waste any time. Every moment the Necromancers' ravel in Ohio exists gets us closer to a point of no return. The Gnarled Fox died preventing the previous ravel. I can't really complain about a little puking.

But I do wish we had time to rest up. I feel awful.

"Here," Crystal says, handing me a canteen to drink from. Louise hovers nearby, making sounds somewhere between a mew and a growl. The Skylark and the Grimalkin round out our group. Malik and Sam had decided to remain behind when Miss Fox told Sam that it would be dangerous to venture back into a Blight with the affliction he'd taken on, and I'm not sad Malik decided to stay with him. The last thing I need right now are his sidelong glances whenever I say something. But mostly I'm happy he and Sam have each other.

Not too far away, the Skylark seems to be trying to remember how to walk as she picks her way toward the water. I watch her, trying to resist looking for the edges of the ravel in Miss Fox's construct. I tried to speak with my mentor before we left, to ask her what had happened to her, if she feels like herself. She had simply asked me to give her some time to sort herself out. For now, I have to be satisfied with what Louise told me: Miss Fox saved the Skylark's life, giving her the option to be placed under a geas and continuing her career or passing on. Perhaps once this is all over the Skylark will tell me the full story—about Tennessee, how she died, and her life after.

I'm not surprised she decided to continue living, even if it meant leading an indentured life. I would've chosen the same thing.

"Are you quite done?" the Grimalkin says, leaping onto my shoulder and digging her claws in to steady herself. She rubs her face against mine, and I sigh. There wasn't time to build the Grimalkin a proper body, but she doesn't seem to mind.

"Look, I'm new at this. Gimme a break," I say, handing the canteen back to Crystal with a grateful smile. She takes it quietly, and I make a note to find time to speak with her as well. She's just had a blow, learning that her teacher is gone forever, passed on. Or perhaps worse, his life and soul tangled up in the weaving of a catastrophic working. Either way, Crystal is doing admirably, and I'm not sure I would be so collected if our positions were reversed. I'm just glad she came along, especially after the boys decided to stay behind at Miss Fox's. I'm going to need all the help I can get. I'm barely keeping it together as it is.

"You'll have to get closer to call the dragon," the Grimalkin says as I start to walk toward the water's edge.

"Right. Remind me again why I need to be the one to do this?"

"Because you're the only one around with any real Faunomantic aptitude," she says. "The Skylark can't sustain a conversation for the necessary amount of time, and I am a cat. I don't have full access to my abilities in this form. Now put your feet in the water. It'll make it easier for them to hear you, and you them."

"Okay, okay." I take a deep breath and let it out. As excited as I was to get to speak to a real-life dragon, now that I'm here about to do it, I'm anxious something awful. I look down at my hastily laced, ill-fitting boots, a parting gift from Miss Fox. I lean down to pull them off, and as I do, the Grimalkin hisses and runs along my back, each step agony.

"Ow, dammit! Watch the claws," I snap.

"Sorry," the Grimalkin replies perfunctorily, and begins to groom herself. "You were getting really close to the water, and I really don't want to get my paws wet. The instinct is strong."

"You keep saying that," I say, ditching the loaner boots and my bandolier and standing barefoot in the grass. The lake before me is manmade and new, created a few years ago by FDR and his Tennessee Valley Authority. This was where the Skylark ran afoul of a Necromancer long ago, and where the Grimalkin remembers the dragon settling in. Dragons like to bury themselves when they take their rest, which can last for decades, and so it makes sense that there should be some dragons in this area.

I'm just hoping they aren't upset at having their rest disturbed.

The water is deeper than I'm expecting. My first step finds me sinking up to my ankles in soft mud, and in two more steps I'm midthigh deep in the water, the dress Miss Fox lent me—a horrible flower-patterned thing that is only marginally better than the nightgown I had on before—gathered up to stay dry. But I don't have much time to consider the picture I present back to the folks on the shore, because stepping into the water is like walking into the middle of a party.

There is so much life in the lake, it's overwhelming. Small fry in the shallows holler warnings to one another, while the far-off sounds of fish in the deeper waters filter back to me in ripples and bubbles. I've never had much reason to talk to fish, but this is beyond any Faunomancy I've ever experienced.

"Now just call the dragon," the Grimalkin offers helpfully from the shoreline.

I clear my throat. "Hey!" I say, scattering a few of the closer fish with my shout. "I'm looking for a dragon. Are there any out there?"

It's stupid to hope it would be that easy, but something slips through my legs, causing me to yelp and jump a little, losing my balance and falling into the water. I sputter, and as I try to regain my footing, there is a liquid voice in my mind.

The dragon sleeps. She is old and does not like visitors. We will not disturb her.

"Is there one who maybe isn't sleeping?" I ask as a water snake pokes its head up just above the surface. I really hope it's not one of those snakes who easily take offense. Or are venomous. Preferably neither. I do not have time to worry about a snakebite.

Young ones, yes, but they only look for mischief and nonsense, the snake responds. *One ate my cousin.*

"I'm very sorry for your loss," I say, inclining my head in respect. "Would you be willing to find one of these younger dragons for me? I am happy to ravel you something in return," I say.

What do you want a dragon for?

"I'm going to stop a death god from waking in Ohio and destroying the continent," I say.

A dangerous adventure? Death more than likely? Lovely. One less cousin eater. Don't go anywhere.

The water snake swims off, and I take the moment to collect myself. I don't look like a great mage is supposed to look, or even a person who has the potential to be a great mage. I look like a girl in ill-fitting clothes who's just gotten dunked in a lake. I don't care how young this dragon is; I can't imagine they'll be impressed.

I smooth my hair the best I can and from behind me comes a shout. "Peregrine! How's it going?" Crystal asks.

I turn around to flash a thumbs-up when a wave hits me mid-chest and sends me back into the water, sputtering and swearing.

When I stand up this time, before me is an honest-to-goodness dragon.

I blink, my scattered thoughts landing somewhere between awe and bone-numbing fear. The dragon's snout is inches from my nose, and it takes my brain a long moment to piece together its face. The thing is a muddy brown, with leathery skin and pointed teeth, the most prominent ones the length of my forearm. The head overall is the size of a coffee table, and I have no doubt that the dragon could very easily devour me if he should so choose.

Human! The snake tells me you're going on an adventure? I want to go on an adventure! I want to eat a human; do you think I'll get the chance to eat a human? Or if not a human, maybe a unicorn. I've never eaten a unicorn before.

"I am sure we could find you a human to eat, if you'd like," I say.

What about those ones back there?

I turn around to see that Crystal and the Skylark have very wisely backed away. Louise stands on the shore with her hands on her hips. "You will not eat us or my Fox," she yells, the sound half snarl.

"Those are my companions, and it's bad form to eat one's companions on an adventure," I explain, my voice somehow calm despite my fear. "But there are some Necromancers raising a god, and I daresay they'd be ripe for eating."

Yay!

One day this will be a very funny story. For now I'm just glad that I've managed to hold on to my bladder. "So, you'll come with us?" I ask.

Yes! I just have to ask my mom.

"What?" I say, but the dragon is already gone, ducking back under the water in such a quick, quiet manner that I realize he could've eaten us all before we even knew such a thing was happening. Once again, I have serious concerns that this is maybe a really bad idea.

"Where'd it go?" Crystal calls from the shore, as I trudge out of the lake.

"It . . . went to go ask its mother if it can come with us," I say, wringing out my dress the best I can.

"Are you serious?" she says.

The Grimalkin sits down and yawns widely. "Of course she's serious. That's a baby."

"Is it up to this?" the Skylark asks.

"I hope so," I say. "If nothing else, it seems excited to eat some Necromancers."

The dragon resurfaces, bursting out of the water, front legs and talons pumping in the air. The movement causes a huge wave to wash up on the shore, soaking everyone except for the Grimalkin, who leaps deftly onto the Skylark's head.

I can go! Let's go eat some humans.

I'm not sure whether this is the best idea I've ever had, or the worst.

If only Pigeon could see me now.

The waters of the lake in Tennessee are cool and blue, but they are nothing compared with the actual sight of a real live dragon. I really wish I had my camera.

THIRTY-FOUR

We take a moment to eat and recharge before setting out for Ohio. It seems like a bad idea to go running right back into the ravel, and everyone else agrees. So we build a small fire to warm ourselves and take a brief moment of respite before charging once more into the breach.

Dragon, as it's implied we should call it, is kind enough to bring back a passel of fish for us to eat, and we figure that the sight of the massive creature is probably enough to keep any threats in the area at bay. The Grimalkin and Louise eat their fish raw; the rest of us roast ours over the open fire, Dragon watching us eat in fascination.

I've never been this close to a human that I haven't eaten, it says. It keeps showing us its teeth, but I think that's just its version of smiling.

"And that is why I avoid dragons," the Skylark says, finally sounding a bit like her old self. The Grimalkin and I take turns translating for Crystal, since Dragon can understand everyone perfectly. Louise seems to be similarly gifted, being able to speak to everyone, human or animal. Though she still seems exceedingly wary around Dragon.

As we talk, the Skylark seems distracted; she keeps tilting her head, as though listening to some faint sound, far off. As for Crystal, she has hardly been her usual chatty self since we left Miss Fox's house, and by the time we have devoured the mountain of fish Dragon brought us, bellies stuffed almost obscenely, I cannot bear to ignore it any longer.

"Do you want to take a walk?" I ask.

Crystal's head snaps up in surprise. But she smiles. "Yes. Thank you," she says, standing. "I'd like that."

"How are you holding up?" I ask once we are out of earshot of the rest of the group. "I'm truly sorry about Onyx, and I wish you had more time to grieve."

"No, this is important," Crystal says. "We have to unravel that spell before more people die. I'll have time to grieve after that."

So much of the sparkle that makes her who she is has been dimmed, and it's painful to see. I realize that I like her more than I thought. Seeing her this way makes me wish there was some way to bring back Onyx, but everyone knows that there is no reviving a person once they have crossed the impermeable threshold between life and death.

"Do you want me to see if I can summon his ghost?" I ask tentatively. I'm not sure if it's a sensitive offer or not; the etiquette of Necromancy is still new to me. "I've done it once, and I think maybe I could do it again. That way you can at least say a proper goodbye."

She shakes her head. "No, but thank you."

"Why don't you tell me about him?" I say. "Sometimes . . . in my family we talk about those who have gone on as a way to remember why we loved them."

"Honestly, I didn't like him very much," she says with a hollow laugh. "He was dismissive and rude, and sometimes he was downright cruel."

"I . . . oh." I'm unsure of how to respond to that.

"But he taught me that I could maybe do some good with this," Crystal says, stopping to hold her hand out over the ground. A narrow quartz pillar rises up, faster and more steadily than anything I saw her do in the Blight. "I'm not grieving Onyx so much as I am the fact that none of that was real. They're never going to just let us live and ravel, are they, Peregrine? Necromancers, the Mechomancers who use their power, the government that seems built to protect it all . . . it's always been nothing more than a new way for those white folks to use us in the same old ways. The bureau was never interested in protecting the mystical arts. They just wanted to enslave us with a different kind of collar."

I have nothing to say to that, because she's right. Every single dream I've had has died in the past few days. I have no doubt that Miss Fox is smarter and better at the mystical arts than whatever suit is running things in Washington, D.C.—it strikes me that the most I can hope for as a Fox is to ravel in the shadows, quiet and unknown. Becoming a great mage doesn't lead to freedom. Just more responsibility, and even less credit.

"I think that's why we fight," I say. "To change that. The Foxes have protected us, making things better little by little, for a long time. I think that's the goal. Not to try and fix everything in one fell swoop, but to keep striving until it's what it could, and should, be." I shrug.

"You sound like Miss Fox," Crystal says, considering me. "It's a big deal to be chosen as a Fox, you know."

"What do you know about Foxes?"

Crystal shrugs. "It's an old story my grandma used to tell, and one that her grandma told her. She said that before the Necromancers and Mechomancers found their way to the Afrikan continent, it was a land full of tribes. Each tribe had a group of gods they worshipped, but the most powerful tribes prayed to the five: Brother Lion, Brother Ant, Sister Bird, Sister Hyena, and the Fox."

The animals are familiar, because they're part of the Wayfaring ravel I learned from the Gnarled Fox. Things are beginning to make sense.

"Wait, just 'the Fox'?" I say, and Crystal gives me a slow nod.

"The Fox wasn't like the others. They were all constant in their temperaments, but Fox was tricksy and mercurial, and was always the champion of the underdog, no matter who it was. If Ant and Bird were fighting, Fox would take Ant's side. If Bird and Lion were fighting, Fox would take Bird's side. Fox was the element that kept the others together."

Uniting the various disciplines, I think. "So what happened?"

"What do you think? The Europeans came, deemed anyone who worshipped the five to be savage and heretical, and talked the tribes that didn't worship the five into warring with their neighbors who did. Our ancestors were brought here in boats, stripped of their abilities, and enslaved. My grandma said that the way we split and divide the mystical arts even now is unnatural, and just more of those old Necromancers and Mechomancers trying to limit our abilities.

"But I heard what the old woman said back there," she continues. "She said you were a Fox, and Peregrine, if that's true, well . . . After our people were brought to this continent it was the Foxes who ran off, who organized the Afrikan Uprisings, who swore to keep our kin safe always, even if they could only do it from the shadows."

"I just . . . don't want to mess this up." I think about Pigeon and the way she always scolded me for the things I did, how I felt like I couldn't ever do anything right. And I think about how I ended up joining the Colored Auxiliary not because I wanted to help anyone, but because I wanted a license.

"You won't mess up," Crystal says. "Of all of us, you were the only one who managed to keep things together."

"Well, I had help. And not just yours," I say, pulling the Necromancer's vessel from the pocket of my bandolier. The Gnarled Fox's journal stated how the souls need to be cleansed, so even though the Skylark told me I should release these souls once I was out of the Blight, I'm still holding on to them. Once this is all done, I will give them a proper send-off.

But for now, the jar is just a reminder of how low some will stoop in the name of progress.

Crystal pats me on the shoulder. "I believe you have everything you need, Peregrine. Now let's go stomp those Necromancers."

We wander back to the rest of the group, but halfway there we are met by the Skylark. She gives us both a nervous smile.

"Hello, girls. Peregrine, can I have a word with you?"

There are some gaps in my memory between the time we entered the Blight and when we were able to unravel the working being done there.

Unfortunately, I have been unable to recover those memories, even with the help of a licensed seer.

Chapter
THIRTY-FIVE

The Skylark is having trouble with her new body.

The first time she really felt it was when she saw Peregrine for the first time, healthy and safe and alive, and her heart did an uncomfortable double beat. The Fox just cackled and hit her on the back. "Emotions are sometimes the last thing to settle in, so try not to get too agitated," the old woman said. But the Skylark didn't know how she was supposed to remain calm when Necromancers were summoning a dead god on the backs of colored folks.

And now, standing alone with the Peregrine, she feels more than a little nervous. Had it been this hard adjusting to a new form the first time the Fox saved her? She didn't think so.

"You have questions," the Skylark says, her voice strange even to her own ears.

"Yeah, a lot," the girl says. "First, do you ask the Fox to spring-load that old eyebrow of yours whenever she ravels you a body? I've been wondering."

The Skylark laughs, and she feels better immediately. "I'm

sorry I didn't tell you about my past."

"Aww, I'm not sore about it. We've known each other less than a week, not exactly enough time to go sharing stories of highly illegal ravels," the girl says with a grin.

"True. Do you have any questions for me? I do think it's best if we clear the air before heading back into the Blight." There was an element of trust that was vital in operations such as this, and the Skylark would not be the obstacle that undermined the difficult job that lay before the girl.

The Peregrine is quiet for a long moment, staring out toward the lake. Then she turns to the Skylark. "Was it worth it?" she asks, voice low.

"Was what worth it?" the Skylark asks.

"Dying. You died twice now for the bureau, near as I can figure it. Once in Tennessee, and again just a few days ago. So, was it worth it?"

The Skylark ponders the girl's words. "It was. But I didn't die for the bureau," the Skylark says with a sad smile. "I died for you. And Crystal. And me, to be honest. I have given my life for the possibility that Negroes can be more than what they allow us to be, that somehow, with the place I've carved out in the bureau, I can push boundaries and widen the bubble we're allowed to exist within."

The Peregrine nods. "I can see that."

"I never wanted to hire you, you know," she begins, throat clogging with emotion. Ah, there they come, at the worst possible time. She swallows the regret away. "When you came in spouting that Mechomancer nonsense, it was easy to turn you away. I only came to find you at the precinct because my boss required that I find an apprentice before setting out for Ohio. If I'd known for sure that . . . Well, I'm truly sorry I pulled you into this mess. I've gone through this before, and as you know too well, it cost me my life. I don't want that for you."

"I don't think it's up to us," the Peregrine says, her expression pensive. "I think we can either take up the mantle or not, but the fight is still there. I would've ended up wrapped up with the Foxes somehow, I'm certain. The Possibilities always try to even themselves out."

"Perhaps. But I'm not finished. More than anything, I'm sorry I didn't trust you enough to have an honest conversation about Craft, and how to balance that with the expectations of the bureau. I've always thought I could change things from the inside, but now I wonder if trying to do that all by myself was the problem. There are allies within the bureau, people who think more like me and less like the others. I should've reached out to them long before I met you, and I should have told you exactly the kind of organization you were joining up with. Not one that would allow you to flourish, but one that would limit you so that you could be a better tool."

The Peregrine laughs and ducks her head. "I'm not sure it would've mattered, to be honest," she says. "Isn't that what the whole world does to us anyway? Tries to put us in the box that suits them? Nah, that wouldn't have mattered. But I am glad that you finally understand that it takes a whole lot of folks to steer the ship, so to speak. You can't go it alone. We need each other. Because we are stronger together."

How did the silly country girl the Skylark met less than a week ago turn into this young woman? A sudden exhaustion washes over her in that moment, and she stumbles, but the Peregrine is there to catch her.

"Let's get back to the others," the girl says. "We've got to head out soon, and it seems like you need to rest before we do."

"What's the plan?" the Skylark asks, leaning heavily on the Peregrine. The girl is stronger than she looks.

"What's ever the plan?" the Peregrine says, expression hard. "We're going to do what we always do: clean up someone else's mess."

I'm not sure what else to say at this point. If we make it, I suppose everyone will know. And if we don't, well, I suppose we won't be around to care.

THIRTY-SIX

When I implied to the Skylark that we were just going to stride right in and take out the Necromancers, I was bluffing, blustering, trying to build myself up. The truth is, I'm terrified to return to Ohio. But when I return to where the rest of the group waits, I realize that's the best plan we have.

"There's no way around it," the Grimalkin says, sunning herself in a patch of grass. "It's not as if stealth is an option. They're going to know the exact moment we enter the ravel. After all, we have a dragon with us."

"How are we going to get the, uh, beast to Ohio in the first place?" Crystal asks.

"Can you fly to Ohio?" I ask Dragon.

I'm not old enough to grow wings, he says. *But I can travel with you*.

I start to explain how that won't work—there's a limit to how many people I can beam with my old-timey ravel—but then Dragon begins to sort of fold into itself, a very nauseating manipulation of space, so that by the time it is finished it is no bigger than my palm. I place my hand out and it scrambles onto it, climbing up my arm and nuzzling into the side of my neck.

You smell good.

"Please do not eat me; that would be rude, and I do not think your mother would like that," I say.

"If it eats you, I will eat it," Louise growls.

"Did anyone know dragons can do that?" Crystal asks, visibly distressed.

"There's a reason their kind have survived so long in a country full of humans while so many others haven't," the Grimalkin says.

"Our goal should be to find the Deathstruck tree," I say. "According to the Gnarled Fox's journal, it was the anchor point for the ravel."

The Skylark frowns. "What is that?"

"I'm not sure," I say. "It's a tree full of some kind of strange fruit, with people inside?"

This sounds like a grand adventure, Dragon says. *I like fruit.*

"I saw something like that in Tennessee," the Skylark says. Her gaze goes distant. "The hearts the Necromancer pulled from us were placed on a misshapen tree like bloody decorations. If it's anything like what I saw before, we won't be able to miss it."

"Well, I guess that's something," Crystal says, some of her usual brightness returning. "Should we get going?"

"Yes. The sooner we handle this the better," the Skylark says. She seems just like her old self, her form fully integrated once more. Looking at her reminds me that I have a lot to learn. I hope I survive Ohio so that I have the chance.

Ugh, I am far too maudlin today.

"Right," I say, walking over to the dirt area I cleared before we ate. I sketch out the Wayfaring path again. It comes easier now that I've done it twice before. The rest of the old Gnarled Fox's ravels are in a grimoire, safe and sound back at Miss Fox's house, held there for when I return. And if I don't, she at least has the contents of the journal, so she can find some other Fox to take over the responsibilities in Ohio and Pennsylvania, the territories the Gnarled Fox covered long ago.

Once I'm finished, I step into the center circle, the one with the fox. Everyone else picks a circle, and once we're ready I take the loaner boots I wear off so that I can feel the leylines running beneath my feet. I reach out to feel the stars and where they touch the Possibilities. Once everything is ready, I send everyone along their assigned path, waiting until I feel them arrive in Ohio before I open my own gate and slip out of existence. The times before I made the mistake of trying to send and travel at the same time, which seems to have been too much. This time, I arrive to the well-vern's house without any nausea or lost consciousness, which is a vast improvement over my previous attempts.

Everyone is waiting for me when I arrive, and I very quickly pull my boots on as I take in the ruined landscape once more. The world is still cast in shades of gray, but with Dragon on my shoulder I don't feel so bad. In fact, it feels almost normal, and everyone's looks of relief at my appearance make me think they were a bit worried they'd be left to deal with the space on their own.

"Baldur approaches," Louise says, her voice a nearly feline hiss. "I can *feel* him."

"Which way?" the Skylark asks.

Louise sniffs and points up the road. "That way."

···

After the arduous journey we endured the last time around, I'm expecting something similar as we set out. But the truth is the walk is surprisingly uneventful.

That doesn't mean we aren't careful.

No one says much as we go, but it's clear something has changed since Crystal, Sam, Malik, and I found our way out. The houses on either side of the road, even those that were occupied only a few days ago, are abandoned. There's not a single soul around as we walk down the road, and the land is as quiet as a tomb. Even the house with the little boy and his father appears now to be empty, the door hanging off the hinges.

"Where do you think everyone went?" Crystal asks softly.

"Dead," the Grimalkin says, blunt as ever.

Louise shifts into her puma form and darts off into the trees that line the side of the road. The closer we get to the center of the ravel, the more nervous she gets, hissing and muttering to herself as she shifts back and then again. She's gotten the scent of something, and I'm just about to ask her what is amiss when we round a bend in the path between the trees and freeze.

"That is worse that I was expecting," the Skylark breathes beside me. "Far bigger than Tennessee."

Before us, towering amid low hills a mile away, is a giant tree. It's larger than any I have ever seen, taller than an oak or a maple, massive like a Mechomancer's skyscraper. The branches twist and split like an oak tree, but there are no leaves, just hundreds of ruby-red sacs that hang heavily from the branches, pulsing and quivering. As we watch, one of the sacs falls, like an overripe fruit gone to rot. Bile burns the back of my throat, and I have to fight to keep my breakfast down.

"Bad place, bad people," Louise says.

"I'm guessing we've found the Deathstruck tree?" the Grimalkin says, leaping once more onto the Skylark's shoulder to avoid walking in the dirt.

My skin begins to tingle, and I realize that this is the center of the ravel. I can feel the energy weaving around me, obvious now that I've left and returned, and the stink of this white brand of Necromancy sours my stomach. Rotting flowers and rancid flesh. Whatever is being worked here is heresy of the highest order.

Prohibition was aimed at keeping folks from abusing the mystical arts. How did the bureau let a ravel like this reach this point? I guess the answer is because they were too busy busting bootlegging mages in small towns to notice. Or, perhaps, there's a darker explanation. . . .

My thoughts are interrupted by a whiff of burning sugar coming from the path beside us. I pull my eyes away from the Deathstruck tree at the same time that I reach inside my bandolier for a walnut, one of many I carry thanks to the generosity of Miss Fox. I roll it along the ground, right toward a normal-looking tree beside us. "Dragon, get ready," I say, low enough that only it can hear, although I notice the Grimalkin's ears twist toward me as well.

And that is when all hell breaks loose.

A nearby tree reveals itself, branches shifted into tentacles, and as it lurches toward us, Dragon reveals its true form, and I ravel the walnut.

The tree is fast, but my ravel is faster, and it catches the tree before it can grab anyone, the walnut warrior holding the thing fast. It writhes in the arms of my ten-foot construct. It reveals its face and roars at us, its mouth full of razor-sharp teeth. It's a lumpen, misshapen thing, like it was created by someone who didn't really know what a face should look like. Tentacles dance around the mouth opening, and the cavernous eyes lock onto us with an inhuman glare.

Monster, Dragon says, hissing.

"Cthulhu spawn," Louise corrects him, spitting as she speaks. "Peregrine, how did you know that was going to happen?"

"I could sense the Illusion," I say. "Dragon, do you want to eat it?"

No, that thing is dead, it says.

I sigh. "I figured you were going to say that." I can sense the ravel of the thing now that my mind isn't clouded by its Illusions, and it's just a matter of tugging on a loose end of the foul Necromancy at work. A dense gray smoke begins to surround the tentacle beast. The creature lets forth another roar as it is unmade, dissolving into a distressing gurgle.

There is a moment of sadness once the thing is reduced to a puddle of goo. Perhaps I'm feeling the souls of those whose lives were lost to raise the thing.

"Abomination," Louise hisses, shifting back into her girl form.

"Agreed." The Grimalkin is all puffed up, tail high and large.

I look down at the puddle that had been the tentacle creature. But I don't have long to ponder the Necromancer's ravel before what sounds like a herd of elephants comes thundering toward us. This was apparently just a scout.

"Get ready," the Skylark says, palming a few walnuts. Crystal kicks off her shoes, so that her bare feet press into the dusty road while Louise shifts once more, this time into a nightmare-inducing form: a golden hunting cat the size of a wagon with vicious fangs and wickedly curved claws, quill-like spikes rising along her spine.

"That is definitely not a puma," Crystal mutters to me, and I snort.

But then there is no time for speech as more of the weird, rotting tentacle monsters descend upon us from the nearby woods, not bothering with any kind of subterfuge.

Dragon and Louise roar before charging into the fray, tearing apart the Necromantic constructs while the Skylark and I ravel a battalion of okra-seed and walnut soldiers. Crystal makes a lifting motion with her hand, and similar rock-shaped constructs appear from the ground, the golems joining the fray with ferocity.

The Necromancer constructs are a hodgepodge of strange creatures: some of them are like the cancerous dog we saw the first day, while others are closer to the thing I fought near the field where Nell died. Large chunks of flesh slough off of them as they move, as though the things find it difficult to hold their form. This is what Necromancy looks like when it's turned to nefarious purposes: a sickening mockery of the constructs that the rest of us have raveled so beautifully.

For a moment it seems that we'll defeat them easily, but then I realize that no matter how much we tear them apart, they rebuild themselves just as quickly, cannibalizing each other and everything around them in order to continue fighting.

This isn't working.

I charge into the fray, my attention on the Necromancy that threads through the constructs. A few of my walnut warriors surround me like a vanguard as I push through the melee, keeping the worst of the Necromantic constructs at bay. Behind me there's yelling, but I ignore it as I begin to unravel the Necromancy.

It isn't easy. This thing in front of me feels nothing like the energy in the soul jar, or the form Miss Fox raveled for the Skylark with her own Necromancy. This power is corrupted and foul, like a long-dead fish washed up on the shore of a lake, putrid and bloated with wrongness. I ignore the ickiness of it and begin to pull at the ravel until I find the edge. It isn't refined or impressive—it's the mage's equivalent of hacking at a body with a hatchet—but it works. The Cthulhu spawn, as Louise called them, begin to fall apart into little more than piles of foul-smelling, fleshy goo.

Once the last creature has fallen, I turn back to my companions, but they watch me in stunned silence. I blink. "What?"

"I felt that," the Skylark says. "Whatever it was you just did."

"Me too," Crystal says.

"I . . . how did it feel?" I ask, afraid of the answer.

"Like a breath of fresh air," Crystal says with a grin. "Like clearing out the old and ushering in the new. Like you fixed the Possibilities."

"Perhaps this is what the mystical arts were truly meant to be," the Skylark says with wonder. "Reparative."

"That's what a Fox does," Louise says, although I have no idea how she can talk in her current form, her massive teeth terrifying. "They fix things. Even the Possibilities."

"Well, I do think everything is better after a little spring-cleaning," I say.

Crystal nods. "Then let's go take care of that blasted tree. And these Necromancers."

Dragon roars approval, and I cannot help but agree.

And so we turn toward the tree looming in the distance and break out into a run.

Chapter
THIRTY-SEVEN

The closer we get to the tree, the worse the smell. It's not just the stink of the Necromancy, but the fruit itself. It moves in some unfelt breeze, the waves of stink assaulting us. Rotting fruit and spoiled meat, excrement and blood. It is every foul thing wrapped up and tied with a bow, a gift no one wants. Except, perhaps, a Death god.

The sun is still watery and weak, even with Dragon at our side. We've been keeping to the road as it winds through the hills toward the base of the tree. We figure that the road would be safer than cutting through the woods, which seem likely to be laced with more creatures, and possibly traps like the flowers that devoured Nell. So it isn't until we round a curve between the last of the hills that we're able to see the base of the tree, and once we do, we slow to a stop. It's not the tree that has our attention any longer, but the buzz of activity around it.

In my mind, I imagined the ravel to be done by a small group of rogue Necromancers working for their own nefarious purposes. But the number of people at the base of the tree paints a much bleaker truth. Dozens of people and Mechomancer constructs move with purpose around the clearing, a few of the Necromancers in the unmistakable garb of the Ku Klux Klan, but far more wearing the business suits and laboratory garb favored by Mechomancers. And nearby, unmistakable in its shape, is a Resonator, though far larger than any of the images I'd seen in the papers.

"Well, I guess the bureau's Mechomancy Division finally found a solution for the Blights," the Grimalkin says darkly.

"Wait, so the Resonator didn't fail?" I ask, but the chug of smoke and blinking electric lights on it answer my question for me. Cables and tubing emanating from the thing surround the tree, wrapping around the massive roots, arranged on a scaffolding of steel girders; it's hard to see where the Resonator ends and the Deathstruck tree begins, and the whole thing stinks of burning Death.

"Oh, it did," says a voice nearby. "But we decided to build it back better."

Suddenly, the road beneath us is pudding, rising to meet us and quickly swallowing me up to my chest. Before I can ravel a single walnut warrior, I am encased in mud that quickly hardens into rock, and next to me, Crystal, the Skylark, Louise, and even Dragon are similarly ensnared. It is only the Grimalkin who retains her freedom, leaping into the air and running off to disappear among the trees that line the road.

Standing before us, wearing his bejeweled Bureau of the Arcane robe, is Onyx. His kinky curly hair has been slicked down and his spectacles are gone, and the smile he turns on us seems friendly.

But there is something off about his eyes.

"I didn't think you'd be so foolish as to return," he says. "But I am glad you did. The ravel is coming up a little short, but between you and the dragon, we should have the tappable energy we need be push this past the finish line. So to speak."

"You're working with them," I say, because everyone else has been stunned to silence. Crystal glares daggers at her former mentor, her expression murderous. The Skylark looks less surprised, but I suppose that's because she always knew what kind of man Onyx was. I thought he was a pill, but I didn't think he was a traitor.

"Of course I'm working with them," he says, coolly gesturing toward the collected mass of people. Looking even closer, I see more than a few mages in bureau robes among them. "Did you really think a ravel this massive could be done by a handful of Klansmen? I told you the night we met that Mechomancy is the future, and that our job as mages is to embrace change instead of railing against it with acorns and what have you." He sighs. "You think I'm the villain here, but I'm not. Things change, progress marches on, and there's no sense clinging to a world that never was."

"And yet, the Mechomancers still have you working as the help," the Skylark says.

Onyx laughs mirthlessly. "What do you care? You aren't even *human*. And you only have yourself to blame for this predicament you're in. If you would've just listened to me and marched on to Mercersburg like I suggested, you would've just slowly fallen asleep and then been consumed by the ravel. Instead, you wanted to hunker down in that old hedge witch's house, calling for help and trying to find a way to undo everything happening here. Ridiculous."

"You lied. About the Hawk," the Skylark says.

"Yes," Onyx says. "The Hawk, like most of our leaders, is a fool. An easily manipulated one at that. He actually thinks that the mystical arts are worth saving. Case in point, he had no idea what was happening here. I had to convince him to let me tag along on your mission; he'd wanted to send Rose Quartz from the Detroit office. As if that woman has the ability to outravel me."

"You wrecked the runes," Crystal says. A tear rolls down her cheek. I cannot imagine the kind of betrayal she must be feeling right now, but I bet she'd like nothing more than to send one of her stone soldiers after him. "You were going to let us all die, and for what? A few Mechomantic constructs?"

"Is that what you think this is all for?" he says, looking at us as though we're the ones who are being unreasonable. "This is going to repair every single Blight on the *continent*. This ravel is going to summon a rising and dying god to power the largest Resonator ever created—an endless source of energy, one that can power Mechomantic constructs indefinitely. No more of this disgusting Necromancy business—as much power as there is to draw from their rituals, I must admit, it is unsavory. Not to mention inconvenient—expendable souls are getting harder and harder to come by. No, this is the future. And I will be right in the middle of it. No one cares where their Mechomancy comes from, not truly—they just care that it works. We're going to be heroes, and you lot will be nothing but a footnote. As for the lower arts, well, the sooner the Negro realizes that we will never find ourselves on the path to acceptance by white society until we give up the old ways, the better. And that begins with this." He gives us a rueful smile. "Ah, my friends, I only wish we could have had this heart-to-heart under better circumstances."

I want to believe that Onyx is insane, but I don't think he is. He truly believes that our deaths are the price to be paid for progress in America, and he has made his peace with that. Horror and rage steal my words, and I am rendered speechless. He is more of a monster than the Necromantic constructs I just destroyed.

Dragon makes a noise somewhere between a squeal and a roar and flails a bit against the hardened earth that holds us fast. *He talks too much. Can I eat him?*

"Yes," I say. "Be my guest."

Dragon lunges forward, roaring, but Onyx's stone prison holds. Louise begins to struggle as well, but neither are any match for Onyx's ravel.

"This is pathetic," the man says, sighing sadly. "Luckily, you won't have long to wait."

In the distance a cloud of dirt rises as riders approach. A group of men on horses, or what appear to be horses, bears down on us. They wear the pointed white hoods of their ilk.

The Necromancers are coming.

But before they arrive, a scream splits the air, and the Grimalkin leaps onto Onyx's face. She is all rage and fur, and he howls in pain as she claws at him.

It's only a moment, but the earthen restraints loosen with his distraction. I pull out a handful of bits while Dragon and Louise explode toward Onyx just as he throws the Grimalkin to the side. I don't have a chance to even toss a ravel before Onyx recovers, and for a moment panic zings through me and the dirt begins to crawl up my legs once more.

But then there is a moment of stillness as everyone freezes. Onyx stands in the middle of the road, a pillar spearing him through the center of his being. The tip of the spear explodes out of the top of his head, and a river of blood flows from the corner of his mouth, eyes rolling back in his skull.

Crystal stands in the middle of the road, hand outstretched, angry tears streaming down her cheeks. I turn to her, slowly. Every line of her body is tense, and I'm half-afraid she might spear me next if I startle her. "Crystal."

"I'm not sorry," she says, angry tears streaming down her face. "He would've watched us die and blamed us for it. *I'm not sorry.*"

"I know," I say, my voice soft. "But we have bigger issues approaching."

The Klansmen are nearly upon us, but they're in for a surprise. The horses the men ride rear up as Dragon surges toward them, scattering the beasts and moving so incredibly fast that I have to thank the Possibilities that Dragon is on our side.

"This is your chance," the Grimalkin says, jumping on my shoulder. "Find the edges of the ravel. We'll hold them off."

I look toward Crystal, and she scrubs her hand across her face. "Go. We've got this."

And they do. There are about twenty men, and they aren't

much match for any of us. Louise rips a Necromancer's throat out, the blood painting the white sheets the man wears in garish scarlet. The Skylark has an army of walnut and okra soldiers surrounding her, and they rush into the melee as well, tearing into the hooded men.

I move off, looking for a particularly strong thread of power. When I find it, I follow it toward the tree, feeling the way the death surges along the line. I still don't like this corrupted kind of Necromancy, and the ravel feels slippery and slimy like Mechomancy when I reach for it, but I appreciate being able to sense it.

I'm chasing the ravel down and through the roots of the massive tree when I hear a sound like crying. I look up and realize that the fetid hanging fruit contain people. A colored man looks down at me through the nearest one, the fleshy wall translucent enough to see through. His eyes are overly large in his face, and his skin is sallow. But even so, I recognize him.

It's Smoke. But he doesn't look like he's going to make it.

I glance around; most of the people dangling from the tree are colored, and I realize these must be the missing Chicago teams who were sent in before us.

What happens to all these people if I undo the Necromancer's ravel? I can't know, but I have a feeling in my gut that it's nothing good.

"Go ahead. Finish what you started," says a voice from behind me. It's a very pretty white woman with blond hair who looks more like a starlet than a member of the Klan. Her hood is pushed back so that her face is clear.

Rage steels me, and I grab a handful of walnuts and hurl them at her. Her eyes widen in surprise before a sharp smile spreads across her face. She lifts her hand, and the stink of decay and rot wafts toward me. Back where my companions still fight, I watch the bodies of dead Klansmen and that of Onyx begin to twitch and dissolve. The Necromancer uses no bits, her workings powered by what remains of the corpses, the energy a shadowy, sickly pull. In the space between her and me appear more of the shape-shifting tentacle creatures, and I pull a few more bits from my bandolier and ravel. And then her creatures are crashing into mine, each of them tearing into each other violently. I toss walnut after walnut at her, and a few okra seeds besides, and she raises dead thing after dead thing to attack.

"Your effort is wasted," she says with a smile. "The ravel is almost complete, and then you will be nothing."

At that moment, from nowhere, Louise streaks past me in a golden blur. She shifts faster than I can see, and I'm swept up into her arms as she runs away from the Necromancer.

"Hey! What's going on?" I shout.

"Dragon says it's too late. This is a trap. Baldur rises!"

Louise sets me down so that I can run alongside her. We move past Necromancers in puddles of red, and before I can ask what happened, Louise says, "They killed themselves. The end of the ravel."

I look over my shoulder, and the white woman waves at me before flipping open a straight razor and parting her throat. The tentacle creatures around her collapse into puddles at her feet.

"What the hell!" I yell as I turn back around, gasping for breath. "She just killed herself!"

"She is a Necromancer," Louise says as we slide to a stop next to the Skylark and company. "She knows she will return. It's most likely part of the ravel, that they will be reborn along with their dead god."

"A life trapped in a Resonator," the Grimalkin says. "That's exactly the kind of hell they deserve."

I say nothing. This is reminding me of how much I don't know about Necromancy. "Is that what Onyx meant about the ravel ending the Blights?"

"It won't, though," the Skylark says with a shake of her head. "The Resonators don't store the energy of the Dynamism. They consume it slowly."

"Maybe this one works differently," Crystal says. "Onyx told us it doesn't amplify mystical energy, but stores it."

"I have a feeling that none of the Resonators worked the way the government said they would," the Skylark says. "They were just there to be batteries, to draw on the mystical arts until Mechomancers needed them."

"I don't think we wait around to find out," I say. "But we can't leave without saving everyone. The strange fruits on the trees? They're people, and Smoke is in one of the sacs. We have to find a way to free them."

"If the ravel is complete, I don't know what else we can do," the Skylark begins, but I grab her arm.

"The tree itself is still a tree. This isn't just Necromancy; the ravel draws on Floramancy and something else as well. We may not be able to stop the Necromantic ravel, but maybe we can turn it against itself. What do we have to lose?"

The Skylark looks to the tree and then back at me. "You're right. I've got this."

Without another word she runs off, toward a fat root of the Deathstruck tree that runs parallel to the road. I start to chase her when a hand grabs my sleeve. Louise gives me a meaningful look.

"We have to stop Baldur. Look."

She points to the top of the tree, where it slices into the sky. A fierce storm has begun above us, a swirling vortex of black and purple. Looking at it fills me with a deep-seated dread, and all I want to do is scribble out a Wayfaring circle and beam myself to another continent. Even the Mechomancers and other people below have begun to flee, the sight too much for their resolve.

But Louise is already shifting into her fearsome quilled cat shape and charging toward the trunk of the tree, so there is nothing for it but to follow her.

Upon arriving back to the Ohio Deep Blight, we were met with a group of Necromancers raveling a particularly complicated spell. That is when the Peregrine revealed her true self: as the leader of the group, intent on ending the world and undermining the safety and security of this great land.

Luckily, my team and I were able to defeat the villains.

THIRTY-EIGHT

The Skylark does not really think she can save the people trapped in the nightmare tree. In fact, she is quite sure that they are all doomed.

But that is not something she is going to tell the girl, who is about to throw herself into the path of a rising god.

"So, what now?" the Grimalkin says, weaving herself through the Skylark's legs when she stops short next to a fat taproot.

She reaches down to pick up the cat, placing her on her shoulder. "I'm going to try to reravel the tree. But I'm going to need some help." The Skylark has always disliked the idea of familiars, as they had always seemed to be a cruel and inhumane practice. Binding an animal to you for greater access to the Dynamism? It was completely unnecessary. Now, however, the Skylark is realizing this will be the greatest undertaking of her life. Well, lives. For once, she needs a little help.

The Grimalkin rubs her face against the Skylark's cheek. "Excellent idea."

"Okay, then. Are you ready?"

The Grimalkin sinks her claws into the Skylark's shoulder. "Whatever you need."

The Skylark has never raveled something as complex as a tree before, and definitely not one tainted with Necromancy. But with the ravel completed, and with her own form being a Necromantic construct, she is willing to try something unorthodox, something she might not survive.

She is going to ravel the tree.

Theoretically it is possible. Just like everything in the world, a tree is technically a ravel made of several basic components, and they can be exploited to create something new. So while she has manipulated the Dynamism to make trees grow faster or produce more nuts and bits, she has never changed the fundamental purpose of one.

But there is, of course, a first time for everything.

The Skylark places her hands upon the taproot, finding that the Peregrine is correct: there is Necromancy here, now fading, but also a good bit of Floramancy. There's nothing the Skylark can do with the Necromancy; it doesn't sing to her like the Floramancy does, but she realizes she doesn't have to do anything but work around it. The Floramancy she can grab hold of with no problem, and so she does and gives it a strong tug.

It doesn't budge.

This working isn't powered by the Dynamism, but by the lives of the Floramancers who were spent in raising the tree. It's so intricately tied to the slow death of the working that the Skylark at first is worried that she won't be able to touch the ravel.

That's when she realizes she's working backward. Instead of starting from the root, she needs to start from the fruit. She runs toward a low-hanging branch, heavy enough that the bloody orb nearly touches the ground, the Grimalkin complaining as she struggles to hold on. When she reaches the fruit, holding a younger colored boy, the Skylark casts through the Dynamism to where the boy and the ravel touch, and she pushes herself into it.

"Whoa, careful there," the Grimalkin says, her claws in the Skylark's shoulder bracing. "Ease yourself into the work."

The Skylark breathes deeply and begins to ravel the already existing ravel. It's no different than using bits to power a working, with the exception that there's so much. She begins by raveling the bloody sacs not into chambers of death but into things that heal, putting a little Sanamancy into the work. Frederick taught her how to repair minor injuries once, and she uses that particular design on the bloody sacs. After all, a uterus could give life. These were no different.

It's nearly enough, but a pounding headache starts up behind her eyes. The Skylark knows what happens if she overexerts herself: the form Miss Fox raveled for her will begin to fray. But the Grimalkin is there, adding her own connection to the Dynamism to that of the Skylark's.

"Just a little more," the Grimalkin says, her voice a near purr. "I can sense it."

The Skylark finds the edge of Floramancy in the ravel and works it to her own purposes, turning it toward life and healing, toward redemption and repair. It's not very different from the ravels she does to tie the beacons to the Dynamism in a Blight, only this time she is using the residual Floramancy in the Death-struck tree to heal the mages and other people it holds. She doesn't even know if it will work.

And then the bloody sac under her fingertips gives a tremble, and begins to *bloom*.

The death-sick scent is gone, along with the iron blood smell. Instead there is the clean fresh scent of life, like holding a baby right after a bath. The little boy in the sac sits on a giant ebony flower, reminiscent of a lotus, and rubs his eyes. "What happened?" he asks, groggy like he has just awoken from a too-long nap. He's pale and too skinny, but he's alive.

All over the tree the sacs, no, *buds*, begin to bloom, a riot of flower. People sit on them at various heights all over the tree, calling out to one another or sobbing in relief. Not everyone makes it, though. There are a number flowers that bloom to reveal naught but withered remains, their captives lost to the Necromancer's ravel. But far more of them reveal colored mages, a few of whom recognize the Skylark and shout questions down at her.

"Look." The sky above the tree still boils, a storm swirling up above. But the tree itself has split down the middle, a silver-hued zigzag separating the trunk. It splits to reveal new growth, a sapling, green and fresh, tying directly to the Dynamism in a way that invigorates the land. The grasses begin to grow, springtime green; trees leaf out and the haze fades away, a scent like fresh air flowing through a stuffy room making the Skylark sigh.

"And that is how you truly repair a Blight," the Skylark says.

She is wiped, bone tired, but she feels happy. Truly ecstatic.

She turns to the sky, and the clouds spinning in a vortex there.

"We need to see to these folks," the Grimalkin says. "Explain to them what has happened."

The Skylark nods. "It's up to the Peregrine now."

THIRTY-NINE

I follow Louise in her headlong dash toward the base of the tree, more than a bit overwhelmed. How am I supposed to stop a god? Up until a couple of days ago I didn't even think it was actually possible to raise one.

At that moment there's a sound like thunder, a huge boom that vibrates across the land. The screaming tree breaks in half, and I watch as the bloody fruits actually bloom, the highest ones floating to the ground and revealing their charges in a way that is mesmerizing.

"Okay, that's weird even for the mystical arts," I say.

"You have to stop him," Louise snarls, sliding to a halt. I stumble and turn to see her expression twisted with fear. "Baldur approaches."

"We have to stop them as well," Crystal says, panting. "You guys run too fast."

"Stop who?" I ask, but Crystal just points to the Mechomancers running toward us. "Dammit. It's always something. A dead god isn't enough?"

Dragon ambles over at that moment, appearing out of the nearby trees. I would wonder what it's been up to, but the blood on its muzzle says it all. *Necromancers are not very good.*

An idea forms in my head, and I turn toward Dragon. "Are you still hungry?"

I am Dragon. I am always hungry.

"You can try sampling those folks over there."

He turns toward the men who run toward us. *They smell funny.*

I shrug. "But they probably taste okay."

Dragon eyes them, but then turns its gaze toward the massive Resonator. *That thing smells the same. Foul arts.*

"So, do you think you can bust it up and all the people inside?" I ask.

Can I eat them?

"Yeah, why not?"

Okay.

"What, are you setting the Dragon on the Mechomancers?" she asks.

"Maybe," I say as Dragon moves toward the men and their approaching constructs. The massive beast crushes them easily and eats the people, a few escaping despite its quickness. But it's enough that I have to look away.

"Dragons are terrifying," Crystal says, voice small.

"I don't like them," Louise reiterates once more. I'm starting to see her point.

My relief is short lived. The funnel of the storm above has grown in size, and if I look closely there is a massive face beginning to appear in the maelstrom. There are bushy eyebrows and a mouth screaming in agony, slowly becoming more and more corporeal, and a sound like a low moan echoes through my bones, growing in intensity.

"Oh, that's bad, right?" Crystal says.

"Baldur wakes," Louise whimpers.

I swallow dryly. I know what I have to do. The Gnarled Fox's ravel is still in the forefront of my mind, and I take a deep breath before grabbing Crystal's hand.

"Tell everyone to stay back," I say to her, before planting a quick kiss on her cheek. "And thank you for being here. You're a good friend, Crystal."

She frowns as I push her away and fall to my knees. I grab a sharp rock in the road and begin to carve out what looks like the Wayfarer's gate I used earlier, only this has a much different purpose.

"What are you doing?" Crystal asks, but I grab an okra seed and fling it at her, the okra warrior gently picking her up and carrying her away. "Hey, stop, I can help!"

But she can't. That I know. This road I have to walk alone.

I continue drawing, and Louise sits back on her haunches. "You don't have to be a girl for me," I say, the words clogging my throat. "I like you either way."

She flashes her teeth at me. "Of course you do; I'm a Ligahoo and you're a Fox. But you don't have to do this alone."

A new roar echoes across the land, and when I glance up Baldur is more defined, the face pale and looming, a rictus of pain and agony. I have to work quickly.

Louise watches as I finish. "You're creating a linking ravel," she says.

"You sure seem to know a lot," I say with a laugh.

"That's my job. I'm your Ligahoo," she says. "I can't ravel, but I know how things work."

"Can I unravel a god?"

"A Fox can unravel anything," she says simply.

Once the design is finished I stand in the center circle, but not before I take my shoes off, my bare feet pressing into the land, anchoring me to this continent I call home. This is not the land of my people, but it isn't the land of the Necromancers or Mechomancers either.

Why do they get to lay claim to a prize they've stolen?

I close my eyes and feel the potential in the design. Not quite the runes that the rest of the Colored Auxiliary uses, but something great in its own way. Once I've opened the beam I direct it up, to Baldur and whatever place is giving him birth.

But I can't quite reach. He's there, just out of my purview, and I swear.

But then there is a push, like someone giving me a boost, and I open my eyes to see Louise in one of the circles surrounding mine. "A Ligahoo follows their Fox," she says. "I go where you go."

I smile, but then Crystal is there as well, and I gasp as she steps into another of the circles. "What kind of friend would I be if I left you in your darkest hour?" she says with a sad smile.

And then the Skylark is there as well, and dozens of other mages that I don't recognize. They place their hands on each other's shoulders, connecting to the circles I drew even if they are standing beyond the channeling barrier. Some of them wear the robes of the Bureau of the Arcane, but far more are dressed simply, just regular colored folks living their lives who got caught up in things bigger than them. Their dark faces are grim or hopeful or scared, but they are there, and we are all connected.

And finally I can reach the dying god trying to enter our world.

I stretch, feeling disconnected from my form. For a moment there is nothing, and then I am light and hope and everything that could be and never was. I am the Possibilities; no, *we* are the Possibilities, and we are made up of fear and anger but also love and trust. We are infinite and yet oh so fragile, trying to keep everything together even while being torn asunder. I am all, and all is me. Regardless of mystic discipline, of race, of *anything*.

I wake, an old voice says in my mind.

Not today, we send back.

In this form, in the complete surrendering of myself and those who came with me, we begin to unmake the old god. We strip away the stolen lives and the corrupted energies. We heal the lesions and the cancerous growths that are a god-given form. And in unmaking Baldur, we remake the world around us, reaching across the continent, no, the *world*, and repairing the damage the Great Rust tried to correct, and failed.

I have a single thought that is mine alone and no one else's: *Looks like Onyx was right after all.*

There's a primal roar that seems to cut through me, and then a high-pitched scream of pain. I gasp for breath and open my eyes.

The storm is gone, the funnel spinning off into downy wisps.

Blue sky. Sunshine. Sweet fresh air.

And the Possibilities? Right there, flush and just waiting for the next ravel.

No one cheers. We are all exhausted and reverent in the face of our accomplishment.

"We did it," Louise says in amazement.

"Of course we did," the Skylark says with a sniff, adjusting her dress, which she has somehow managed to keep pristine. "We're the Colored Auxiliary. Fixing problems is what we do."

And for some reason that sends me into a fit of the giggles.

And so, the lost mages of the Chicago branch of the Colored Auxiliary were recovered, as you well know from their statements. The Colored Auxiliary not only managed to fix, once and for all, the break in the Dynamism at the heart of the Ohio Deep Blight, but also repaired every single Blight across the continent.

And the Peregrine and her coconspirators were given the end they deserved.

FORTY

The Skylark steps out of the Bureau of the Arcane's headquarters into the Washington, D.C., sunshine and adjusts her hat. The inquiry went better than expected. Having approximately 105 Negroes, the majority of them colored mages, willing to testify to the horrors they had experienced in Ohio was a big part of that. That, and the number of Bureau of the Arcane employees who had suddenly disappeared, many of them suspected of either participating in the activities in the Ohio Deep Blight or having gone missing after the story had come to light. Even Congress was taking the matter to heart, with talk about revisiting the Prohibition, since it was so very clear now that the mystical arts were necessary to keep the balance in the Dynamism.

Quite unexpected from the whole situation was a call for stronger regulation of Mechomancy by the president, a move the Skylark never thought she would see. But everyone was enjoying the new era of prosperity that had suddenly spread across the land, the mystical arts falling into favor in light of the new push from Congress, so while the Skylark wasn't hopeful it would last, she could definitely enjoy it for the moment.

Not only that, but just yesterday she agreed to be part of FDR's Black Caucus, a terrible name for a group of colored mages who would be responsible for advising the president on matters pertaining to colored mages and colored folks as a whole. It was an exceptionally good day to be the Skylark.

She only wished it hadn't cost them quite so many lives to make such advancements.

The Skylark walks down the street toward the Wayfarer's station, past a group of rough-looking white men demanding back pay for mages exploited by the Mechomancer's Union, and across the National Mall. She is more than ready to return to her office in New York and only half-surprised when a smartly dressed girl falls into step next to her.

"How did it go?" Crystal asks, handing the Skylark the carrier that held the Grimalkin. The old cat snores softly. As much as she hated the carrier, she always fell right asleep once she was inside.

"Excellent. I actually think they might lift the Prohibition by the end of the month. Just think of how many people won't have to worry about going to jail for petty crimes."

"And the missing Necromancers and Mechomancers?" Crystal asks, skipping along. She looks much younger in the bright yellow dress she wears. It makes the Skylark feel old, which is not an emotion she ever thought she would feel. She quite likes it.

"Ah, yes. The list." The Skylark opens the handbag she carries and withdraws a list that looks like nothing more than a dollar bill. Crystal takes it and tucks it away.

"Thank you. And the Fox Cub sends her thanks," Crystal says.

"Is that what she's calling herself?" the Skylark wonders aloud.

"Ah, no, she hasn't quite settled into the role enough to choose a name just yet," Crystal says with a laugh. "But she's getting better every day. She hopes to be able to have you over for a meal once this whole thing has died down a bit, all the inquiries and whatever. She said something about corned beef hash?"

A bark of laughter escapes the Skylark, and she nods. "I totally understand. Tell her I will bring the eggs."

Crystal nods, not in on the joke but smiling anyway. "If you need help, you know how to find us. Be careful. The danger is still out there. Somewhere."

"Oh, I know," the Skylark says, waving goodbye to Crystal as she returns to her own business.

"Wha—what did I miss?" the Grimalkin yowls, waking and stretching in her carrier.

"Nothing, just talking to Crystal. We're heading back to New York. Do you need me to let you out for a stretch before we catch the beam?"

"Yes. What kind of question is that?"

The Skylark finds an area that is relatively vacant and lets the Grimalkin out to attend to her business. The Skylark pretends not to notice. The cat, who sometimes still remembers what it was like to be a woman, but less and less these days, takes herself off behind a tree.

"Did you ask the girl about the geas? About having it removed?" the Grimalkin calls.

"No," the Skylark says, looking to the sky. She would never get tired of seeing a normal blue sky and breathing fresh air. "I think I'm glad for the insurance for now."

"Huh. That sounds like you're planning on putting yourself in the path of something dangerous. I hope that's not the case."

"No, it isn't," the Skylark says, scooping the Grimalkin up when she returns and putting her back in the carrier. "But that doesn't mean trouble won't find me."

EPILOGUE

I did not die, though it was a near thing. Every day Louise finds some way to remind me that I don't have to work alone, that I'm stronger with others. And she's right. But I still sometimes forget, and when I do, it results in a lecture from both her and Crystal. They are both adorable, and I'm thankful to be surrounded by such great friends.

Louise, Crystal, and I returned to the Gnarled Fox's cabin, since I couldn't very well return to New York with the Skylark. Crystal could have gone back, but after Onyx's betrayal I think she decided she'd rather pursue other options. I don't blame her. The government might be reconsidering some things, but I still don't think they're ready for colored girls who can do Necromancy, talk to dragons, and maybe have a bit of a crush on a shape-shifter, so I just figured it would be easier to be dead. Louise and Crystal agreed, so they tagged along with me.

After a few days at the Gnarled Fox's house, we got a visit from the hedge witch whose family owned the big homestead with the well-vern. Turned out she was a widow who'd never had children but she knew us from the day we unraveled Baldur, since she was there. She invited us to stay with her. She's been a big help in getting me better at all the things I don't know, which is a lot. Those public schools keep a lot of the mystical arts secret. But I'm willing to bet the Skylark will change that. Crystal said she's already nagging at the well-known school reformer, Miss Bethune, to put that on her list of reforms.

I still have the grimoire from the Gnarled Fox, but I've found I much prefer visiting old Miss Fox to listen to her wisdom as well. She has a philosophy that matches mine a bit more than the Gnarled Fox, whose spells tend to be a bit more direct. And solitary! I work much better in a group. I've already learned a Wayfarer's circle that doesn't leave me dizzy, although Crystal keeps complaining it makes her crave meat loaf.

Malik and Sam both ended up in California after Sam recovered. Hollywood is always looking for Illusionists. Last I heard Malik was working for a studio with his dad while he and Sam are living together in an apartment. It seems being trapped in a ravel made the Smoke give up the government service and realize that who his son loved wasn't all that big of a deal, though I have to wonder if it ever was. Either way I hope things continue to work out for them. I really do love a happy ending.

The Skylark's raveled tree still stands, and it is a beauty. The locals don't know where the giant twisted tree the size of a ten-story building and covered in purple flowers came from, but they like the way it smells. It also improves attitudes greatly. They may not understand much about the Possibilities, but they really do like that tree.

All in all, life is pretty great. That doesn't mean we don't still have work to do. We have the list of missing mages from the bureau and missing Mechomancers besides. I'm getting better at scrying, and once I'm good enough, Dragon and I are going to go on another adventure. I'll make sure it's hungry when we do. It seems Dragon developed a taste for Mechomancers last time. Something about the meat being smoky.

And most importantly, I finally wrote that letter to Pigeon. I sent it by way of a peregrine who was heading that way, a sheet of paper with three words.

I did it.

AUTHOR'S NOTE

We all know the old adage "a picture is worth a thousand words," and while researching *Deathless Divide*, the sequel to *Dread Nation*, I kept finding myself distracted by the number of pictures available in the digitized archive at the Library of Congress. I was supposed to be reading about the lives of Black folks in the late 1800s, but instead I kept finding myself drawn to the pictures of real Black Americans who had once loved and fought and struggled in the same places I have loved and fought and struggled. There was a connection there, and I wanted to know more about the lives of these Black Americans, their names lost to history but their likeness frozen forever in electrons.

Rust in the Root is the culmination of those musings, a love letter to what never was but could have been.

Each image within these pages was carefully selected from the archives of the Library of Congress, mostly from the Farm Security Administration/Office of War Information collections, which you can learn more about at www.loc.gov/pictures/collection/fsa/. Information and image reproduction numbers for each of the photos can be found on the following page; you can request links via my website at justinaireland.com/connect.

For all of the ills and woes the internet has brought us, digitized historical collections have to be one of the finest offerings in the Internet Age, because history no longer belongs to stuffy academics in universities with grants to research their favorite topics. It belongs to all of us.

Happy researching!
Justina Ireland
September 2022

PHOTO INFORMATION